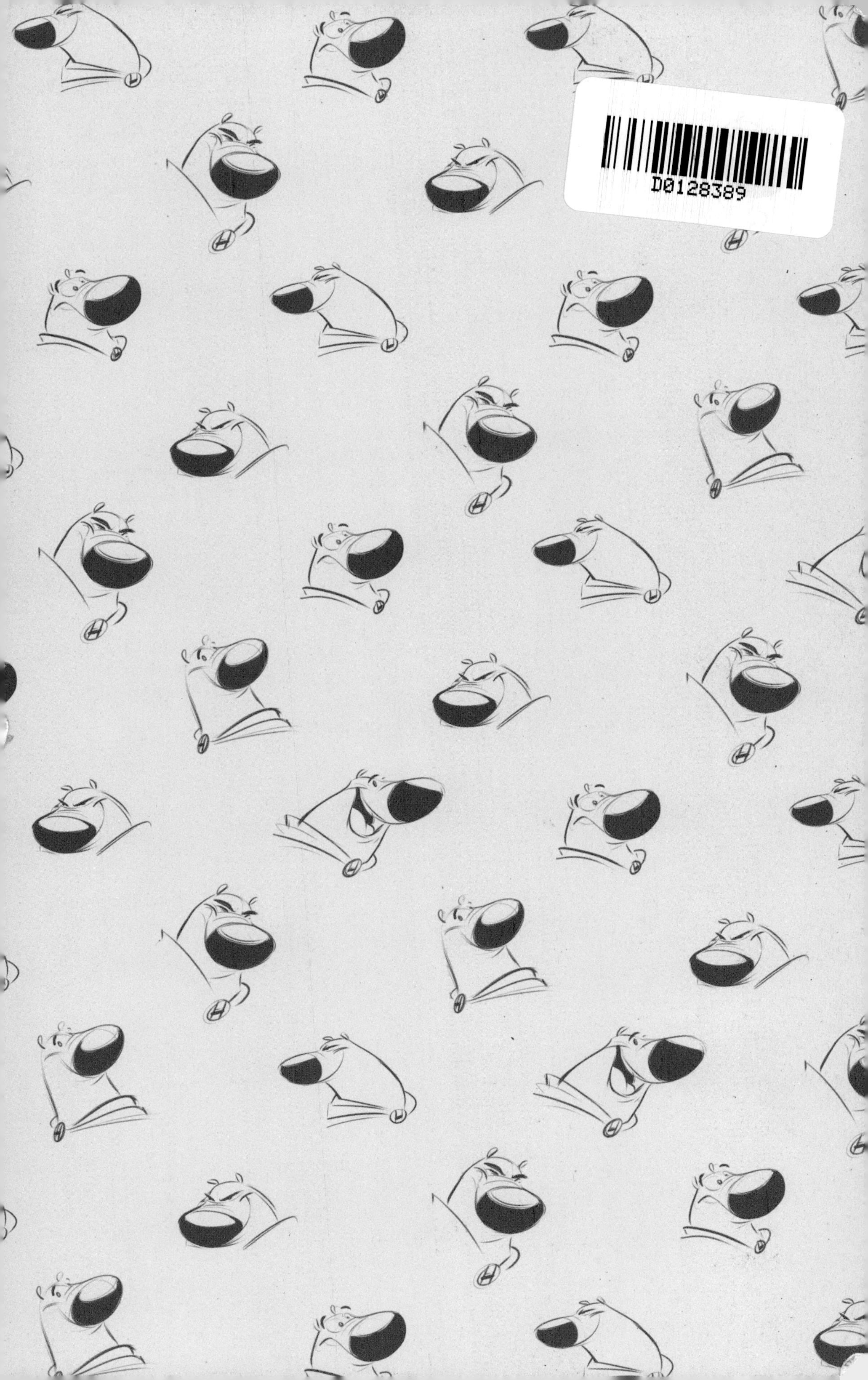

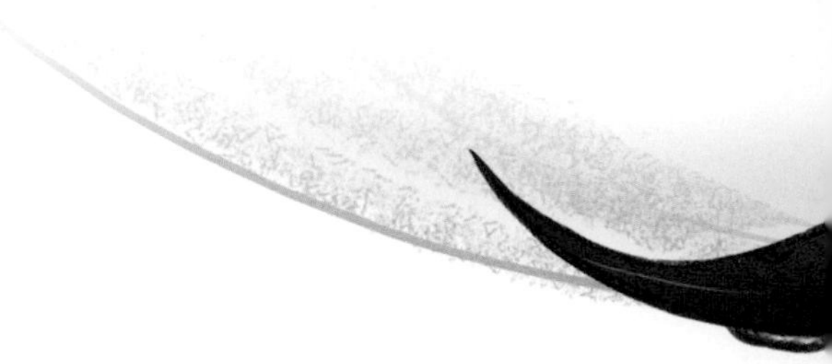

MiKE KU

HERO

and the

~ THE iNHE

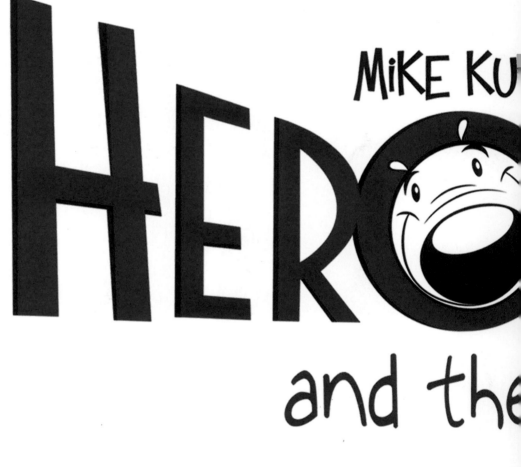

EL'S

BEAR
KID

RITANCE ~

Published by

kaboom!™

ROSS RICHIE CEO & Founder
JACK CUMMINS COO & President
MARK SMYLIE Chief Creative Officer
MATT GAGNON Editor-in-Chief
FILIP SABLIK VP of Publishing & Marketing
STEPHEN CHRISTY VP of Development
LANCE KREITER VP of Licensing & Merchandising
PHIL BARBARO VP of Finance
BRYCE CARLSON Managing Editor
MEL CAYLO Marketing Manager
SCOTT NEWMAN Production Design Manager
IRENE BRADISH Operations Manager
DAFNA PLEBAN Editor
SHANNON WATTERS Editor
ERIC HARBURN Editor
REBECCA TAYLOR Editor
IAN BRILL Editor
CHRIS ROSA Assistant Editor
ALEX GALER Assistant Editor
WHITNEY LEOPARD Assistant Editor
JASMINE AMIRI Assistant Editor
CAMERON CHITTOCK Assistant Editor
HANNAH NANCE PARTLOW Production Designer
KELSEY DIETERICH Production Designer
DEVIN FUNCHES E-Commerce & Inventory Coordinator
ANDY LIEGL Event Coordinator
BRIANNA HART Executive Assistant
AARON FERRARA Operations Assistant
JOSÉ MEZA Sales Assistant

HEROBEAR AND THE KID Volume One: The Inheritance, May 2014. Published by KaBOOM!, a division of Boom Entertainment, Inc. HEROBEAR AND THE KID, the logos, and all related characters and elements are trademarks of Mike Kunkel. Copyright © Mike Kunkel 2014. Originally published in single magazine form as HEROBEAR AND THE KID: THE INHERITANCE No. 1-5, FCBD Summer Blast 2013. © Mike Kunkel 2013. All rights reserved. KaBOOM!™ and the KaBOOM! logo are trademarks of Boom Entertainment, Inc., registered in various countries and categories. All characters, events, and institutions depicted herein are fictional. Any similarity between any of the names, characters, persons, events, and/or institutions in this publication to actual names, characters, and persons, whether living or dead, events, and/or institutions is unintended and purely coincidental. KaBOOM! does not read or accept unsolicited submissions of ideas, stories, or artwork.

A catalog record of this book is available from OCLC and from the KaBOOM! website, www.kaboom-studios.com, on the Librarians Page.

BOOM! Studios, 5670 Wilshire Boulevard, Suite 450, Los Angeles, CA 90036-5679. Printed in China. First Printing. ISBN: 978-1-60886-366-2, eISBN: 978-1-61398-220-4

Created, Written, and Illustrated by

MIKE KUNKEL

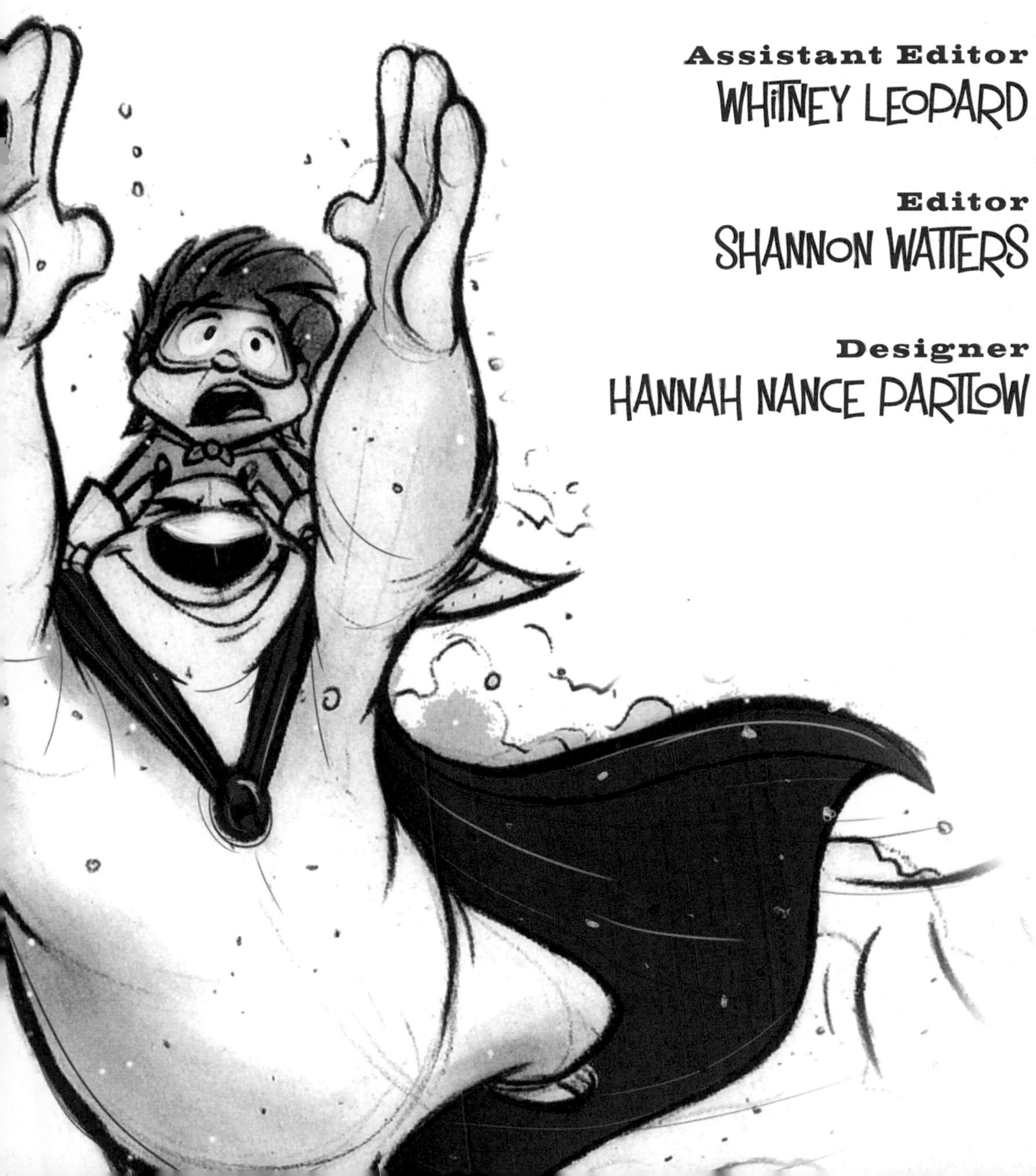

Assistant Editor
WHITNEY LEOPARD

Editor
SHANNON WATTERS

Designer
HANNAH NANCE PARTLOW

Chapter One

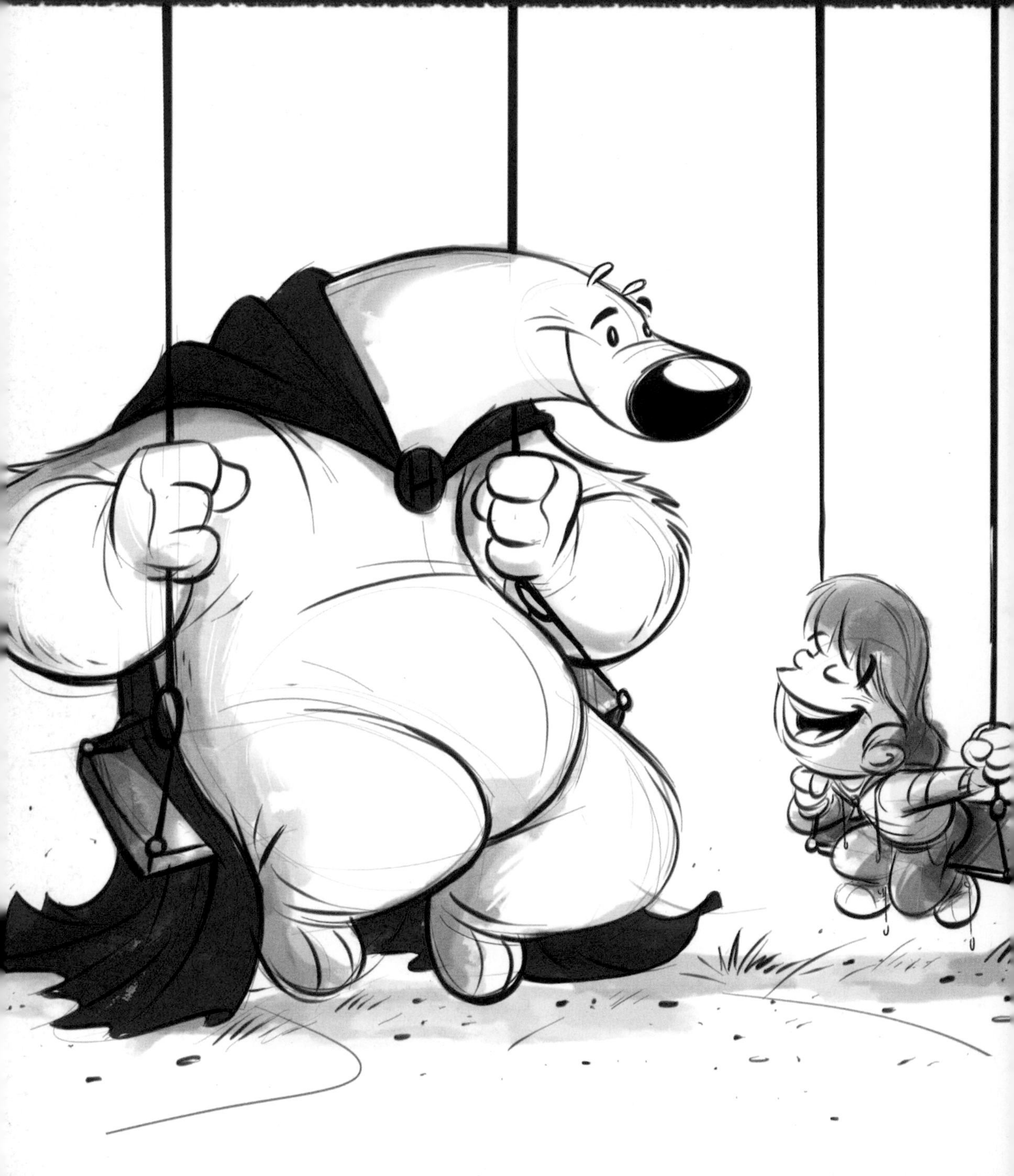

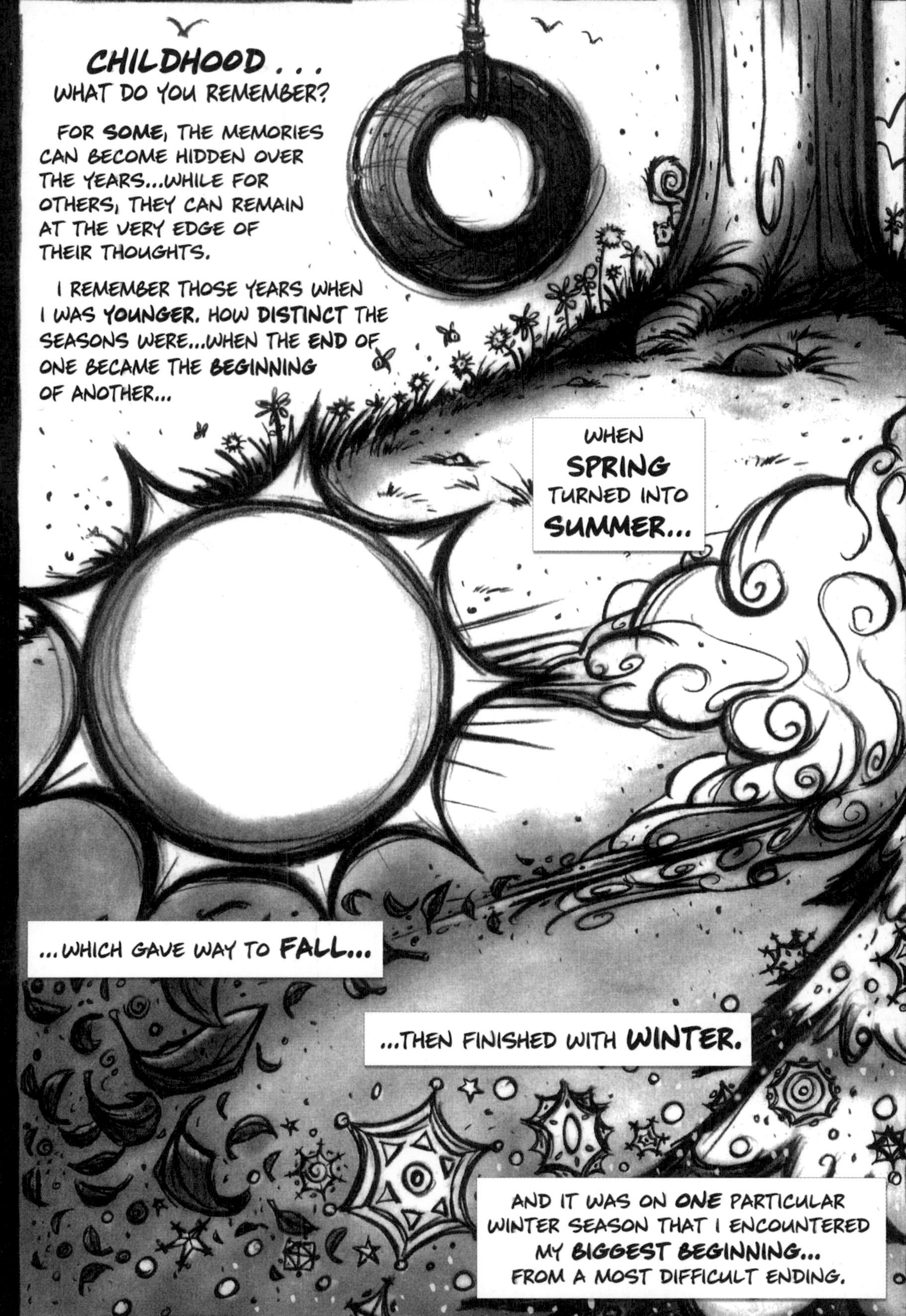
CHILDHOOD . . .
WHAT DO YOU REMEMBER?
FOR SOME, THE MEMORIES CAN BECOME HIDDEN OVER THE YEARS...WHILE FOR OTHERS, THEY CAN REMAIN AT THE VERY EDGE OF THEIR THOUGHTS.
I REMEMBER THOSE YEARS WHEN I WAS YOUNGER. HOW DISTINCT THE SEASONS WERE...WHEN THE END OF ONE BECAME THE BEGINNING OF ANOTHER...
WHEN SPRING TURNED INTO SUMMER...
...WHICH GAVE WAY TO FALL...
...THEN FINISHED WITH WINTER.
AND IT WAS ON ONE PARTICULAR WINTER SEASON THAT I ENCOUNTERED MY BIGGEST BEGINNING... FROM A MOST DIFFICULT ENDING.

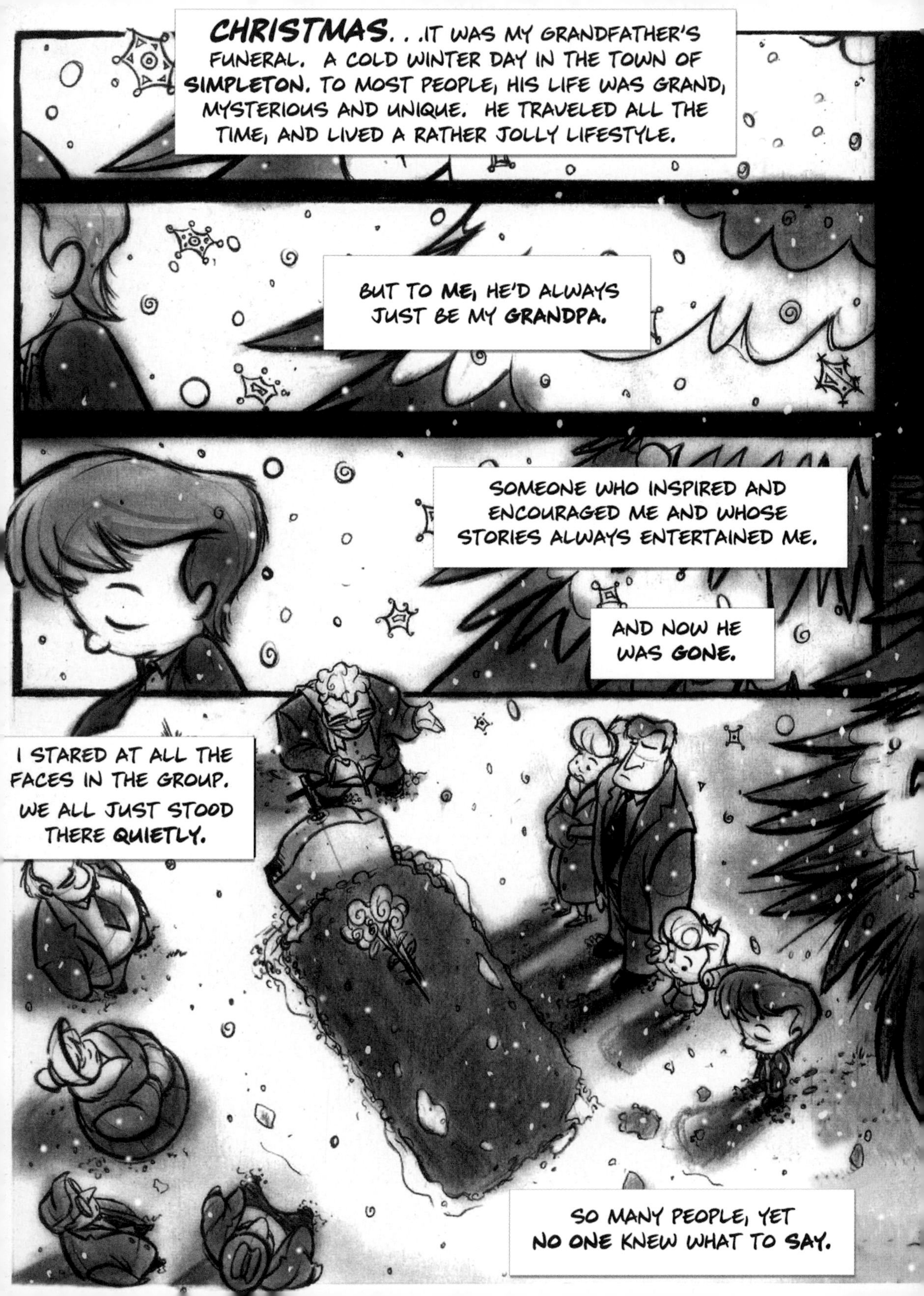
CHRISTMAS. . .IT WAS MY GRANDFATHER'S FUNERAL. A COLD WINTER DAY IN THE TOWN OF SIMPLETON. TO MOST PEOPLE, HIS LIFE WAS GRAND, MYSTERIOUS AND UNIQUE. HE TRAVELED ALL THE TIME, AND LIVED A RATHER JOLLY LIFESTYLE.
BUT TO ME, HE'D ALWAYS JUST BE MY GRANDPA.
SOMEONE WHO INSPIRED AND ENCOURAGED ME AND WHOSE STORIES ALWAYS ENTERTAINED ME.
AND NOW HE WAS GONE.
I STARED AT ALL THE FACES IN THE GROUP.
WE ALL JUST STOOD THERE QUIETLY.
SO MANY PEOPLE, YET NO ONE KNEW WHAT TO SAY.

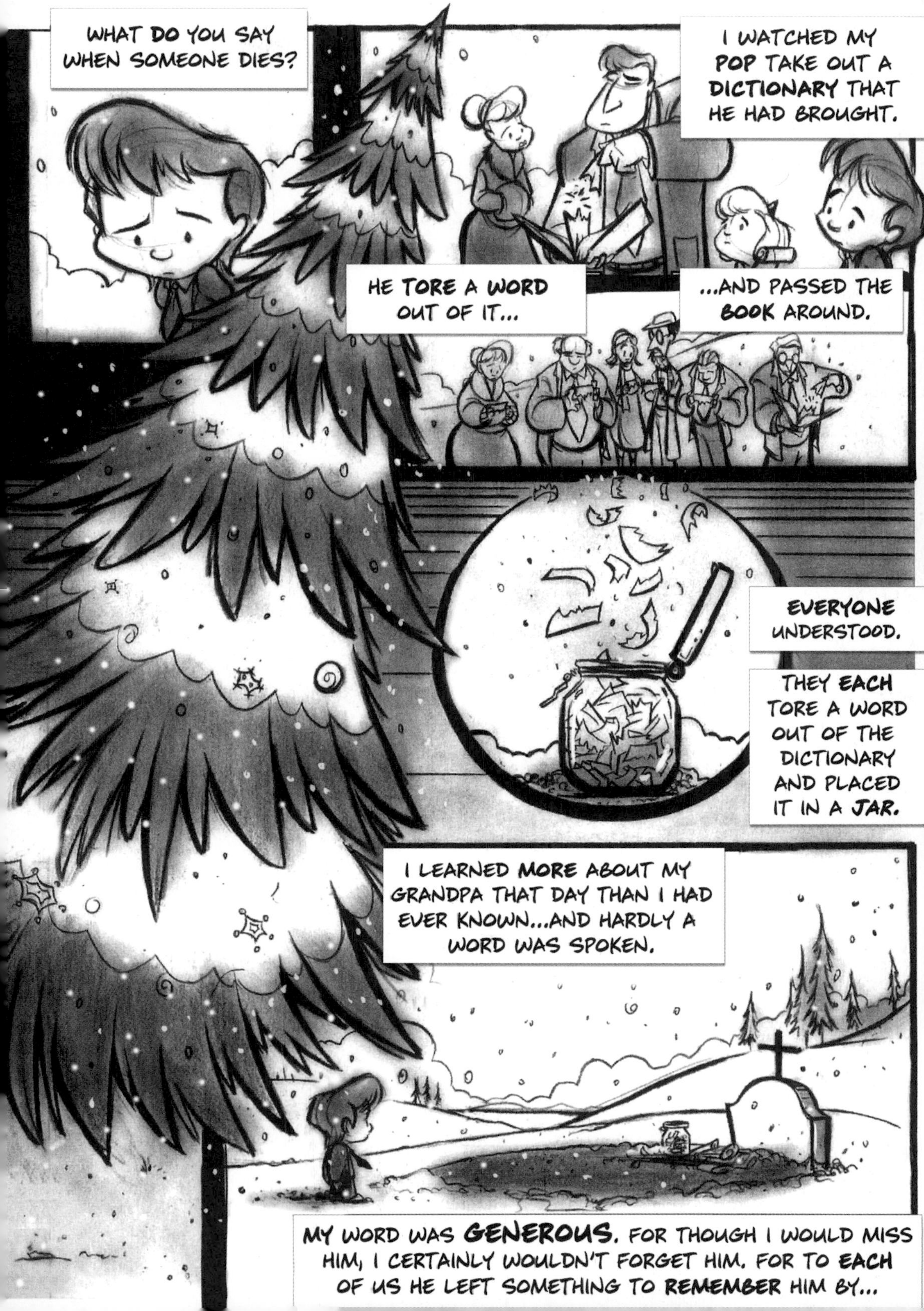
WHAT DO YOU SAY WHEN SOMEONE DIES?
I WATCHED MY POP TAKE OUT A DICTIONARY THAT HE HAD BROUGHT.
HE TORE A WORD OUT OF IT...
...AND PASSED THE BOOK AROUND.
EVERYONE UNDERSTOOD.
THEY EACH TORE A WORD OUT OF THE DICTIONARY AND PLACED IT IN A JAR.
I LEARNED MORE ABOUT MY GRANDPA THAT DAY THAN I HAD EVER KNOWN...AND HARDLY A WORD WAS SPOKEN.
MY WORD WAS GENEROUS. FOR THOUGH I WOULD MISS HIM, I CERTAINLY WOULDN'T FORGET HIM. FOR TO EACH OF US HE LEFT SOMETHING TO REMEMBER HIM BY...

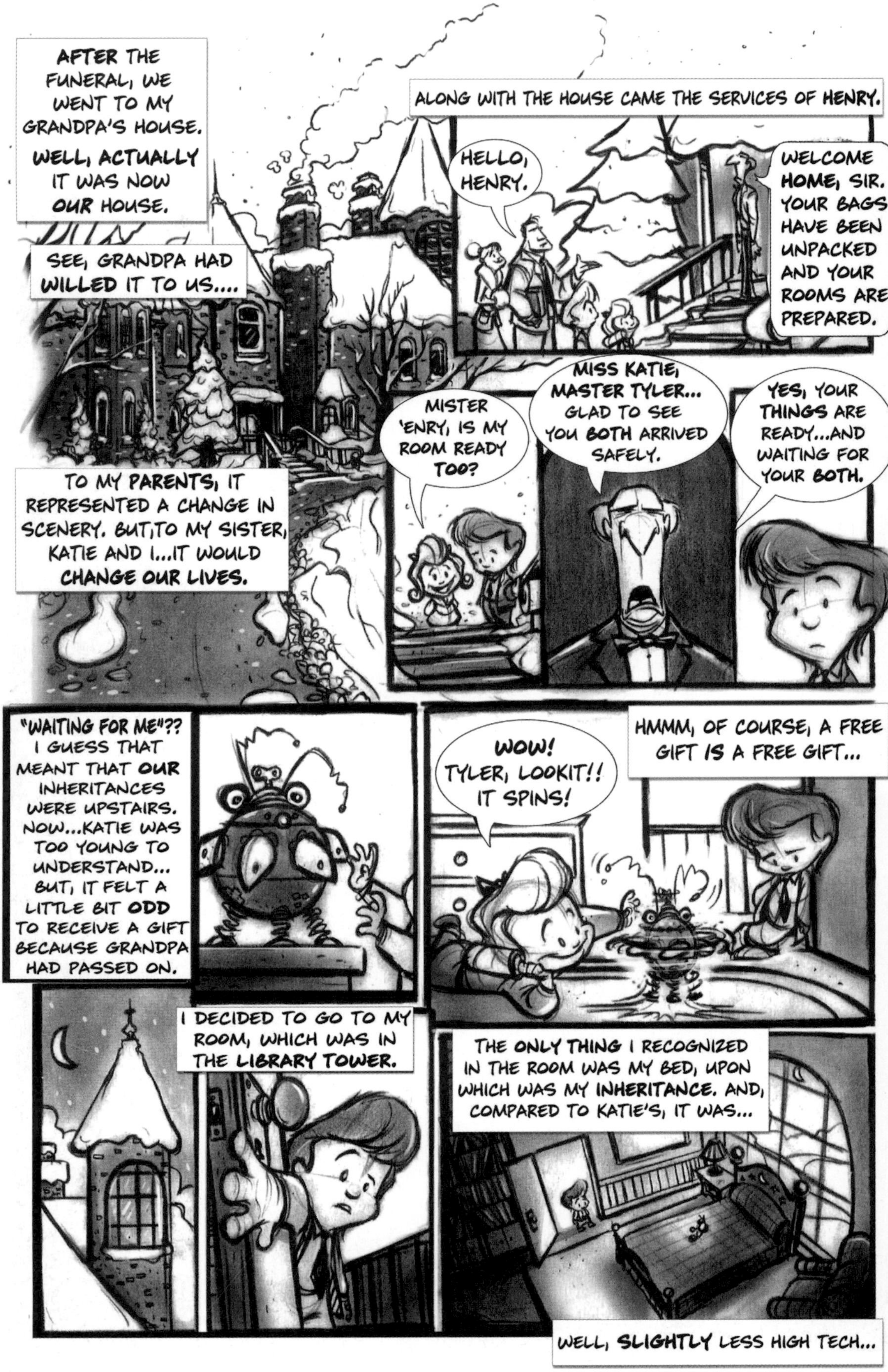
AFTER THE FUNERAL, WE WENT TO MY GRANDPA'S HOUSE.
WELL, ACTUALLY IT WAS NOW OUR HOUSE.
SEE, GRANDPA HAD WILLED IT TO US....
TO MY PARENTS, IT REPRESENTED A CHANGE IN SCENERY. BUT, TO MY SISTER, KATIE AND I...IT WOULD CHANGE OUR LIVES.
ALONG WITH THE HOUSE CAME THE SERVICES OF HENRY.
HELLO, HENRY.
WELCOME HOME, SIR. YOUR BAGS HAVE BEEN UNPACKED AND YOUR ROOMS ARE PREPARED.
MISTER 'ENRY, IS MY ROOM READY TOO?
MISS KATIE, MASTER TYLER... GLAD TO SEE YOU BOTH ARRIVED SAFELY.
YES, YOUR THINGS ARE READY...AND WAITING FOR YOUR BOTH.
"WAITING FOR ME"?? I GUESS THAT MEANT THAT OUR INHERITANCES WERE UPSTAIRS. NOW...KATIE WAS TOO YOUNG TO UNDERSTAND... BUT, IT FELT A LITTLE BIT ODD TO RECEIVE A GIFT BECAUSE GRANDPA HAD PASSED ON.
WOW! TYLER, LOOKIT!! IT SPINS!
HMMM, OF COURSE, A FREE GIFT IS A FREE GIFT...
I DECIDED TO GO TO MY ROOM, WHICH WAS IN THE LIBRARY TOWER.
THE ONLY THING I RECOGNIZED IN THE ROOM WAS MY BED, UPON WHICH WAS MY INHERITANCE. AND, COMPARED TO KATIE'S, IT WAS...
WELL, SLIGHTLY LESS HIGH TECH...

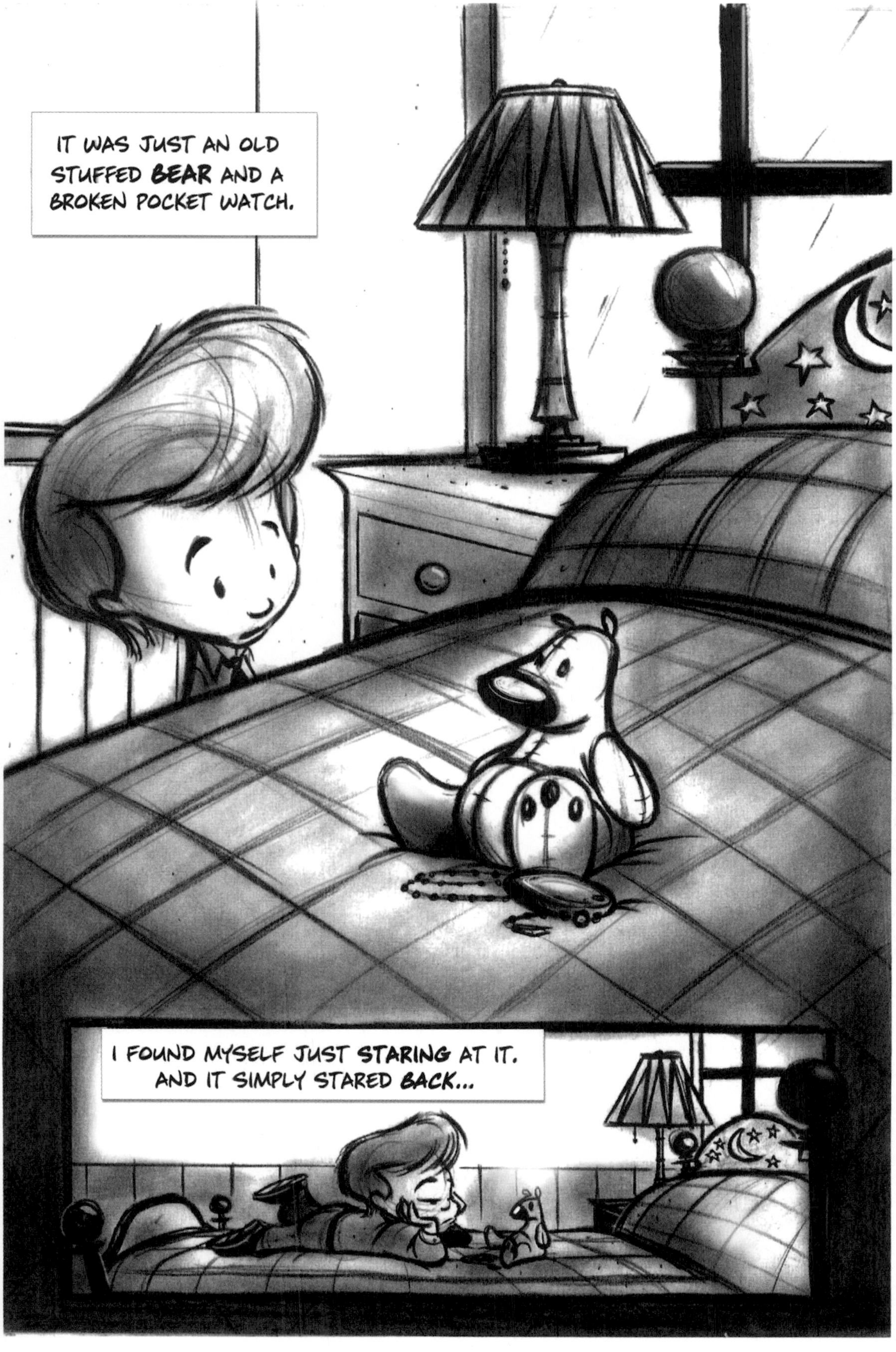

IT WAS JUST AN OLD STUFFED BEAR AND A BROKEN POCKET WATCH.
I FOUND MYSELF JUST STARING AT IT. AND IT SIMPLY STARED BACK...

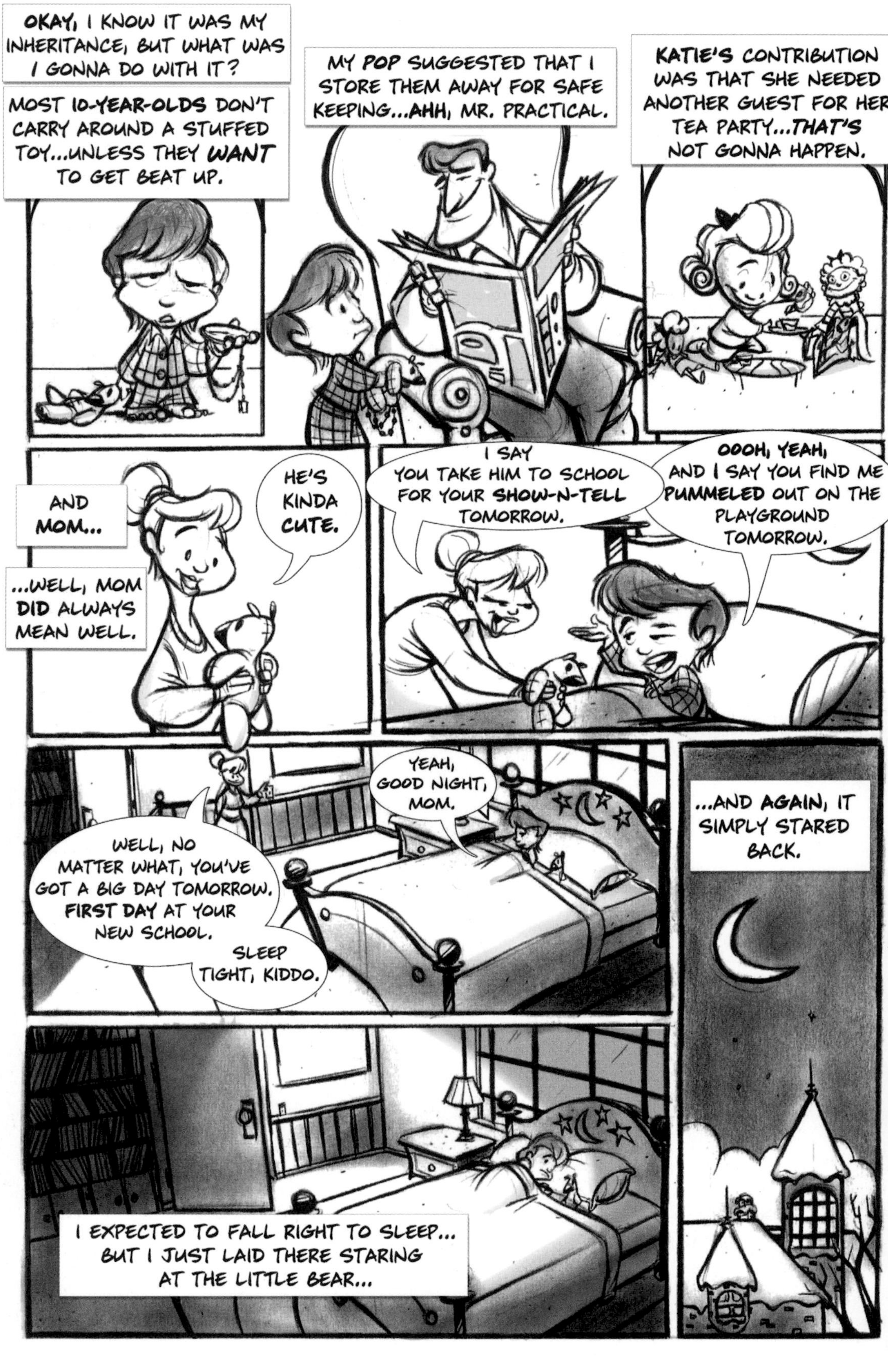
OKAY, I KNOW IT WAS MY INHERITANCE, BUT WHAT WAS I GONNA DO WITH IT?
MOST 10-YEAR-OLDS DON'T CARRY AROUND A STUFFED TOY...UNLESS THEY WANT TO GET BEAT UP.
MY POP SUGGESTED THAT I STORE THEM AWAY FOR SAFE KEEPING...AHH, MR. PRACTICAL.
KATIE'S CONTRIBUTION WAS THAT SHE NEEDED ANOTHER GUEST FOR HER TEA PARTY...THAT'S NOT GONNA HAPPEN.
AND MOM...
HE'S KINDA CUTE.
...WELL, MOM DID ALWAYS MEAN WELL.
I SAY YOU TAKE HIM TO SCHOOL FOR YOUR SHOW-N-TELL TOMORROW.
OOOH, YEAH, AND I SAY YOU FIND ME PUMMELED OUT ON THE PLAYGROUND TOMORROW.
WELL, NO MATTER WHAT, YOU'VE GOT A BIG DAY TOMORROW. FIRST DAY AT YOUR NEW SCHOOL.
SLEEP TIGHT, KIDDO.
YEAH, GOOD NIGHT, MOM.
...AND AGAIN, IT SIMPLY STARED BACK.
I EXPECTED TO FALL RIGHT TO SLEEP... BUT I JUST LAID THERE STARING AT THE LITTLE BEAR...

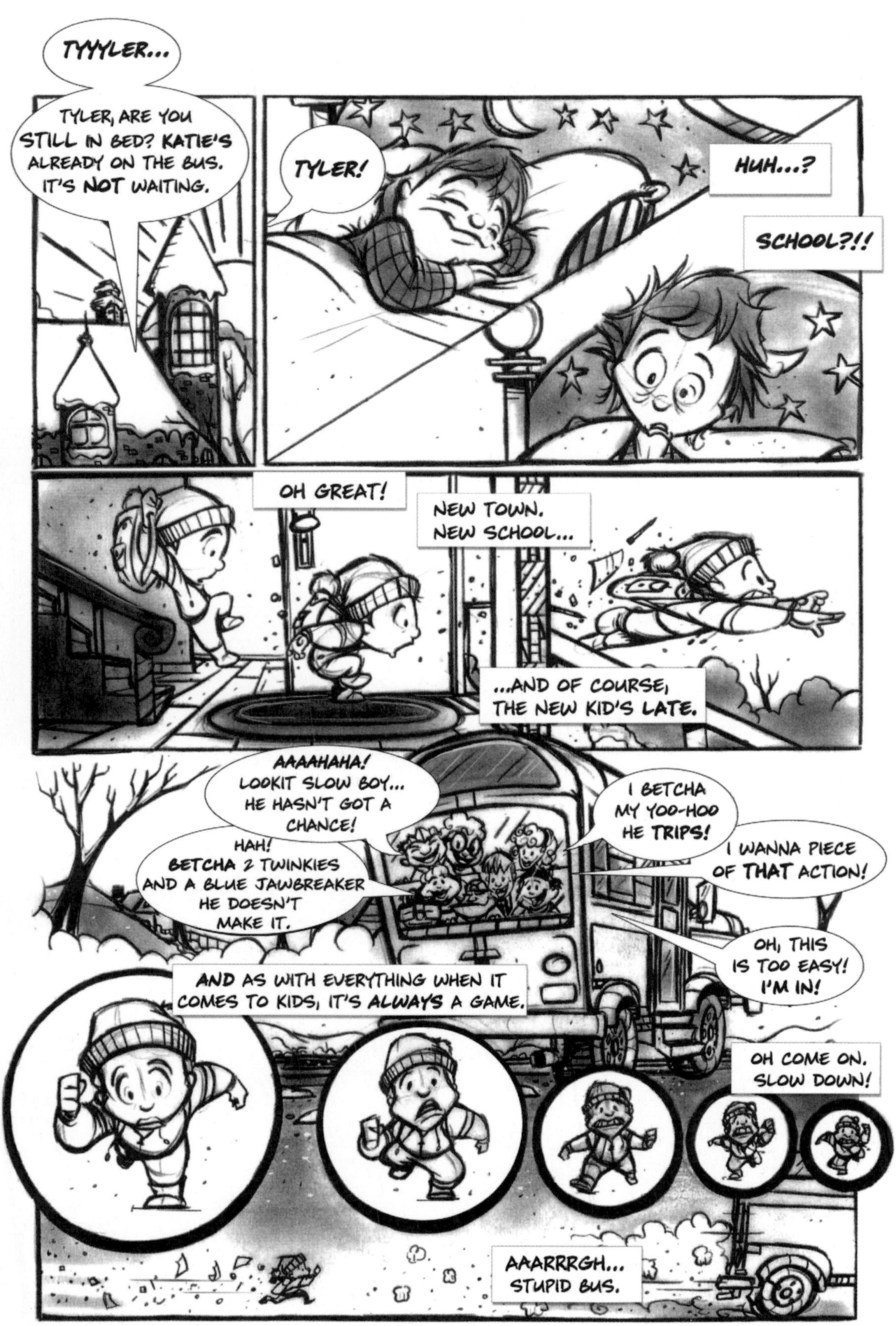
TYYYLER...
TYLER, ARE YOU STILL IN BED? KATIE'S ALREADY ON THE BUS. IT'S NOT WAITING.
TYLER!
HUH...?
SCHOOL?!!
OH GREAT!
NEW TOWN. NEW SCHOOL...
...AND OF COURSE, THE NEW KID'S LATE.
AAAAHAHA! LOOKIT SLOW BOY... HE HASN'T GOT A CHANCE!
HAH! BETCHA 2 TWINKIES AND A BLUE JAWBREAKER HE DOESN'T MAKE IT.
I BETCHA MY YOO-HOO HE TRIPS!
I WANNA PIECE OF THAT ACTION!
OH, THIS IS TOO EASY! I'M IN!
AND AS WITH EVERYTHING WHEN IT COMES TO KIDS, IT'S ALWAYS A GAME.
OH COME ON. SLOW DOWN!
AAARRRGH... STUPID BUS.

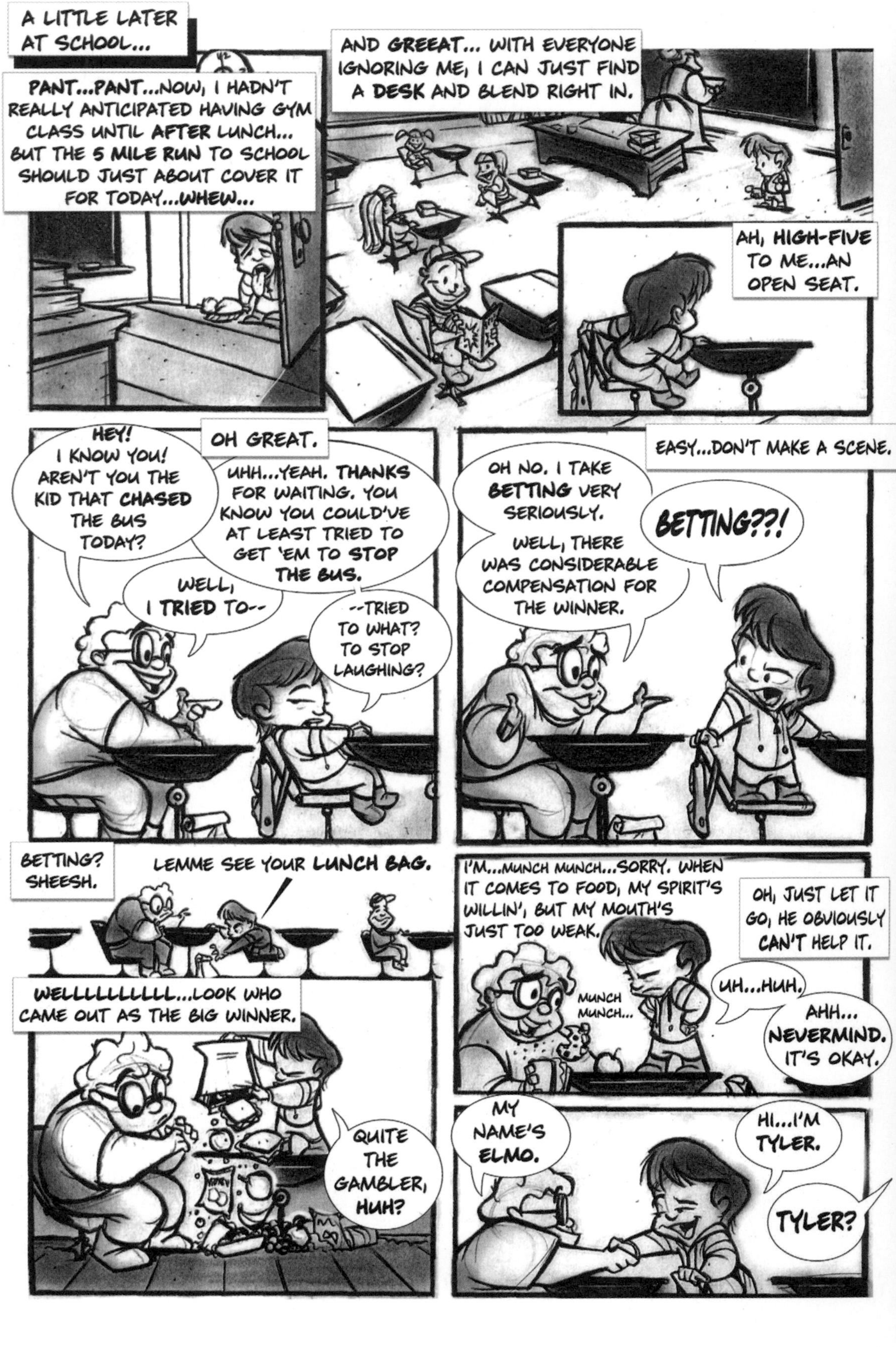
A LITTLE LATER AT SCHOOL...
PANT...PANT...NOW, I HADN'T REALLY ANTICIPATED HAVING GYM CLASS UNTIL AFTER LUNCH... BUT THE 5 MILE RUN TO SCHOOL SHOULD JUST ABOUT COVER IT FOR TODAY...WHEW...
AND GREEAT... WITH EVERYONE IGNORING ME, I CAN JUST FIND A DESK AND BLEND RIGHT IN.
AH, HIGH-FIVE TO ME...AN OPEN SEAT.
HEY! I KNOW YOU! AREN'T YOU THE KID THAT CHASED THE BUS TODAY?
OH GREAT.
UHH...YEAH. THANKS FOR WAITING. YOU KNOW YOU COULD'VE AT LEAST TRIED TO GET 'EM TO STOP THE BUS.
WELL, I TRIED TO--
--TRIED TO WHAT? TO STOP LAUGHING?
EASY...DON'T MAKE A SCENE.
OH NO. I TAKE BETTING VERY SERIOUSLY.
WELL, THERE WAS CONSIDERABLE COMPENSATION FOR THE WINNER.
BETTING??!
BETTING? SHEESH.
LEMME SEE YOUR LUNCH BAG.
WELLLLLLLLLL...LOOK WHO CAME OUT AS THE BIG WINNER.
QUITE THE GAMBLER, HUH?
I'M...MUNCH MUNCH...SORRY. WHEN IT COMES TO FOOD, MY SPIRIT'S WILLIN', BUT MY MOUTH'S JUST TOO WEAK.
OH, JUST LET IT GO, HE OBVIOUSLY CAN'T HELP IT.
MUNCH MUNCH...
UH...HUH.
AHH... NEVERMIND. IT'S OKAY.
MY NAME'S ELMO.
HI...I'M TYLER.
TYLER?

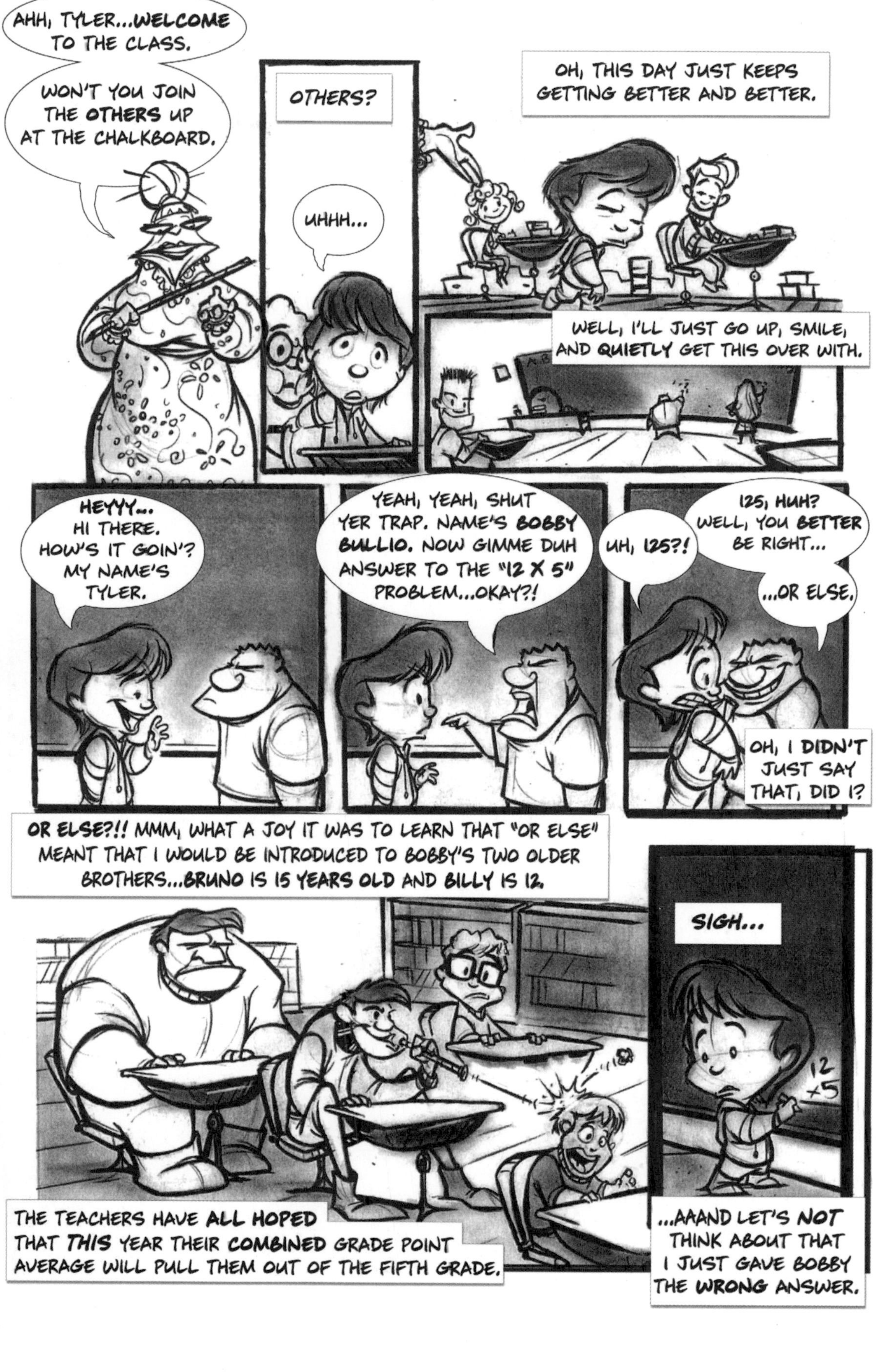
AHH, TYLER...WELCOME TO THE CLASS.
WON'T YOU JOIN THE OTHERS UP AT THE CHALKBOARD.
OTHERS?
UHHH...
OH, THIS DAY JUST KEEPS GETTING BETTER AND BETTER.
WELL, I'LL JUST GO UP, SMILE, AND QUIETLY GET THIS OVER WITH.
HEYYY... HI THERE. HOW'S IT GOIN'? MY NAME'S TYLER.
YEAH, YEAH, SHUT YER TRAP. NAME'S BOBBY BULLIO. NOW GIMME DUH ANSWER TO THE "12 X 5" PROBLEM...OKAY?!
UH, 125?!
125, HUH? WELL, YOU BETTER BE RIGHT...
...OR ELSE.
OH, I DIDN'T JUST SAY THAT, DID I?
OR ELSE?!! MMM, WHAT A JOY IT WAS TO LEARN THAT "OR ELSE" MEANT THAT I WOULD BE INTRODUCED TO BOBBY'S TWO OLDER BROTHERS...BRUNO IS 15 YEARS OLD AND BILLY IS 12.
SIGH...
12 x5
THE TEACHERS HAVE ALL HOPED THAT THIS YEAR THEIR COMBINED GRADE POINT AVERAGE WILL PULL THEM OUT OF THE FIFTH GRADE.
...AAAND LET'S NOT THINK ABOUT THAT I JUST GAVE BOBBY THE WRONG ANSWER.

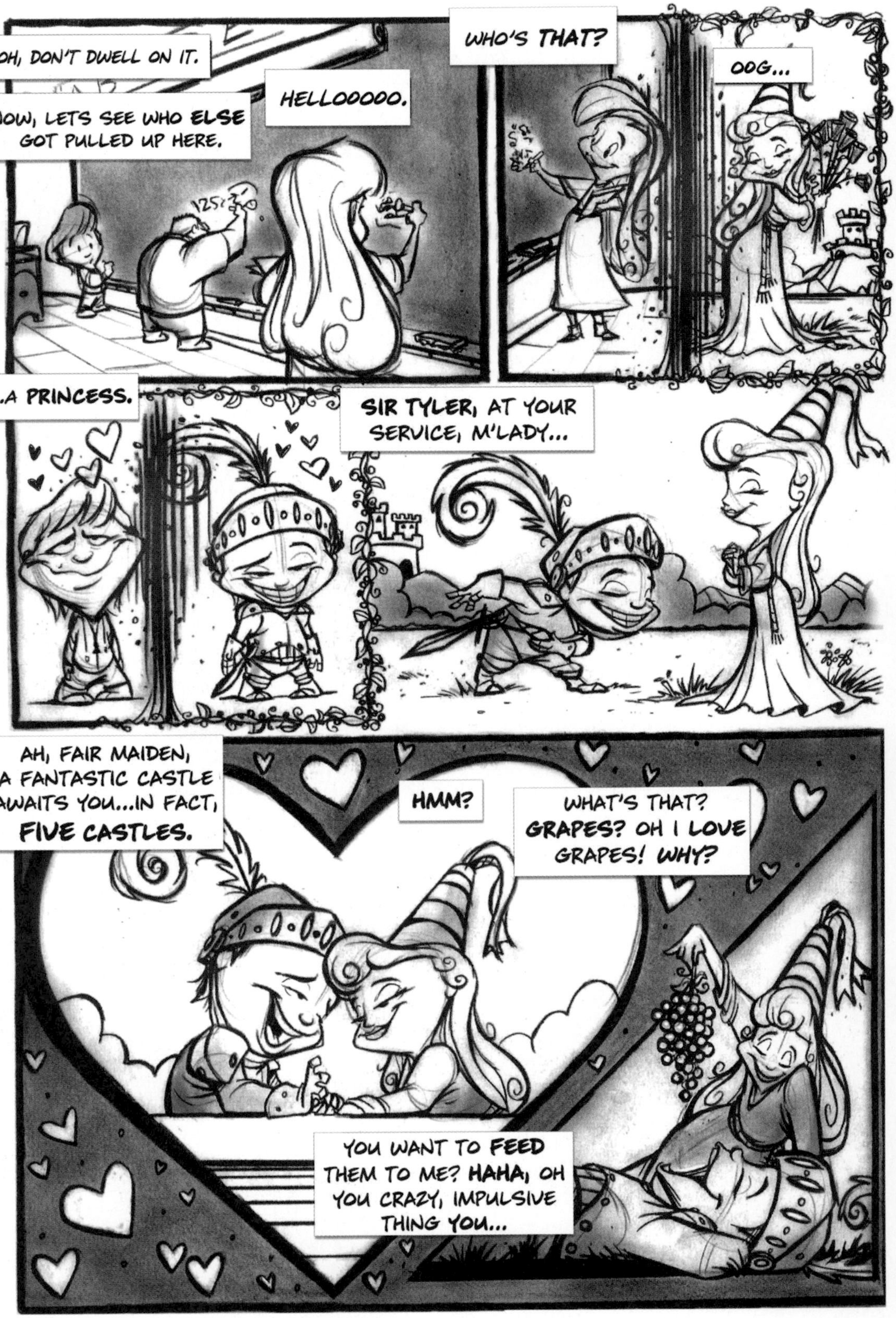
OH, DON'T DWELL ON IT.
NOW, LETS SEE WHO ELSE GOT PULLED UP HERE.
HELLOOOOO.
WHO'S THAT?
OOG...
...A PRINCESS.
SIR TYLER, AT YOUR SERVICE, M'LADY...
AH, FAIR MAIDEN, A FANTASTIC CASTLE AWAITS YOU...IN FACT, FIVE CASTLES.
HMM?
WHAT'S THAT? GRAPES? OH I LOVE GRAPES! WHY?
YOU WANT TO FEED THEM TO ME? HAHA, OH YOU CRAZY, IMPULSIVE THING YOU...

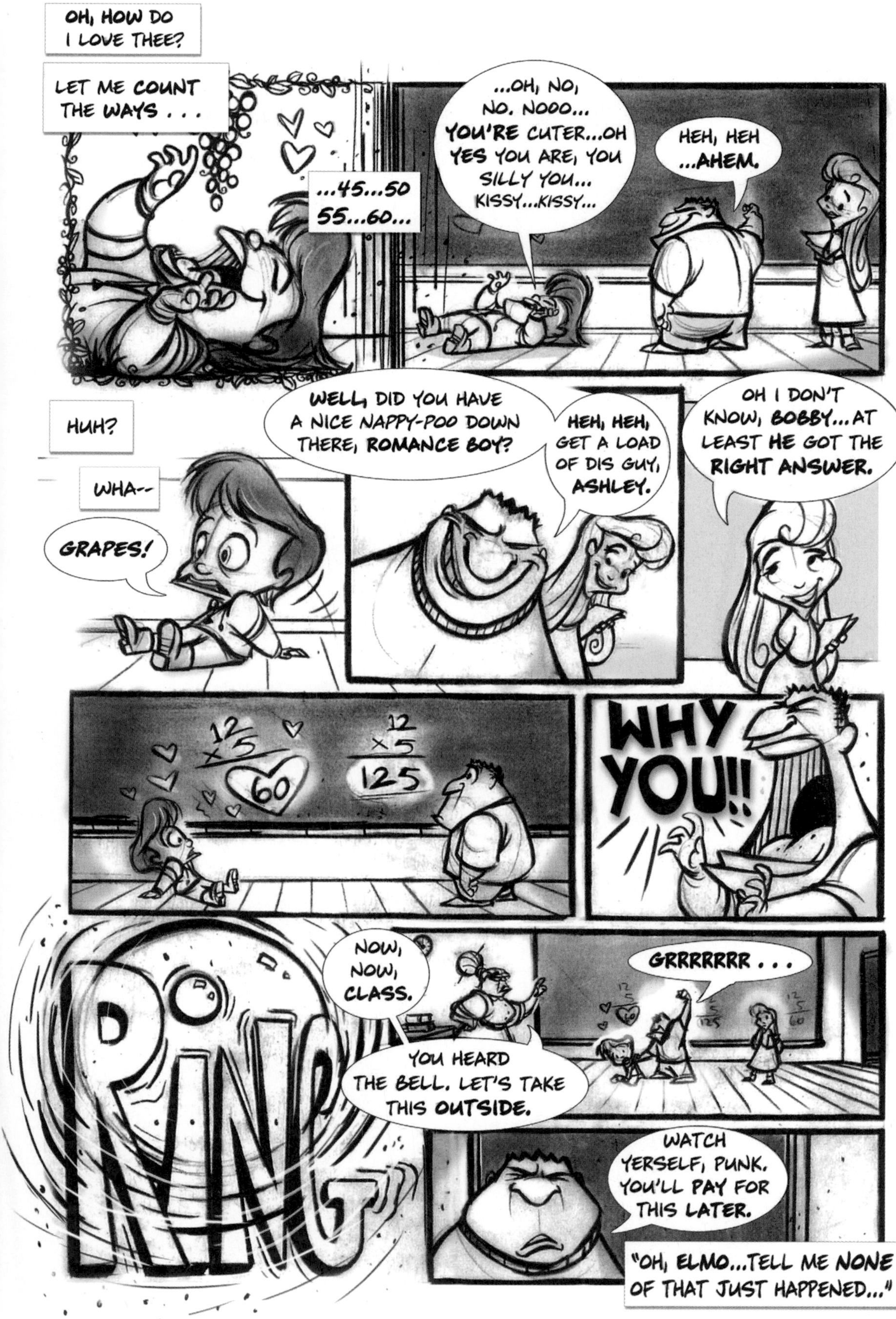
OH, HOW DO I LOVE THEE?
LET ME COUNT THE WAYS . . .
...45...50 55...60...
...OH, NO, NO. NOOO... YOU'RE CUTER...OH YES YOU ARE, YOU SILLY YOU... KISSY...KISSY...
HEH, HEH ...AHEM.
HUH?
WHA--
GRAPES!
WELL, DID YOU HAVE A NICE NAPPY-POO DOWN THERE, ROMANCE BOY?
HEH, HEH, GET A LOAD OF DIS GUY, ASHLEY.
OH I DON'T KNOW, BOBBY... AT LEAST HE GOT THE RIGHT ANSWER.
12 ×5 60
12 ×5 125
WHY YOU!!
RING
NOW, NOW, CLASS.
GRRRRRRR . . .
YOU HEARD THE BELL. LET'S TAKE THIS OUTSIDE.
WATCH YERSELF, PUNK. YOU'LL PAY FOR THIS LATER.
"OH, ELMO...TELL ME NONE OF THAT JUST HAPPENED..."

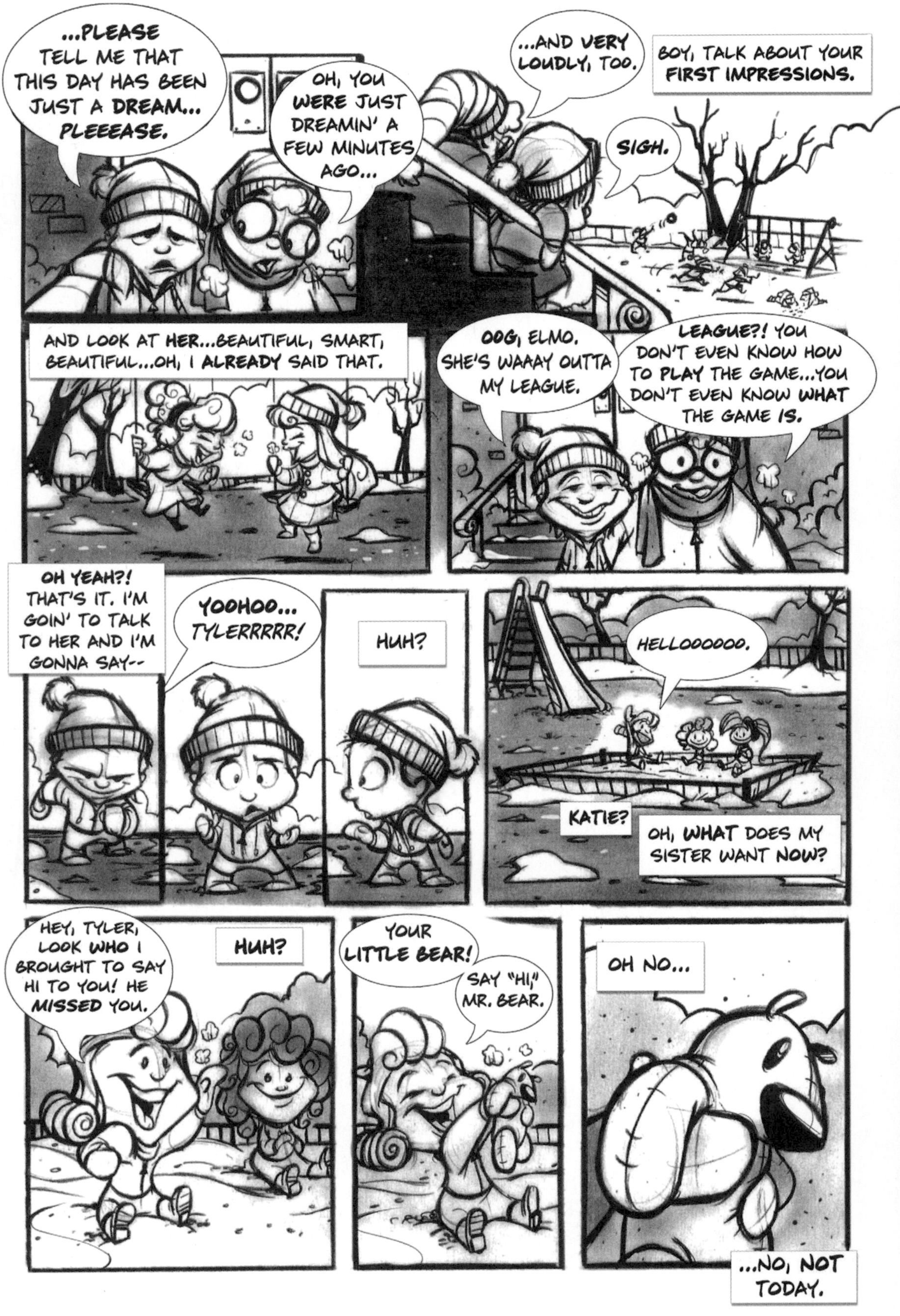
...PLEASE TELL ME THAT THIS DAY HAS BEEN JUST A DREAM... PLEEEASE.
OH, YOU WERE JUST DREAMIN' A FEW MINUTES AGO...
...AND VERY LOUDLY, TOO.
BOY, TALK ABOUT YOUR FIRST IMPRESSIONS.
SIGH.
AND LOOK AT HER...BEAUTIFUL, SMART, BEAUTIFUL...OH, I ALREADY SAID THAT.
OOG, ELMO. SHE'S WAAAY OUTTA MY LEAGUE.
LEAGUE?! YOU DON'T EVEN KNOW HOW TO PLAY THE GAME...YOU DON'T EVEN KNOW WHAT THE GAME IS.
OH YEAH?! THAT'S IT. I'M GOIN' TO TALK TO HER AND I'M GONNA SAY--
YOOHOO... TYLERRRRR!
HUH?
HELLOOOOOO.
KATIE?
OH, WHAT DOES MY SISTER WANT NOW?
HEY, TYLER, LOOK WHO I BROUGHT TO SAY HI TO YOU! HE MISSED YOU.
HUH?
YOUR LITTLE BEAR!
SAY "HI," MR. BEAR.
OH NO...
...NO, NOT TODAY.

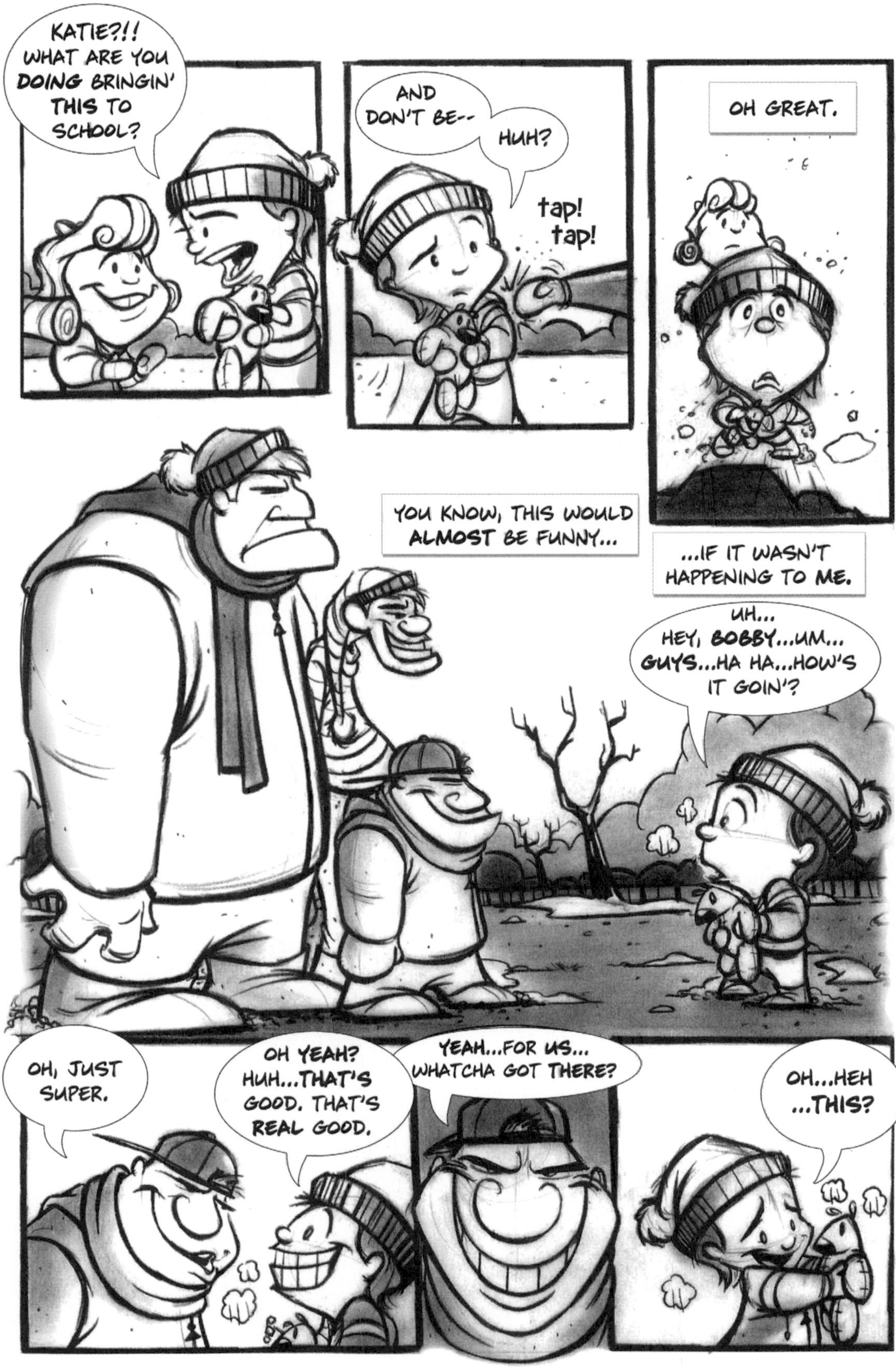
KATIE?!! WHAT ARE YOU DOING BRINGIN' THIS TO SCHOOL?
AND DON'T BE--
HUH?
tap! tap!
OH GREAT.
YOU KNOW, THIS WOULD ALMOST BE FUNNY...
...IF IT WASN'T HAPPENING TO ME.
UH... HEY, BOBBY...UM... GUYS...HA HA...HOW'S IT GOIN'?
OH, JUST SUPER.
OH YEAH? HUH...THAT'S GOOD. THAT'S REAL GOOD.
YEAH...FOR US... WHATCHA GOT THERE?
OH...HEH ...THIS?

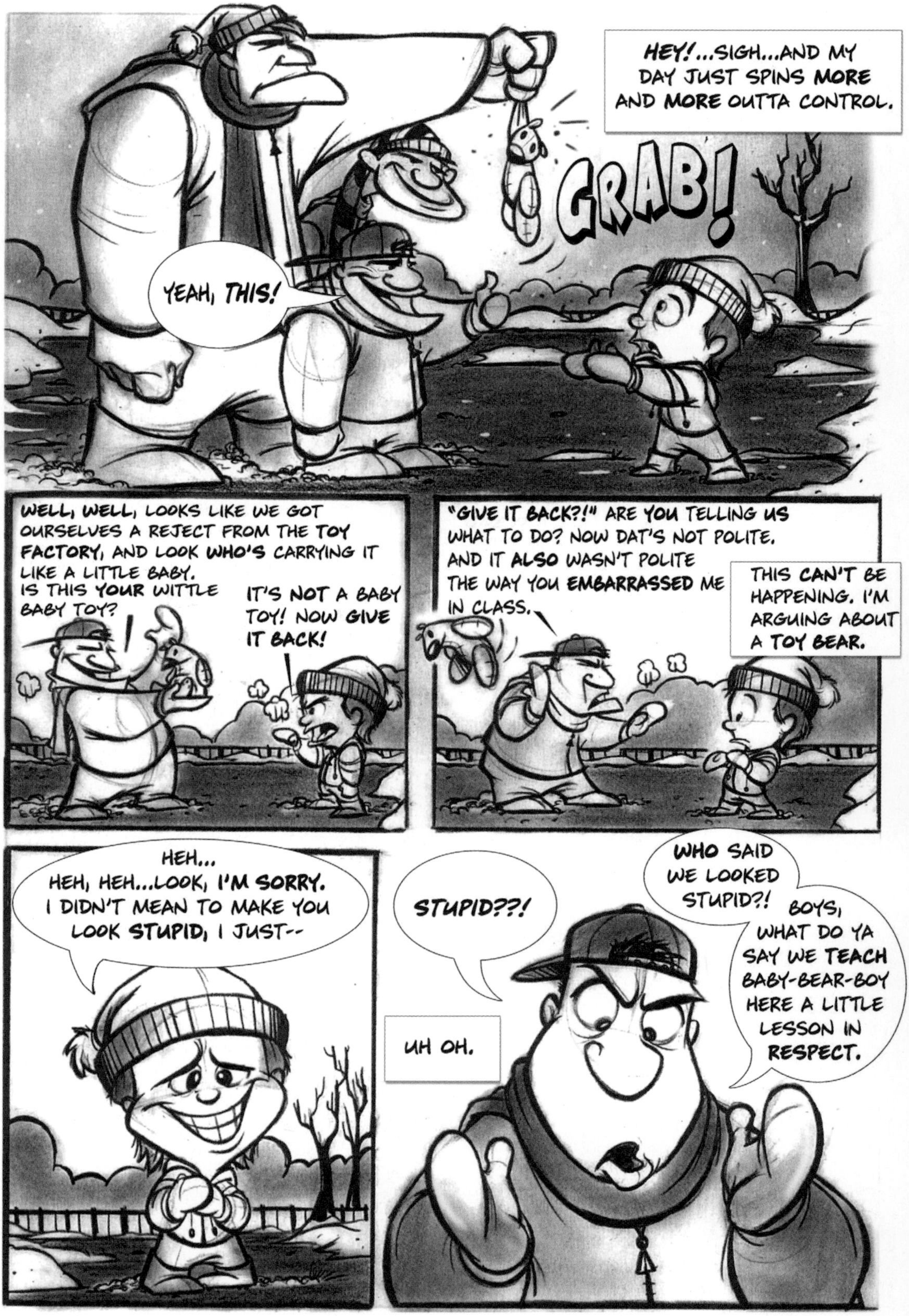
HEY!...SIGH...AND MY DAY JUST SPINS MORE AND MORE OUTTA CONTROL.
GRAB!
YEAH, THIS!
WELL, WELL, LOOKS LIKE WE GOT OURSELVES A REJECT FROM THE TOY FACTORY, AND LOOK WHO'S CARRYING IT LIKE A LITTLE BABY. IS THIS YOUR WITTLE BABY TOY?
IT'S NOT A BABY TOY! NOW GIVE IT BACK!
"GIVE IT BACK?!" ARE YOU TELLING US WHAT TO DO? NOW DAT'S NOT POLITE. AND IT ALSO WASN'T POLITE THE WAY YOU EMBARRASSED ME IN CLASS.
THIS CAN'T BE HAPPENING. I'M ARGUING ABOUT A TOY BEAR.
HEH... HEH, HEH...LOOK, I'M SORRY. I DIDN'T MEAN TO MAKE YOU LOOK STUPID, I JUST--
STUPID??!
UH OH.
WHO SAID WE LOOKED STUPID?!
BOYS, WHAT DO YA SAY WE TEACH BABY-BEAR-BOY HERE A LITTLE LESSON IN RESPECT.

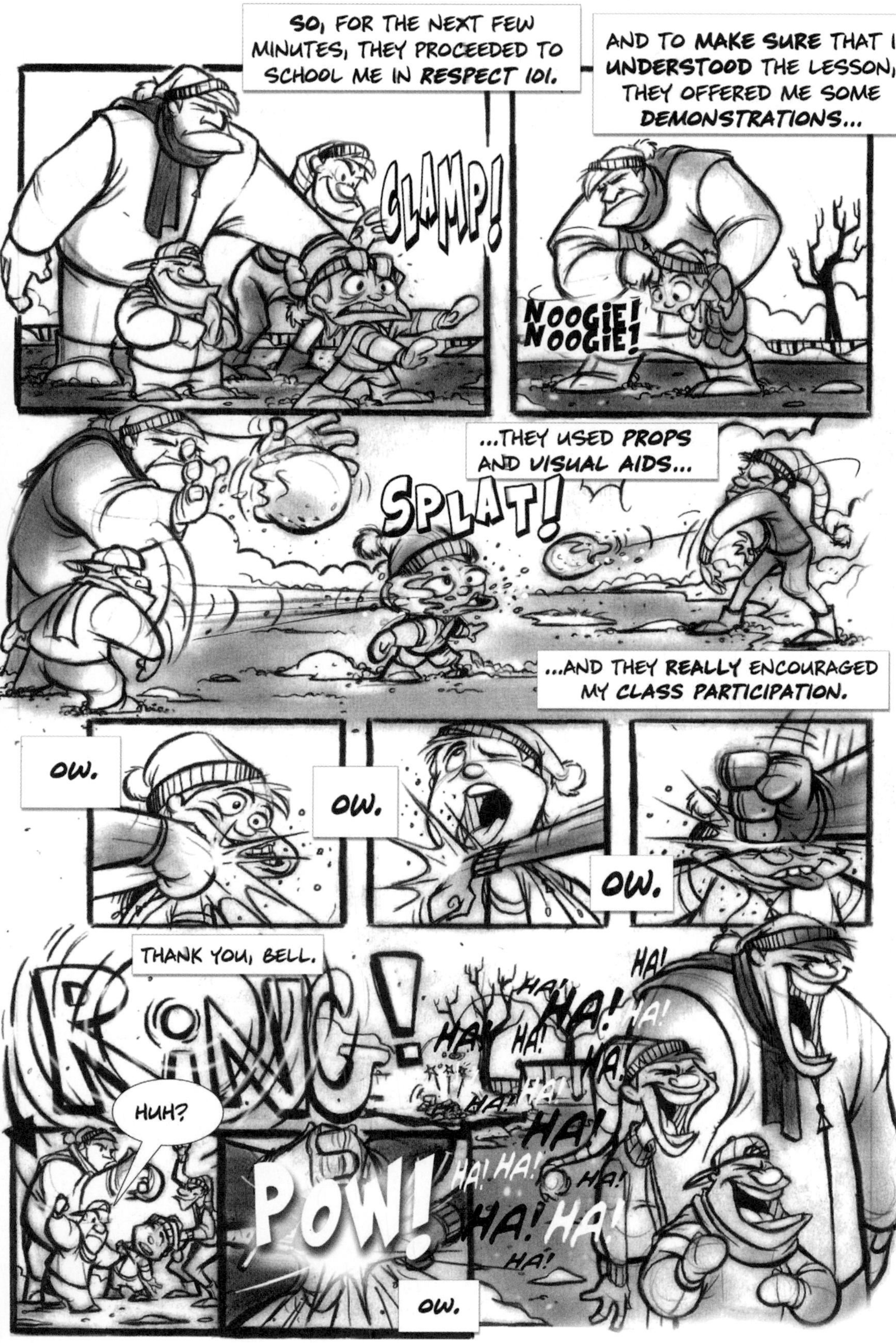
SO, FOR THE NEXT FEW MINUTES, THEY PROCEEDED TO SCHOOL ME IN RESPECT 101.
CLAMP!
AND TO MAKE SURE THAT I UNDERSTOOD THE LESSON, THEY OFFERED ME SOME DEMONSTRATIONS...
NOOGIE! NOOGIE!
...THEY USED PROPS AND VISUAL AIDS...
SPLAT!
...AND THEY REALLY ENCOURAGED MY CLASS PARTICIPATION.
OW.
OW.
OW.
THANK YOU, BELL.
RING!
HA! HA! HA! HA! HA! HA! HA! HA! HA! HA! HA! HA! HA! HA! HA!
HUH?
POW!
OW.

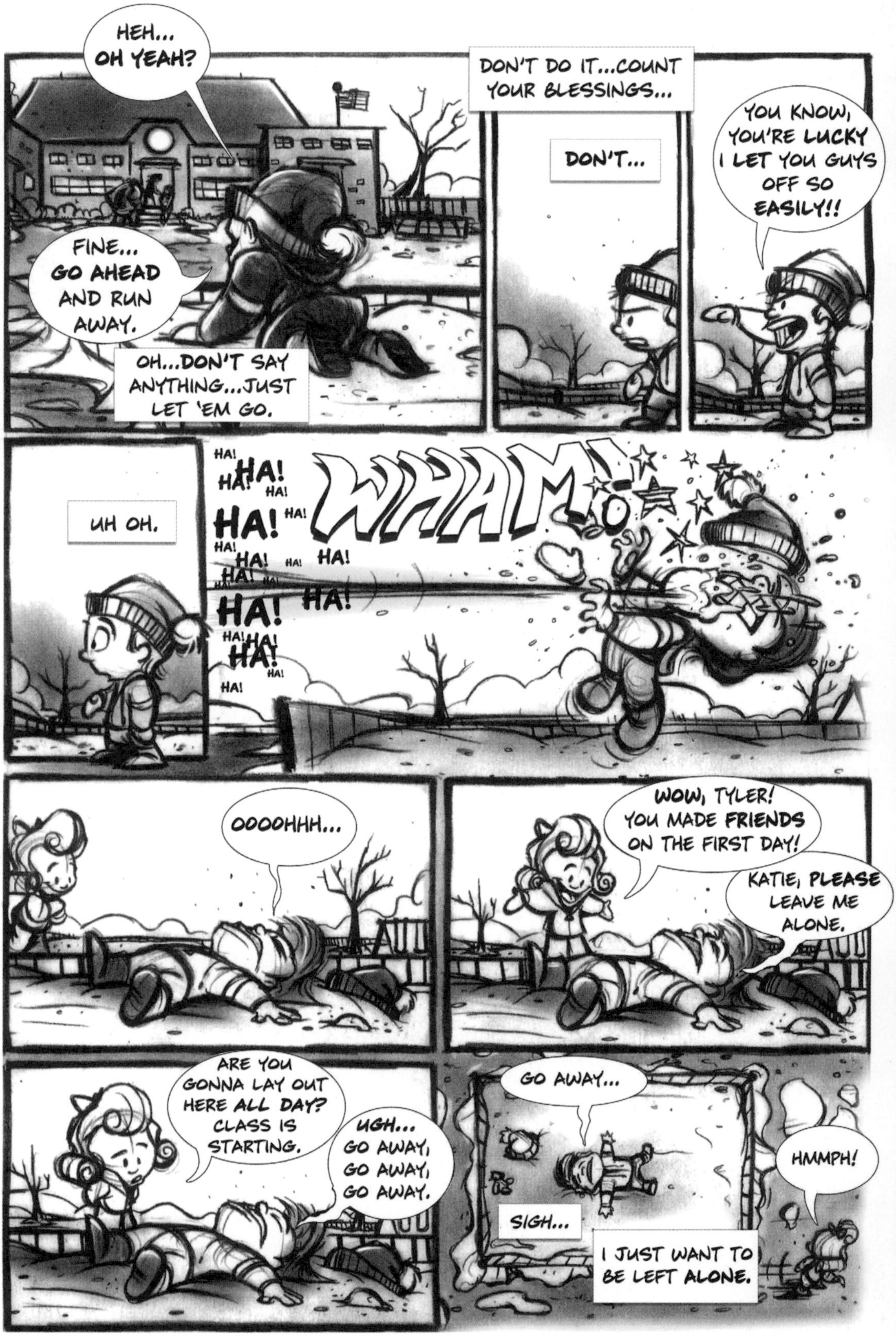
HEH... OH YEAH?
FINE... GO AHEAD AND RUN AWAY.
OH...DON'T SAY ANYTHING...JUST LET 'EM GO.
DON'T DO IT...COUNT YOUR BLESSINGS...
DON'T...
YOU KNOW, YOU'RE LUCKY I LET YOU GUYS OFF SO EASILY!!
UH OH.
HA! HA! HA! HA! HA! HA! HA! HA! HA! HA! HA! HA! HA! HA! HA! HA! HA! HA! HA!
WHAM!
OOOOHHH...
WOW, TYLER! YOU MADE FRIENDS ON THE FIRST DAY!
KATIE, PLEASE LEAVE ME ALONE.
ARE YOU GONNA LAY OUT HERE ALL DAY? CLASS IS STARTING.
UGH... GO AWAY, GO AWAY, GO AWAY.
GO AWAY...
SIGH...
I JUST WANT TO BE LEFT ALONE.
HMMPH!

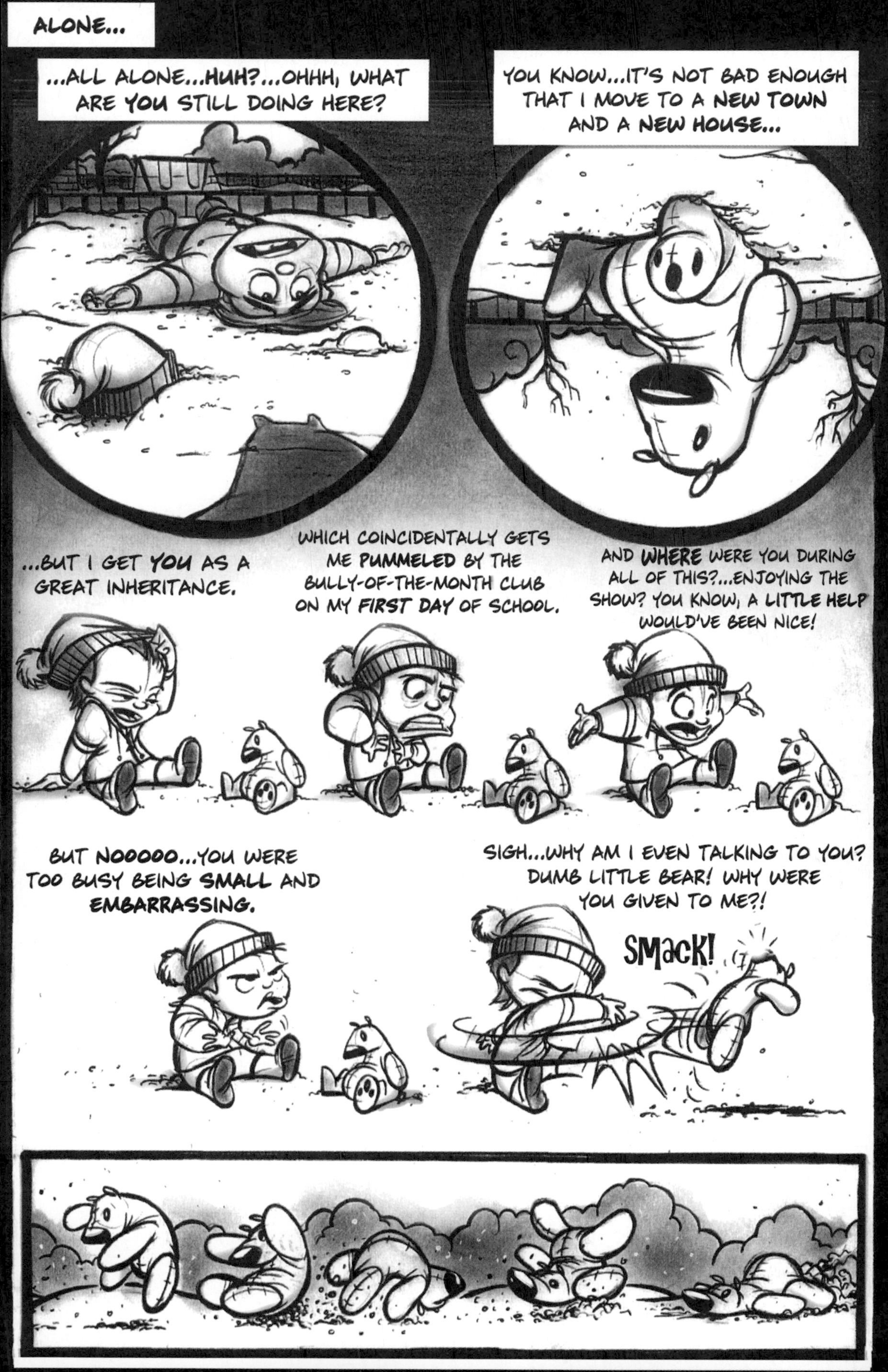
ALONE...
...ALL ALONE...HUH?...OHHH, WHAT ARE YOU STILL DOING HERE?
YOU KNOW...IT'S NOT BAD ENOUGH THAT I MOVE TO A NEW TOWN AND A NEW HOUSE...
...BUT I GET YOU AS A GREAT INHERITANCE.
WHICH COINCIDENTALLY GETS ME PUMMELED BY THE BULLY-OF-THE-MONTH CLUB ON MY FIRST DAY OF SCHOOL.
AND WHERE WERE YOU DURING ALL OF THIS?...ENJOYING THE SHOW? YOU KNOW, A LITTLE HELP WOULD'VE BEEN NICE!
BUT NOOOOO...YOU WERE TOO BUSY BEING SMALL AND EMBARRASSING.
SIGH...WHY AM I EVEN TALKING TO YOU? DUMB LITTLE BEAR! WHY WERE YOU GIVEN TO ME?!
SMACK!

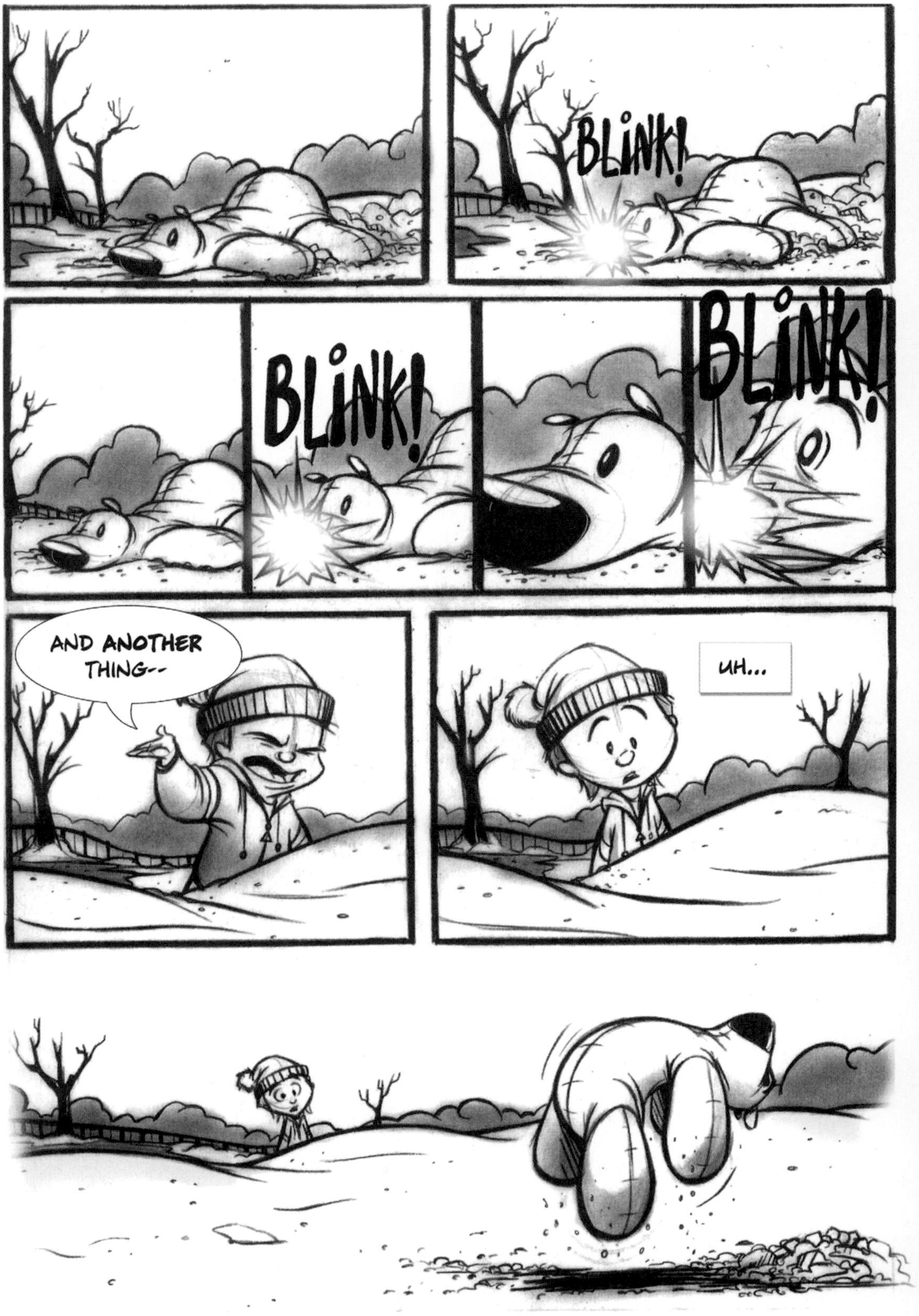
BLINK!
BLINK!
BLINK!
AND ANOTHER THING--
UH...

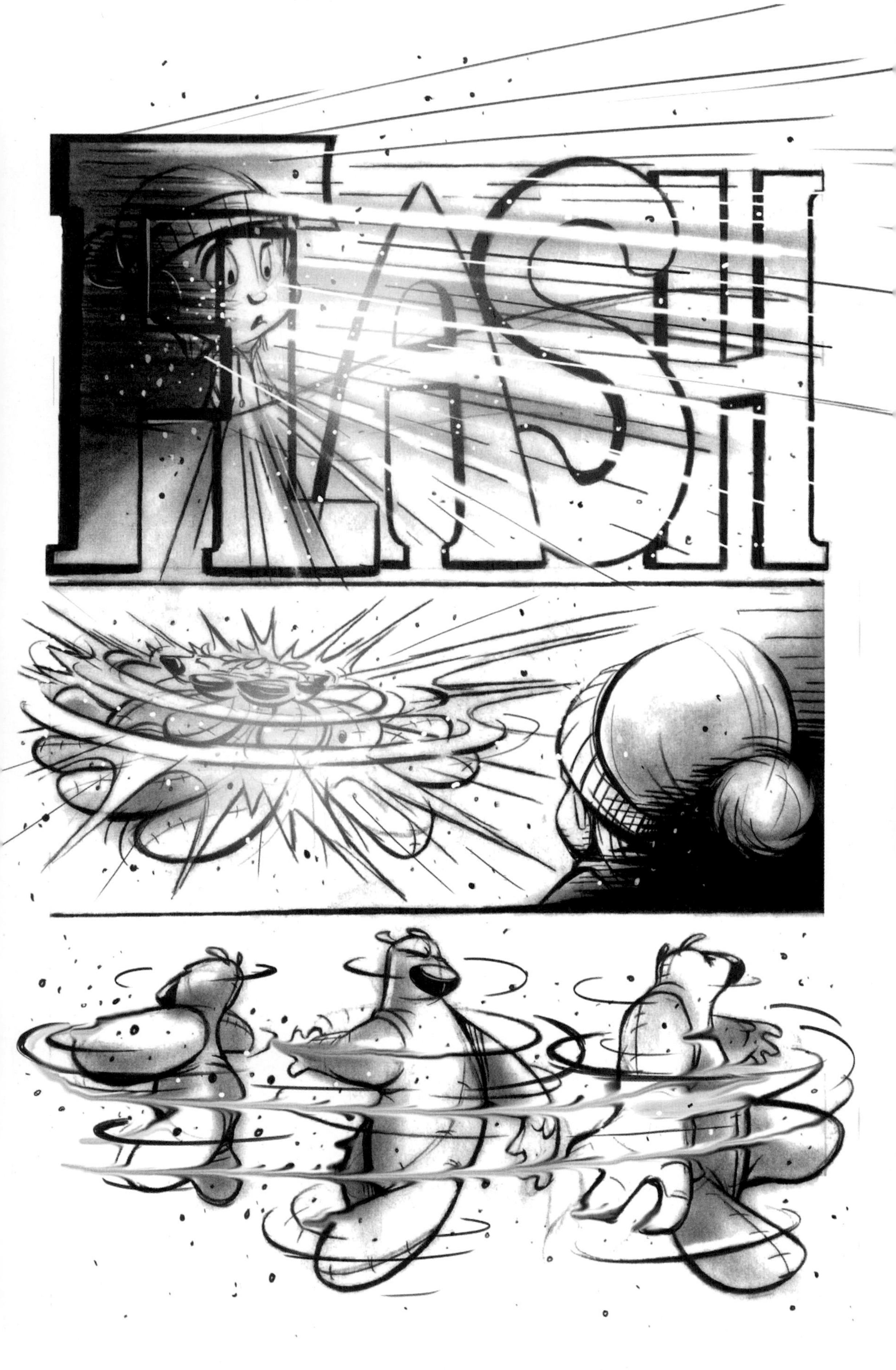
FLASH

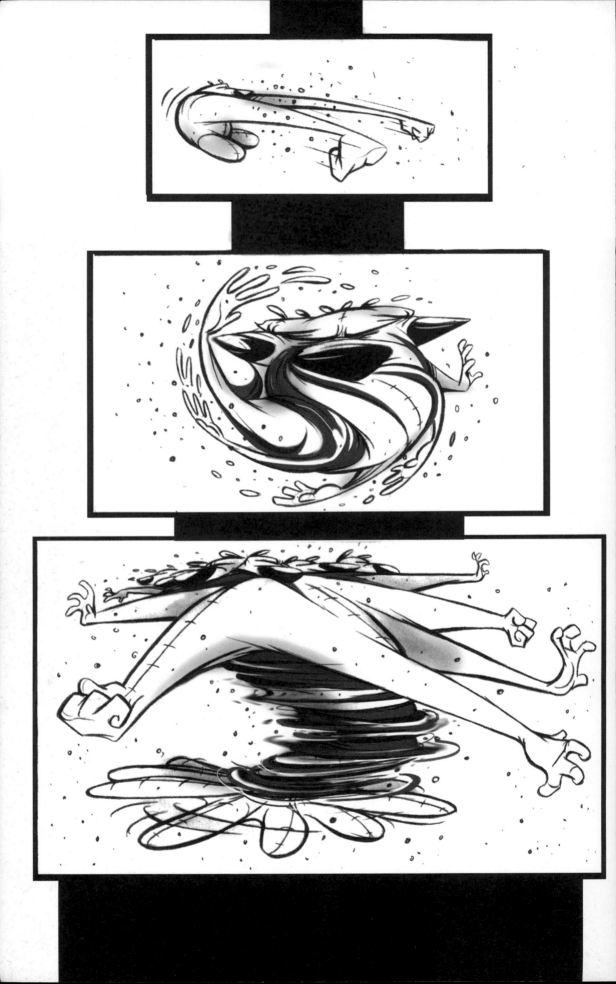

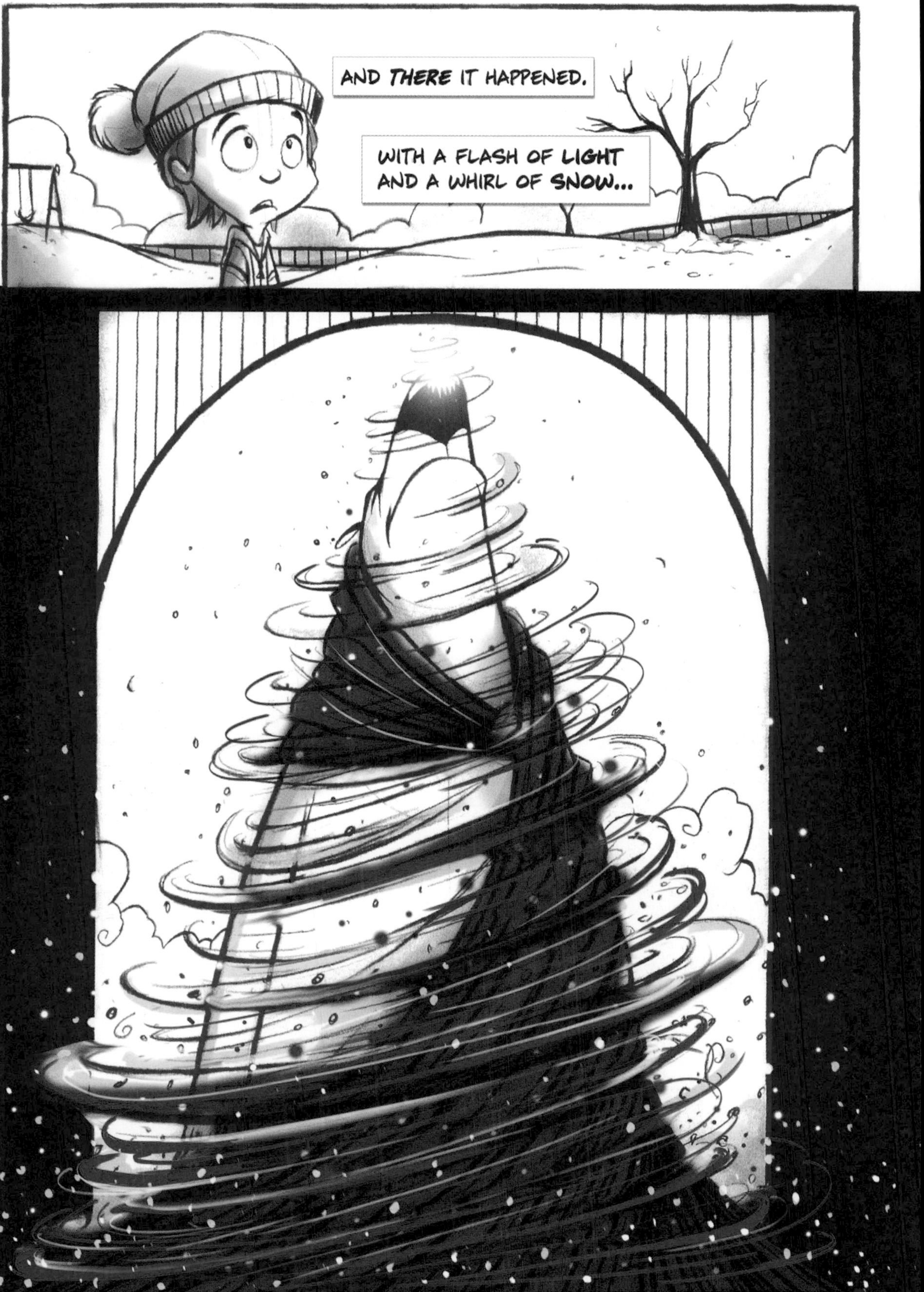
AND *THERE* IT HAPPENED.
WITH A FLASH OF LIGHT AND A WHIRL OF SNOW...

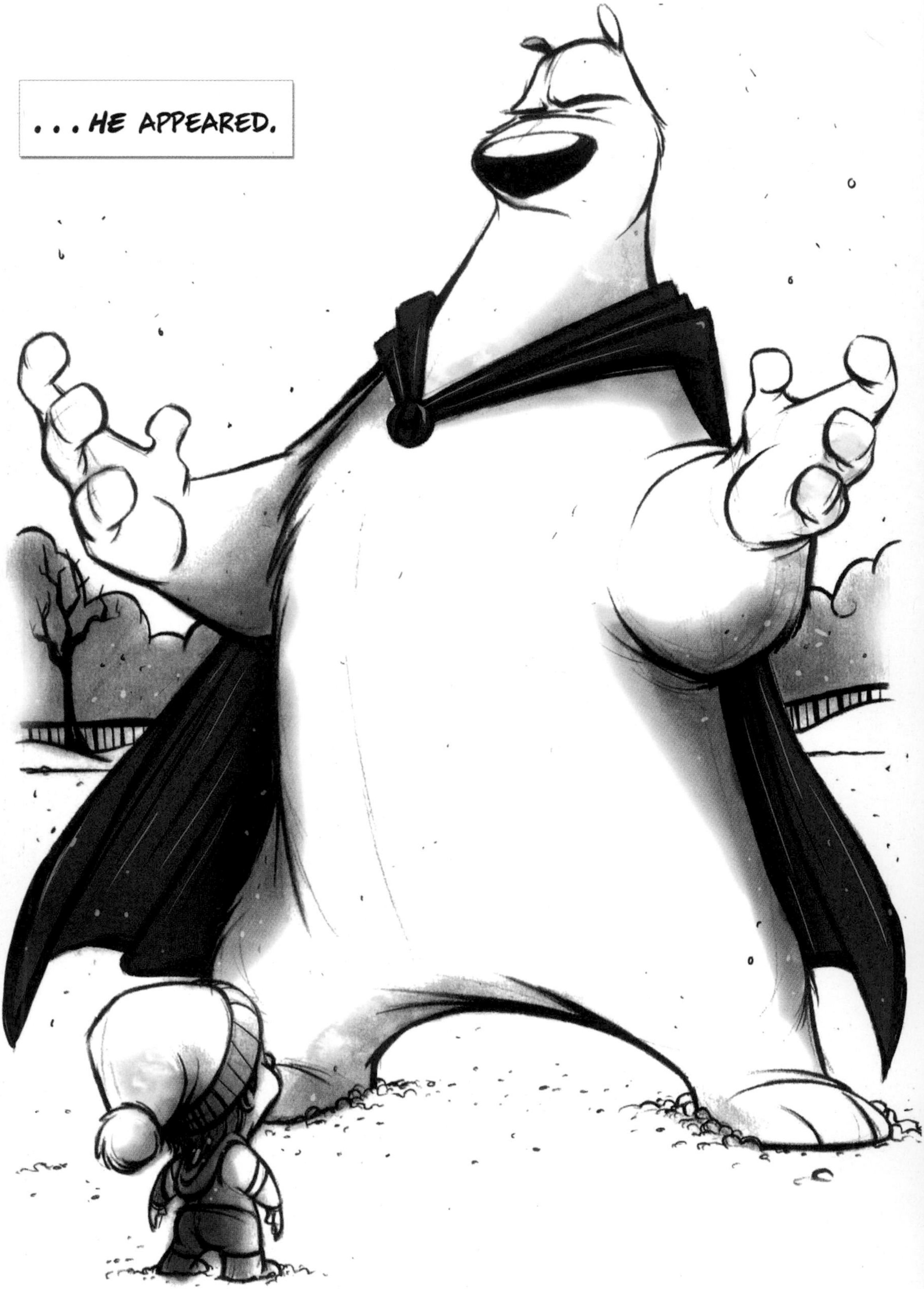
. . . HE APPEARED.

Chapter Two

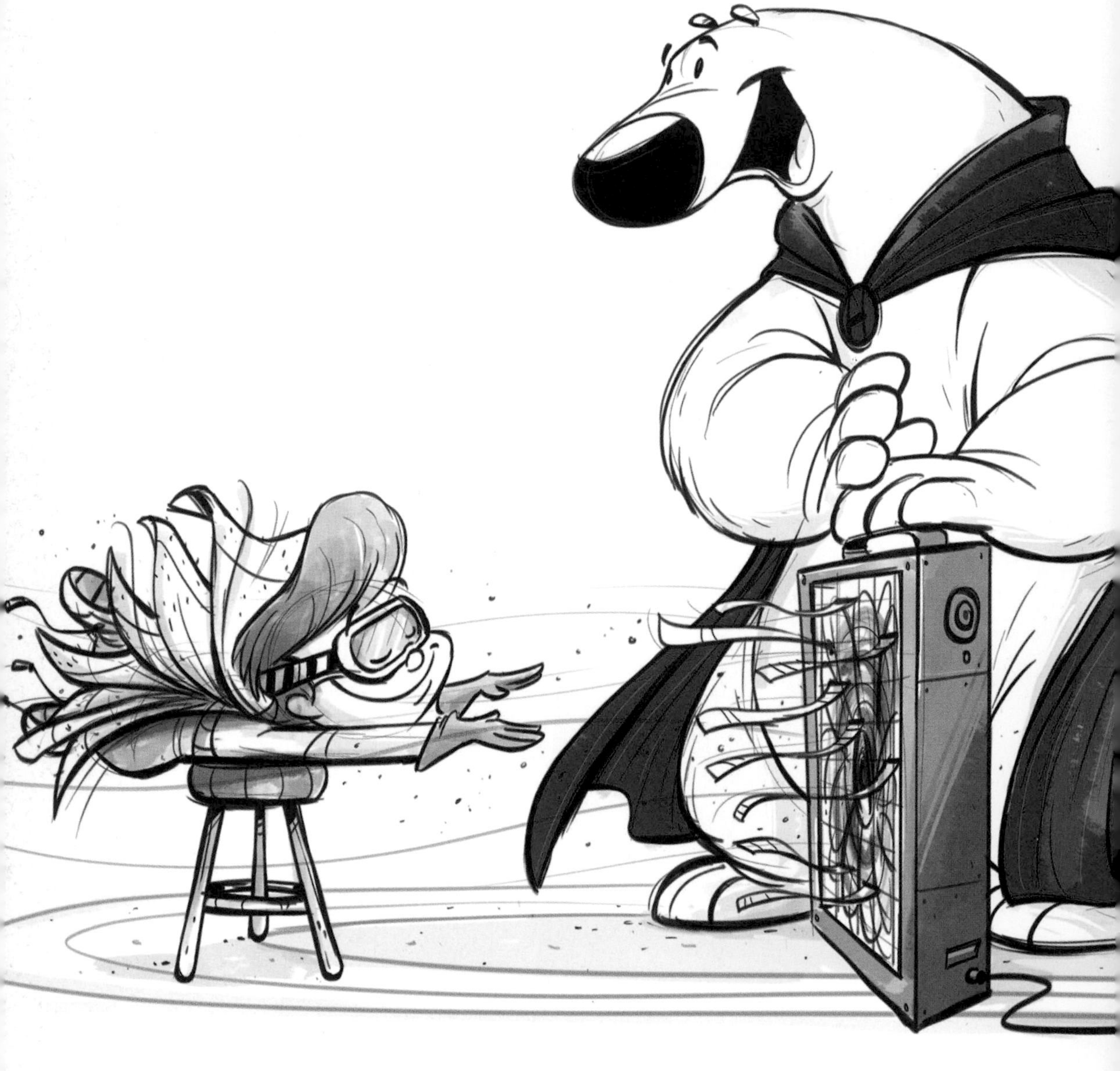

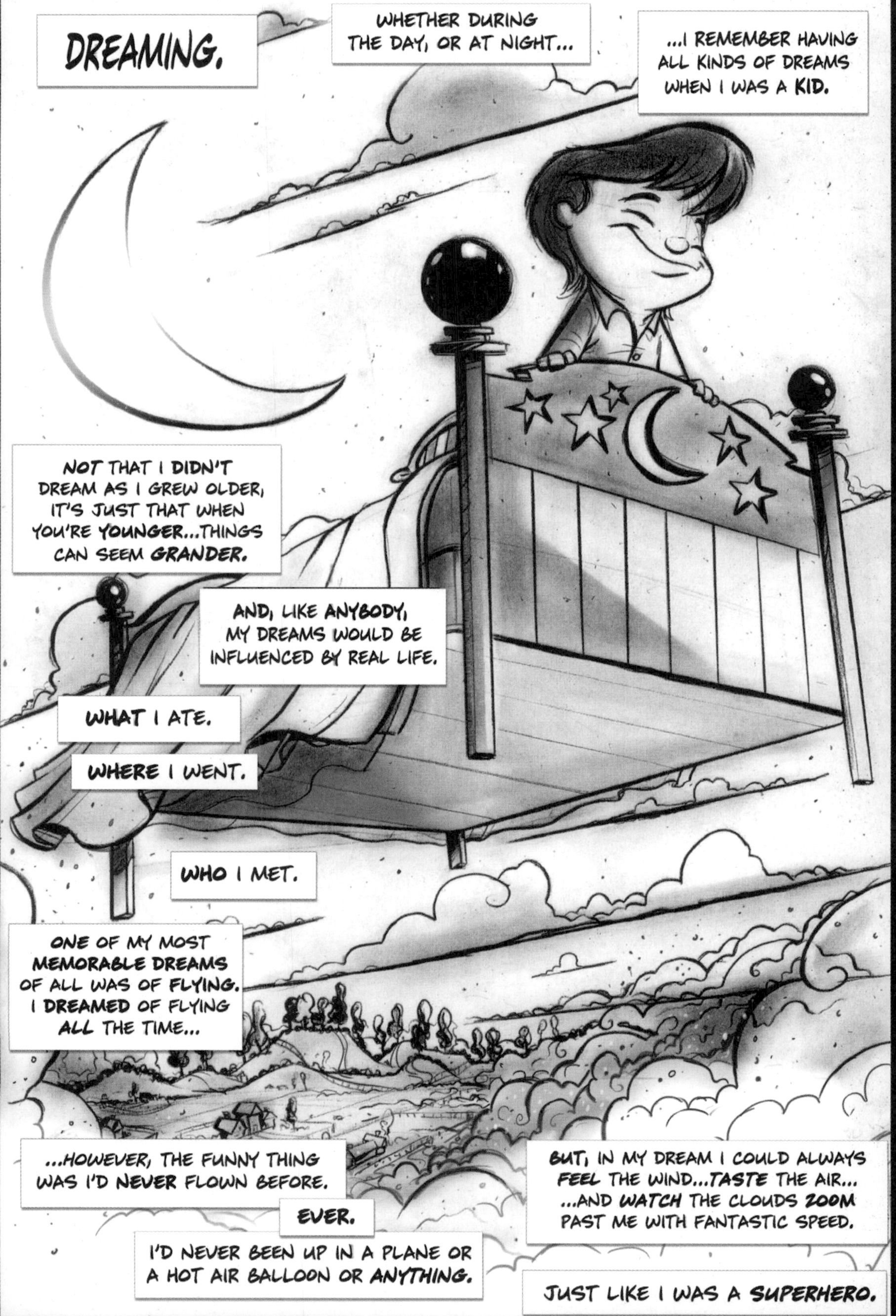
DREAMING.
WHETHER DURING THE DAY, OR AT NIGHT...
...I REMEMBER HAVING ALL KINDS OF DREAMS WHEN I WAS A KID.
NOT THAT I DIDN'T DREAM AS I GREW OLDER, IT'S JUST THAT WHEN YOU'RE YOUNGER...THINGS CAN SEEM GRANDER.
AND, LIKE ANYBODY, MY DREAMS WOULD BE INFLUENCED BY REAL LIFE.
WHAT I ATE.
WHERE I WENT.
WHO I MET.
ONE OF MY MOST MEMORABLE DREAMS OF ALL WAS OF FLYING. I DREAMED OF FLYING ALL THE TIME...
...HOWEVER, THE FUNNY THING WAS I'D NEVER FLOWN BEFORE.
EVER.
I'D NEVER BEEN UP IN A PLANE OR A HOT AIR BALLOON OR ANYTHING.
BUT, IN MY DREAM I COULD ALWAYS FEEL THE WIND...TASTE THE AIR... ...AND WATCH THE CLOUDS ZOOM PAST ME WITH FANTASTIC SPEED.
JUST LIKE I WAS A SUPERHERO.

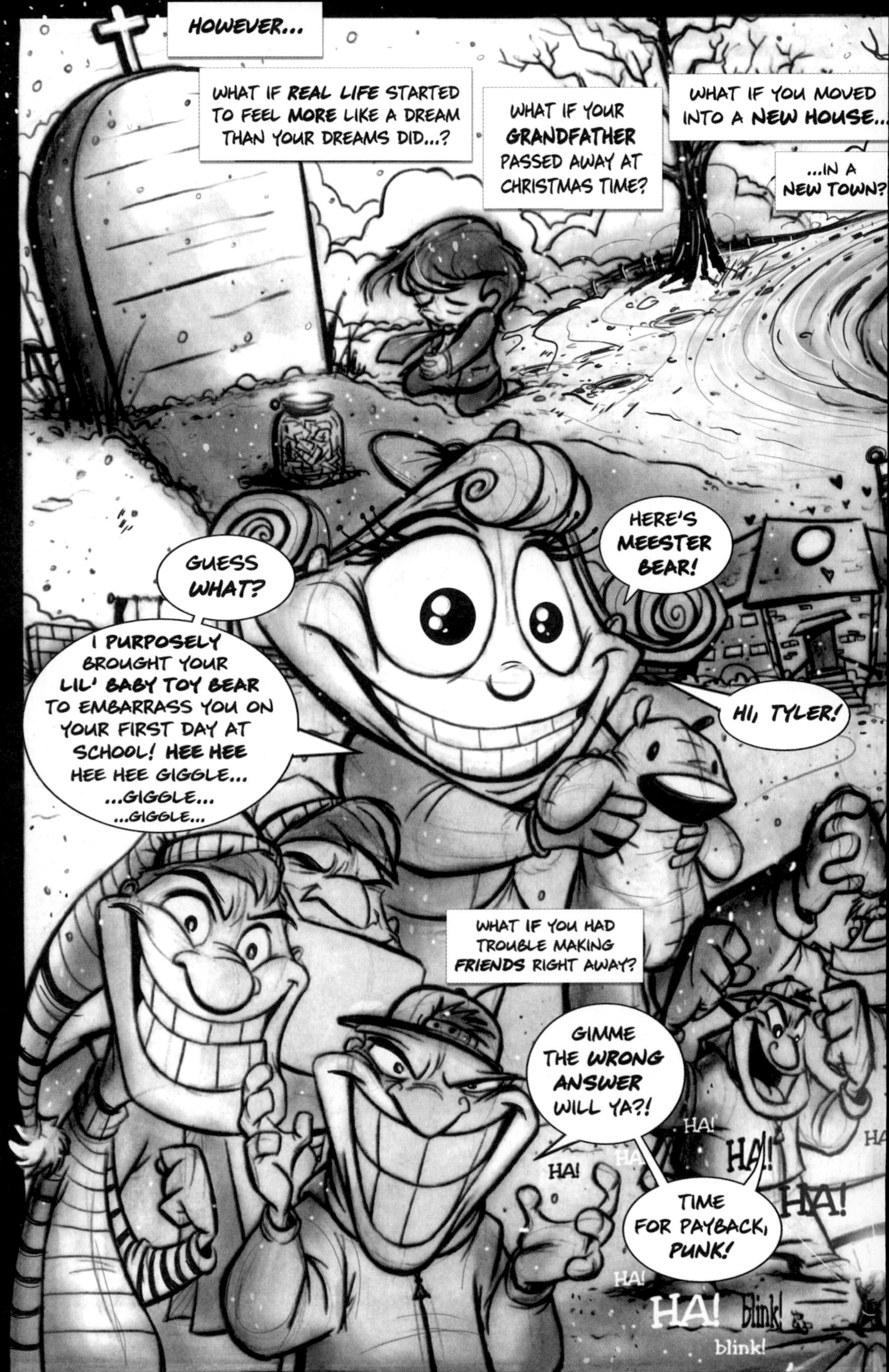
HOWEVER...
WHAT IF REAL LIFE STARTED TO FEEL MORE LIKE A DREAM THAN YOUR DREAMS DID...?
WHAT IF YOUR GRANDFATHER PASSED AWAY AT CHRISTMAS TIME?
WHAT IF YOU MOVED INTO A NEW HOUSE...
...IN A NEW TOWN?
GUESS WHAT?
HERE'S MEESTER BEAR!
I PURPOSELY BROUGHT YOUR LIL' BABY TOY BEAR TO EMBARRASS YOU ON YOUR FIRST DAY AT SCHOOL! HEE HEE HEE HEE GIGGLE... ...GIGGLE... ...GIGGLE...
HI, TYLER!
WHAT IF YOU HAD TROUBLE MAKING FRIENDS RIGHT AWAY?
GIMME THE WRONG ANSWER WILL YA?!
TIME FOR PAYBACK, PUNK!
HA!
HA!
HA!
HA!
HA!
HA!
HA!
blink!
blink!

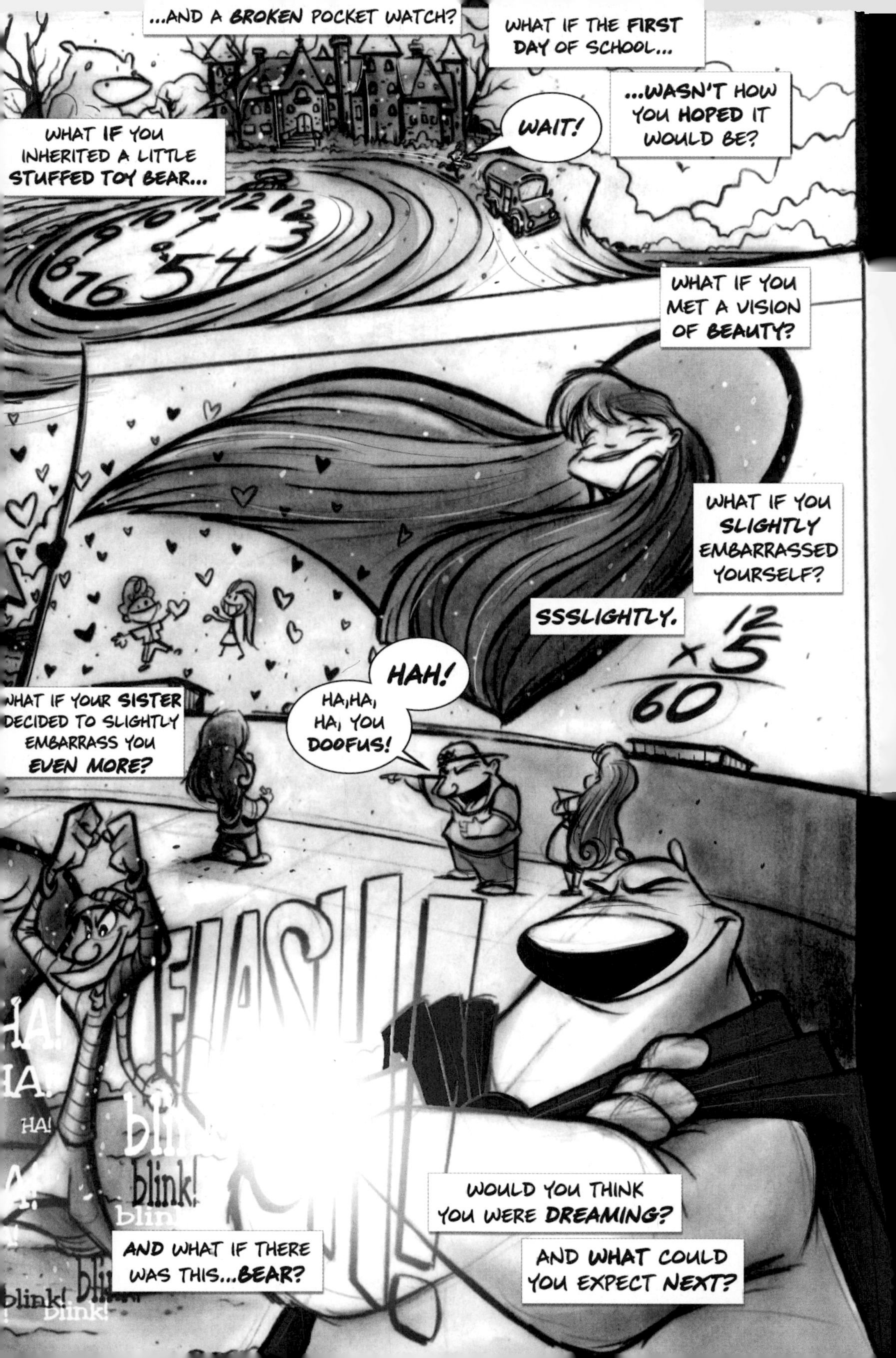
WHAT IF THE FIRST DAY OF SCHOOL...
...WASN'T HOW YOU HOPED IT WOULD BE?
WAIT!
WHAT IF YOU INHERITED A LITTLE STUFFED TOY BEAR...
...AND A BROKEN POCKET WATCH?
WHAT IF YOU MET A VISION OF BEAUTY?
WHAT IF YOU SLIGHTLY EMBARRASSED YOURSELF?
SSSLIGHTLY.
12
×5
60
WHAT IF YOUR SISTER DECIDED TO SLIGHTLY EMBARRASS YOU EVEN MORE?
HAH!
HA, HA, HA, YOU DOOFUS!
FLASH!
HA!
HA.
HA!
blink!
blink!
blink!
WOULD YOU THINK YOU WERE DREAMING?
AND WHAT IF THERE WAS THIS...BEAR?
AND WHAT COULD YOU EXPECT NEXT?

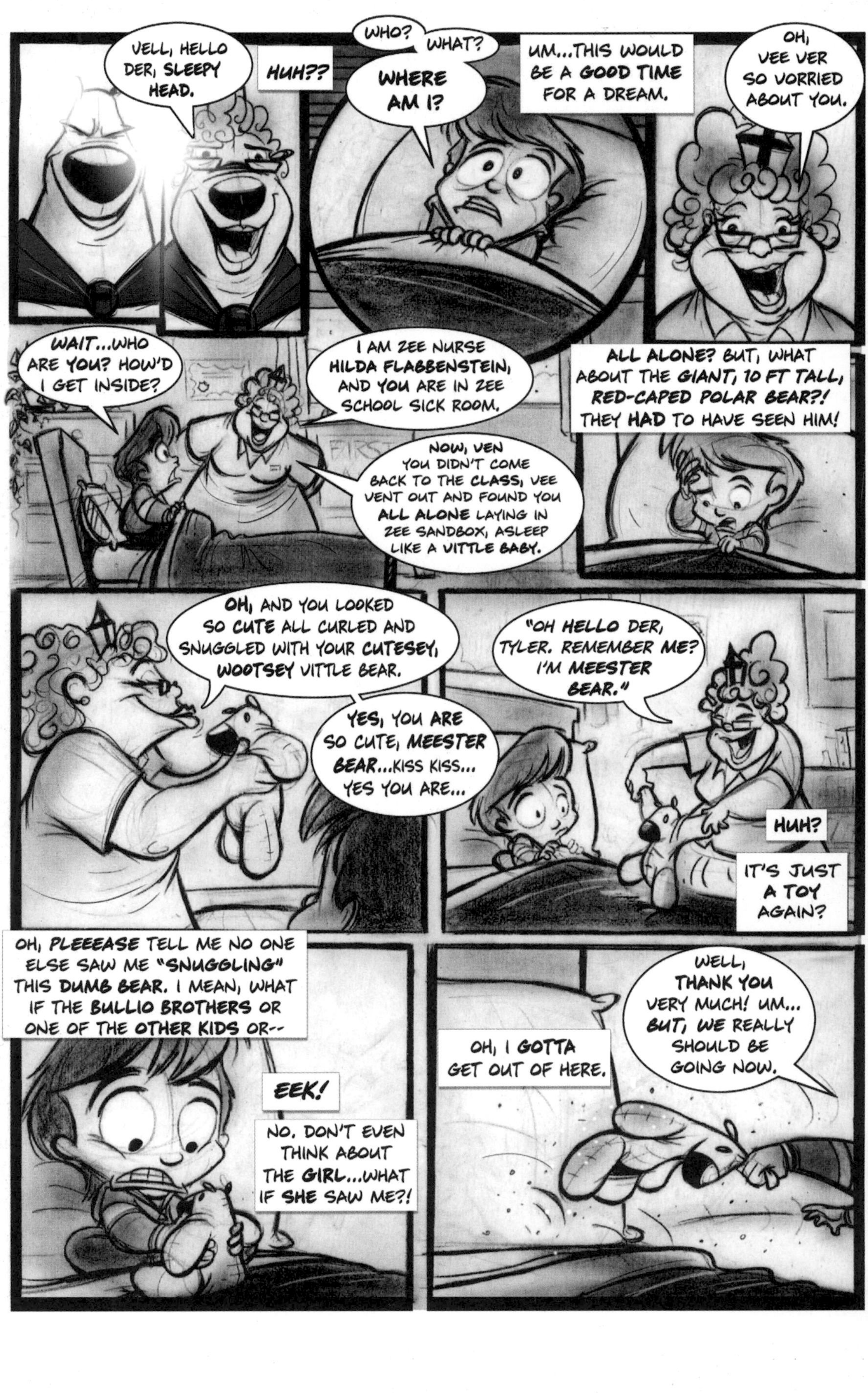
VELL, HELLO DER, SLEEPY HEAD.
HUH??
WHO?
WHAT?
WHERE AM I?
UM...THIS WOULD BE A GOOD TIME FOR A DREAM.
OH, VEE VER SO VORRIED ABOUT YOU.
WAIT...WHO ARE YOU? HOW'D I GET INSIDE?
I AM ZEE NURSE HILDA FLABBENSTEIN, AND YOU ARE IN ZEE SCHOOL SICK ROOM.
NOW, VEN YOU DIDN'T COME BACK TO THE CLASS, VEE VENT OUT AND FOUND YOU ALL ALONE LAYING IN ZEE SANDBOX, ASLEEP LIKE A VITTLE BABY.
ALL ALONE? BUT, WHAT ABOUT THE GIANT, 10 FT TALL, RED-CAPED POLAR BEAR?! THEY HAD TO HAVE SEEN HIM!
OH, AND YOU LOOKED SO CUTE ALL CURLED AND SNUGGLED WITH YOUR CUTESEY, WOOTSEY VITTLE BEAR.
YES, YOU ARE SO CUTE, MEESTER BEAR...KISS KISS... YES YOU ARE...
"OH HELLO DER, TYLER. REMEMBER ME? I'M MEESTER BEAR."
HUH?
IT'S JUST A TOY AGAIN?
OH, PLEEEASE TELL ME NO ONE ELSE SAW ME "SNUGGLING" THIS DUMB BEAR. I MEAN, WHAT IF THE BULLIO BROTHERS OR ONE OF THE OTHER KIDS OR--
EEK!
NO. DON'T EVEN THINK ABOUT THE GIRL...WHAT IF SHE SAW ME?!
OH, I GOTTA GET OUT OF HERE.
WELL, THANK YOU VERY MUCH! UM... BUT, WE REALLY SHOULD BE GOING NOW.

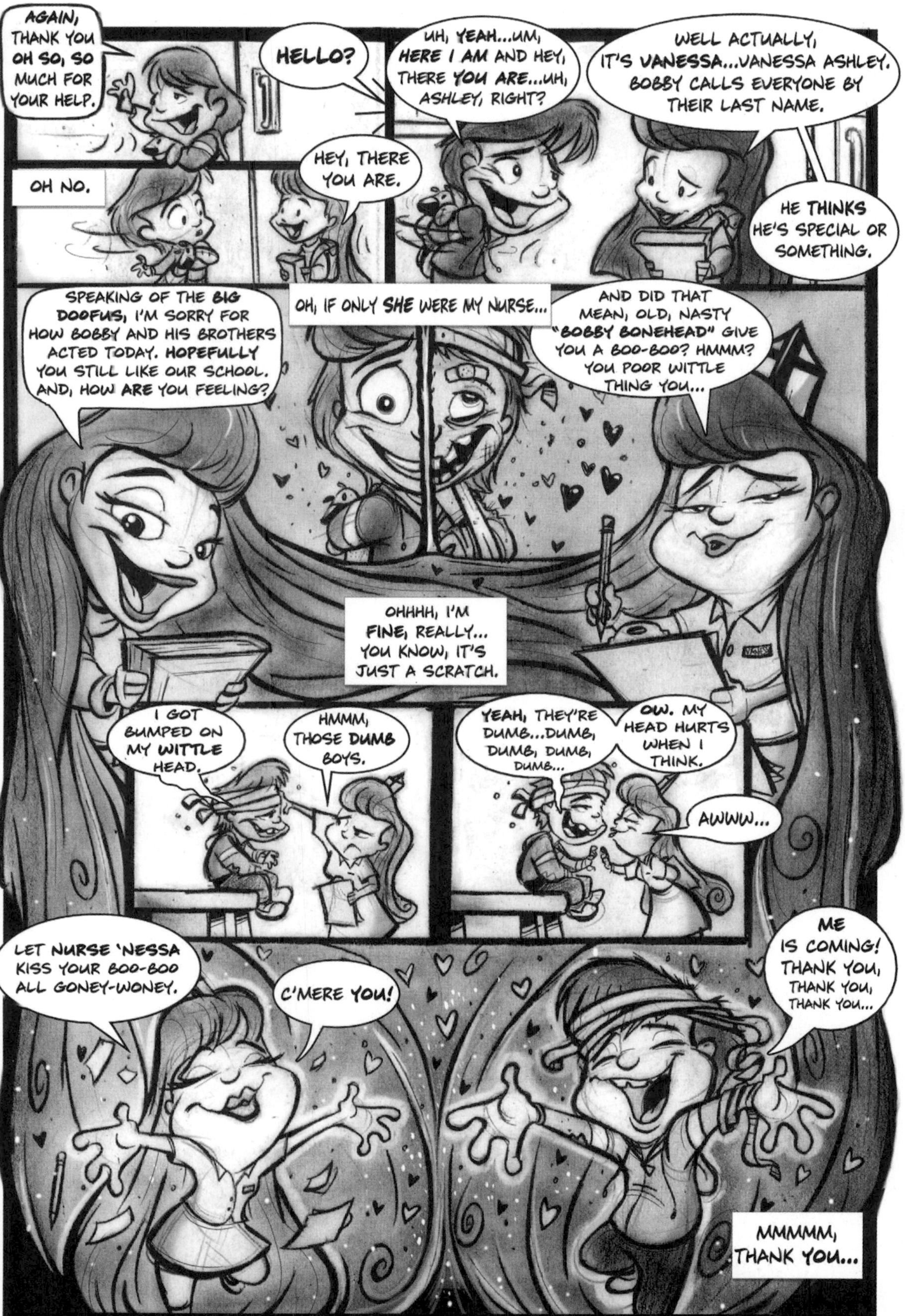
AGAIN, THANK YOU OH SO, SO MUCH FOR YOUR HELP.
HELLO?
UH, YEAH...UM, HERE I AM AND HEY, THERE YOU ARE...UH, ASHLEY, RIGHT?
WELL ACTUALLY, IT'S VANESSA...VANESSA ASHLEY. BOBBY CALLS EVERYONE BY THEIR LAST NAME.
OH NO.
HEY, THERE YOU ARE.
HE THINKS HE'S SPECIAL OR SOMETHING.
SPEAKING OF THE BIG DOOFUS, I'M SORRY FOR HOW BOBBY AND HIS BROTHERS ACTED TODAY. HOPEFULLY YOU STILL LIKE OUR SCHOOL. AND, HOW ARE YOU FEELING?
OH, IF ONLY SHE WERE MY NURSE...
AND DID THAT MEAN, OLD, NASTY "BOBBY BONEHEAD" GIVE YOU A BOO-BOO? HMMM? YOU POOR WITTLE THING YOU...
OHHHH, I'M FINE, REALLY... YOU KNOW, IT'S JUST A SCRATCH.
I GOT BUMPED ON MY WITTLE HEAD.
HMMM, THOSE DUMB BOYS.
YEAH, THEY'RE DUMB...DUMB, DUMB, DUMB, DUMB...
OW. MY HEAD HURTS WHEN I THINK.
AWWW...
LET NURSE 'NESSA KISS YOUR BOO-BOO ALL GONEY-WONEY.
C'MERE YOU!
ME IS COMING! THANK YOU, THANK YOU, THANK YOU...
MMMMM, THANK YOU...

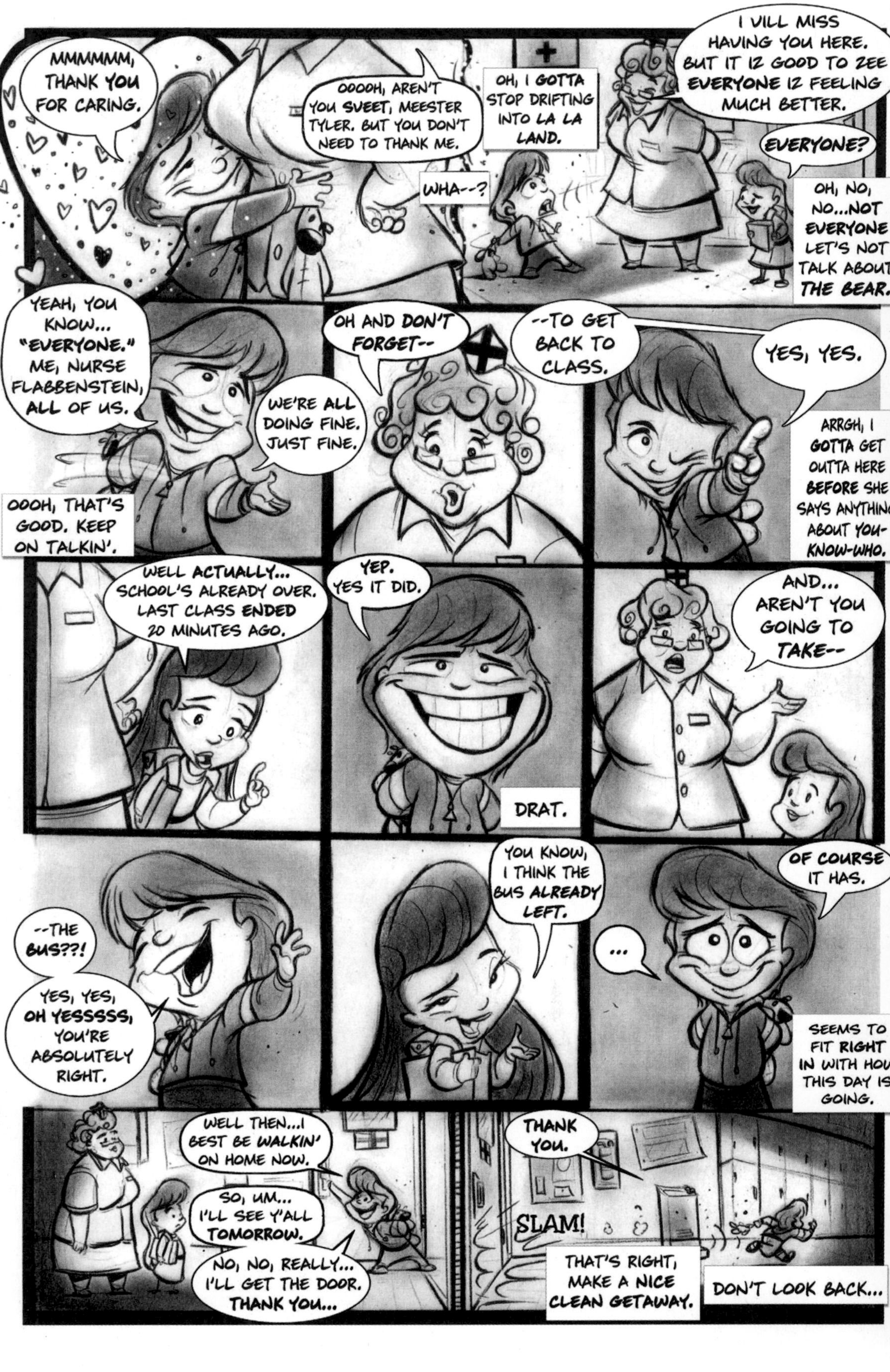
MMMMMM, THANK YOU FOR CARING.
OOOOH, AREN'T YOU SVEET, MEESTER TYLER. BUT YOU DON'T NEED TO THANK ME.
WHA--?
OH, I GOTTA STOP DRIFTING INTO LA LA LAND.
I VILL MISS HAVING YOU HERE. BUT IT IZ GOOD TO ZEE EVERYONE IZ FEELING MUCH BETTER.
EVERYONE?
OH, NO, NO...NOT EVERYONE LET'S NOT TALK ABOUT THE BEAR.
YEAH, YOU KNOW... "EVERYONE." ME, NURSE FLABBENSTEIN, ALL OF US.
WE'RE ALL DOING FINE. JUST FINE.
OOOH, THAT'S GOOD. KEEP ON TALKIN'.
OH AND DON'T FORGET--
--TO GET BACK TO CLASS.
YES, YES.
ARRGH, I GOTTA GET OUTTA HERE BEFORE SHE SAYS ANYTHING ABOUT YOU-KNOW-WHO.
WELL ACTUALLY... SCHOOL'S ALREADY OVER. LAST CLASS ENDED 20 MINUTES AGO.
YEP. YES IT DID.
DRAT.
AND... AREN'T YOU GOING TO TAKE--
--THE BUS??!
YES, YES, OH YESSSSS, YOU'RE ABSOLUTELY RIGHT.
YOU KNOW, I THINK THE BUS ALREADY LEFT.
...
OF COURSE IT HAS.
SEEMS TO FIT RIGHT IN WITH HOW THIS DAY IS GOING.
WELL THEN...I BEST BE WALKIN' ON HOME NOW.
SO, UM... I'LL SEE Y'ALL TOMORROW.
NO, NO, REALLY... I'LL GET THE DOOR. THANK YOU...
THANK YOU.
SLAM!
THAT'S RIGHT, MAKE A NICE CLEAN GETAWAY.
DON'T LOOK BACK...

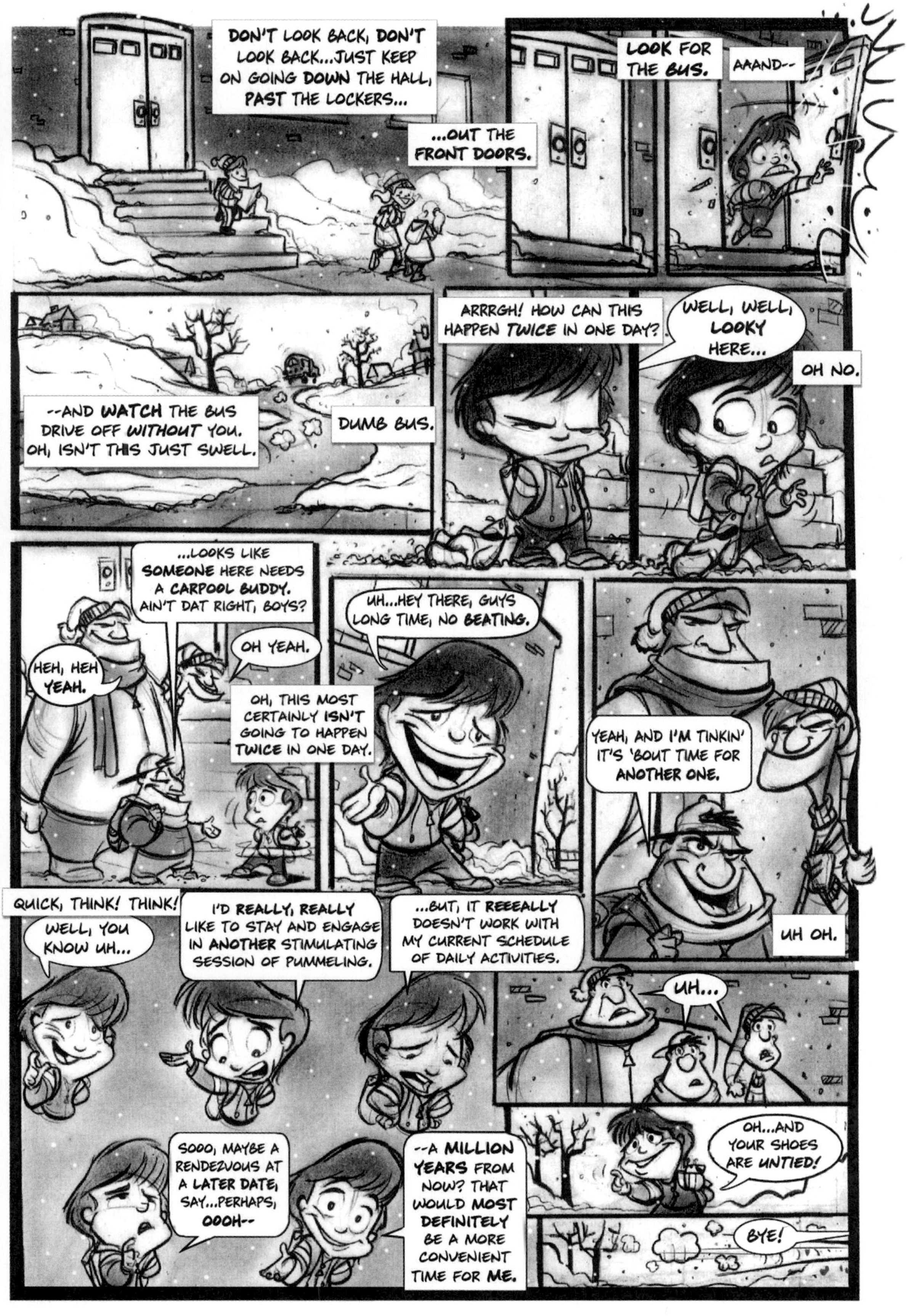
DON'T LOOK BACK, DON'T LOOK BACK...JUST KEEP ON GOING DOWN THE HALL, PAST THE LOCKERS...
...OUT THE FRONT DOORS.
LOOK FOR THE BUS.
AAAND--
--AND WATCH THE BUS DRIVE OFF WITHOUT YOU. OH, ISN'T THIS JUST SWELL.
DUMB BUS.
ARRRGH! HOW CAN THIS HAPPEN TWICE IN ONE DAY?
WELL, WELL, LOOKY HERE...
OH NO.
...LOOKS LIKE SOMEONE HERE NEEDS A CARPOOL BUDDY. AIN'T DAT RIGHT, BOYS?
HEH, HEH YEAH.
OH YEAH.
OH, THIS MOST CERTAINLY ISN'T GOING TO HAPPEN TWICE IN ONE DAY.
UH...HEY THERE, GUYS LONG TIME, NO BEATING.
YEAH, AND I'M TINKIN' IT'S 'BOUT TIME FOR ANOTHER ONE.
UH OH.
QUICK, THINK! THINK!
WELL, YOU KNOW UH...
I'D REALLY, REALLY LIKE TO STAY AND ENGAGE IN ANOTHER STIMULATING SESSION OF PUMMELING.
...BUT, IT REEEALLY DOESN'T WORK WITH MY CURRENT SCHEDULE OF DAILY ACTIVITIES.
UH...
SOOO, MAYBE A RENDEZVOUS AT A LATER DATE, SAY...PERHAPS, OOOH--
--A MILLION YEARS FROM NOW? THAT WOULD MOST DEFINITELY BE A MORE CONVENIENT TIME FOR ME.
OH...AND YOUR SHOES ARE UNTIED!
BYE!

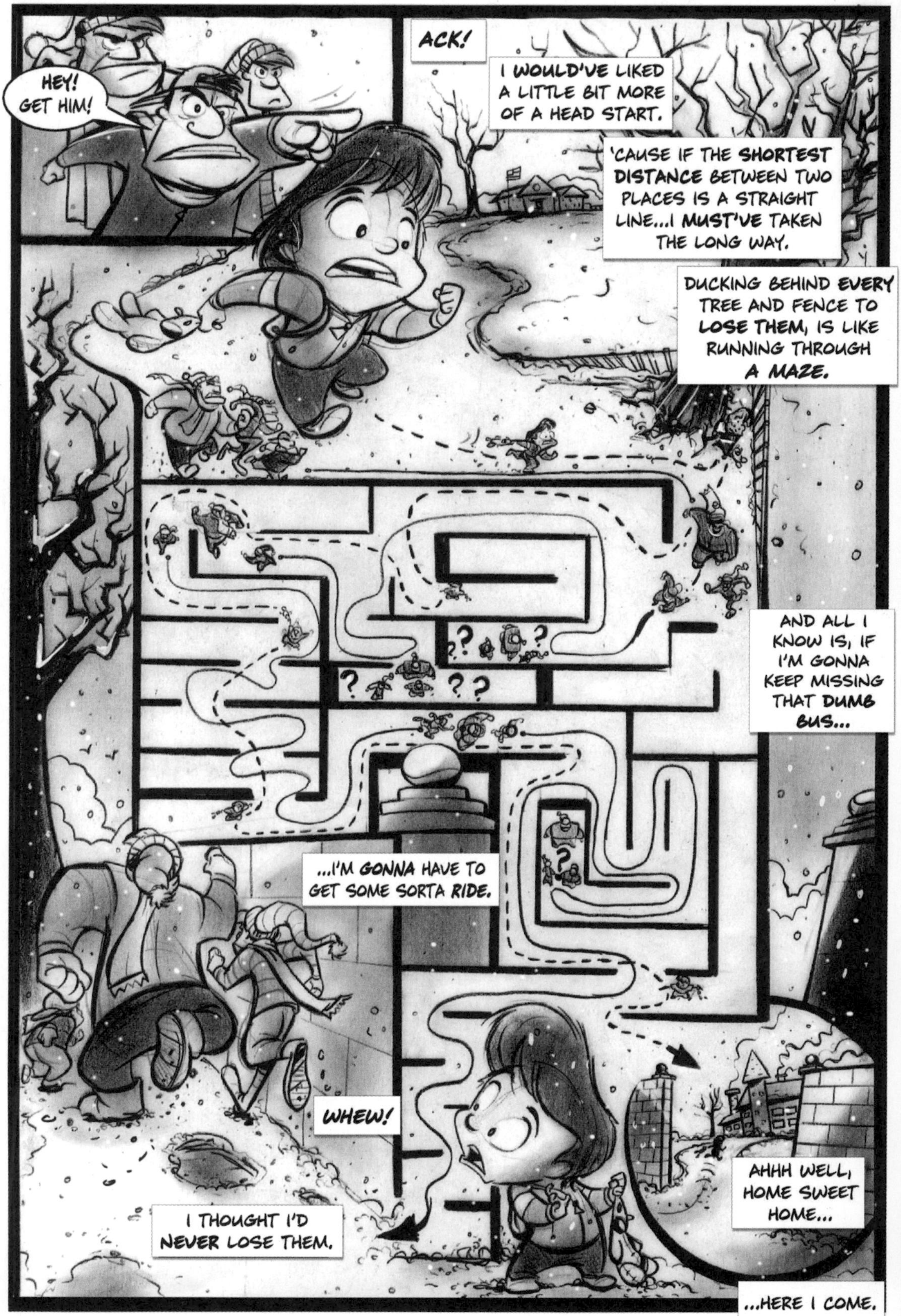
HEY! GET HIM!
ACK!
I WOULD'VE LIKED A LITTLE BIT MORE OF A HEAD START.
'CAUSE IF THE SHORTEST DISTANCE BETWEEN TWO PLACES IS A STRAIGHT LINE...I MUST'VE TAKEN THE LONG WAY.
DUCKING BEHIND EVERY TREE AND FENCE TO LOSE THEM, IS LIKE RUNNING THROUGH A MAZE.
AND ALL I KNOW IS, IF I'M GONNA KEEP MISSING THAT DUMB BUS...
...I'M GONNA HAVE TO GET SOME SORTA RIDE.
WHEW!
I THOUGHT I'D NEVER LOSE THEM.
AHHH WELL, HOME SWEET HOME...
...HERE I COME.

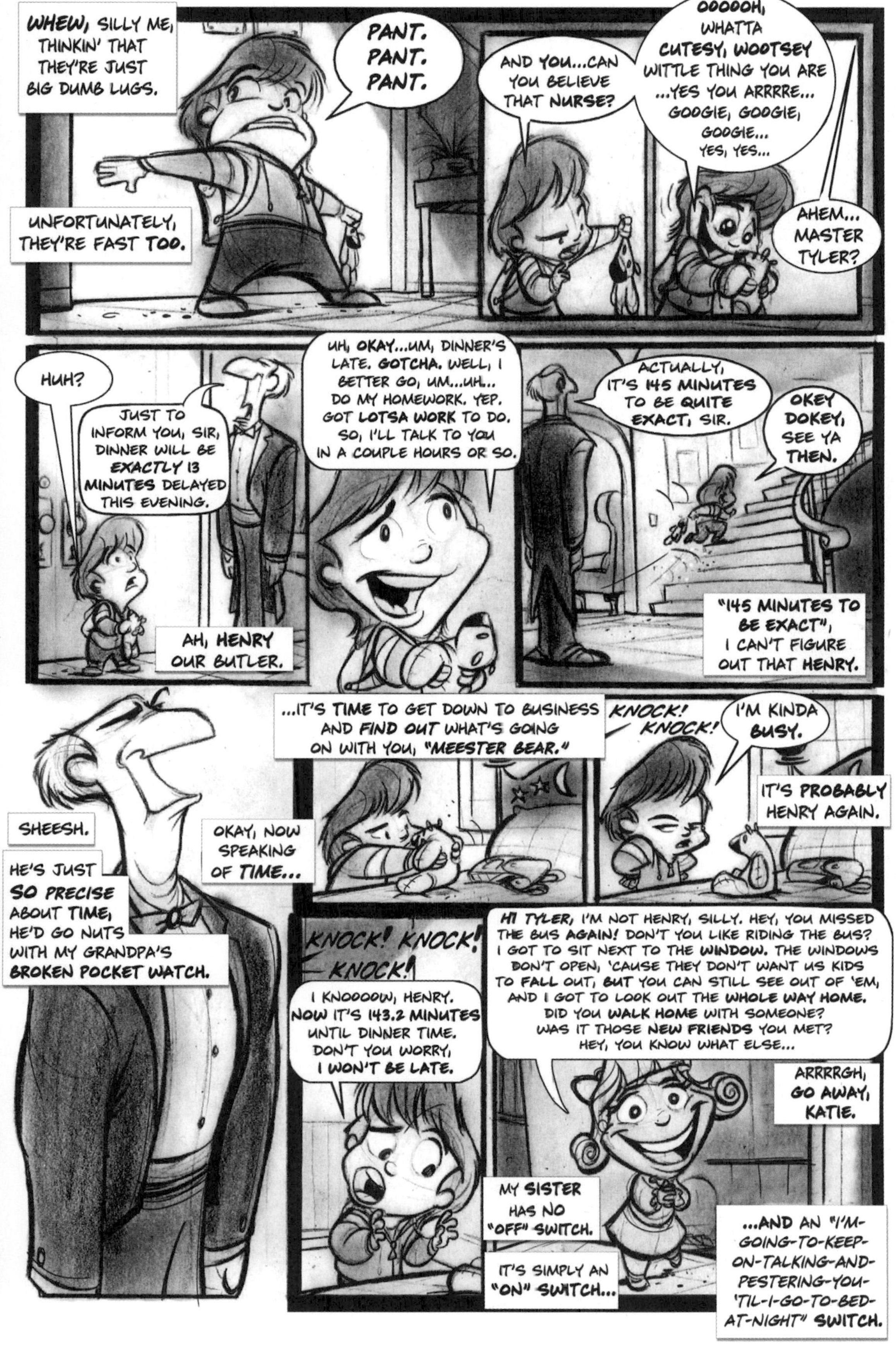

WHEW, SILLY ME, THINKIN' THAT THEY'RE JUST BIG DUMB LUGS.
PANT. PANT. PANT.
UNFORTUNATELY, THEY'RE FAST TOO.
AND YOU...CAN YOU BELIEVE THAT NURSE?
OOOOOH, WHATTA CUTESY, WOOTSEY WITTLE THING YOU ARE ...YES YOU ARRRRE... GOOGIE, GOOGIE, GOOGIE... YES, YES...
AHEM... MASTER TYLER?
HUH?
JUST TO INFORM YOU, SIR, DINNER WILL BE EXACTLY 13 MINUTES DELAYED THIS EVENING.
AH, HENRY OUR BUTLER.
UH, OKAY...UM, DINNER'S LATE. GOTCHA. WELL, I BETTER GO, UM...UH... DO MY HOMEWORK. YEP. GOT LOTSA WORK TO DO. SO, I'LL TALK TO YOU IN A COUPLE HOURS OR SO.
ACTUALLY, IT'S 145 MINUTES TO BE QUITE EXACT, SIR.
OKEY DOKEY, SEE YA THEN.
"145 MINUTES TO BE EXACT", I CAN'T FIGURE OUT THAT HENRY.
SHEESH.
HE'S JUST SO PRECISE ABOUT TIME, HE'D GO NUTS WITH MY GRANDPA'S BROKEN POCKET WATCH.
OKAY, NOW SPEAKING OF TIME...
...IT'S TIME TO GET DOWN TO BUSINESS AND FIND OUT WHAT'S GOING ON WITH YOU, "MEESTER BEAR."
KNOCK! KNOCK!
I'M KINDA BUSY.
IT'S PROBABLY HENRY AGAIN.
KNOCK! KNOCK! KNOCK!
I KNOOOOW, HENRY. NOW IT'S 143.2 MINUTES UNTIL DINNER TIME. DON'T YOU WORRY, I WON'T BE LATE.
HI TYLER, I'M NOT HENRY, SILLY. HEY, YOU MISSED THE BUS AGAIN! DON'T YOU LIKE RIDING THE BUS? I GOT TO SIT NEXT TO THE WINDOW. THE WINDOWS DON'T OPEN, 'CAUSE THEY DON'T WANT US KIDS TO FALL OUT, BUT YOU CAN STILL SEE OUT OF 'EM, AND I GOT TO LOOK OUT THE WHOLE WAY HOME. DID YOU WALK HOME WITH SOMEONE? WAS IT THOSE NEW FRIENDS YOU MET? HEY, YOU KNOW WHAT ELSE...
ARRRRGH, GO AWAY, KATIE.
MY SISTER HAS NO "OFF" SWITCH.
IT'S SIMPLY AN "ON" SWITCH...
...AND AN "I'M-GOING-TO-KEEP-ON-TALKING-AND-PESTERING-YOU-'TIL-I-GO-TO-BED-AT-NIGHT" SWITCH.

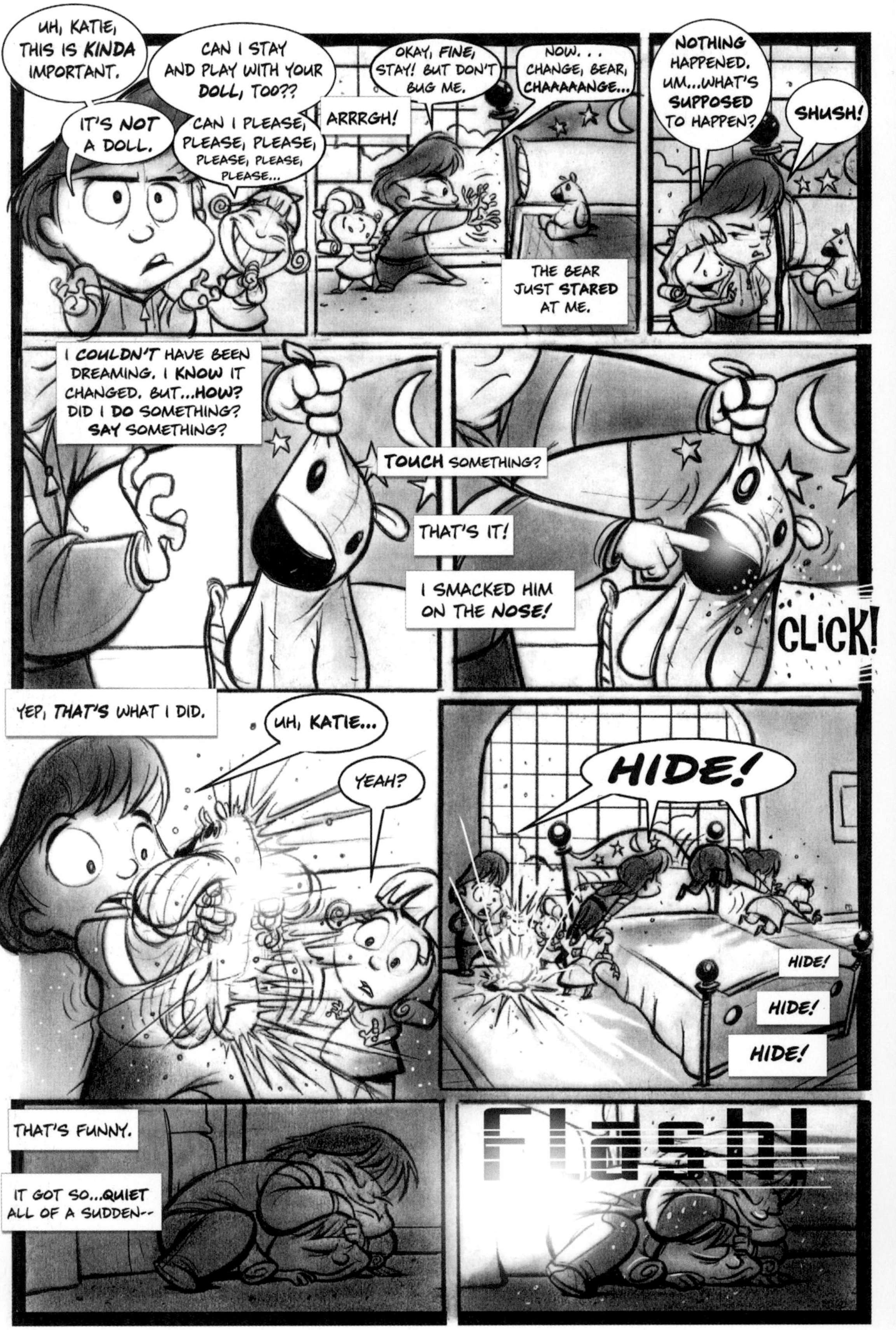
UH, KATIE, THIS IS KINDA IMPORTANT.
CAN I STAY AND PLAY WITH YOUR DOLL, TOO??
IT'S NOT A DOLL.
CAN I PLEASE, PLEASE, PLEASE, PLEASE, PLEASE, PLEASE...
ARRRGH!
OKAY, FINE, STAY! BUT DON'T BUG ME.
NOW. . . CHANGE, BEAR, CHAAAAANGE...
THE BEAR JUST STARED AT ME.
NOTHING HAPPENED. UM...WHAT'S SUPPOSED TO HAPPEN?
SHUSH!
I COULDN'T HAVE BEEN DREAMING. I KNOW IT CHANGED. BUT...HOW? DID I DO SOMETHING? SAY SOMETHING?
TOUCH SOMETHING?
THAT'S IT!
I SMACKED HIM ON THE NOSE!
CLICK!
YEP, THAT'S WHAT I DID.
UH, KATIE...
YEAH?
HIDE!
HIDE!
HIDE!
HIDE!
THAT'S FUNNY.
IT GOT SO...QUIET ALL OF A SUDDEN--
Flash!

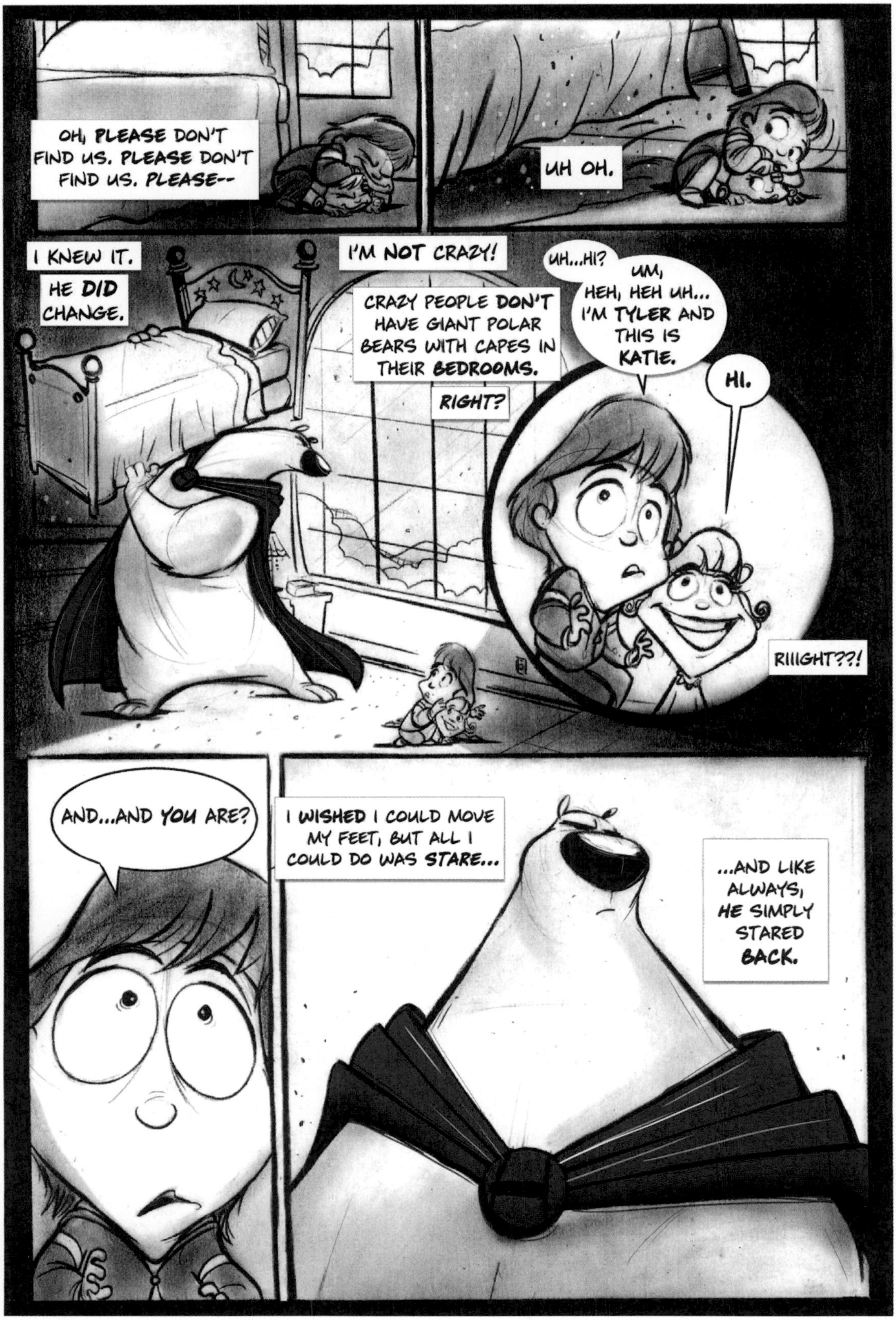
OH, PLEASE DON'T FIND US. PLEASE DON'T FIND US. PLEASE--
UH OH.
I KNEW IT.
HE DID CHANGE.
I'M NOT CRAZY!
CRAZY PEOPLE DON'T HAVE GIANT POLAR BEARS WITH CAPES IN THEIR BEDROOMS.
RIGHT?
UH...HI?
UM, HEH, HEH UH... I'M TYLER AND THIS IS KATIE.
HI.
RIIIGHT??!
AND...AND YOU ARE?
I WISHED I COULD MOVE MY FEET, BUT ALL I COULD DO WAS STARE...
...AND LIKE ALWAYS, HE SIMPLY STARED BACK.

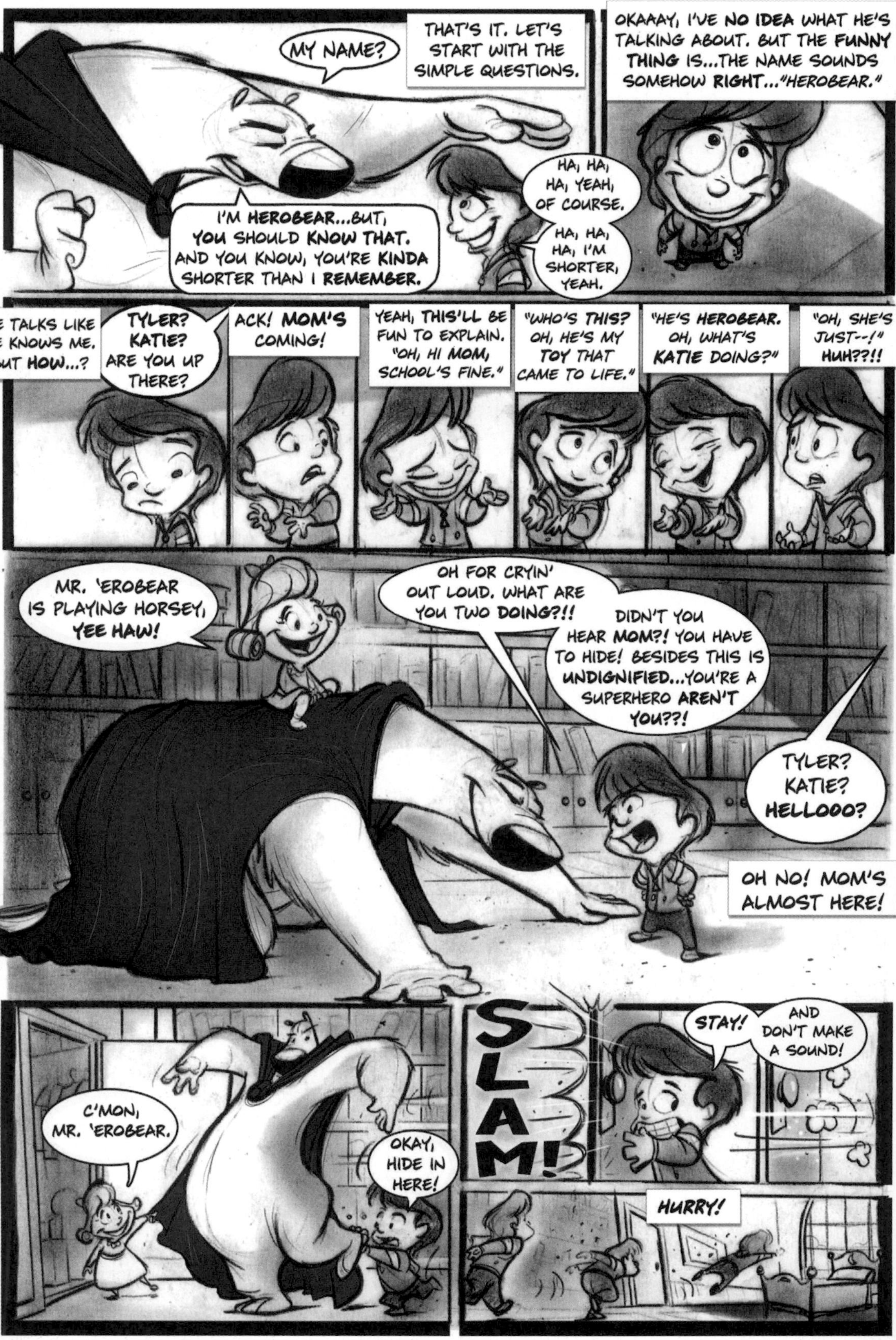
MY NAME?
THAT'S IT. LET'S START WITH THE SIMPLE QUESTIONS.
I'M HEROBEAR...BUT, YOU SHOULD KNOW THAT. AND YOU KNOW, YOU'RE KINDA SHORTER THAN I REMEMBER.
HA, HA, HA, YEAH, OF COURSE.
HA, HA, HA, I'M SHORTER, YEAH.
OKAAAY, I'VE NO IDEA WHAT HE'S TALKING ABOUT. BUT THE FUNNY THING IS...THE NAME SOUNDS SOMEHOW RIGHT..."HEROBEAR."
HE TALKS LIKE HE KNOWS ME. BUT HOW...?
TYLER? KATIE? ARE YOU UP THERE?
ACK! MOM'S COMING!
YEAH, THIS'LL BE FUN TO EXPLAIN. "OH, HI MOM, SCHOOL'S FINE."
"WHO'S THIS? OH, HE'S MY TOY THAT CAME TO LIFE."
"HE'S HEROBEAR. OH, WHAT'S KATIE DOING?"
"OH, SHE'S JUST--!" HUH??!!
MR. 'EROBEAR IS PLAYING HORSEY, YEE HAW!
OH FOR CRYIN' OUT LOUD. WHAT ARE YOU TWO DOING?!!
DIDN'T YOU HEAR MOM?! YOU HAVE TO HIDE! BESIDES THIS IS UNDIGNIFIED...YOU'RE A SUPERHERO AREN'T YOU??!
TYLER? KATIE? HELLOOO?
OH NO! MOM'S ALMOST HERE!
C'MON, MR. 'EROBEAR.
OKAY, HIDE IN HERE!
SLAM!
STAY!
AND DON'T MAKE A SOUND!
HURRY!

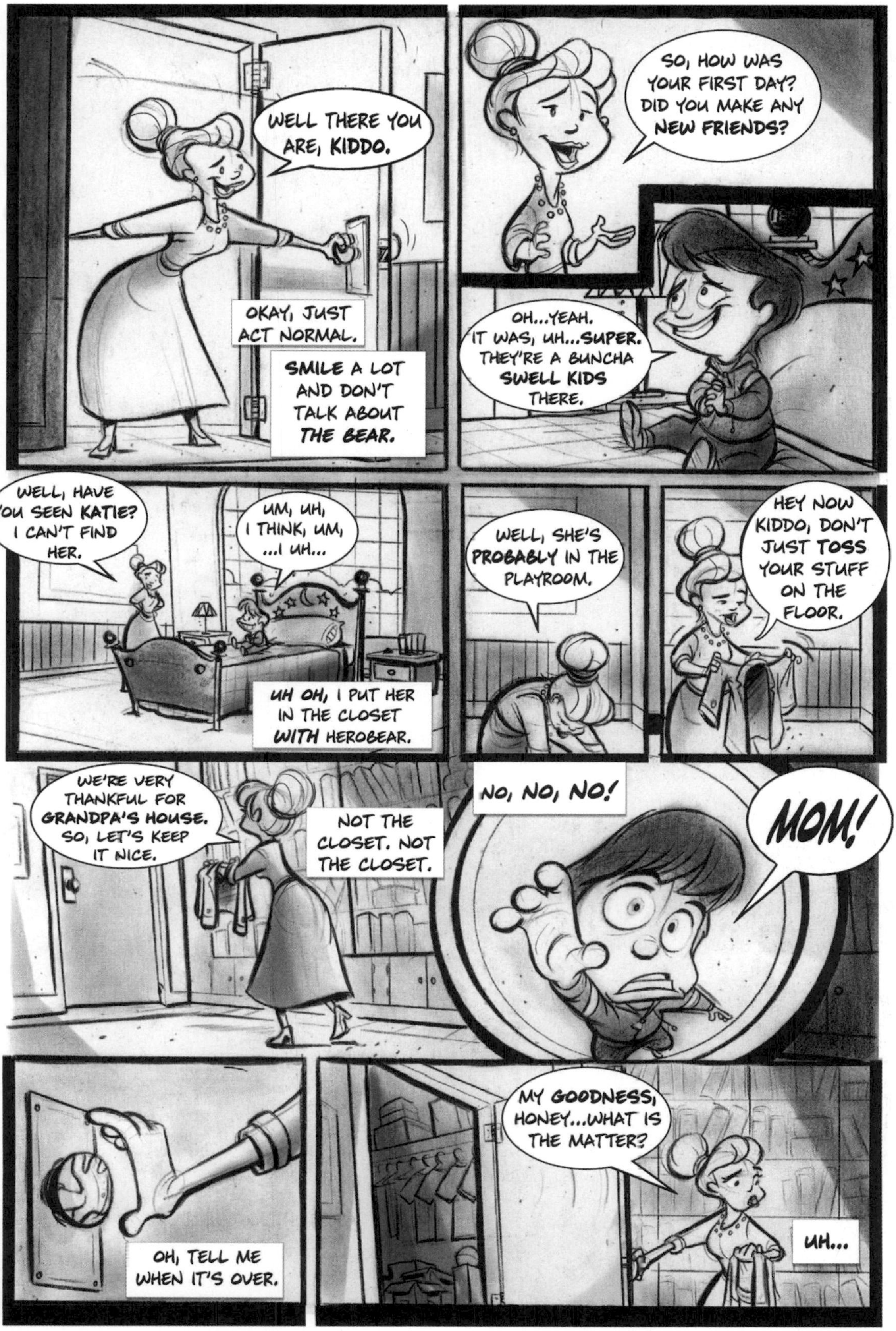
WELL THERE YOU ARE, KIDDO.
OKAY, JUST ACT NORMAL.
SMILE A LOT AND DON'T TALK ABOUT THE BEAR.
SO, HOW WAS YOUR FIRST DAY? DID YOU MAKE ANY NEW FRIENDS?
OH...YEAH. IT WAS, UH...SUPER. THEY'RE A BUNCHA SWELL KIDS THERE.
WELL, HAVE YOU SEEN KATIE? I CAN'T FIND HER.
UM, UH, I THINK, UM, ...I UH...
UH OH, I PUT HER IN THE CLOSET WITH HEROBEAR.
WELL, SHE'S PROBABLY IN THE PLAYROOM.
HEY NOW KIDDO, DON'T JUST TOSS YOUR STUFF ON THE FLOOR.
WE'RE VERY THANKFUL FOR GRANDPA'S HOUSE. SO, LET'S KEEP IT NICE.
NOT THE CLOSET. NOT THE CLOSET.
NO, NO, NO!
MOM!
OH, TELL ME WHEN IT'S OVER.
MY GOODNESS, HONEY...WHAT IS THE MATTER?
UH...

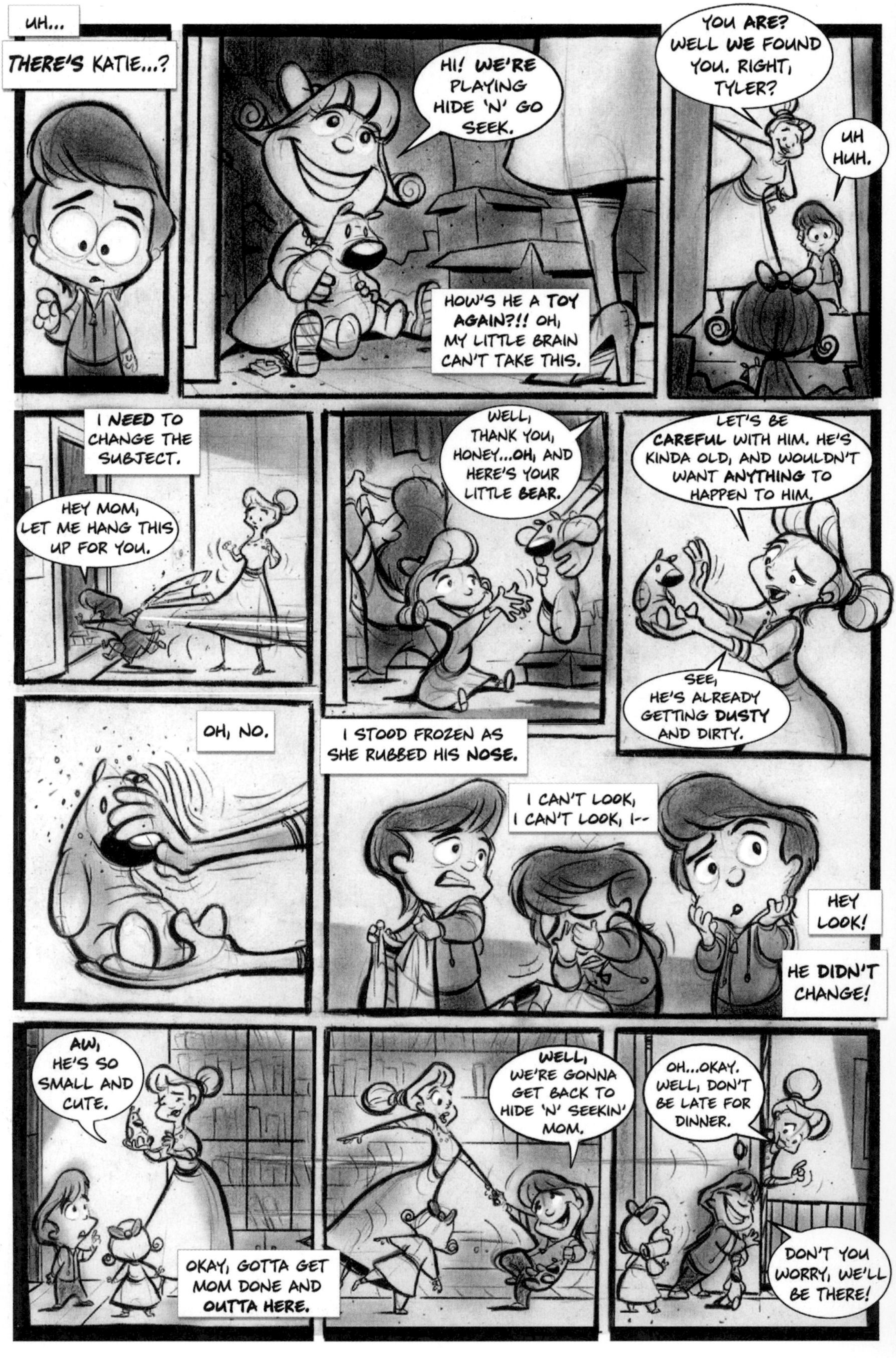
UH...
THERE'S KATIE...?
HI! WE'RE PLAYING HIDE 'N' GO SEEK.
HOW'S HE A TOY AGAIN?!! OH, MY LITTLE BRAIN CAN'T TAKE THIS.
YOU ARE? WELL WE FOUND YOU. RIGHT, TYLER?
UH HUH.
I NEED TO CHANGE THE SUBJECT.
HEY MOM, LET ME HANG THIS UP FOR YOU.
WELL, THANK YOU, HONEY...OH, AND HERE'S YOUR LITTLE BEAR.
LET'S BE CAREFUL WITH HIM. HE'S KINDA OLD, AND WOULDN'T WANT ANYTHING TO HAPPEN TO HIM.
SEE, HE'S ALREADY GETTING DUSTY AND DIRTY.
OH, NO.
I STOOD FROZEN AS SHE RUBBED HIS NOSE.
I CAN'T LOOK, I CAN'T LOOK, I--
HEY LOOK!
HE DIDN'T CHANGE!
AW, HE'S SO SMALL AND CUTE.
OKAY, GOTTA GET MOM DONE AND OUTTA HERE.
WELL, WE'RE GONNA GET BACK TO HIDE 'N' SEEKIN' MOM.
OH...OKAY. WELL, DON'T BE LATE FOR DINNER.
DON'T YOU WORRY, WE'LL BE THERE!

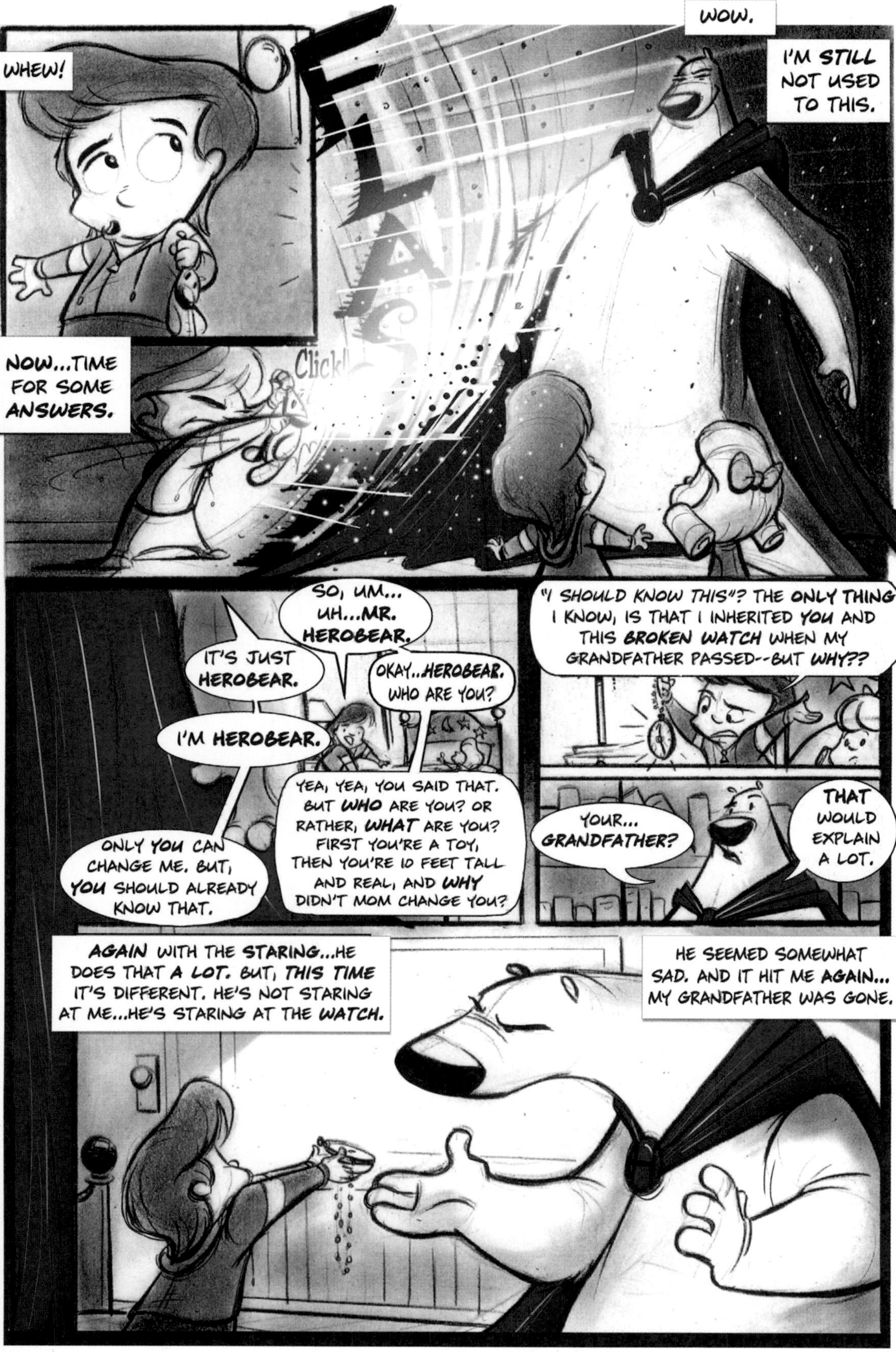
WHEW!
FLASH
Click!
WOW.
I'M STILL NOT USED TO THIS.
NOW...TIME FOR SOME ANSWERS.
SO, UM... UH...MR. HEROBEAR.
IT'S JUST HEROBEAR.
OKAY...HEROBEAR. WHO ARE YOU?
I'M HEROBEAR.
YEA, YEA, YOU SAID THAT. BUT WHO ARE YOU? OR RATHER, WHAT ARE YOU? FIRST YOU'RE A TOY, THEN YOU'RE 10 FEET TALL AND REAL, AND WHY DIDN'T MOM CHANGE YOU?
ONLY YOU CAN CHANGE ME. BUT, YOU SHOULD ALREADY KNOW THAT.
"I SHOULD KNOW THIS"? THE ONLY THING I KNOW, IS THAT I INHERITED YOU AND THIS BROKEN WATCH WHEN MY GRANDFATHER PASSED--BUT WHY??
YOUR... GRANDFATHER?
THAT WOULD EXPLAIN A LOT.
AGAIN WITH THE STARING...HE DOES THAT A LOT. BUT, THIS TIME IT'S DIFFERENT. HE'S NOT STARING AT ME...HE'S STARING AT THE WATCH.
HE SEEMED SOMEWHAT SAD. AND IT HIT ME AGAIN... MY GRANDFATHER WAS GONE.

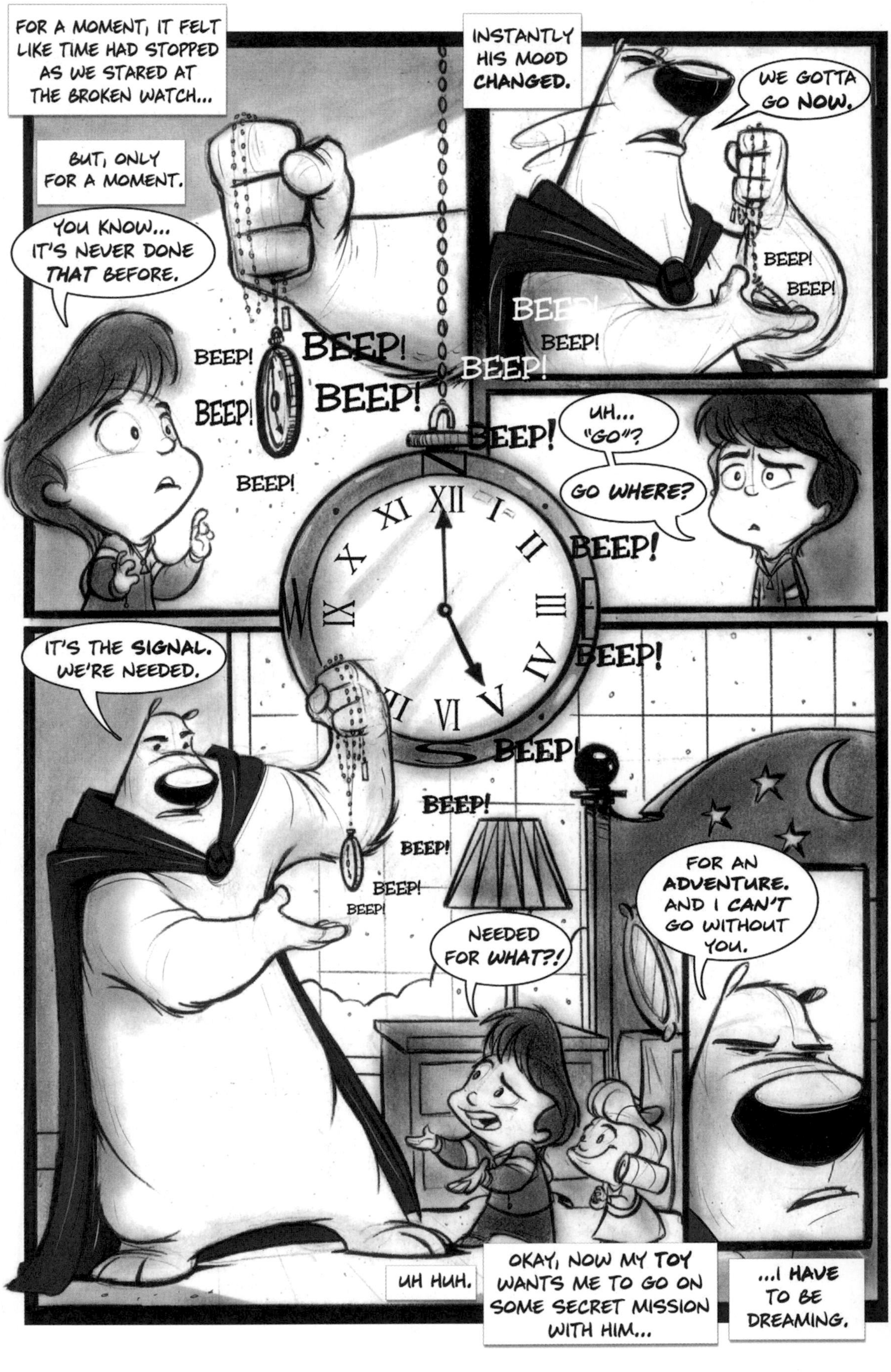

FOR A MOMENT, IT FELT LIKE TIME HAD STOPPED AS WE STARED AT THE BROKEN WATCH...
BUT, ONLY FOR A MOMENT.
YOU KNOW... IT'S NEVER DONE THAT BEFORE.
BEEP! BEEP! BEEP! BEEP! BEEP!
INSTANTLY HIS MOOD CHANGED.
WE GOTTA GO NOW.
BEEP! BEEP! BEEP! BEEP! BEEP!
UH... "GO"?
GO WHERE?
BEEP! BEEP! BEEP! BEEP! BEEP!
IT'S THE SIGNAL. WE'RE NEEDED.
BEEP! BEEP! BEEP! BEEP!
NEEDED FOR WHAT?!
FOR AN ADVENTURE. AND I CAN'T GO WITHOUT YOU.
UH HUH.
OKAY, NOW MY TOY WANTS ME TO GO ON SOME SECRET MISSION WITH HIM...
...I HAVE TO BE DREAMING.

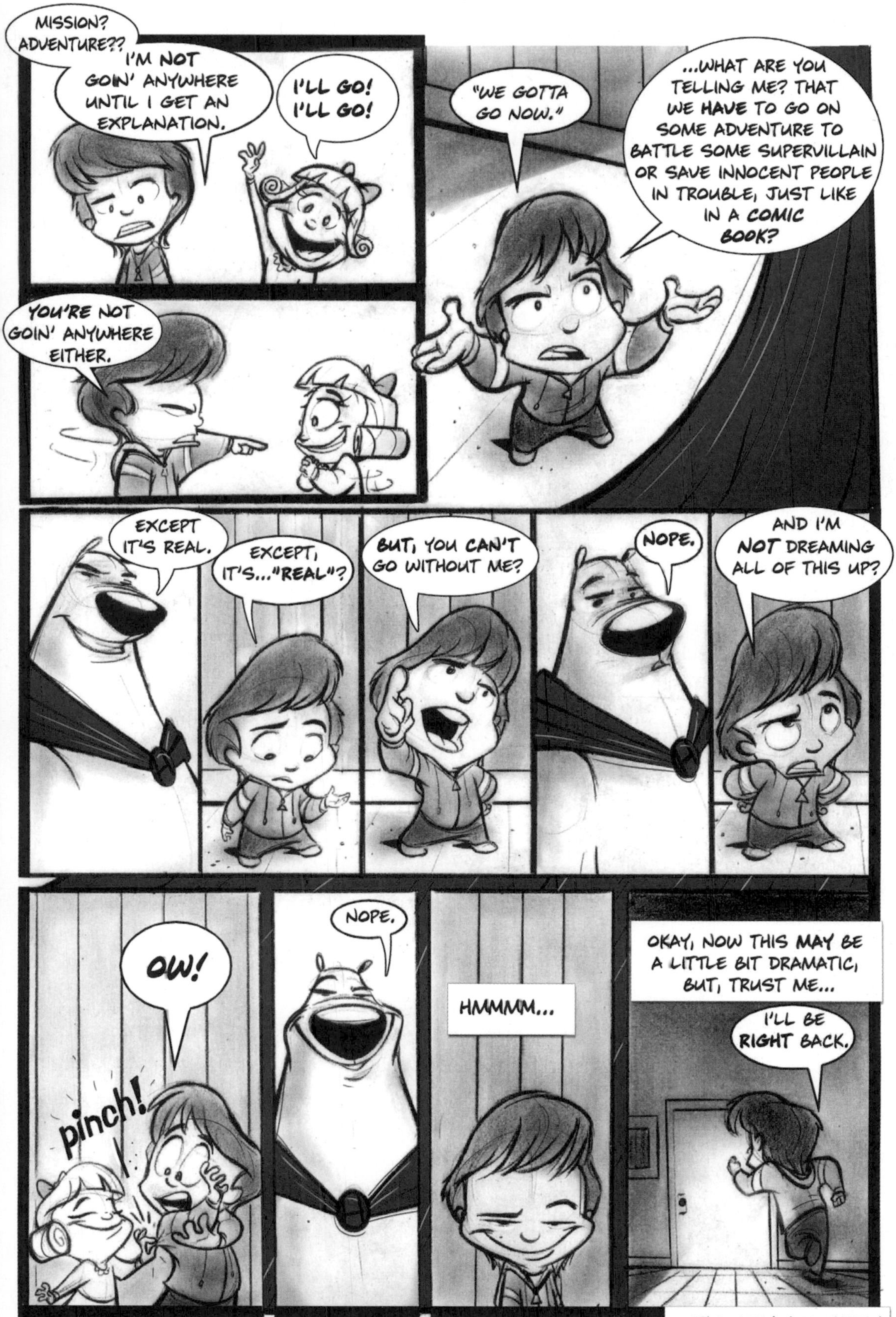
MISSION? ADVENTURE??
I'M NOT GOIN' ANYWHERE UNTIL I GET AN EXPLANATION.
I'LL GO! I'LL GO!
YOU'RE NOT GOIN' ANYWHERE EITHER.
"WE GOTTA GO NOW."
...WHAT ARE YOU TELLING ME? THAT WE HAVE TO GO ON SOME ADVENTURE TO BATTLE SOME SUPERVILLAIN OR SAVE INNOCENT PEOPLE IN TROUBLE, JUST LIKE IN A COMIC BOOK?
EXCEPT IT'S REAL.
EXCEPT, IT'S..."REAL"?
BUT, YOU CAN'T GO WITHOUT ME?
NOPE.
AND I'M NOT DREAMING ALL OF THIS UP?
OW!
pinch!
NOPE.
HMMMM...
OKAY, NOW THIS MAY BE A LITTLE BIT DRAMATIC, BUT, TRUST ME...
I'LL BE RIGHT BACK.
...IT'S VERY NECESSARY.

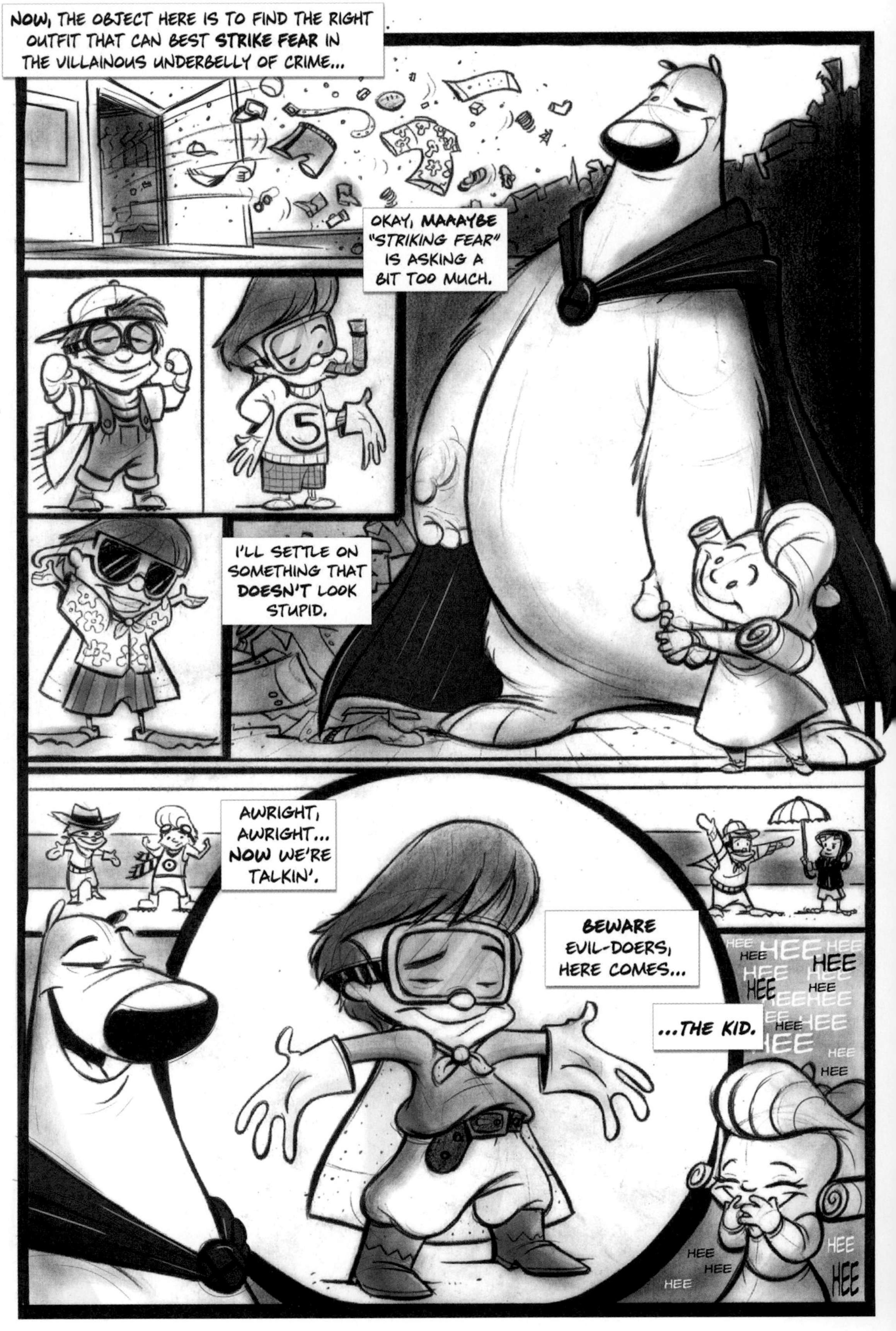
NOW, THE OBJECT HERE IS TO FIND THE RIGHT OUTFIT THAT CAN BEST STRIKE FEAR IN THE VILLAINOUS UNDERBELLY OF CRIME...
OKAY, MAAAYBE "STRIKING FEAR" IS ASKING A BIT TOO MUCH.
5
I'LL SETTLE ON SOMETHING THAT DOESN'T LOOK STUPID.
AWRIGHT, AWRIGHT... NOW WE'RE TALKIN'.
BEWARE EVIL-DOERS, HERE COMES...
...THE KID.
HEE HEE HEE HEE HEE HEE HEE HEE HEE HEE HEE HEE HEE
HEE HEE HEE HEE HEE

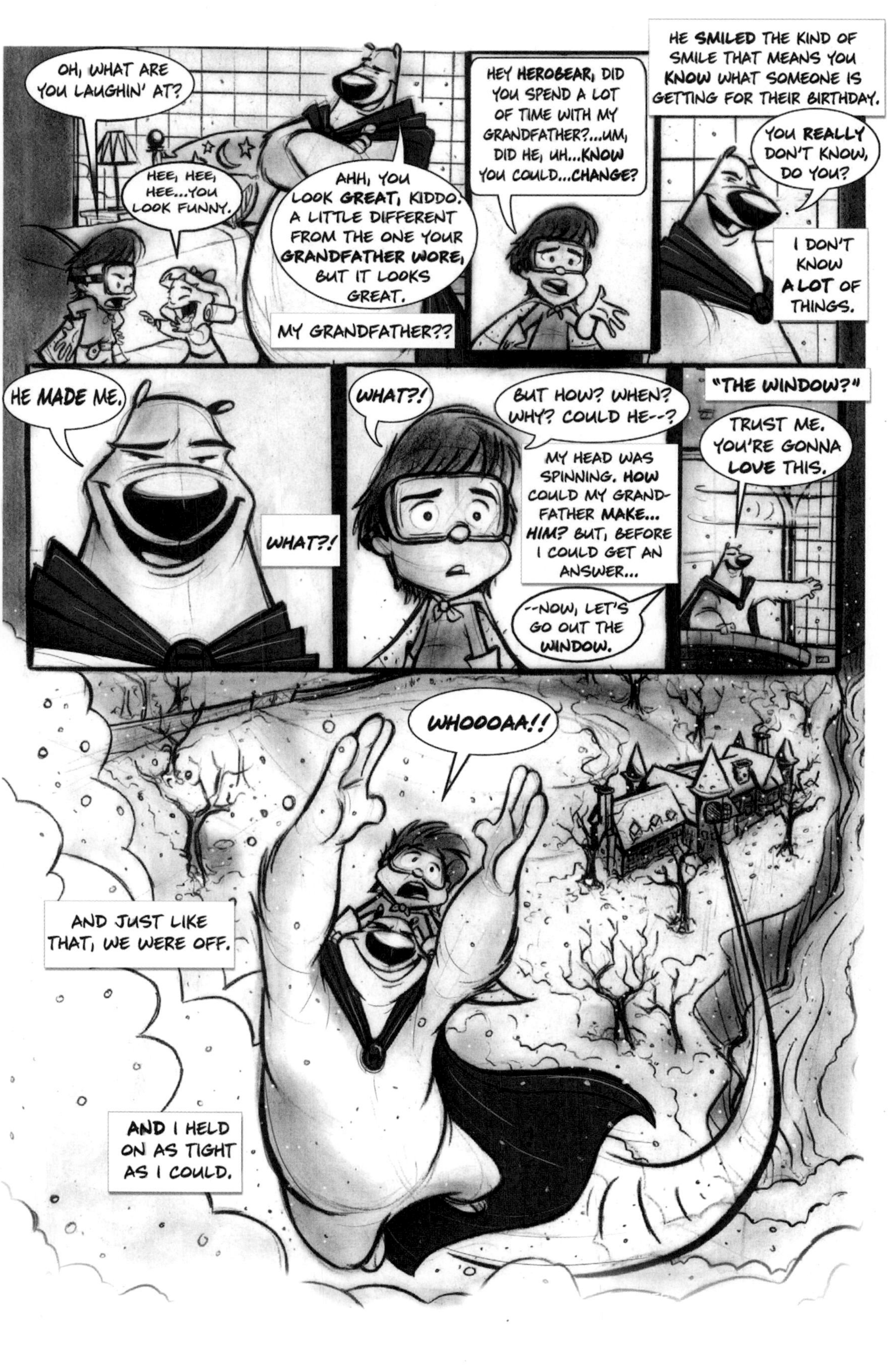
OH, WHAT ARE YOU LAUGHIN' AT?
HEE, HEE, HEE...YOU LOOK FUNNY.
AHH, YOU LOOK GREAT, KIDDO. A LITTLE DIFFERENT FROM THE ONE YOUR GRANDFATHER WORE, BUT IT LOOKS GREAT.
MY GRANDFATHER??
HEY HEROBEAR, DID YOU SPEND A LOT OF TIME WITH MY GRANDFATHER?...UM, DID HE, UH...KNOW YOU COULD...CHANGE?
HE SMILED THE KIND OF SMILE THAT MEANS YOU KNOW WHAT SOMEONE IS GETTING FOR THEIR BIRTHDAY.
YOU REALLY DON'T KNOW, DO YOU?
I DON'T KNOW A LOT OF THINGS.
HE MADE ME.
WHAT?!
WHAT?!
BUT HOW? WHEN? WHY? COULD HE--?
MY HEAD WAS SPINNING. HOW COULD MY GRANDFATHER MAKE... HIM? BUT, BEFORE I COULD GET AN ANSWER...
--NOW, LET'S GO OUT THE WINDOW.
"THE WINDOW?"
TRUST ME. YOU'RE GONNA LOVE THIS.
WHOOOAA!!
AND JUST LIKE THAT, WE WERE OFF.
AND I HELD ON AS TIGHT AS I COULD.

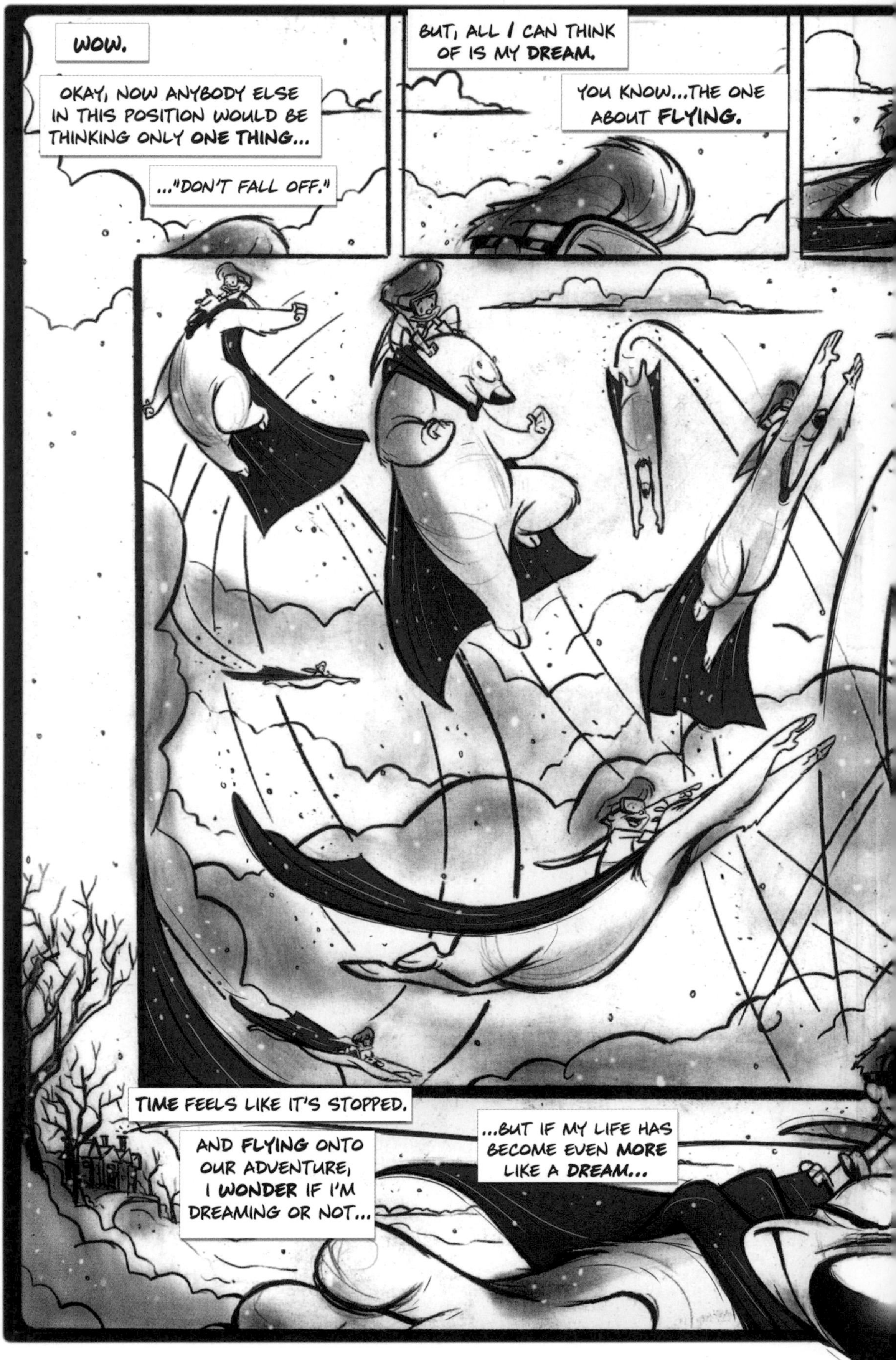
WOW.
OKAY, NOW ANYBODY ELSE IN THIS POSITION WOULD BE THINKING ONLY ONE THING...
..."DON'T FALL OFF."
BUT, ALL I CAN THINK OF IS MY DREAM.
YOU KNOW...THE ONE ABOUT FLYING.
TIME FEELS LIKE IT'S STOPPED.
AND FLYING ONTO OUR ADVENTURE, I WONDER IF I'M DREAMING OR NOT...
...BUT IF MY LIFE HAS BECOME EVEN MORE LIKE A DREAM...

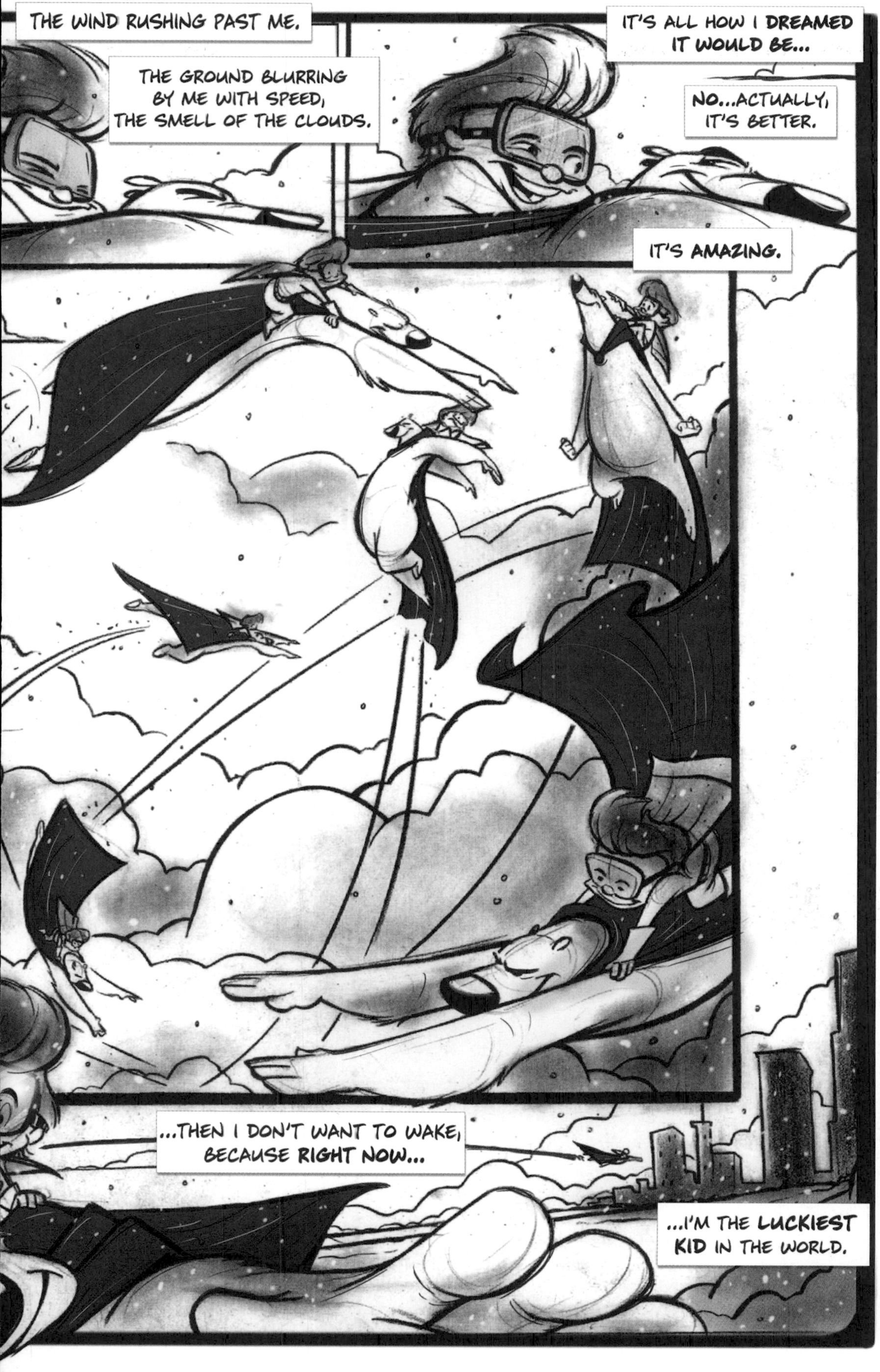
THE WIND RUSHING PAST ME.
THE GROUND BLURRING BY ME WITH SPEED, THE SMELL OF THE CLOUDS.
IT'S ALL HOW I DREAMED IT WOULD BE...
NO...ACTUALLY, IT'S BETTER.
IT'S AMAZING.
...THEN I DON'T WANT TO WAKE, BECAUSE RIGHT NOW...
...I'M THE LUCKIEST KID IN THE WORLD.

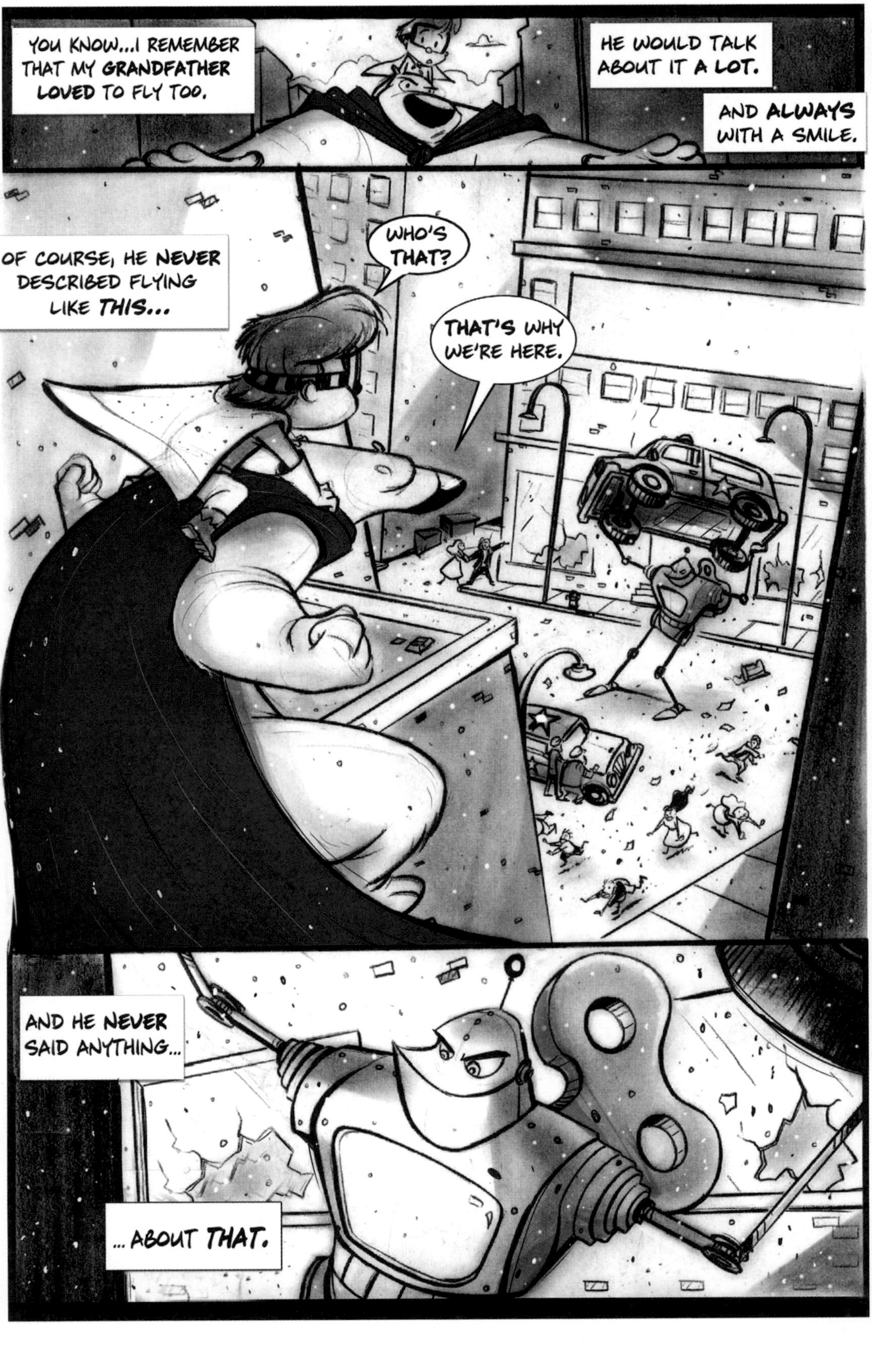
YOU KNOW...I REMEMBER THAT MY GRANDFATHER LOVED TO FLY TOO.
HE WOULD TALK ABOUT IT A LOT.
AND ALWAYS WITH A SMILE.
OF COURSE, HE NEVER DESCRIBED FLYING LIKE THIS...
WHO'S THAT?
THAT'S WHY WE'RE HERE.
AND HE NEVER SAID ANYTHING...
...ABOUT THAT.

Chapter Three

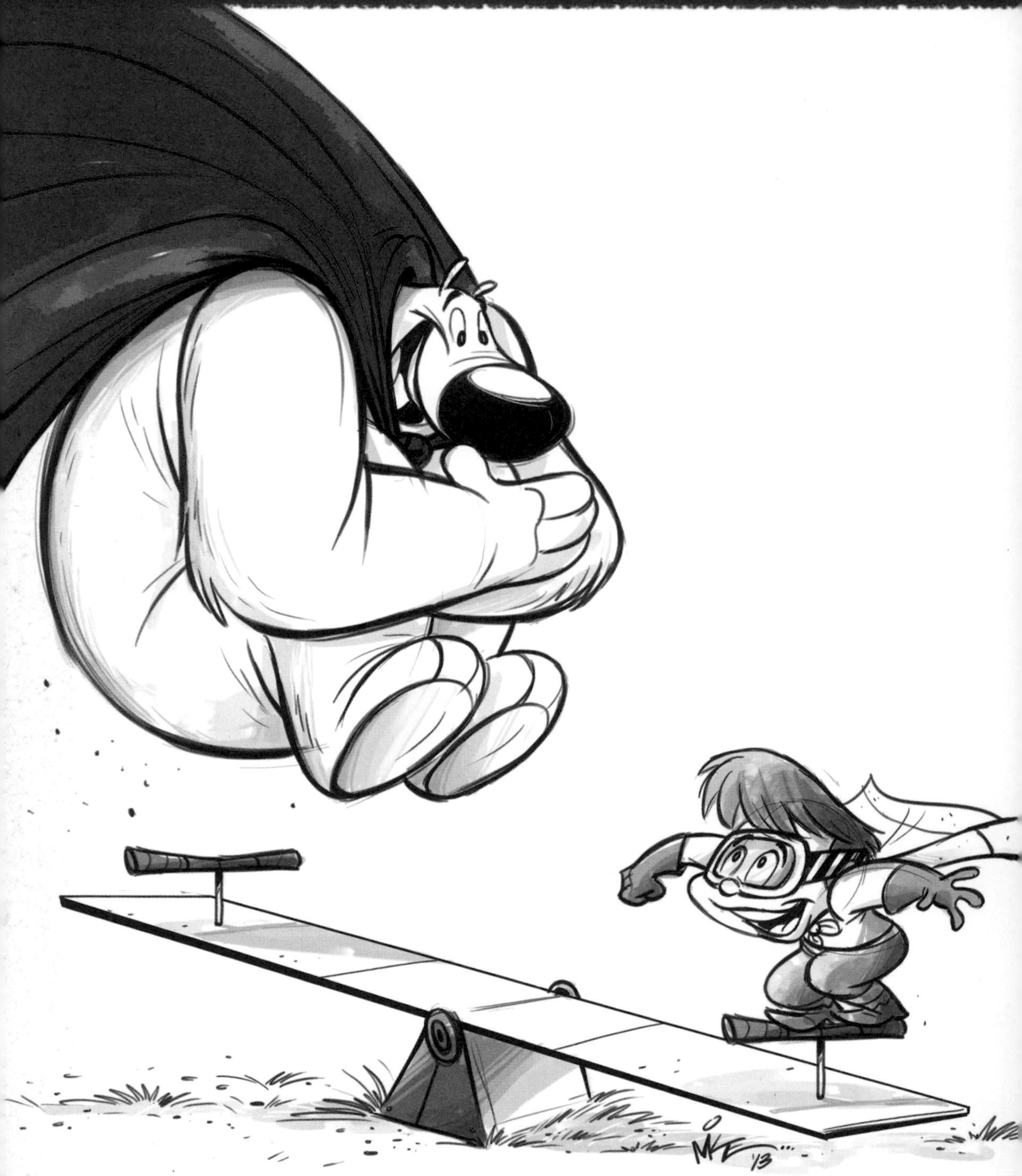

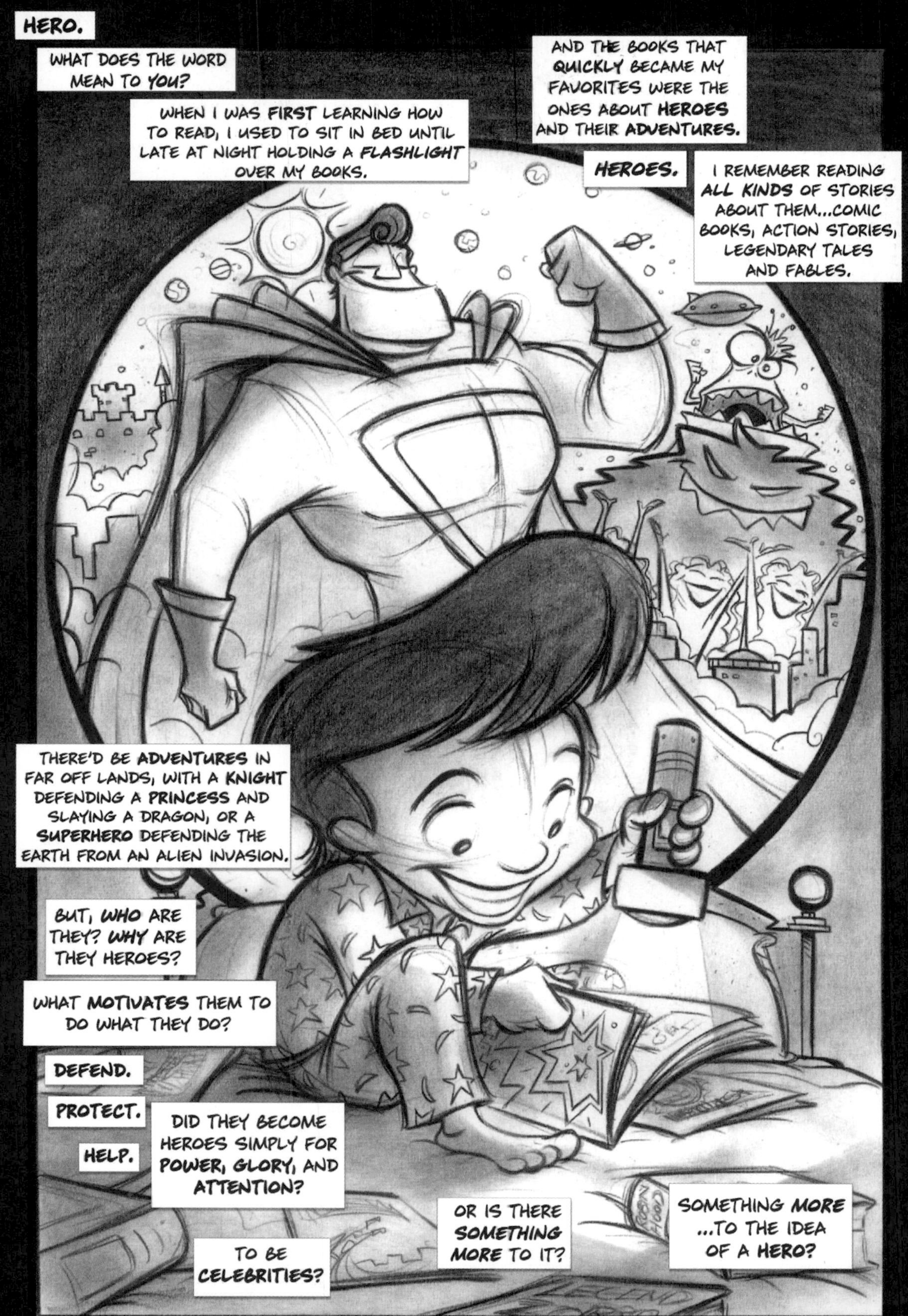
HERO.
WHAT DOES THE WORD MEAN TO YOU?
WHEN I WAS FIRST LEARNING HOW TO READ, I USED TO SIT IN BED UNTIL LATE AT NIGHT HOLDING A FLASHLIGHT OVER MY BOOKS.
AND THE BOOKS THAT QUICKLY BECAME MY FAVORITES WERE THE ONES ABOUT HEROES AND THEIR ADVENTURES.
HEROES.
I REMEMBER READING ALL KINDS OF STORIES ABOUT THEM...COMIC BOOKS, ACTION STORIES, LEGENDARY TALES AND FABLES.
THERE'D BE ADVENTURES IN FAR OFF LANDS, WITH A KNIGHT DEFENDING A PRINCESS AND SLAYING A DRAGON, OR A SUPERHERO DEFENDING THE EARTH FROM AN ALIEN INVASION.
BUT, WHO ARE THEY? WHY ARE THEY HEROES?
WHAT MOTIVATES THEM TO DO WHAT THEY DO?
DEFEND.
PROTECT.
HELP.
DID THEY BECOME HEROES SIMPLY FOR POWER, GLORY, AND ATTENTION?
TO BE CELEBRITIES?
OR IS THERE SOMETHING MORE TO IT?
SOMETHING MORE ...TO THE IDEA OF A HERO?

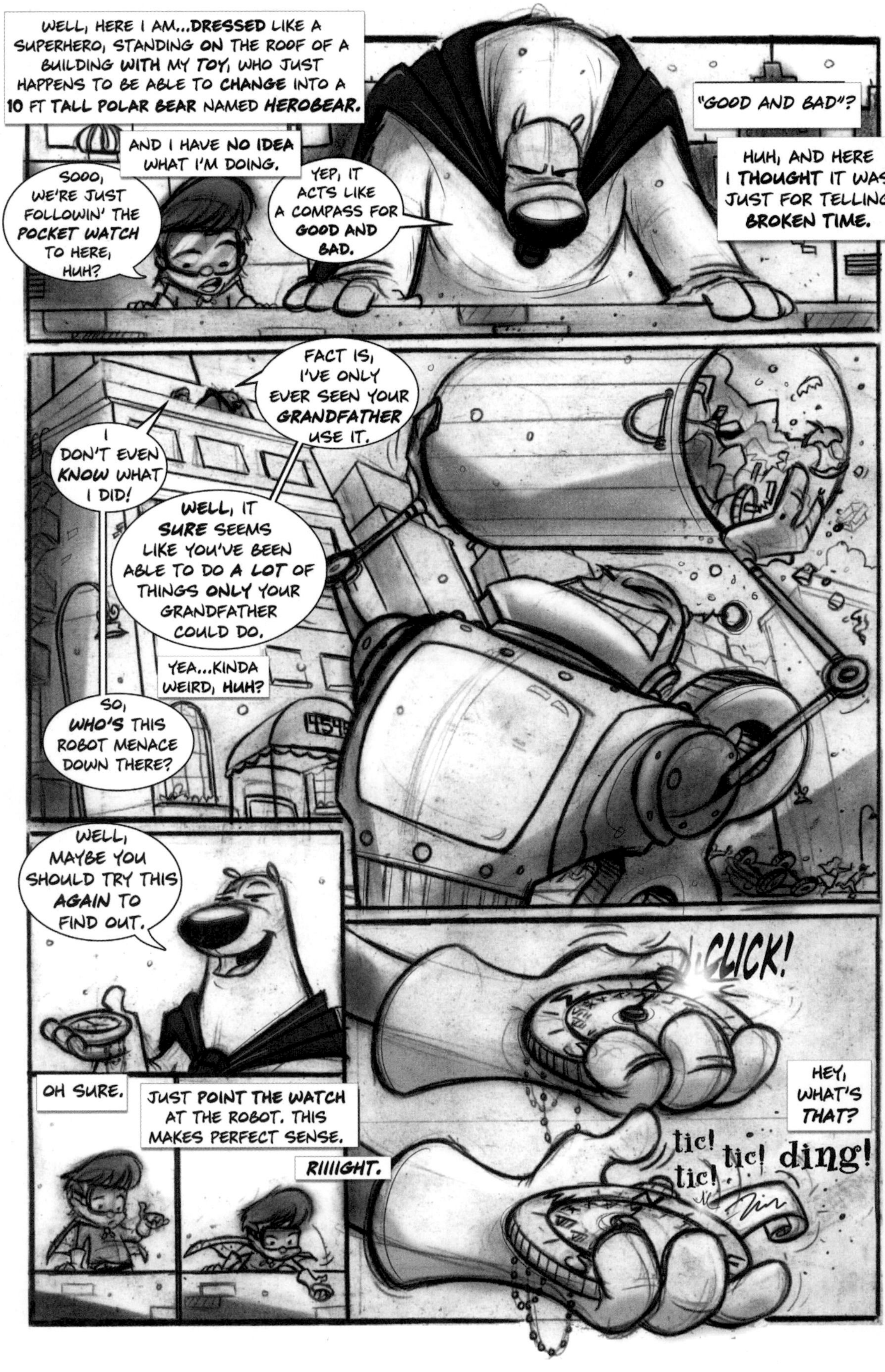
WELL, HERE I AM...DRESSED LIKE A SUPERHERO, STANDING ON THE ROOF OF A BUILDING WITH MY TOY, WHO JUST HAPPENS TO BE ABLE TO CHANGE INTO A 10 FT TALL POLAR BEAR NAMED HEROBEAR.
AND I HAVE NO IDEA WHAT I'M DOING.
SOOO, WE'RE JUST FOLLOWIN' THE POCKET WATCH TO HERE, HUH?
YEP, IT ACTS LIKE A COMPASS FOR GOOD AND BAD.
"GOOD AND BAD"?
HUH, AND HERE I THOUGHT IT WAS JUST FOR TELLING BROKEN TIME.
FACT IS, I'VE ONLY EVER SEEN YOUR GRANDFATHER USE IT.
I DON'T EVEN KNOW WHAT I DID!
WELL, IT SURE SEEMS LIKE YOU'VE BEEN ABLE TO DO A LOT OF THINGS ONLY YOUR GRANDFATHER COULD DO.
YEA...KINDA WEIRD, HUH?
SO, WHO'S THIS ROBOT MENACE DOWN THERE?
WELL, MAYBE YOU SHOULD TRY THIS AGAIN TO FIND OUT.
OH SURE.
JUST POINT THE WATCH AT THE ROBOT. THIS MAKES PERFECT SENSE.
RIIIIGHT.
CLICK!
HEY, WHAT'S THAT?
tic! tic! tic! ding!

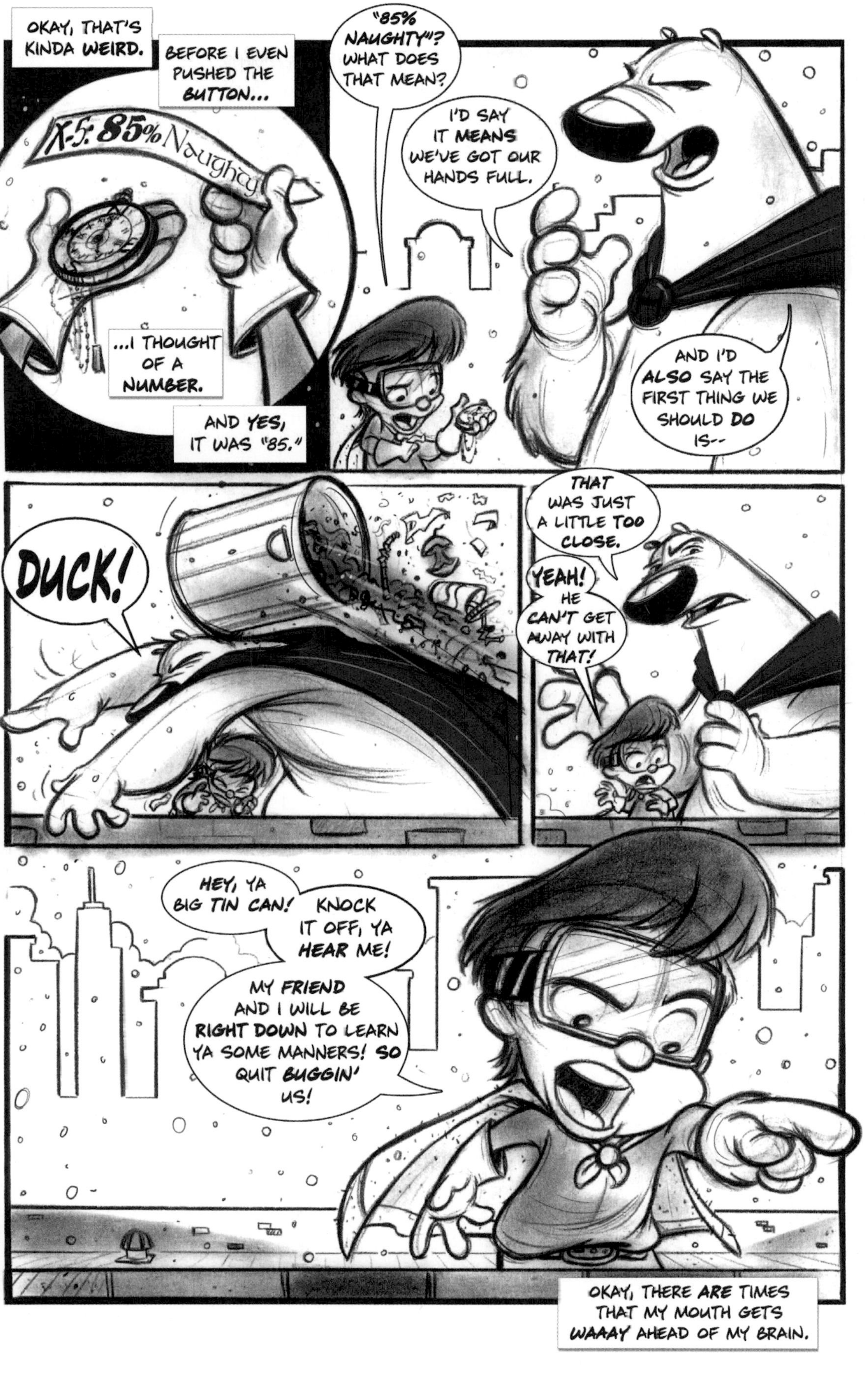
OKAY, THAT'S KINDA WEIRD.
BEFORE I EVEN PUSHED THE BUTTON...
X-5: 85% Naughty
...I THOUGHT OF A NUMBER.
AND YES, IT WAS "85."
"85% NAUGHTY"? WHAT DOES THAT MEAN?
I'D SAY IT MEANS WE'VE GOT OUR HANDS FULL.
AND I'D ALSO SAY THE FIRST THING WE SHOULD DO IS--
DUCK!
THAT WAS JUST A LITTLE TOO CLOSE.
YEAH! HE CAN'T GET AWAY WITH THAT!
HEY, YA BIG TIN CAN!
KNOCK IT OFF, YA HEAR ME!
MY FRIEND AND I WILL BE RIGHT DOWN TO LEARN YA SOME MANNERS! SO QUIT BUGGIN' US!
OKAY, THERE ARE TIMES THAT MY MOUTH GETS WAAAY AHEAD OF MY BRAIN.

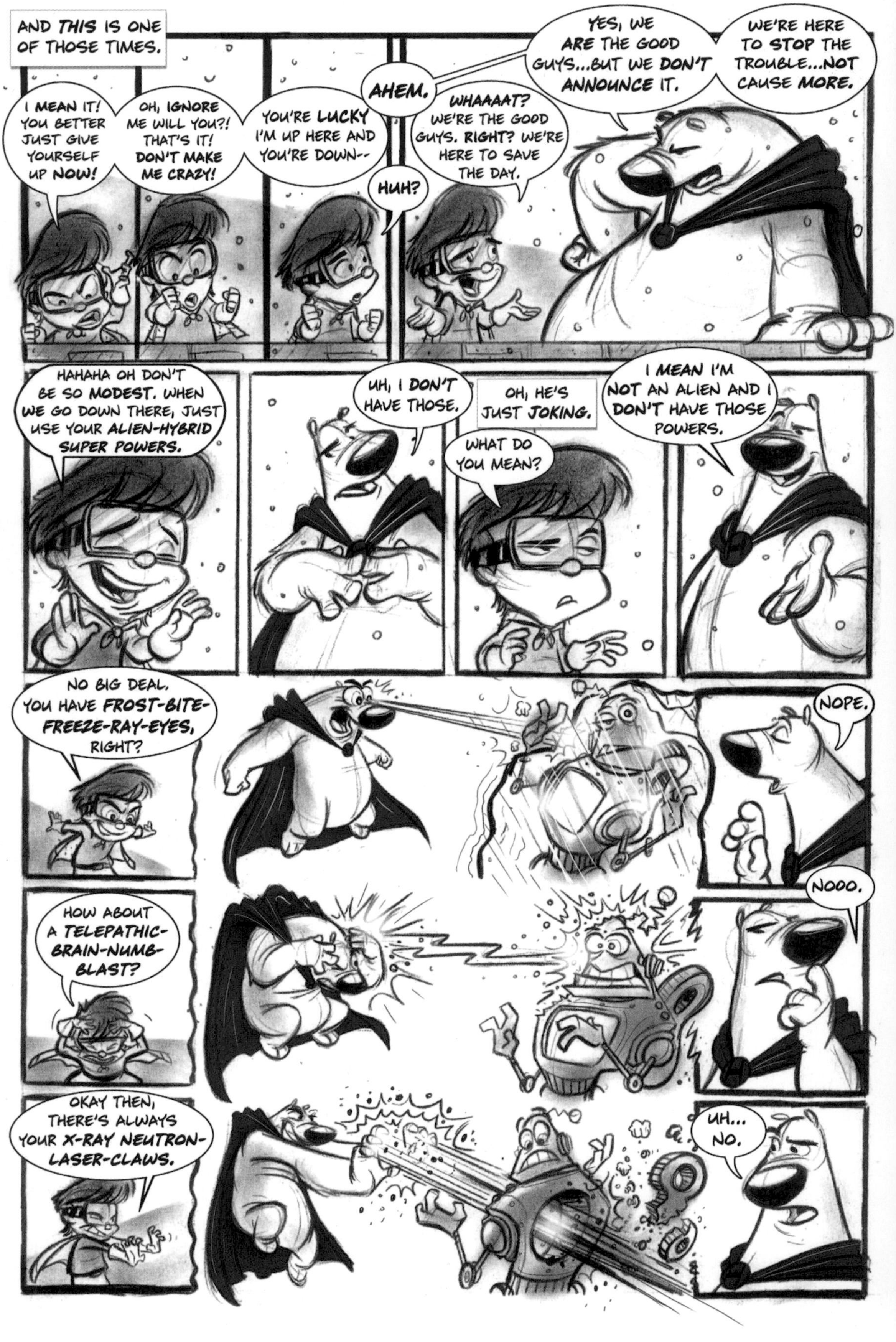
AND THIS IS ONE OF THOSE TIMES.
I MEAN IT! YOU BETTER JUST GIVE YOURSELF UP NOW!
OH, IGNORE ME WILL YOU?! THAT'S IT! DON'T MAKE ME CRAZY!
YOU'RE LUCKY I'M UP HERE AND YOU'RE DOWN--
AHEM.
HUH?
WHAAAAT? WE'RE THE GOOD GUYS. RIGHT? WE'RE HERE TO SAVE THE DAY.
YES, WE ARE THE GOOD GUYS...BUT WE DON'T ANNOUNCE IT.
WE'RE HERE TO STOP THE TROUBLE...NOT CAUSE MORE.
HAHAHA OH DON'T BE SO MODEST. WHEN WE GO DOWN THERE, JUST USE YOUR ALIEN-HYBRID SUPER POWERS.
UH, I DON'T HAVE THOSE.
OH, HE'S JUST JOKING.
WHAT DO YOU MEAN?
I MEAN I'M NOT AN ALIEN AND I DON'T HAVE THOSE POWERS.
NO BIG DEAL. YOU HAVE FROST-BITE-FREEZE-RAY-EYES, RIGHT?
NOPE.
HOW ABOUT A TELEPATHIC-BRAIN-NUMB-BLAST?
NOOO.
OKAY THEN, THERE'S ALWAYS YOUR X-RAY NEUTRON-LASER-CLAWS.
UH... NO.

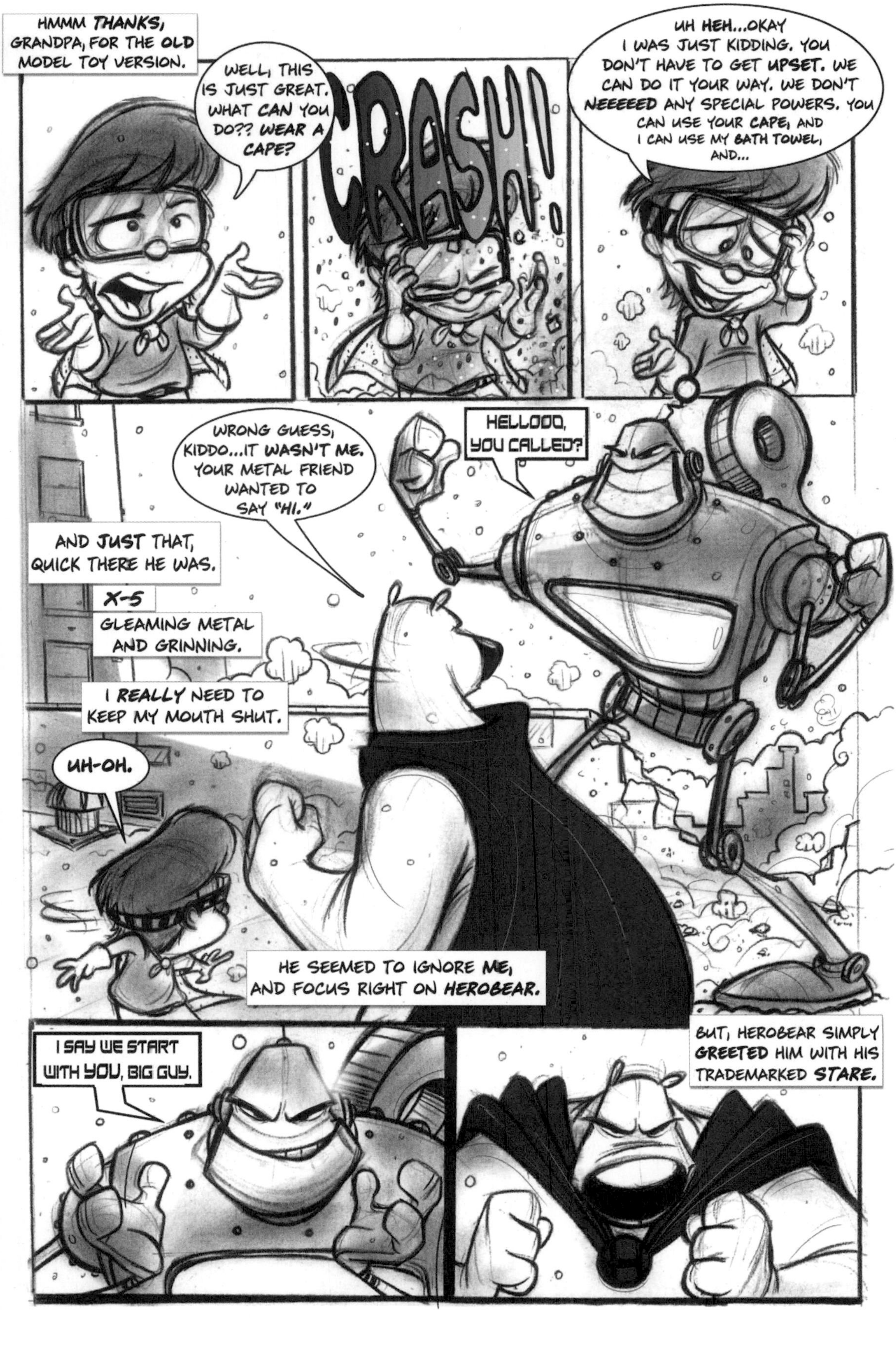
HMMM THANKS, GRANDPA, FOR THE OLD MODEL TOY VERSION.
WELL, THIS IS JUST GREAT. WHAT CAN YOU DO?? WEAR A CAPE?
CRASH!
UH HEH...OKAY I WAS JUST KIDDING. YOU DON'T HAVE TO GET UPSET. WE CAN DO IT YOUR WAY. WE DON'T NEEEEED ANY SPECIAL POWERS. YOU CAN USE YOUR CAPE, AND I CAN USE MY BATH TOWEL, AND...
WRONG GUESS, KIDDO...IT WASN'T ME. YOUR METAL FRIEND WANTED TO SAY "HI."
HELLOOO, YOU CALLED?
AND JUST THAT, QUICK THERE HE WAS.
X-5
GLEAMING METAL AND GRINNING.
I REALLY NEED TO KEEP MY MOUTH SHUT.
UH-OH.
HE SEEMED TO IGNORE ME, AND FOCUS RIGHT ON HEROBEAR.
I SAY WE START WITH YOU, BIG GUY.
BUT, HEROBEAR SIMPLY GREETED HIM WITH HIS TRADEMARKED STARE.

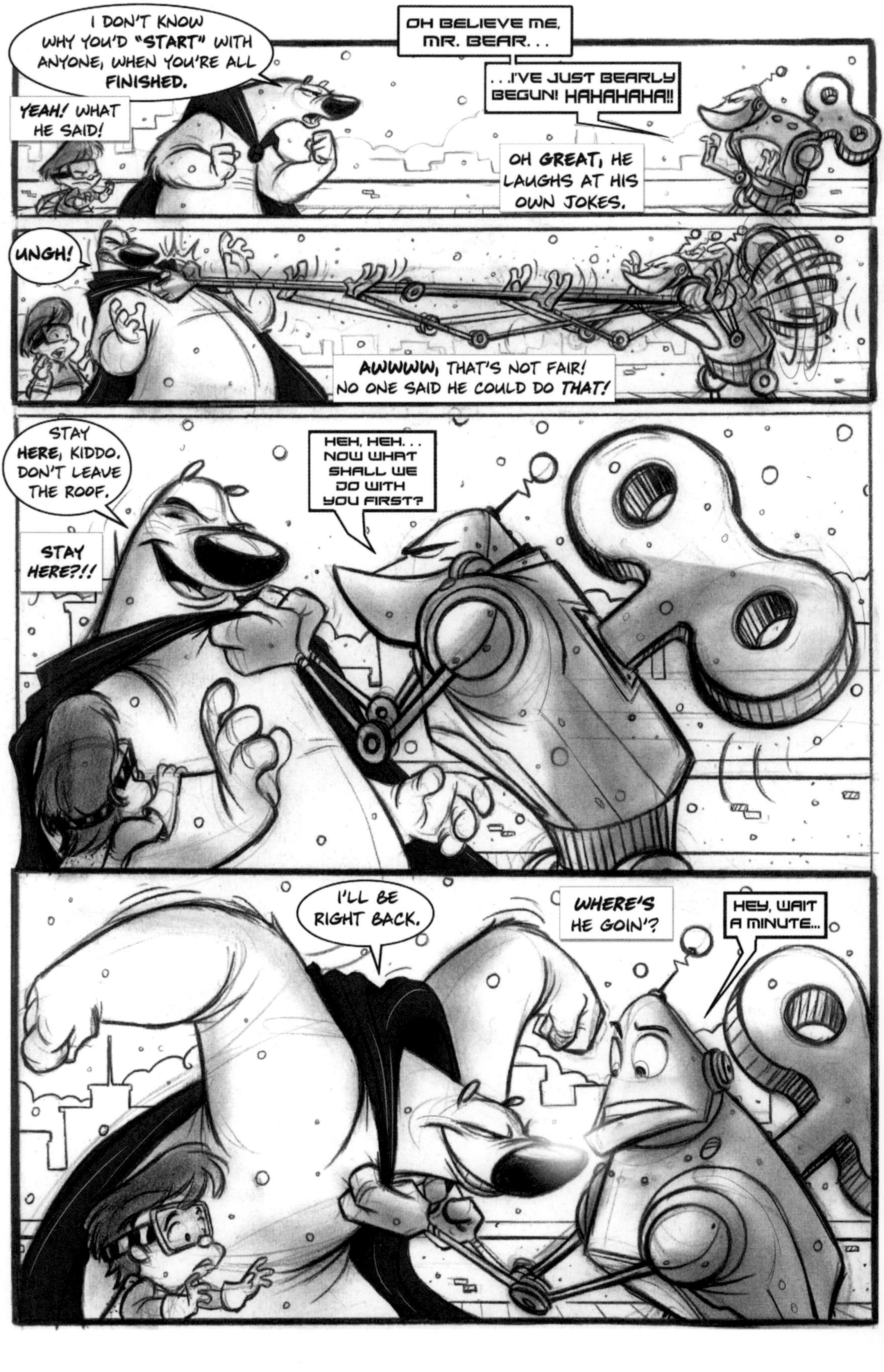

I DON'T KNOW WHY YOU'D "START" WITH ANYONE, WHEN YOU'RE ALL FINISHED.
YEAH! WHAT HE SAID!
OH BELIEVE ME, MR. BEAR. . .
. . .I'VE JUST BEARLY BEGUN! HAHAHAHA!!
OH GREAT, HE LAUGHS AT HIS OWN JOKES.
UNGH!
AWWWW, THAT'S NOT FAIR! NO ONE SAID HE COULD DO THAT!
STAY HERE, KIDDO. DON'T LEAVE THE ROOF.
STAY HERE?!!
HEH, HEH. . . NOW WHAT SHALL WE DO WITH YOU FIRST?
I'LL BE RIGHT BACK.
WHERE'S HE GOIN'?
HEY, WAIT A MINUTE...

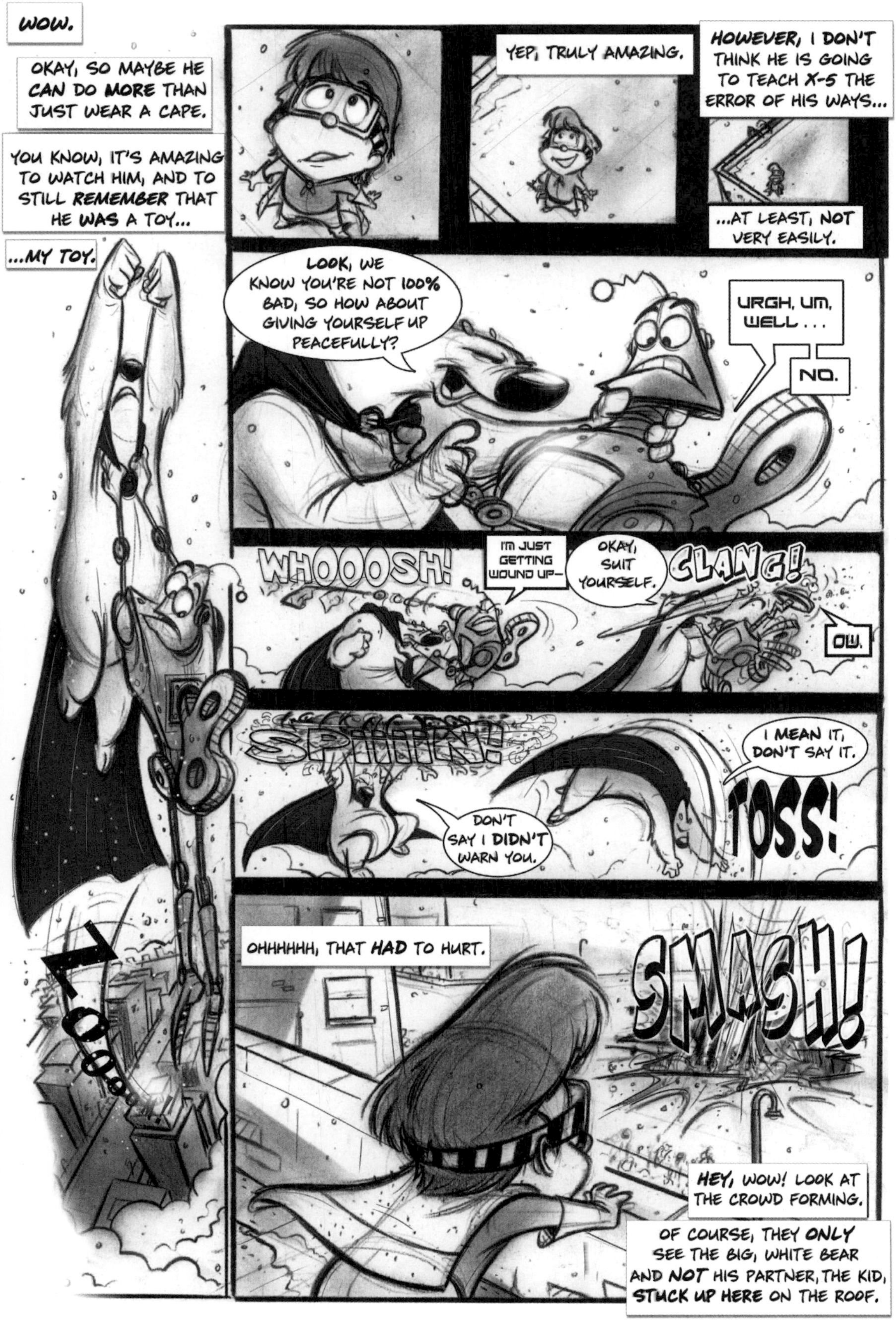

WOW.
OKAY, SO MAYBE HE CAN DO MORE THAN JUST WEAR A CAPE.
YOU KNOW, IT'S AMAZING TO WATCH HIM, AND TO STILL REMEMBER THAT HE WAS A TOY...
...MY TOY.
YEP, TRULY AMAZING.
HOWEVER, I DON'T THINK HE IS GOING TO TEACH X-5 THE ERROR OF HIS WAYS...
...AT LEAST, NOT VERY EASILY.
LOOK, WE KNOW YOU'RE NOT 100% BAD, SO HOW ABOUT GIVING YOURSELF UP PEACEFULLY?
URGH, UM, WELL . . .
NO.
WHOOOSH!
I'M JUST GETTING WOUND UP—
OKAY, SUIT YOURSELF.
CLANG!
OW.
DON'T SAY I DIDN'T WARN YOU.
I MEAN IT, DON'T SAY IT.
TOSS!
OHHHHHH, THAT HAD TO HURT.
SMASH!
HEY, WOW! LOOK AT THE CROWD FORMING.
OF COURSE, THEY ONLY SEE THE BIG, WHITE BEAR AND NOT HIS PARTNER, THE KID, STUCK UP HERE ON THE ROOF.

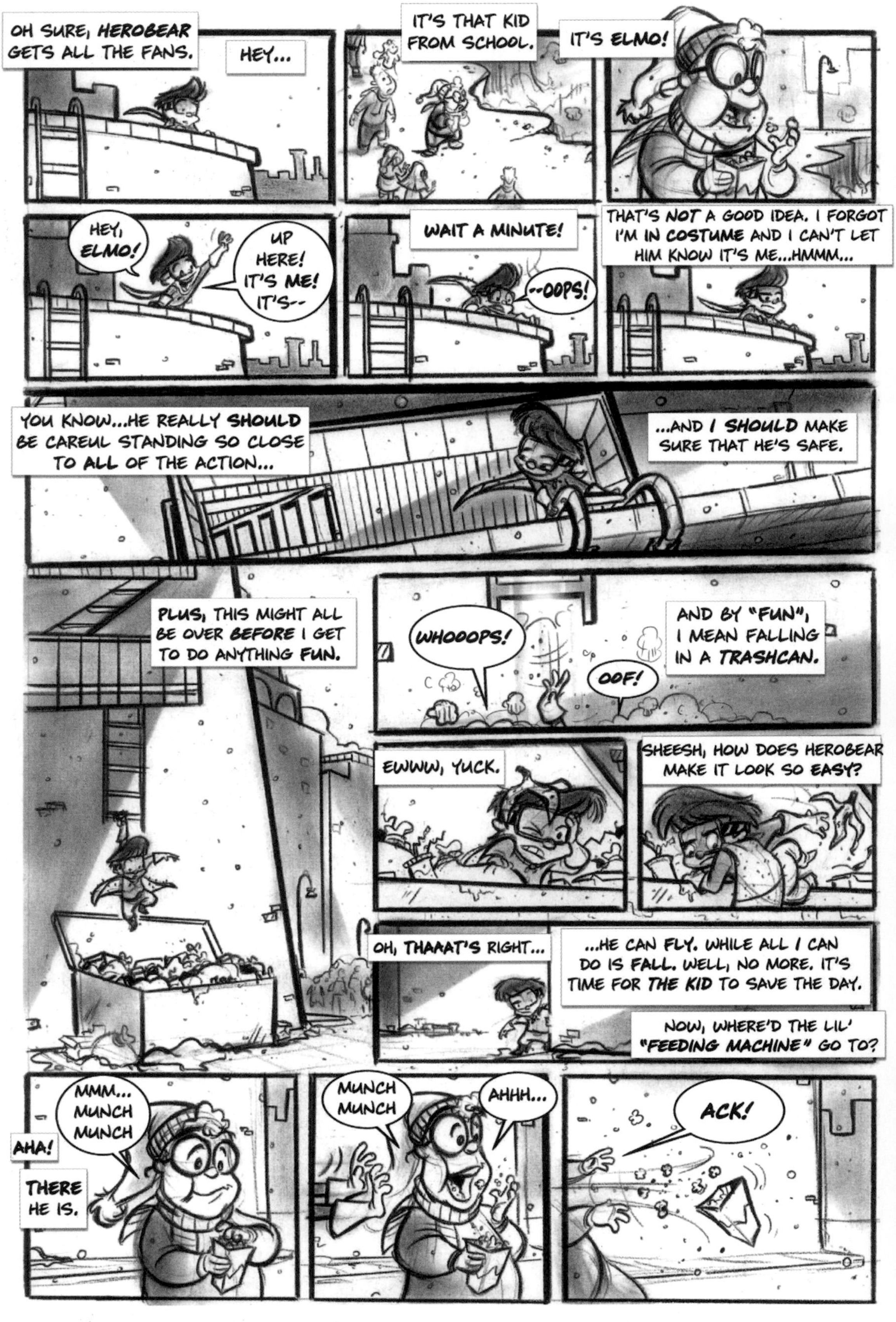
OH SURE, HEROBEAR GETS ALL THE FANS.
HEY...
IT'S THAT KID FROM SCHOOL.
IT'S ELMO!
HEY, ELMO!
UP HERE! IT'S ME! IT'S--
WAIT A MINUTE!
--OOPS!
THAT'S NOT A GOOD IDEA. I FORGOT I'M IN COSTUME AND I CAN'T LET HIM KNOW IT'S ME...HMMM...
YOU KNOW...HE REALLY SHOULD BE CAREUL STANDING SO CLOSE TO ALL OF THE ACTION...
...AND I SHOULD MAKE SURE THAT HE'S SAFE.
PLUS, THIS MIGHT ALL BE OVER BEFORE I GET TO DO ANYTHING FUN.
WHOOOPS!
OOF!
AND BY "FUN", I MEAN FALLING IN A TRASHCAN.
EWWW, YUCK.
SHEESH, HOW DOES HEROBEAR MAKE IT LOOK SO EASY?
OH, THAAAT'S RIGHT...
...HE CAN FLY. WHILE ALL I CAN DO IS FALL. WELL, NO MORE. IT'S TIME FOR THE KID TO SAVE THE DAY.
NOW, WHERE'D THE LIL' "FEEDING MACHINE" GO TO?
AHA!
THERE HE IS.
MMM... MUNCH MUNCH
MUNCH MUNCH
AHHH...
ACK!

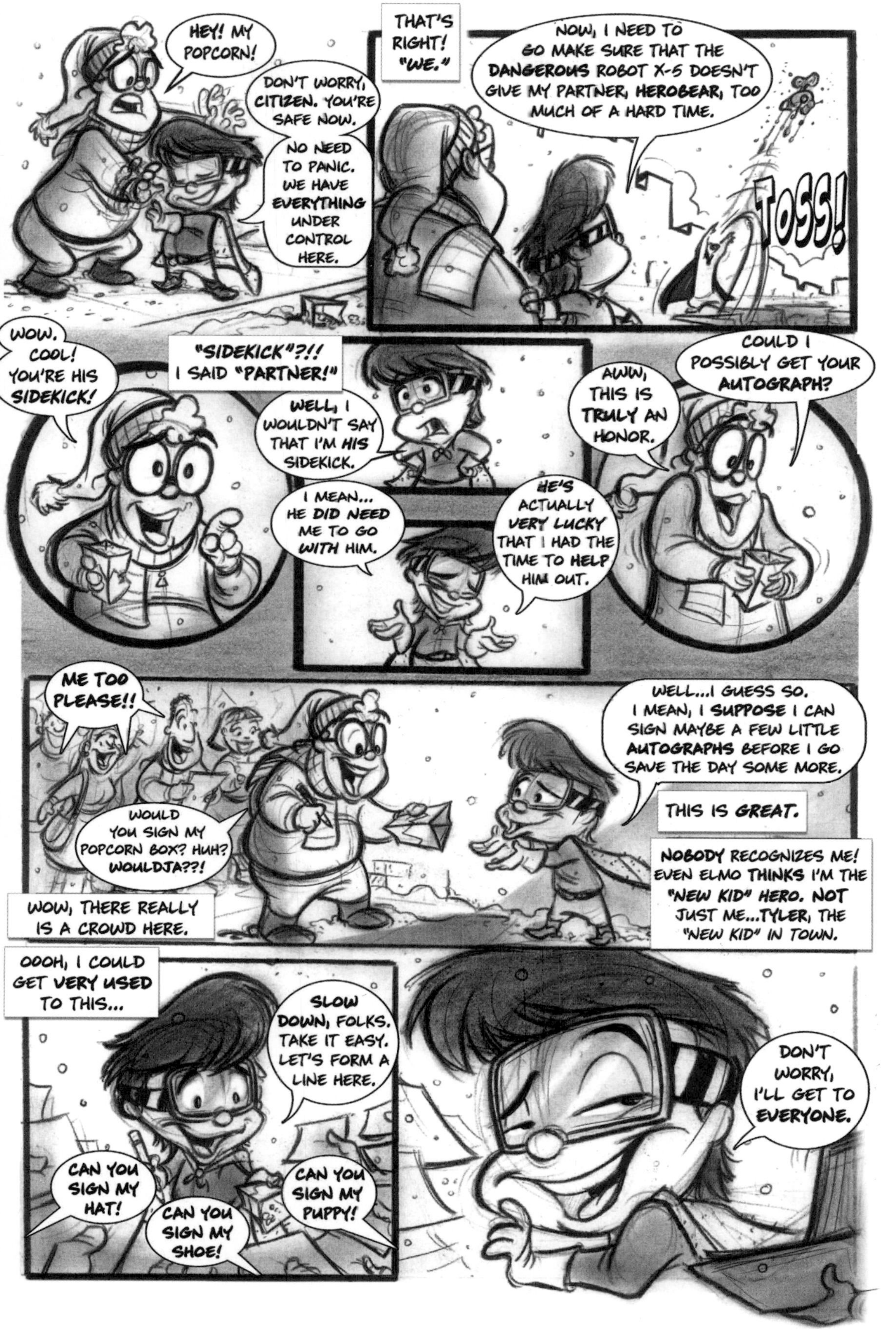
HEY! MY POPCORN!
DON'T WORRY, CITIZEN. YOU'RE SAFE NOW.
NO NEED TO PANIC. WE HAVE EVERYTHING UNDER CONTROL HERE.
THAT'S RIGHT! "WE."
NOW, I NEED TO GO MAKE SURE THAT THE DANGEROUS ROBOT X-5 DOESN'T GIVE MY PARTNER, HEROBEAR, TOO MUCH OF A HARD TIME.
TOSS!
WOW. COOL! YOU'RE HIS SIDEKICK!
"SIDEKICK"?!! I SAID "PARTNER!"
WELL, I WOULDN'T SAY THAT I'M HIS SIDEKICK.
I MEAN... HE DID NEED ME TO GO WITH HIM.
HE'S ACTUALLY VERY LUCKY THAT I HAD THE TIME TO HELP HIM OUT.
AWW, THIS IS TRULY AN HONOR.
COULD I POSSIBLY GET YOUR AUTOGRAPH?
ME TOO PLEASE!!
WOULD YOU SIGN MY POPCORN BOX? HUH? WOULDJA??!
WOW, THERE REALLY IS A CROWD HERE.
WELL...I GUESS SO. I MEAN, I SUPPOSE I CAN SIGN MAYBE A FEW LITTLE AUTOGRAPHS BEFORE I GO SAVE THE DAY SOME MORE.
THIS IS GREAT.
NOBODY RECOGNIZES ME! EVEN ELMO THINKS I'M THE "NEW KID" HERO. NOT JUST ME...TYLER, THE "NEW KID" IN TOWN.
OOOH, I COULD GET VERY USED TO THIS...
SLOW DOWN, FOLKS. TAKE IT EASY. LET'S FORM A LINE HERE.
CAN YOU SIGN MY HAT!
CAN YOU SIGN MY SHOE!
CAN YOU SIGN MY PUPPY!
DON'T WORRY, I'LL GET TO EVERYONE.

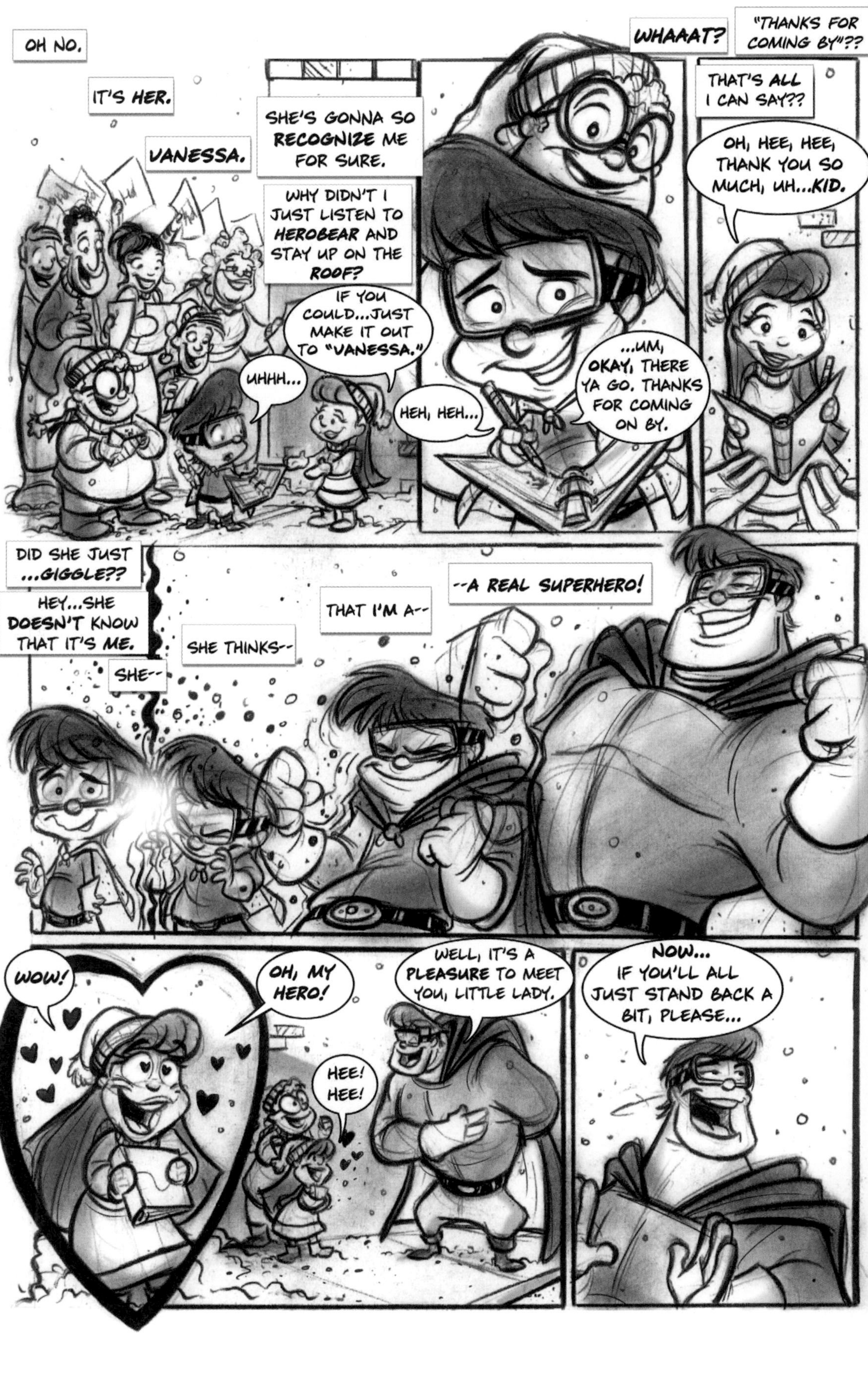
OH NO.
IT'S HER.
VANESSA.
SHE'S GONNA SO RECOGNIZE ME FOR SURE.
WHY DIDN'T I JUST LISTEN TO HEROBEAR AND STAY UP ON THE ROOF?
IF YOU COULD...JUST MAKE IT OUT TO "VANESSA."
UHHH...
HEH, HEH...
...UM, OKAY, THERE YA GO. THANKS FOR COMING ON BY.
WHAAAT?
"THANKS FOR COMING BY"??
THAT'S ALL I CAN SAY??
OH, HEE, HEE, THANK YOU SO MUCH, UH...KID.
DID SHE JUST ...GIGGLE??
HEY...SHE DOESN'T KNOW THAT IT'S ME.
SHE--
SHE THINKS--
THAT I'M A--
--A REAL SUPERHERO!
WOW!
OH, MY HERO!
HEE! HEE!
WELL, IT'S A PLEASURE TO MEET YOU, LITTLE LADY.
NOW... IF YOU'LL ALL JUST STAND BACK A BIT, PLEASE...

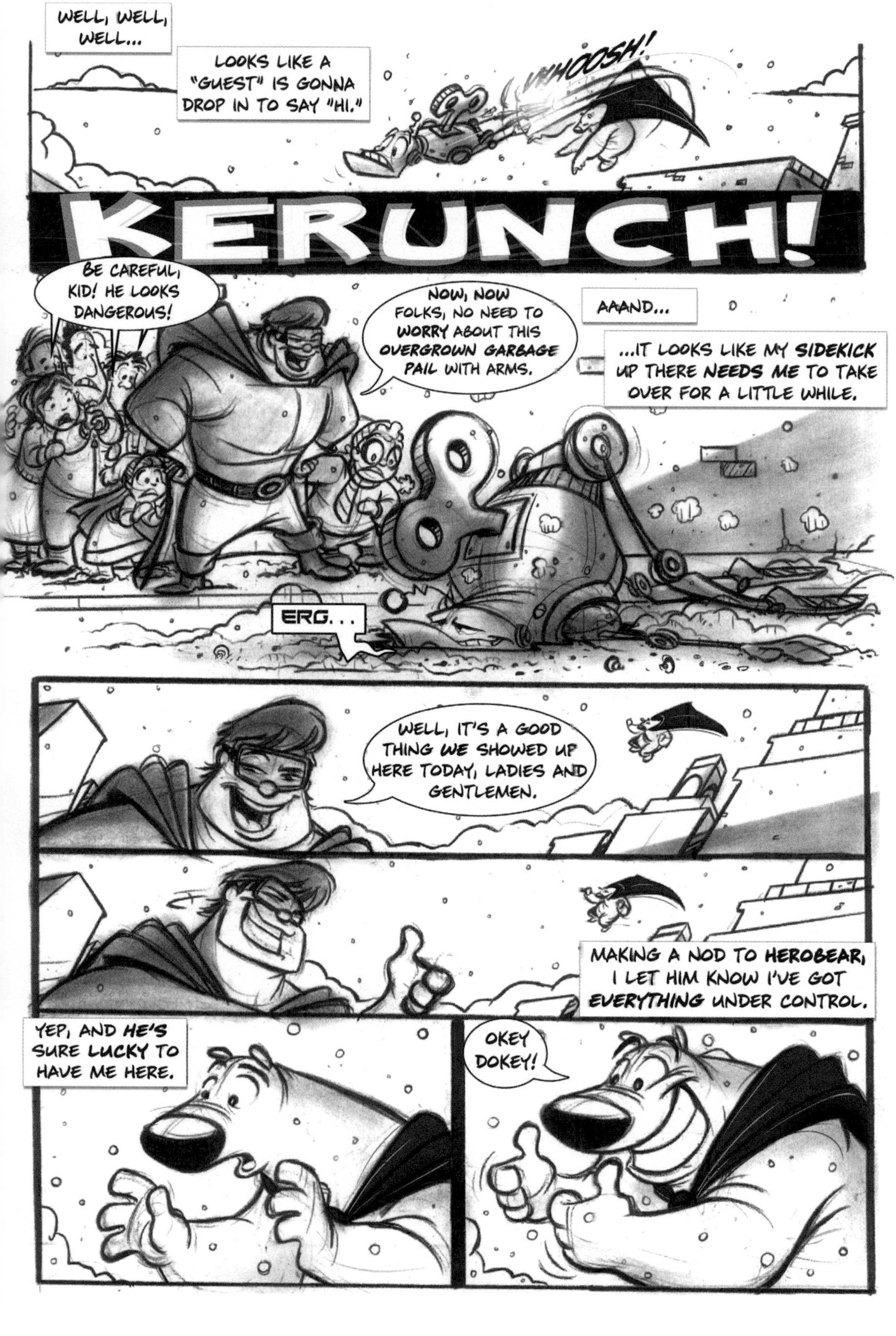
WELL, WELL, WELL...
LOOKS LIKE A "GUEST" IS GONNA DROP IN TO SAY "HI."
WHOOSH!
KERUNCH!
BE CAREFUL, KID! HE LOOKS DANGEROUS!
NOW, NOW FOLKS, NO NEED TO WORRY ABOUT THIS OVERGROWN GARBAGE PAIL WITH ARMS.
AAAND...
...IT LOOKS LIKE MY SIDEKICK UP THERE NEEDS ME TO TAKE OVER FOR A LITTLE WHILE.
ERG...
WELL, IT'S A GOOD THING WE SHOWED UP HERE TODAY, LADIES AND GENTLEMEN.
MAKING A NOD TO HEROBEAR, I LET HIM KNOW I'VE GOT EVERYTHING UNDER CONTROL.
YEP, AND HE'S SURE LUCKY TO HAVE ME HERE.
OKEY DOKEY!

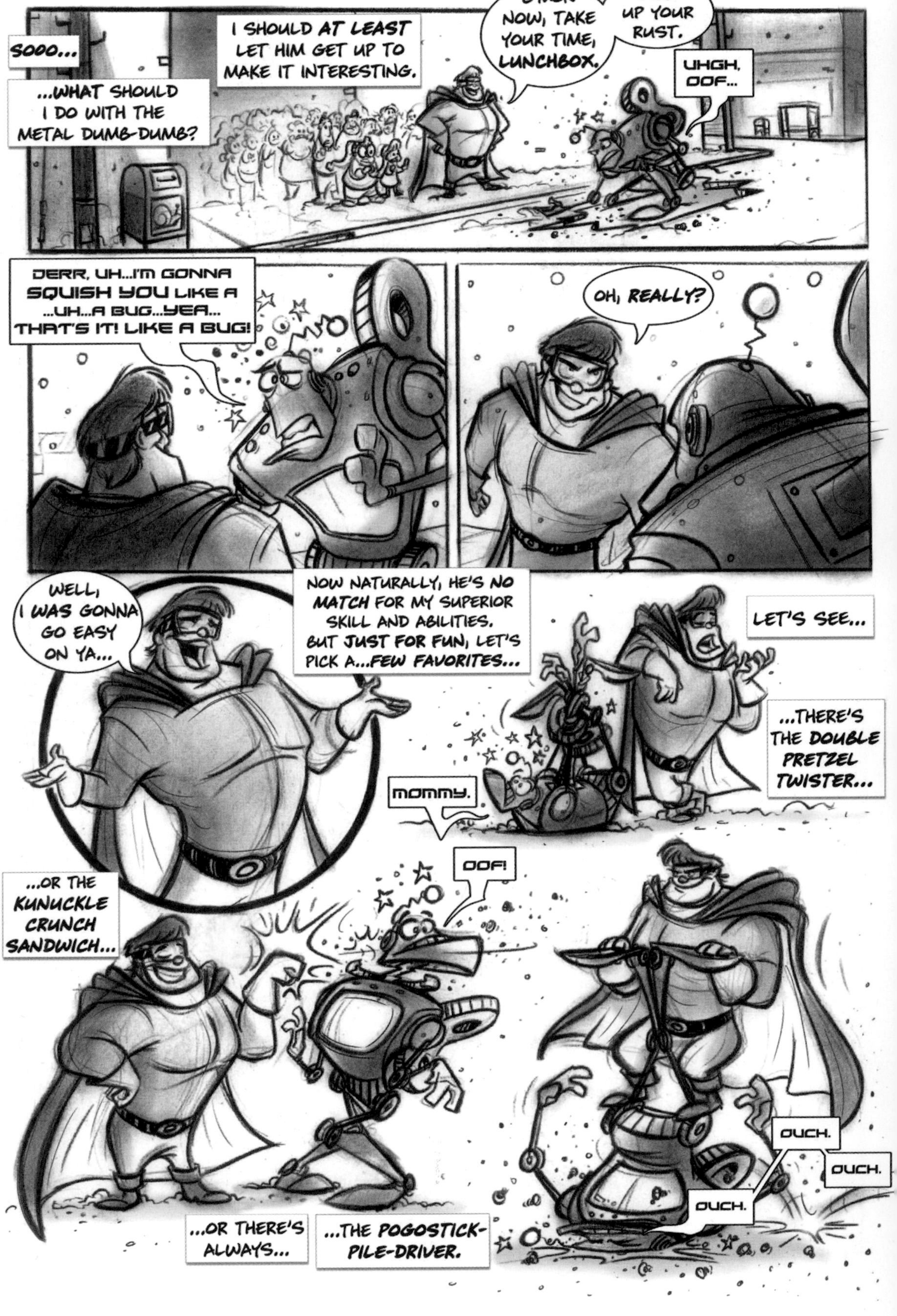

SOOO...
...WHAT SHOULD I DO WITH THE METAL DUMB-DUMB?
I SHOULD AT LEAST LET HIM GET UP TO MAKE IT INTERESTING.
C'MON NOW, TAKE YOUR TIME, LUNCHBOX.
PICK UP YOUR RUST.
UHGH, OOF...
DERR, UH...I'M GONNA SQUISH YOU LIKE A ...UH...A BUG...YEA... THAT'S IT! LIKE A BUG!
OH, REALLY?
WELL, I WAS GONNA GO EASY ON YA...
NOW NATURALLY, HE'S NO MATCH FOR MY SUPERIOR SKILL AND ABILITIES. BUT JUST FOR FUN, LET'S PICK A...FEW FAVORITES...
LET'S SEE...
...THERE'S THE DOUBLE PRETZEL TWISTER...
MOMMY.
...OR THE KUNUCKLE CRUNCH SANDWICH...
OOF!
...OR THERE'S ALWAYS...
...THE POGOSTICK-PILE-DRIVER.
OUCH.
OUCH.
OUCH.

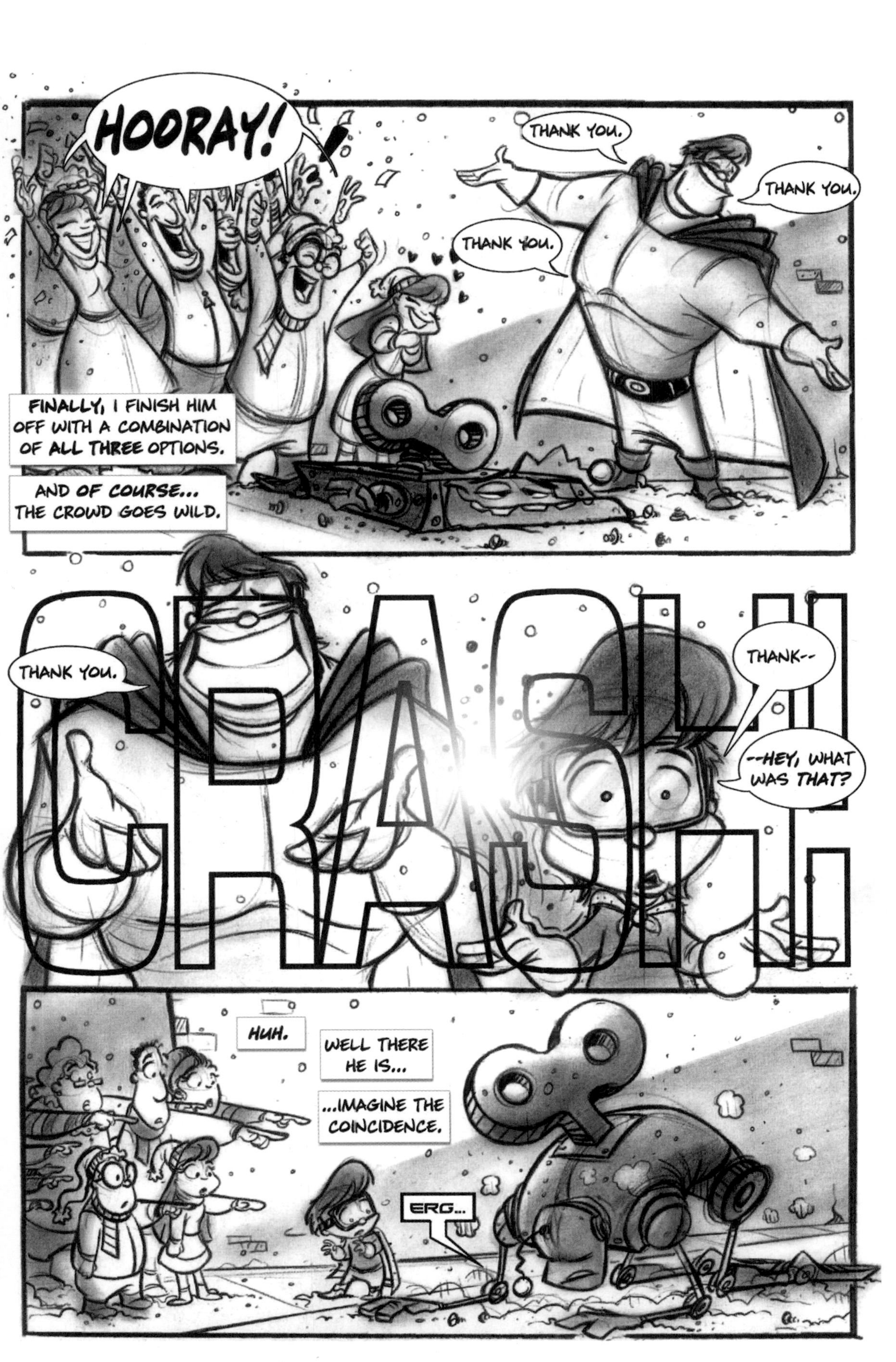
HOORAY!
THANK YOU.
THANK YOU.
THANK YOU.
FINALLY, I FINISH HIM OFF WITH A COMBINATION OF ALL THREE OPTIONS.
AND OF COURSE... THE CROWD GOES WILD.
CRASH!!
THANK YOU.
THANK--
--HEY, WHAT WAS THAT?
HUH.
WELL THERE HE IS...
...IMAGINE THE COINCIDENCE.
ERG...

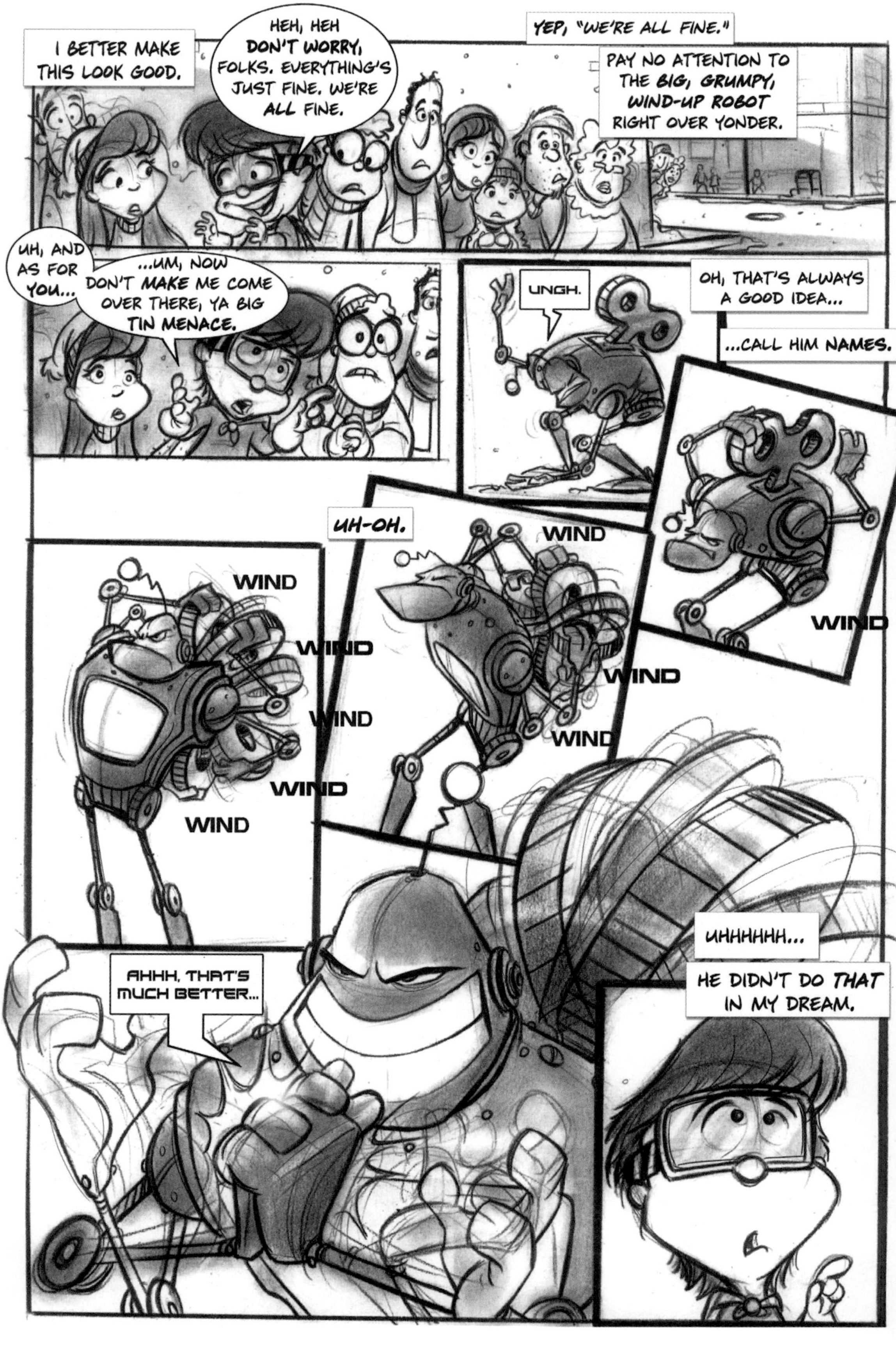
I BETTER MAKE THIS LOOK GOOD.
HEH, HEH DON'T WORRY, FOLKS. EVERYTHING'S JUST FINE. WE'RE ALL FINE.
YEP, "WE'RE ALL FINE."
PAY NO ATTENTION TO THE BIG, GRUMPY, WIND-UP ROBOT RIGHT OVER YONDER.
UH, AND AS FOR YOU...
...UM, NOW DON'T MAKE ME COME OVER THERE, YA BIG TIN MENACE.
UNGH.
OH, THAT'S ALWAYS A GOOD IDEA...
...CALL HIM NAMES.
UH-OH.
WIND
WIND
WIND
WIND
WIND
WIND
WIND
WIND
WIND
AHHH, THAT'S MUCH BETTER...
UHHHHHH...
HE DIDN'T DO THAT IN MY DREAM.

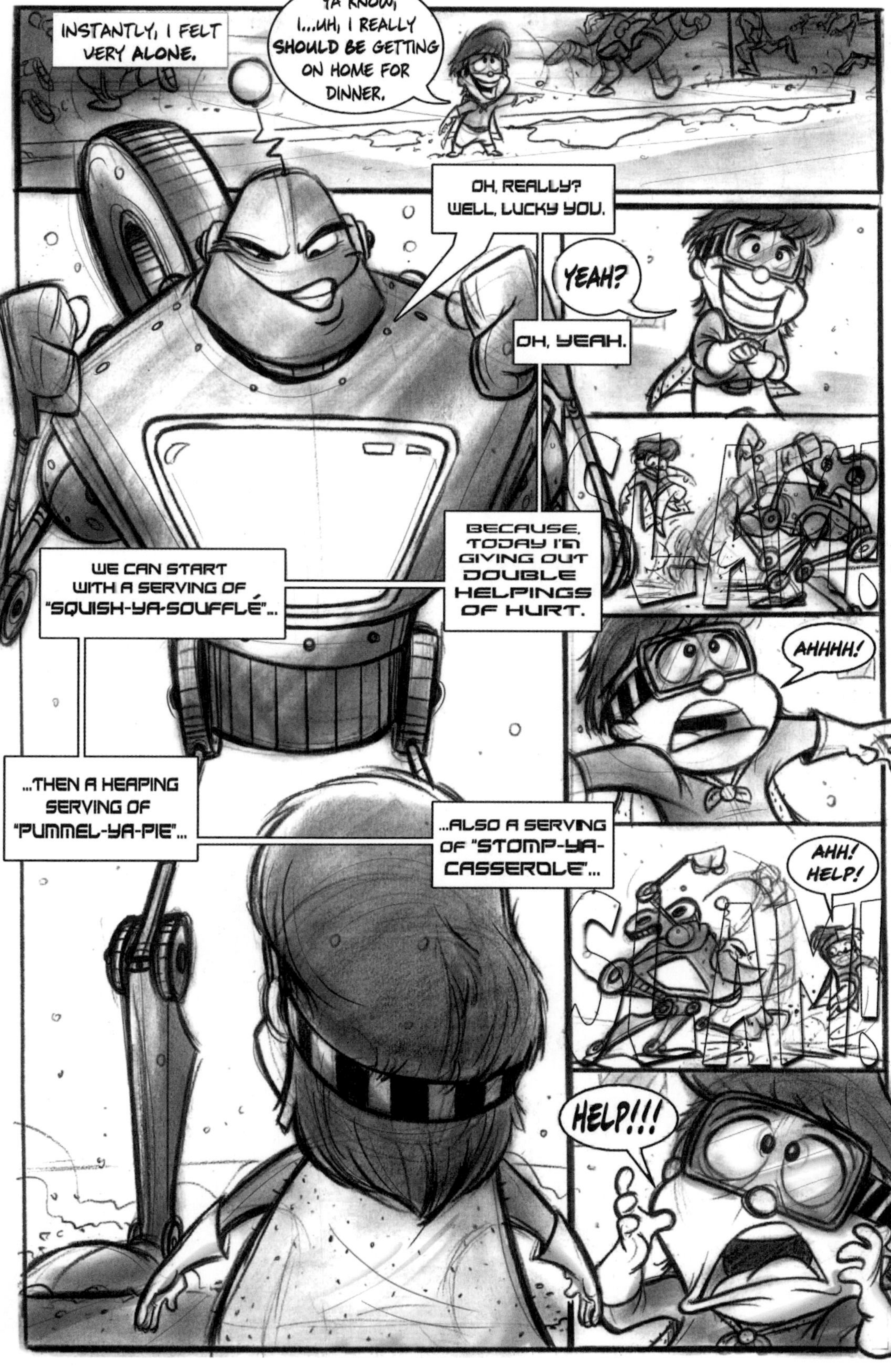
INSTANTLY, I FELT VERY ALONE.
YA KNOW, I...UH, I REALLY SHOULD BE GETTING ON HOME FOR DINNER.
OH, REALLY? WELL, LUCKY YOU.
YEAH?
OH, YEAH.
BECAUSE, TODAY I'M GIVING OUT DOUBLE HELPINGS OF HURT.
WE CAN START WITH A SERVING OF "SQUISH-YA-SOUFFLÉ"...
AHHHH!
...THEN A HEAPING SERVING OF "PUMMEL-YA-PIE"...
...ALSO A SERVING OF "STOMP-YA-CASSEROLE"...
AHH! HELP!
HELP!!!

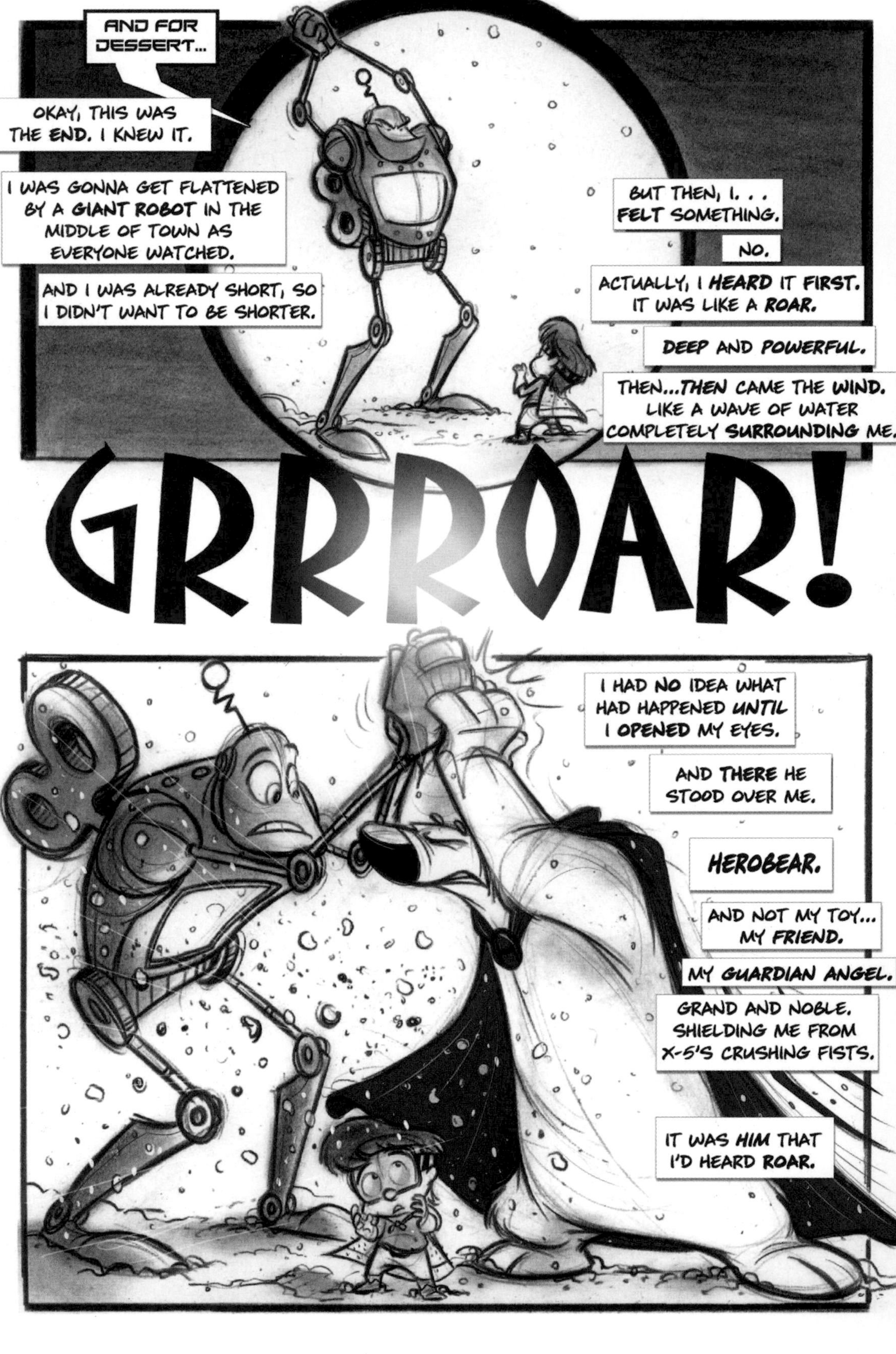
AND FOR DESSERT...
OKAY, THIS WAS THE END. I KNEW IT.
I WAS GONNA GET FLATTENED BY A GIANT ROBOT IN THE MIDDLE OF TOWN AS EVERYONE WATCHED.
AND I WAS ALREADY SHORT, SO I DIDN'T WANT TO BE SHORTER.
BUT THEN, I. . . FELT SOMETHING.
NO.
ACTUALLY, I HEARD IT FIRST. IT WAS LIKE A ROAR.
DEEP AND POWERFUL.
THEN...THEN CAME THE WIND. LIKE A WAVE OF WATER COMPLETELY SURROUNDING ME.
GRRROAR!
I HAD NO IDEA WHAT HAD HAPPENED UNTIL I OPENED MY EYES.
AND THERE HE STOOD OVER ME.
HEROBEAR.
AND NOT MY TOY... MY FRIEND.
MY GUARDIAN ANGEL.
GRAND AND NOBLE. SHIELDING ME FROM X-5'S CRUSHING FISTS.
IT WAS HIM THAT I'D HEARD ROAR.

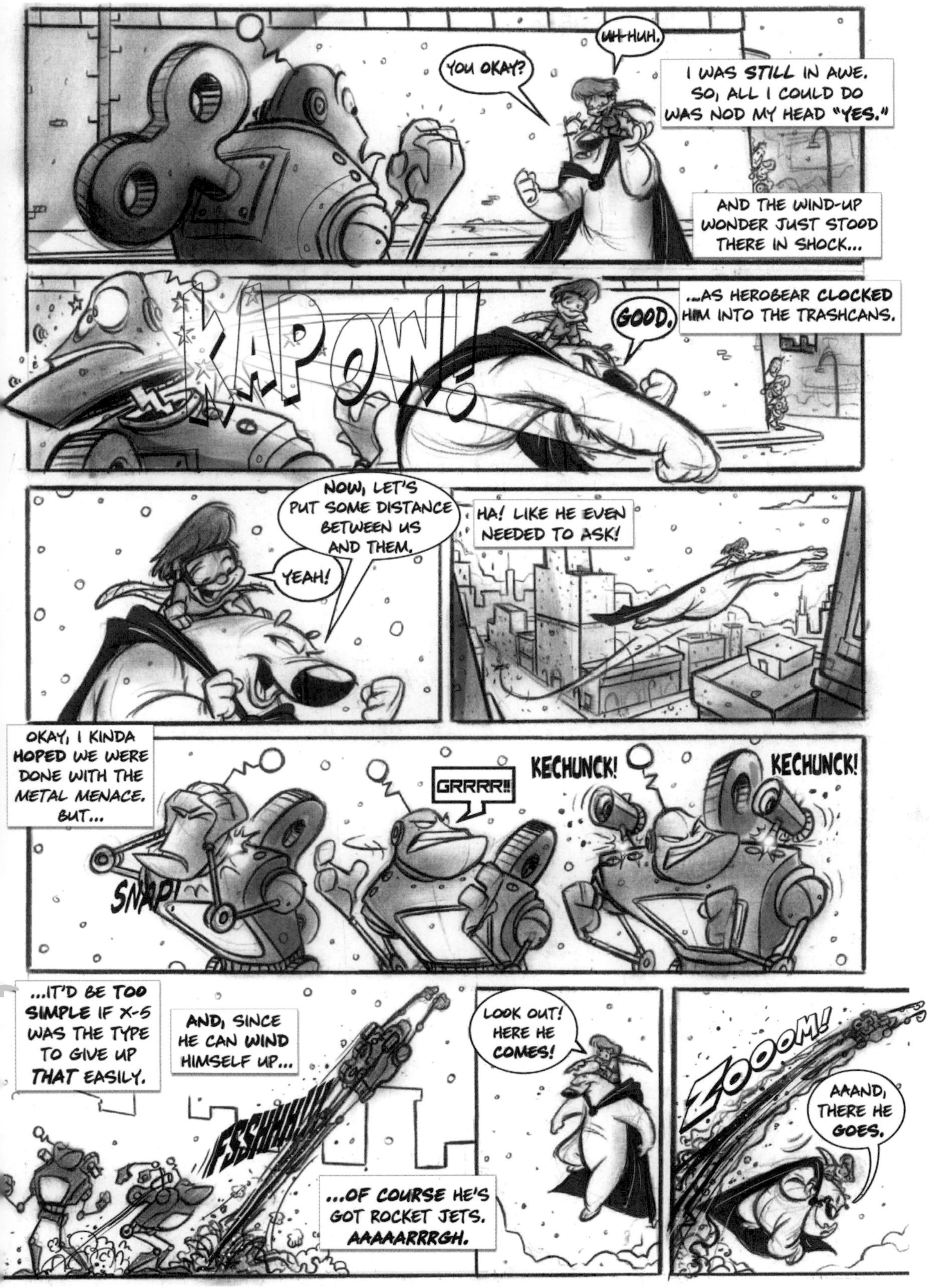
YOU OKAY?
UH-HUH.
I WAS STILL IN AWE. SO, ALL I COULD DO WAS NOD MY HEAD "YES."
AND THE WIND-UP WONDER JUST STOOD THERE IN SHOCK...
KAPOW!!
GOOD.
...AS HEROBEAR CLOCKED HIM INTO THE TRASHCANS.
NOW, LET'S PUT SOME DISTANCE BETWEEN US AND THEM.
YEAH!
HA! LIKE HE EVEN NEEDED TO ASK!
OKAY, I KINDA HOPED WE WERE DONE WITH THE METAL MENACE. BUT...
SNAP!
GRRRR!!
KECHUNCK!
KECHUNCK!
...IT'D BE TOO SIMPLE IF X-5 WAS THE TYPE TO GIVE UP THAT EASILY.
AND, SINCE HE CAN WIND HIMSELF UP...
FSSHHH!!
...OF COURSE HE'S GOT ROCKET JETS. AAAAARRRGH.
LOOK OUT! HERE HE COMES!
ZOOOOM!
AAAND, THERE HE GOES.

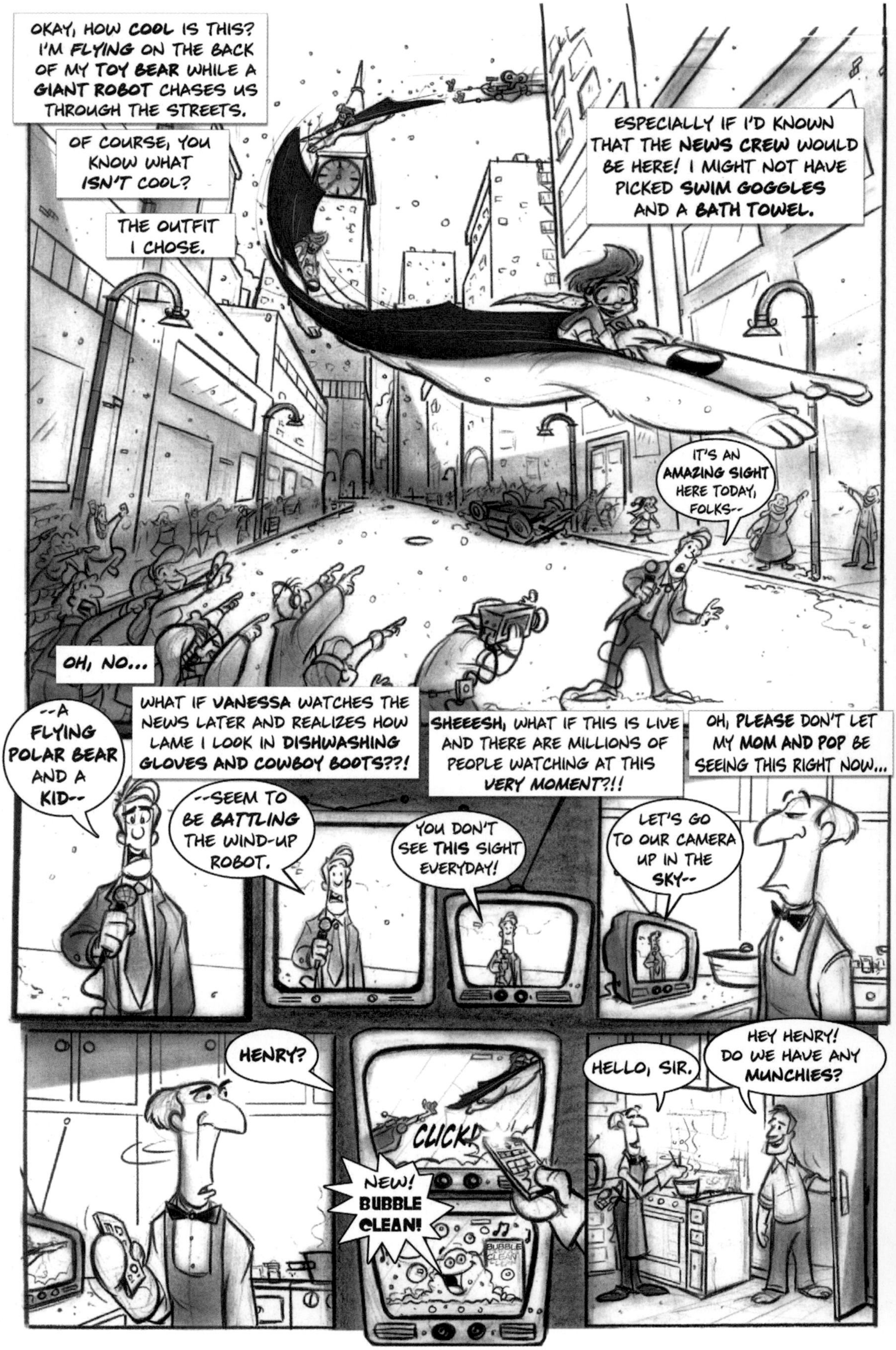

OKAY, HOW COOL IS THIS? I'M FLYING ON THE BACK OF MY TOY BEAR WHILE A GIANT ROBOT CHASES US THROUGH THE STREETS.
OF COURSE, YOU KNOW WHAT ISN'T COOL?
THE OUTFIT I CHOSE.
ESPECIALLY IF I'D KNOWN THAT THE NEWS CREW WOULD BE HERE! I MIGHT NOT HAVE PICKED SWIM GOGGLES AND A BATH TOWEL.
IT'S AN AMAZING SIGHT HERE TODAY, FOLKS--
OH, NO...
--A FLYING POLAR BEAR AND A KID--
WHAT IF VANESSA WATCHES THE NEWS LATER AND REALIZES HOW LAME I LOOK IN DISHWASHING GLOVES AND COWBOY BOOTS??!
--SEEM TO BE BATTLING THE WIND-UP ROBOT.
SHEEESH, WHAT IF THIS IS LIVE AND THERE ARE MILLIONS OF PEOPLE WATCHING AT THIS VERY MOMENT?!!
YOU DON'T SEE THIS SIGHT EVERYDAY!
OH, PLEASE DON'T LET MY MOM AND POP BE SEEING THIS RIGHT NOW...
LET'S GO TO OUR CAMERA UP IN THE SKY--
HENRY?
CLICK!
NEW! BUBBLE CLEAN!
BUBBLE CLEAN
HELLO, SIR.
HEY HENRY! DO WE HAVE ANY MUNCHIES?

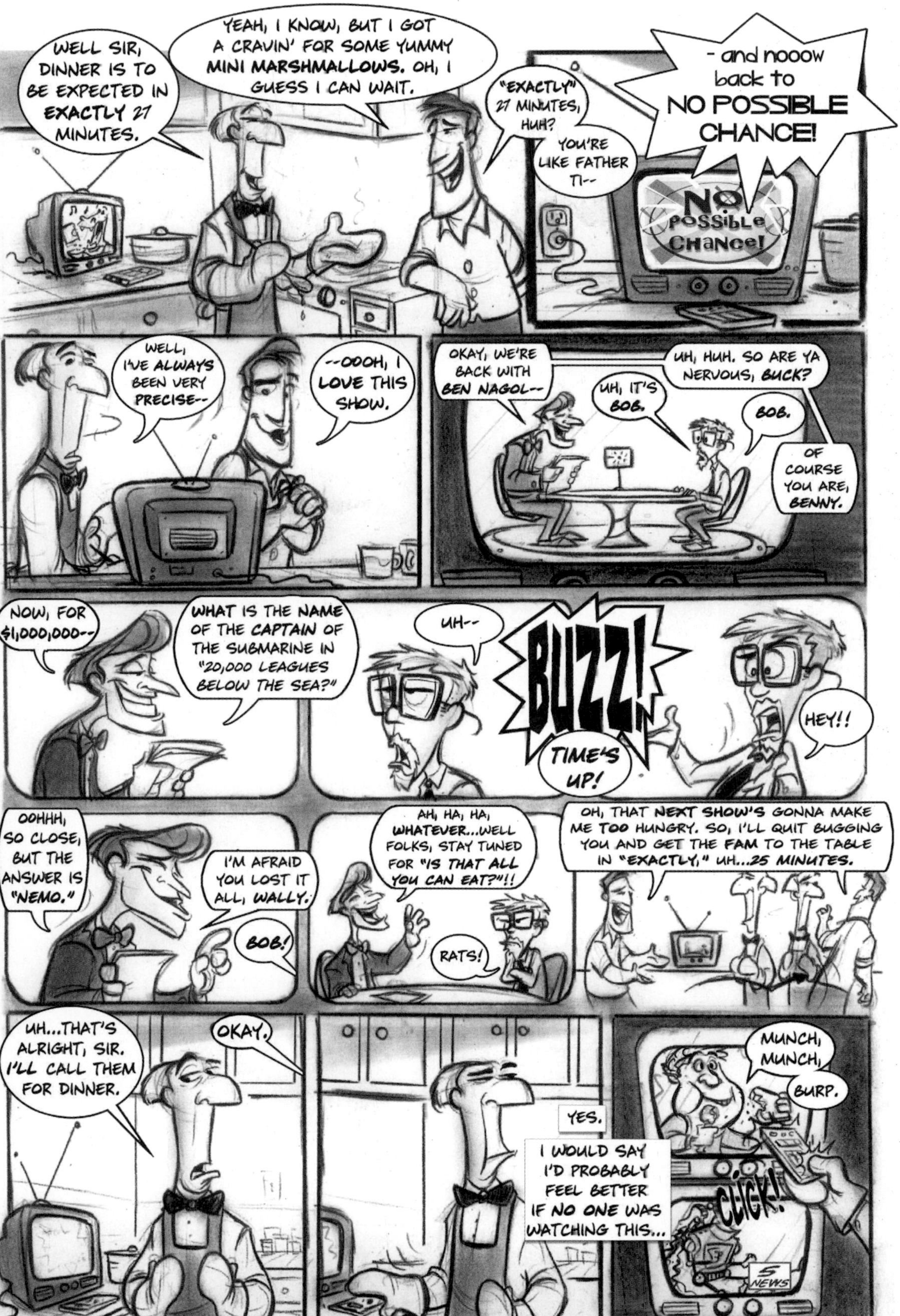
WELL SIR, DINNER IS TO BE EXPECTED IN EXACTLY 27 MINUTES.
YEAH, I KNOW, BUT I GOT A CRAVIN' FOR SOME YUMMY MINI MARSHMALLOWS. OH, I GUESS I CAN WAIT.
"EXACTLY" 27 MINUTES, HUH?
YOU'RE LIKE FATHER TI--
- and nooow back to NO POSSIBLE CHANCE!
NO POSSIBLE CHANCE!
WELL, I'VE ALWAYS BEEN VERY PRECISE--
--OOOH, I LOVE THIS SHOW.
OKAY, WE'RE BACK WITH BEN NAGOL--
UH, IT'S BOB.
UH, HUH. SO ARE YA NERVOUS, BUCK?
BOB.
OF COURSE YOU ARE, BENNY.
NOW, FOR $1,000,000--
WHAT IS THE NAME OF THE CAPTAIN OF THE SUBMARINE IN "20,000 LEAGUES BELOW THE SEA?"
UH--
BUZZ!
TIME'S UP!
HEY!!
OOHHH, SO CLOSE, BUT THE ANSWER IS "NEMO."
I'M AFRAID YOU LOST IT ALL, WALLY.
BOB!
AH, HA, HA, WHATEVER...WELL FOLKS, STAY TUNED FOR "IS THAT ALL YOU CAN EAT?"!!
RATS!
OH, THAT NEXT SHOW'S GONNA MAKE ME TOO HUNGRY. SO, I'LL QUIT BUGGING YOU AND GET THE FAM TO THE TABLE IN "EXACTLY," UH...25 MINUTES.
UH...THAT'S ALRIGHT, SIR. I'LL CALL THEM FOR DINNER.
OKAY.
YES.
I WOULD SAY I'D PROBABLY FEEL BETTER IF NO ONE WAS WATCHING THIS...
MUNCH, MUNCH,
BURP.
CLICK!
5 NEWS

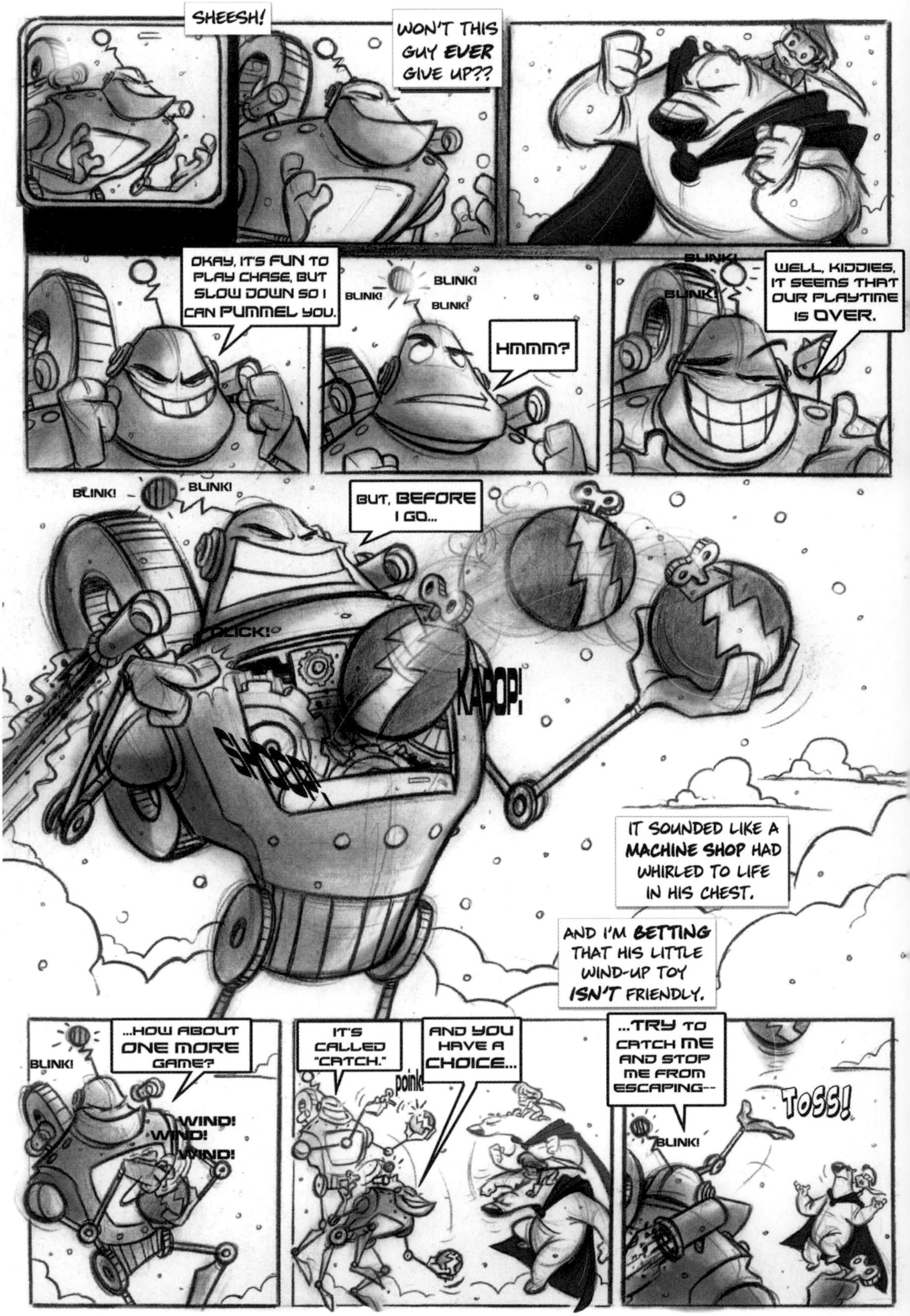
SHEESH!
WON'T THIS GUY EVER GIVE UP??
OKAY, IT'S FUN TO PLAY CHASE, BUT SLOW DOWN SO I CAN PUMMEL YOU.
BLINK!
BLINK!
BLINK!
HMMM?
BLINK!
BLINK!
WELL, KIDDIES, IT SEEMS THAT OUR PLAYTIME IS OVER.
BLINK!
BLINK!
BUT, BEFORE I GO...
CLICK!
KAPOP!
SHOOP!
IT SOUNDED LIKE A MACHINE SHOP HAD WHIRLED TO LIFE IN HIS CHEST.
AND I'M BETTING THAT HIS LITTLE WIND-UP TOY ISN'T FRIENDLY.
BLINK!
...HOW ABOUT ONE MORE GAME?
WIND!
WIND!
WIND!
IT'S CALLED "CATCH."
poink!
AND YOU HAVE A CHOICE...
...TRY TO CATCH ME AND STOP ME FROM ESCAPING--
BLINK!
TOSS!

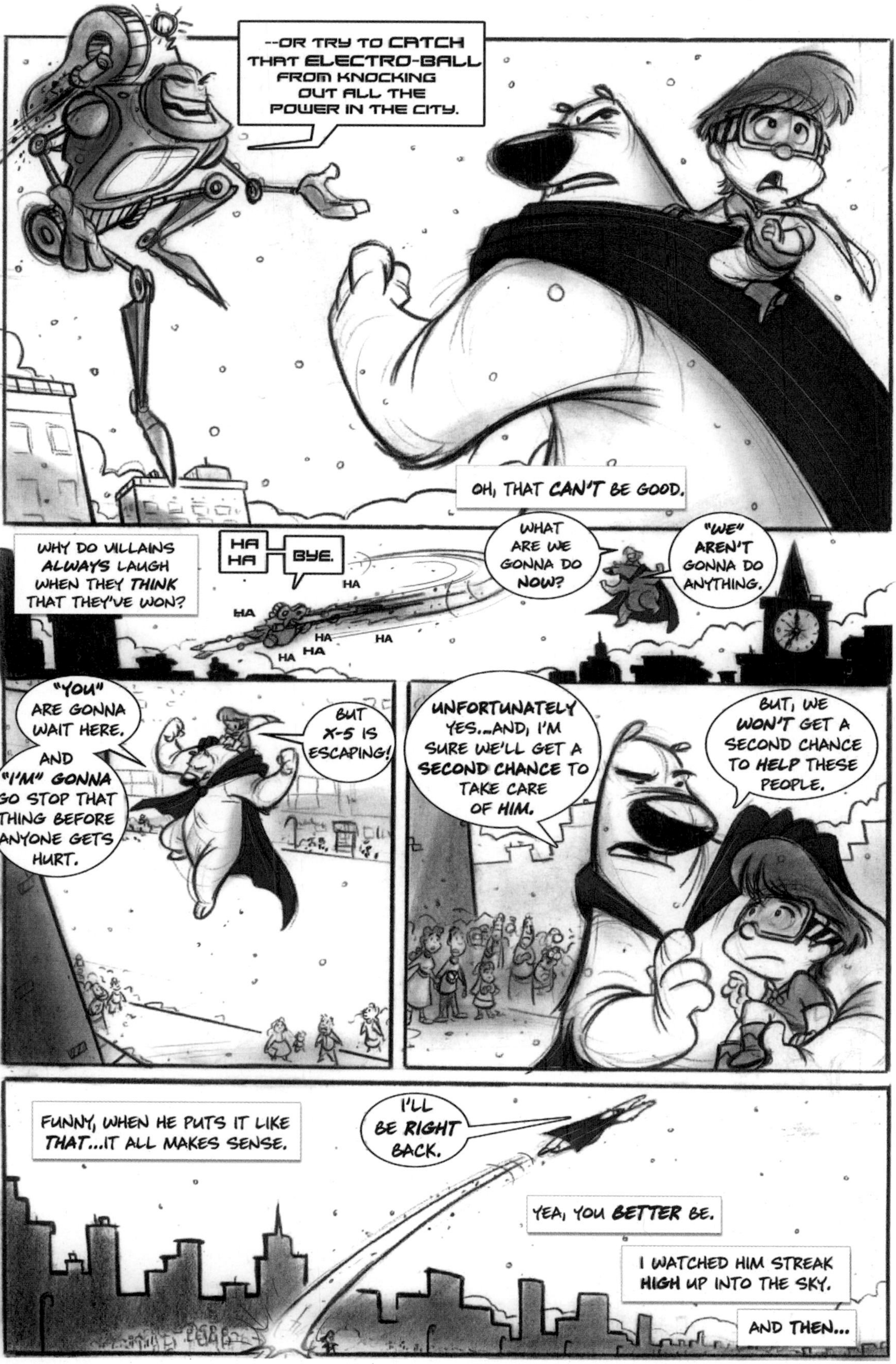
--OR TRY TO CATCH THAT ELECTRO-BALL FROM KNOCKING OUT ALL THE POWER IN THE CITY.
OH, THAT CAN'T BE GOOD.
WHY DO VILLAINS ALWAYS LAUGH WHEN THEY THINK THAT THEY'VE WON?
HA HA
BYE.
HA HA HA HA HA HA
WHAT ARE WE GONNA DO NOW?
"WE" AREN'T GONNA DO ANYTHING.
"YOU" ARE GONNA WAIT HERE.
AND "I'M" GONNA GO STOP THAT THING BEFORE ANYONE GETS HURT.
BUT X-5 IS ESCAPING!
UNFORTUNATELY YES...AND, I'M SURE WE'LL GET A SECOND CHANCE TO TAKE CARE OF HIM.
BUT, WE WON'T GET A SECOND CHANCE TO HELP THESE PEOPLE.
FUNNY, WHEN HE PUTS IT LIKE THAT...IT ALL MAKES SENSE.
I'LL BE RIGHT BACK.
YEA, YOU BETTER BE.
I WATCHED HIM STREAK HIGH UP INTO THE SKY.
AND THEN...

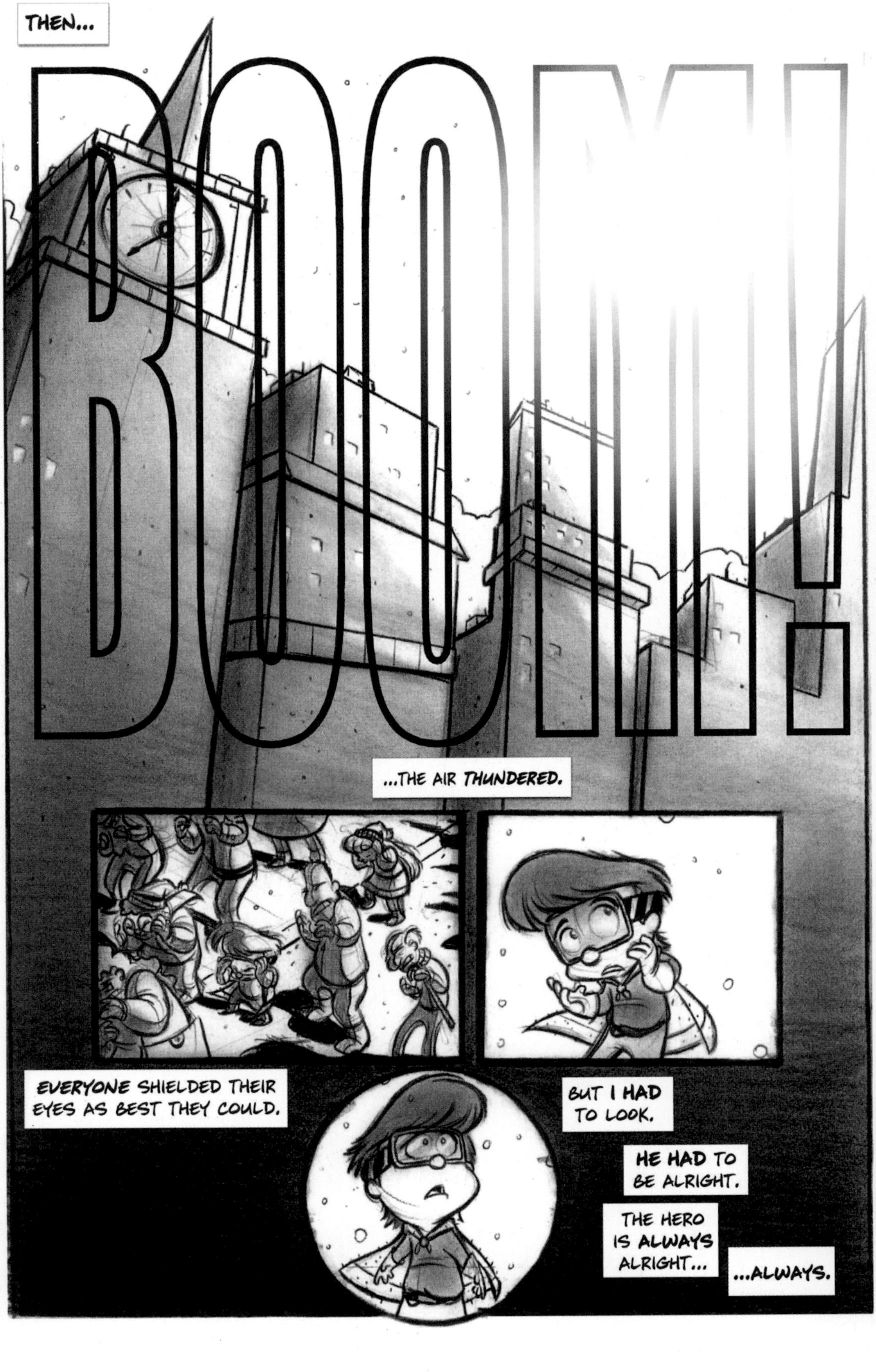
THEN...
BOOM!
...THE AIR THUNDERED.
EVERYONE SHIELDED THEIR EYES AS BEST THEY COULD.
BUT I HAD TO LOOK.
HE HAD TO BE ALRIGHT.
THE HERO IS ALWAYS ALRIGHT...
...ALWAYS.

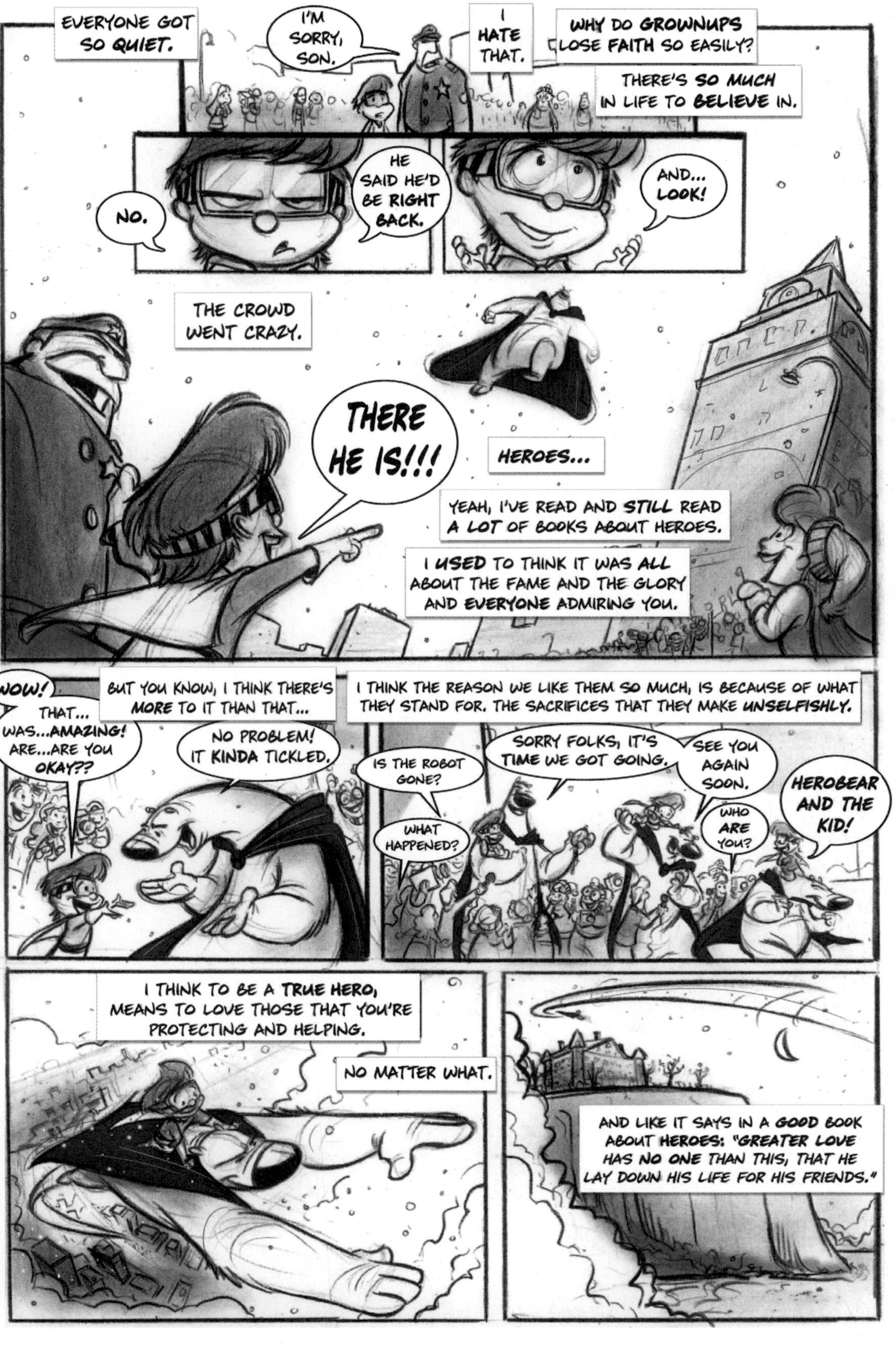
EVERYONE GOT SO QUIET.
I'M SORRY, SON.
I HATE THAT.
WHY DO GROWNUPS LOSE FAITH SO EASILY?
THERE'S SO MUCH IN LIFE TO BELIEVE IN.
NO.
HE SAID HE'D BE RIGHT BACK.
AND... LOOK!
THE CROWD WENT CRAZY.
THERE HE IS!!!
HEROES...
YEAH, I'VE READ AND STILL READ A LOT OF BOOKS ABOUT HEROES.
I USED TO THINK IT WAS ALL ABOUT THE FAME AND THE GLORY AND EVERYONE ADMIRING YOU.
WOW! THAT... WAS...AMAZING! ARE...ARE YOU OKAY??
BUT YOU KNOW, I THINK THERE'S MORE TO IT THAN THAT...
NO PROBLEM! IT KINDA TICKLED.
I THINK THE REASON WE LIKE THEM SO MUCH, IS BECAUSE OF WHAT THEY STAND FOR. THE SACRIFICES THAT THEY MAKE UNSELFISHLY.
IS THE ROBOT GONE?
WHAT HAPPENED?
SORRY FOLKS, IT'S TIME WE GOT GOING.
SEE YOU AGAIN SOON.
WHO ARE YOU?
HEROBEAR AND THE KID!
I THINK TO BE A TRUE HERO, MEANS TO LOVE THOSE THAT YOU'RE PROTECTING AND HELPING.
NO MATTER WHAT.
AND LIKE IT SAYS IN A GOOD BOOK ABOUT HEROES: "GREATER LOVE HAS NO ONE THAN THIS, THAT HE LAY DOWN HIS LIFE FOR HIS FRIENDS."

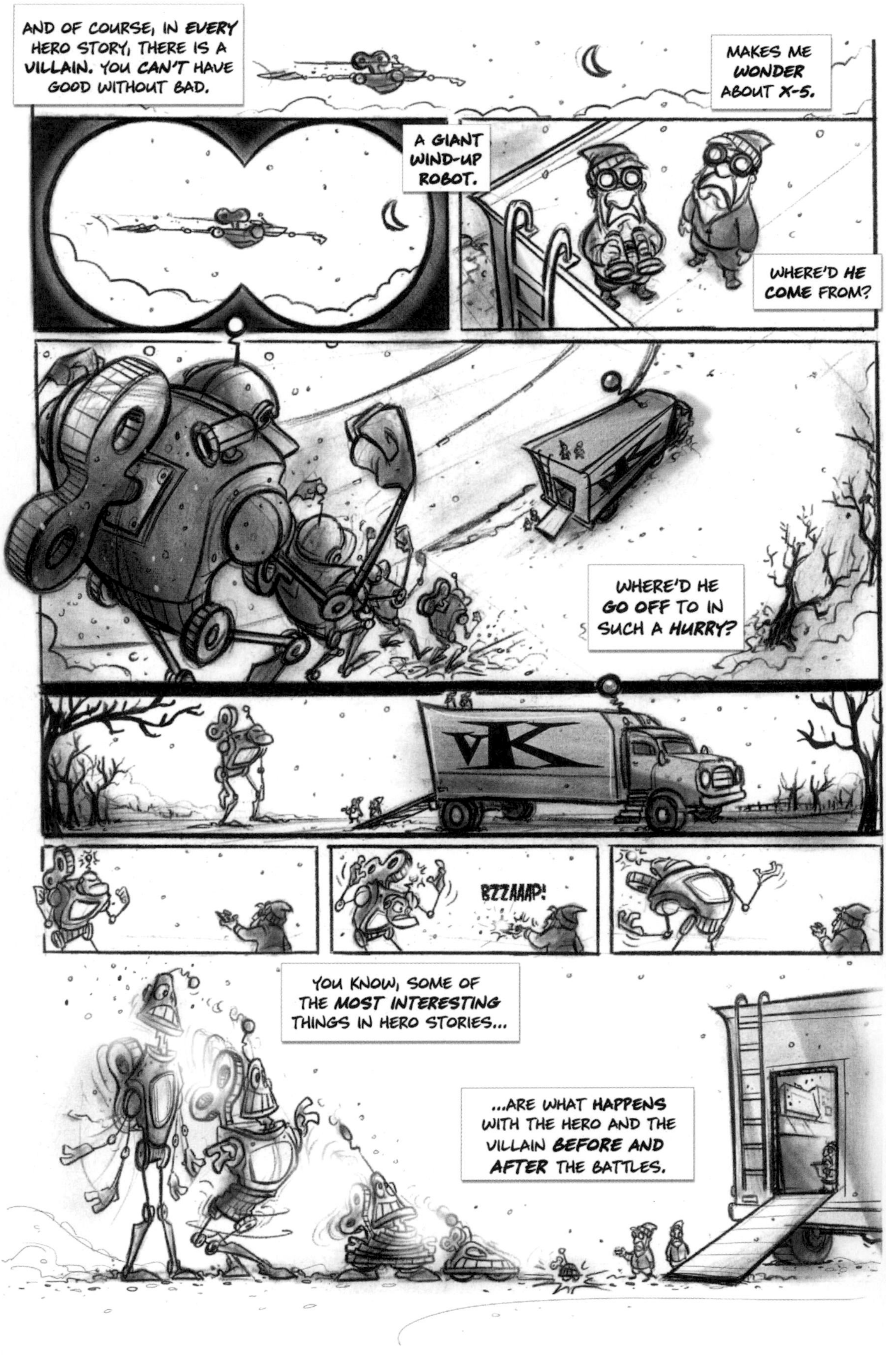
AND OF COURSE, IN EVERY HERO STORY, THERE IS A VILLAIN. YOU CAN'T HAVE GOOD WITHOUT BAD.
MAKES ME WONDER ABOUT X-5.
A GIANT WIND-UP ROBOT.
WHERE'D HE COME FROM?
WHERE'D HE GO OFF TO IN SUCH A HURRY?
VK
BZZZAAAP!
YOU KNOW, SOME OF THE MOST INTERESTING THINGS IN HERO STORIES...
...ARE WHAT HAPPENS WITH THE HERO AND THE VILLAIN BEFORE AND AFTER THE BATTLES.

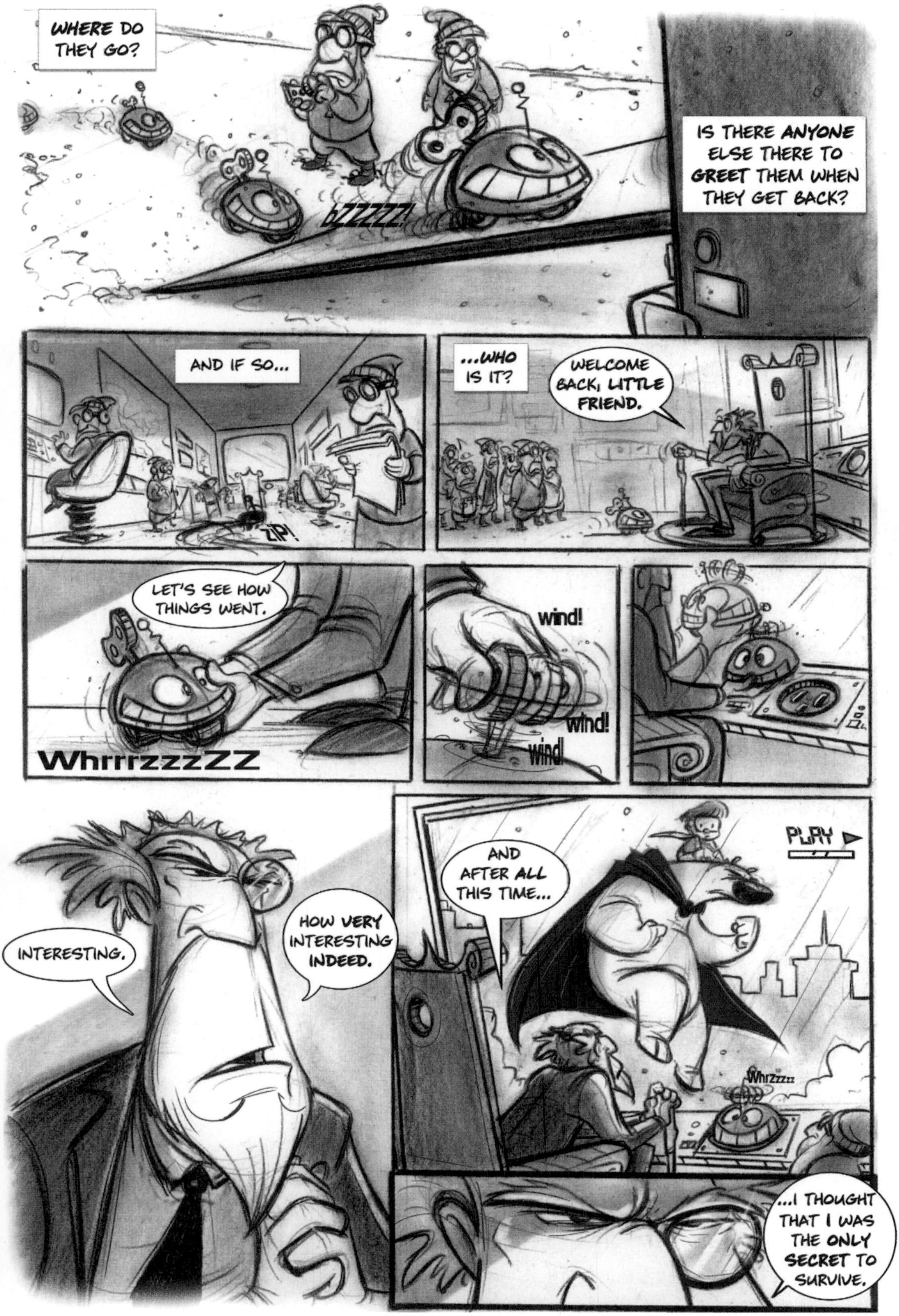
WHERE DO THEY GO?
bZZZZZ!
IS THERE ANYONE ELSE THERE TO GREET THEM WHEN THEY GET BACK?
AND IF SO...
ZIP!
...WHO IS IT?
WELCOME BACK, LITTLE FRIEND.
LET'S SEE HOW THINGS WENT.
WhrrrzzzZZ
wind!
wind!
wind!
INTERESTING.
HOW VERY INTERESTING INDEED.
AND AFTER ALL THIS TIME...
PLAY
Whrzzzzz
...I THOUGHT THAT I WAS THE ONLY SECRET TO SURVIVE.

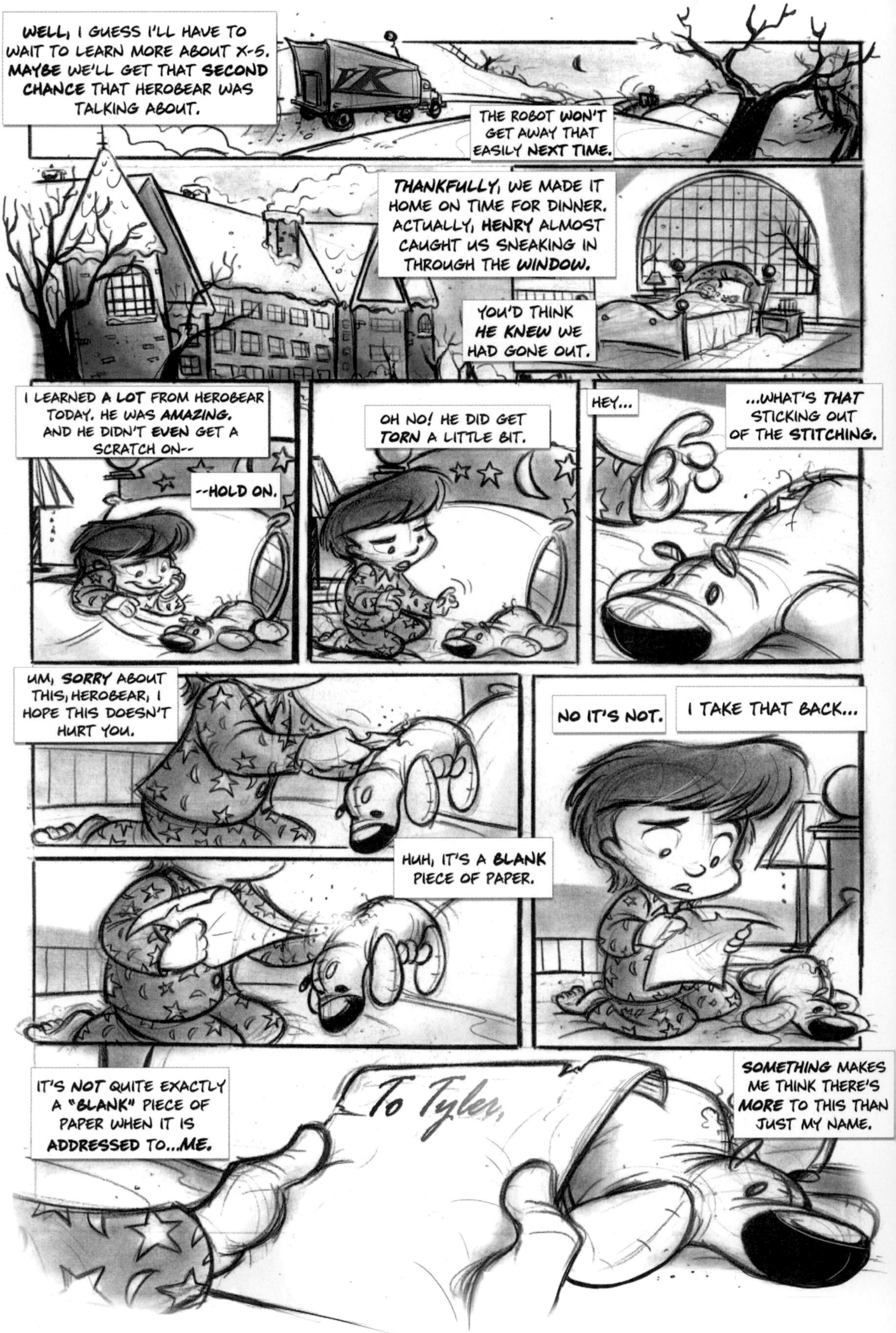
WELL, I GUESS I'LL HAVE TO WAIT TO LEARN MORE ABOUT X-5. MAYBE WE'LL GET THAT SECOND CHANCE THAT HEROBEAR WAS TALKING ABOUT.
THE ROBOT WON'T GET AWAY THAT EASILY NEXT TIME.
THANKFULLY, WE MADE IT HOME ON TIME FOR DINNER. ACTUALLY, HENRY ALMOST CAUGHT US SNEAKING IN THROUGH THE WINDOW.
YOU'D THINK HE KNEW WE HAD GONE OUT.
I LEARNED A LOT FROM HEROBEAR TODAY. HE WAS AMAZING. AND HE DIDN'T EVEN GET A SCRATCH ON--
--HOLD ON.
OH NO! HE DID GET TORN A LITTLE BIT.
HEY...
...WHAT'S THAT STICKING OUT OF THE STITCHING.
UM, SORRY ABOUT THIS, HEROBEAR, I HOPE THIS DOESN'T HURT YOU.
HUH, IT'S A BLANK PIECE OF PAPER.
I TAKE THAT BACK...
NO IT'S NOT.
IT'S NOT QUITE EXACTLY A "BLANK" PIECE OF PAPER WHEN IT IS ADDRESSED TO...ME.
To Tyler,
SOMETHING MAKES ME THINK THERE'S MORE TO THIS THAN JUST MY NAME.

Chapter Four

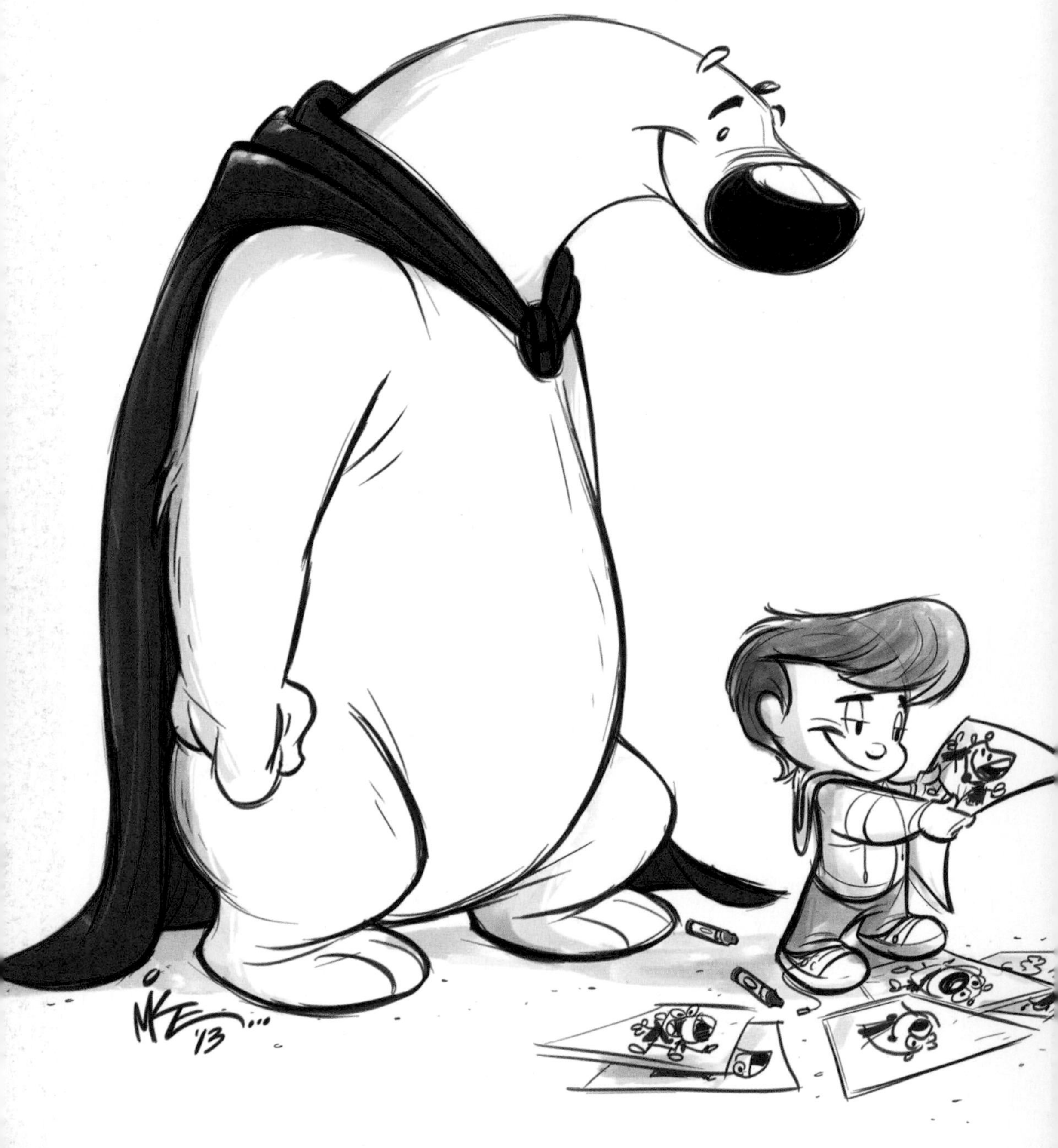

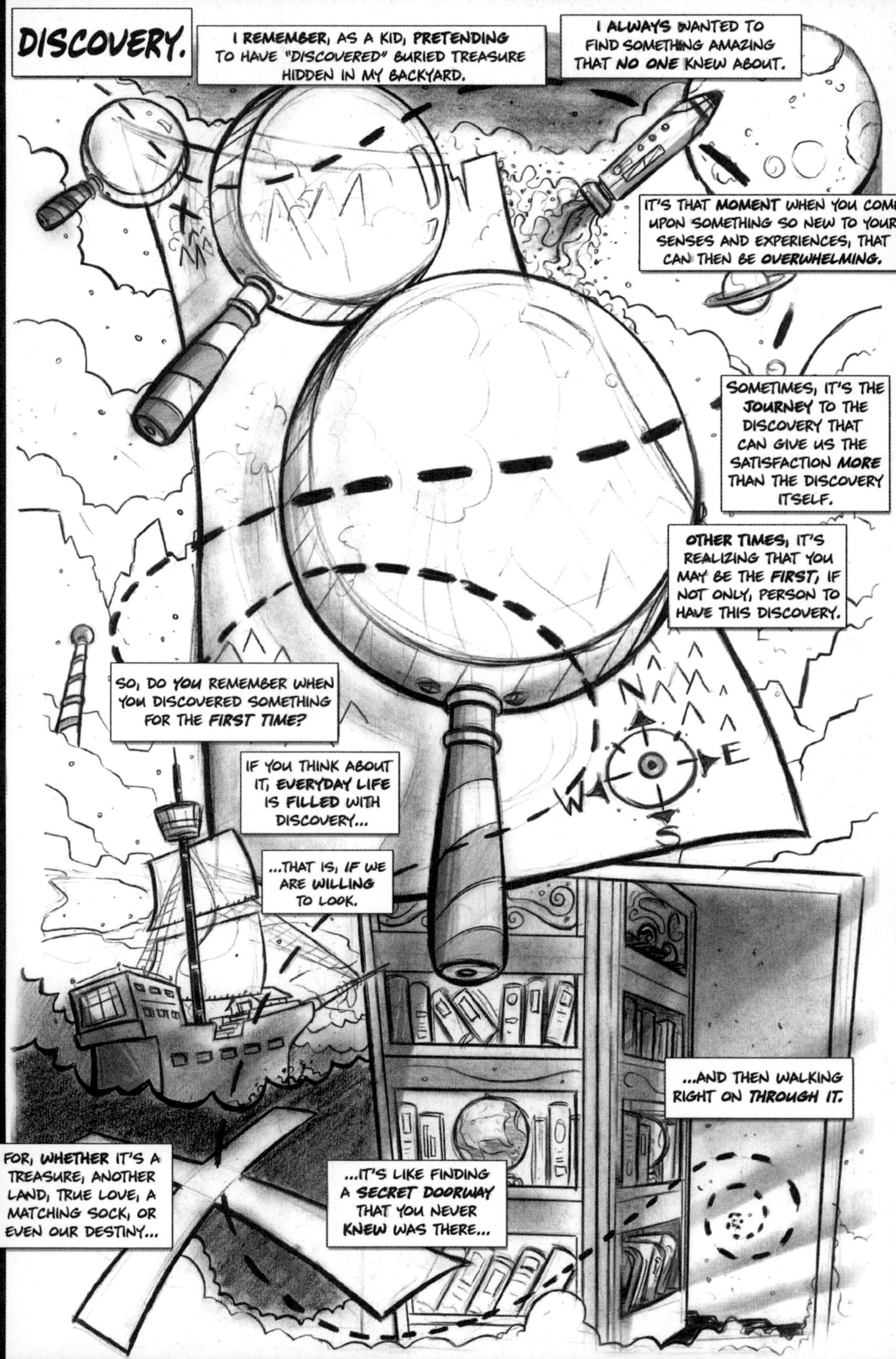
DISCOVERY.
I REMEMBER, AS A KID, PRETENDING TO HAVE "DISCOVERED" BURIED TREASURE HIDDEN IN MY BACKYARD.
I ALWAYS WANTED TO FIND SOMETHING AMAZING THAT NO ONE KNEW ABOUT.
IT'S THAT MOMENT WHEN YOU COME UPON SOMETHING SO NEW TO YOUR SENSES AND EXPERIENCES, THAT CAN THEN BE OVERWHELMING.
SOMETIMES, IT'S THE JOURNEY TO THE DISCOVERY THAT CAN GIVE US THE SATISFACTION MORE THAN THE DISCOVERY ITSELF.
OTHER TIMES, IT'S REALIZING THAT YOU MAY BE THE FIRST, IF NOT ONLY, PERSON TO HAVE THIS DISCOVERY.
SO, DO YOU REMEMBER WHEN YOU DISCOVERED SOMETHING FOR THE FIRST TIME?
N
E
W
S
IF YOU THINK ABOUT IT, EVERYDAY LIFE IS FILLED WITH DISCOVERY...
...THAT IS, IF WE ARE WILLING TO LOOK.
FOR, WHETHER IT'S A TREASURE, ANOTHER LAND, TRUE LOVE, A MATCHING SOCK, OR EVEN OUR DESTINY...
...IT'S LIKE FINDING A SECRET DOORWAY THAT YOU NEVER KNEW WAS THERE...
...AND THEN WALKING RIGHT ON THROUGH IT.

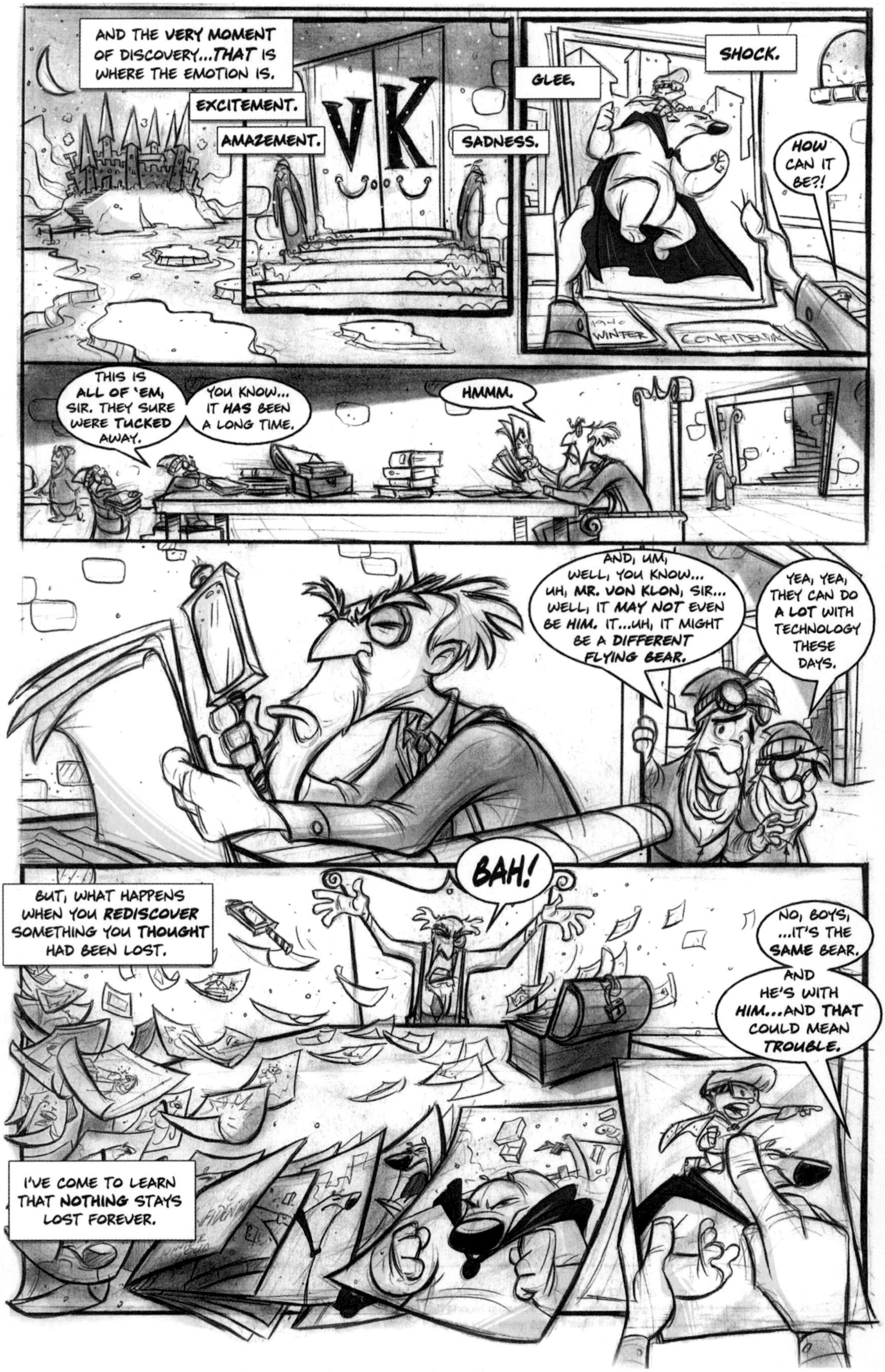
AND THE VERY MOMENT OF DISCOVERY...THAT IS WHERE THE EMOTION IS.
EXCITEMENT.
AMAZEMENT.
VK
GLEE.
SADNESS.
SHOCK.
HOW CAN IT BE?!
WINTER
CONFIDENTIAL
THIS IS ALL OF 'EM, SIR. THEY SURE WERE TUCKED AWAY.
YOU KNOW... IT HAS BEEN A LONG TIME.
HMMM.
AND, UM, WELL, YOU KNOW... UH, MR. VON KLON, SIR... WELL, IT MAY NOT EVEN BE HIM. IT...UH, IT MIGHT BE A DIFFERENT FLYING BEAR.
YEA, YEA, THEY CAN DO A LOT WITH TECHNOLOGY THESE DAYS.
BAH!
BUT, WHAT HAPPENS WHEN YOU REDISCOVER SOMETHING YOU THOUGHT HAD BEEN LOST.
NO, BOYS, ...IT'S THE SAME BEAR.
AND HE'S WITH HIM...AND THAT COULD MEAN TROUBLE.
I'VE COME TO LEARN THAT NOTHING STAYS LOST FOREVER.

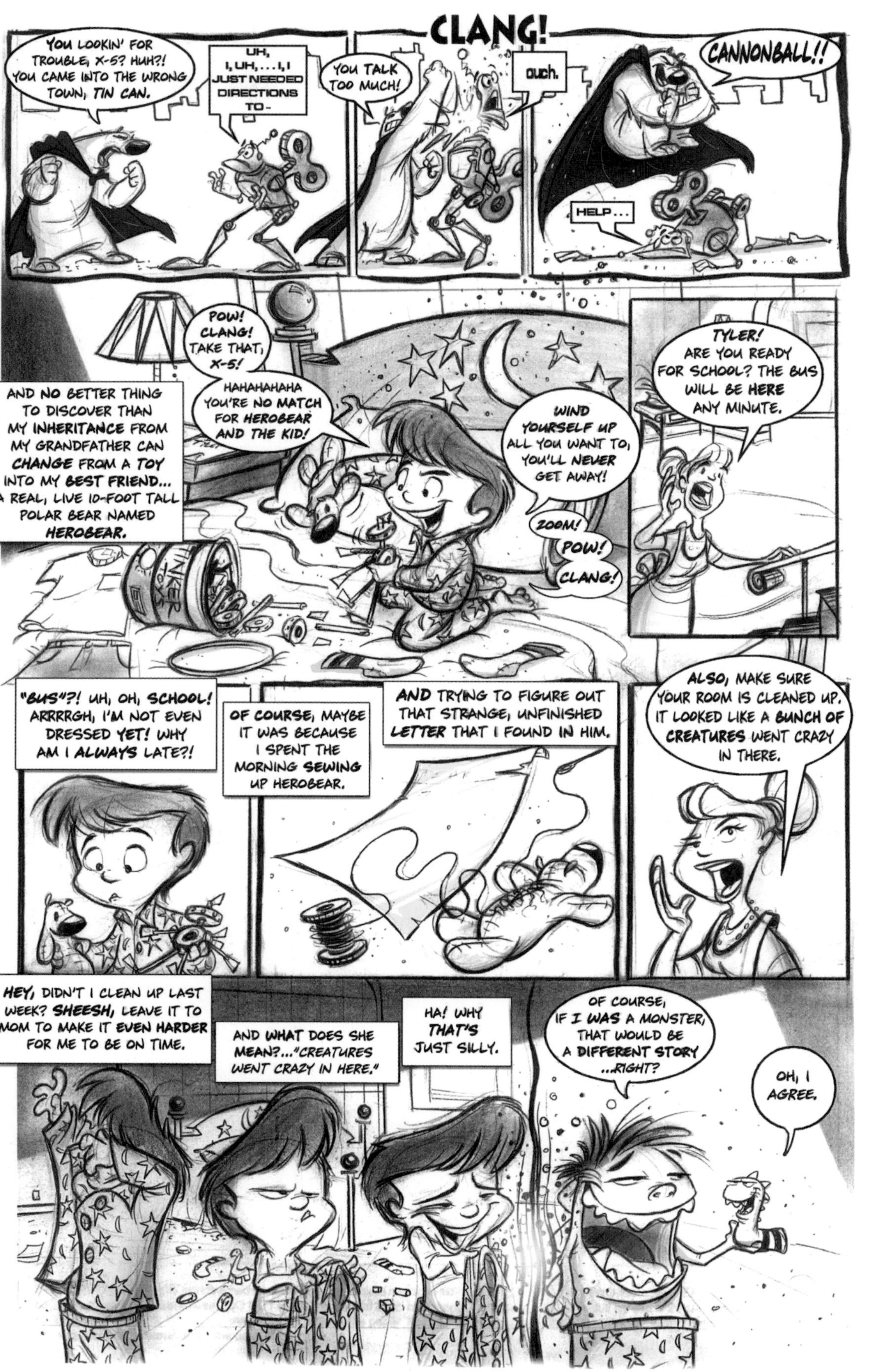

CLANG!
YOU LOOKIN' FOR TROUBLE, X-5? HUH?! YOU CAME INTO THE WRONG TOWN, TIN CAN.
UH, I, UH, . . . I, I JUST NEEDED DIRECTIONS TO -
YOU TALK TOO MUCH!
ouch.
CANNONBALL!!
HELP . . .
POW! CLANG! TAKE THAT, X-5!
HAHAHAHAHA YOU'RE NO MATCH FOR HEROBEAR AND THE KID!
AND NO BETTER THING TO DISCOVER THAN MY INHERITANCE FROM MY GRANDFATHER CAN CHANGE FROM A TOY INTO MY BEST FRIEND... A REAL, LIVE 10-FOOT TALL POLAR BEAR NAMED HEROBEAR.
WIND YOURSELF UP ALL YOU WANT TO, YOU'LL NEVER GET AWAY!
ZOOM! POW! CLANG!
TINKER TOYS
TYLER! ARE YOU READY FOR SCHOOL? THE BUS WILL BE HERE ANY MINUTE.
"BUS"?! UH, OH, SCHOOL! ARRRRGH, I'M NOT EVEN DRESSED YET! WHY AM I ALWAYS LATE?!
OF COURSE, MAYBE IT WAS BECAUSE I SPENT THE MORNING SEWING UP HEROBEAR.
AND TRYING TO FIGURE OUT THAT STRANGE, UNFINISHED LETTER THAT I FOUND IN HIM.
ALSO, MAKE SURE YOUR ROOM IS CLEANED UP. IT LOOKED LIKE A BUNCH OF CREATURES WENT CRAZY IN THERE.
HEY, DIDN'T I CLEAN UP LAST WEEK? SHEESH, LEAVE IT TO MOM TO MAKE IT EVEN HARDER FOR ME TO BE ON TIME.
AND WHAT DOES SHE MEAN?..."CREATURES WENT CRAZY IN HERE."
HA! WHY THAT'S JUST SILLY.
OF COURSE, IF I WAS A MONSTER, THAT WOULD BE A DIFFERENT STORY ...RIGHT?
OH, I AGREE.

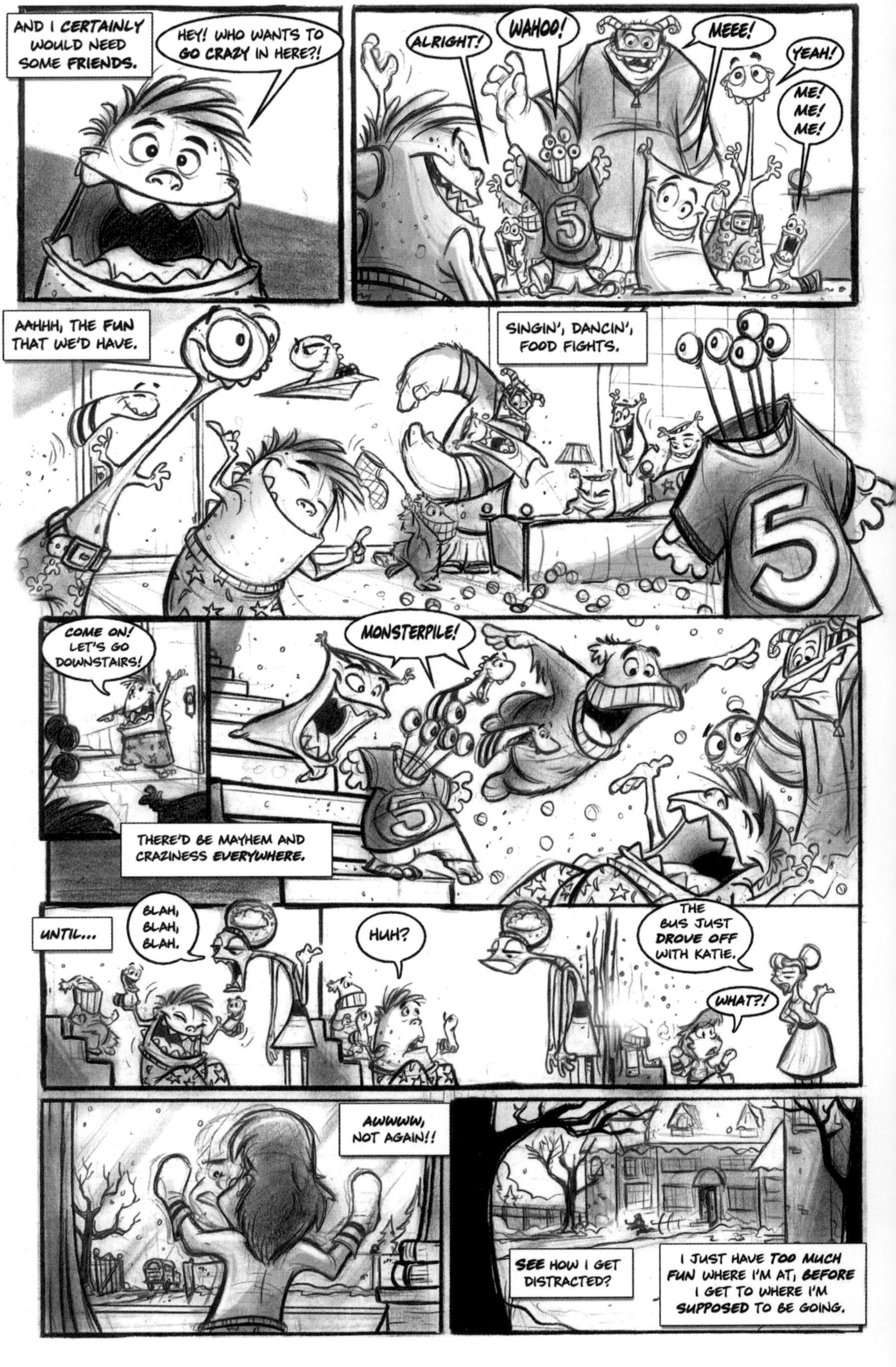
AND I CERTAINLY WOULD NEED SOME FRIENDS.
HEY! WHO WANTS TO GO CRAZY IN HERE?!
ALRIGHT!
WAHOO!
MEEE!
YEAH!
ME! ME! ME!
AAHHH, THE FUN THAT WE'D HAVE.
SINGIN', DANCIN', FOOD FIGHTS.
COME ON! LET'S GO DOWNSTAIRS!
MONSTERPILE!
THERE'D BE MAYHEM AND CRAZINESS EVERYWHERE.
UNTIL...
BLAH, BLAH, BLAH.
HUH?
THE BUS JUST DROVE OFF WITH KATIE.
WHAT?!
AWWWW, NOT AGAIN!!
SEE HOW I GET DISTRACTED?
I JUST HAVE TOO MUCH FUN WHERE I'M AT, BEFORE I GET TO WHERE I'M SUPPOSED TO BE GOING.

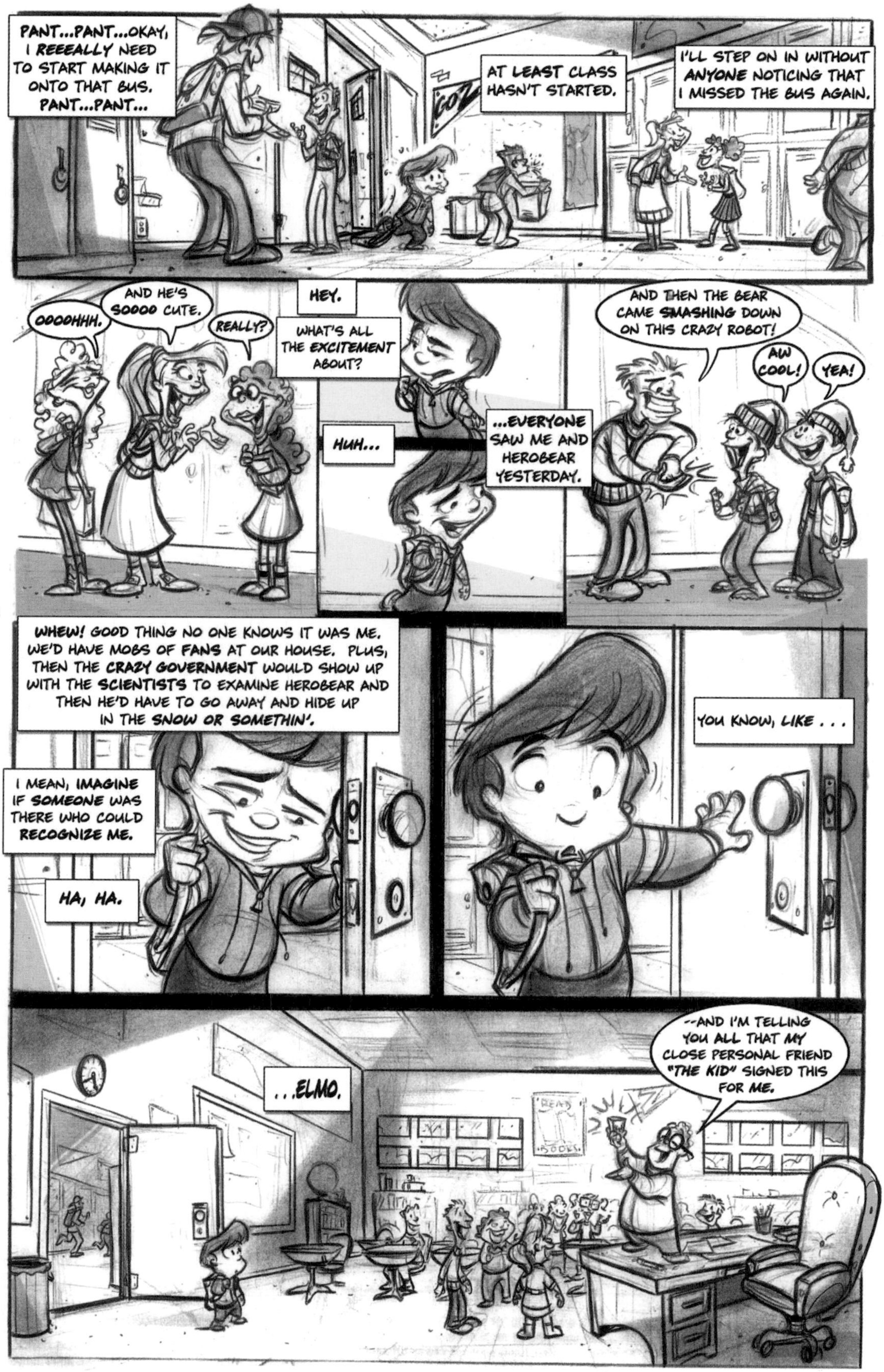
PANT...PANT...OKAY, I REEEALLY NEED TO START MAKING IT ONTO THAT BUS. PANT...PANT...
AT LEAST CLASS HASN'T STARTED.
I'LL STEP ON IN WITHOUT ANYONE NOTICING THAT I MISSED THE BUS AGAIN.
OOOOHHH.
AND HE'S SOOOO CUTE.
REALLY?
HEY.
WHAT'S ALL THE EXCITEMENT ABOUT?
HUH...
...EVERYONE SAW ME AND HEROBEAR YESTERDAY.
AND THEN THE BEAR CAME SMASHING DOWN ON THIS CRAZY ROBOT!
AW COOL!
YEA!
WHEW! GOOD THING NO ONE KNOWS IT WAS ME. WE'D HAVE MOBS OF FANS AT OUR HOUSE. PLUS, THEN THE CRAZY GOVERNMENT WOULD SHOW UP WITH THE SCIENTISTS TO EXAMINE HEROBEAR AND THEN HE'D HAVE TO GO AWAY AND HIDE UP IN THE SNOW OR SOMETHIN'.
I MEAN, IMAGINE IF SOMEONE WAS THERE WHO COULD RECOGNIZE ME.
HA, HA.
YOU KNOW, LIKE . . .
. . .ELMO.
--AND I'M TELLING YOU ALL THAT MY CLOSE PERSONAL FRIEND "THE KID" SIGNED THIS FOR ME.

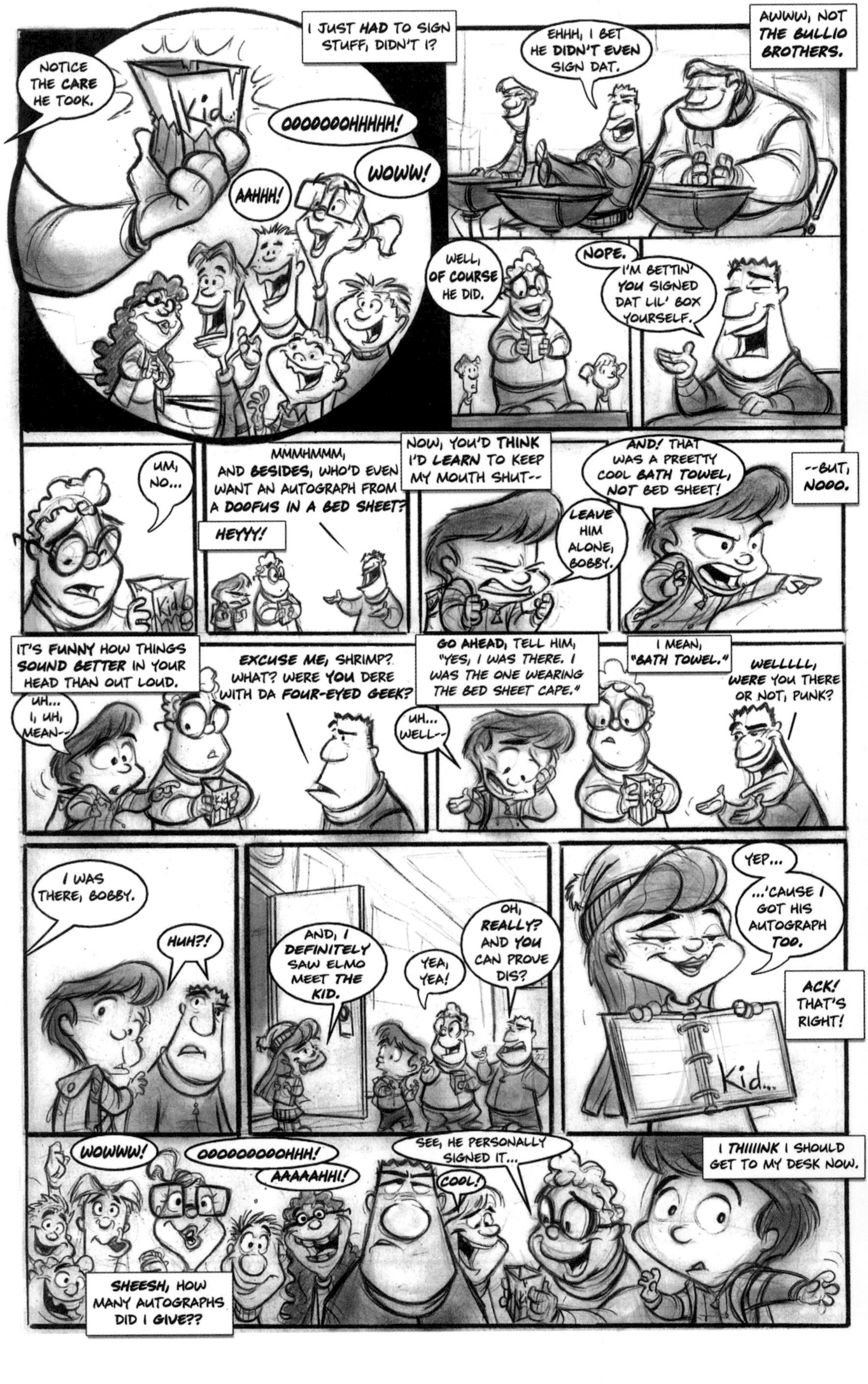

I JUST HAD TO SIGN STUFF, DIDN'T I?
NOTICE THE CARE HE TOOK.
OOOOOOOHHHHH!
WOWW!
AAHHH!
Kid
EHHH, I BET HE DIDN'T EVEN SIGN DAT.
AWWW, NOT THE BULLIO BROTHERS.
WELL, OF COURSE HE DID.
NOPE.
I'M BETTIN' YOU SIGNED DAT LIL' BOX YOURSELF.
UM, NO...
MMMHMMM, AND BESIDES, WHO'D EVEN WANT AN AUTOGRAPH FROM A DOOFUS IN A BED SHEET?
HEYYY!
NOW, YOU'D THINK I'D LEARN TO KEEP MY MOUTH SHUT--
LEAVE HIM ALONE, BOBBY.
AND! THAT WAS A PREETTY COOL BATH TOWEL, NOT BED SHEET!
--BUT, NOOO.
IT'S FUNNY HOW THINGS SOUND BETTER IN YOUR HEAD THAN OUT LOUD.
UH... I, UH, MEAN--
EXCUSE ME, SHRIMP? WHAT? WERE YOU DERE WITH DA FOUR-EYED GEEK?
GO AHEAD, TELL HIM, "YES, I WAS THERE. I WAS THE ONE WEARING THE BED SHEET CAPE."
UH... WELL--
I MEAN, "BATH TOWEL."
WELLLLL, WERE YOU THERE OR NOT, PUNK?
I WAS THERE, BOBBY.
HUH?!
AND, I DEFINITELY SAW ELMO MEET THE KID.
YEA, YEA!
OH, REALLY? AND YOU CAN PROVE DIS?
YEP...
...'CAUSE I GOT HIS AUTOGRAPH TOO.
ACK! THAT'S RIGHT!
Kid...
WOWWW!
OOOOOOOOOHHH!
AAAAAHH!
SEE, HE PERSONALLY SIGNED IT...
COOL!
I THIIIINK I SHOULD GET TO MY DESK NOW.
SHEESH, HOW MANY AUTOGRAPHS DID I GIVE??

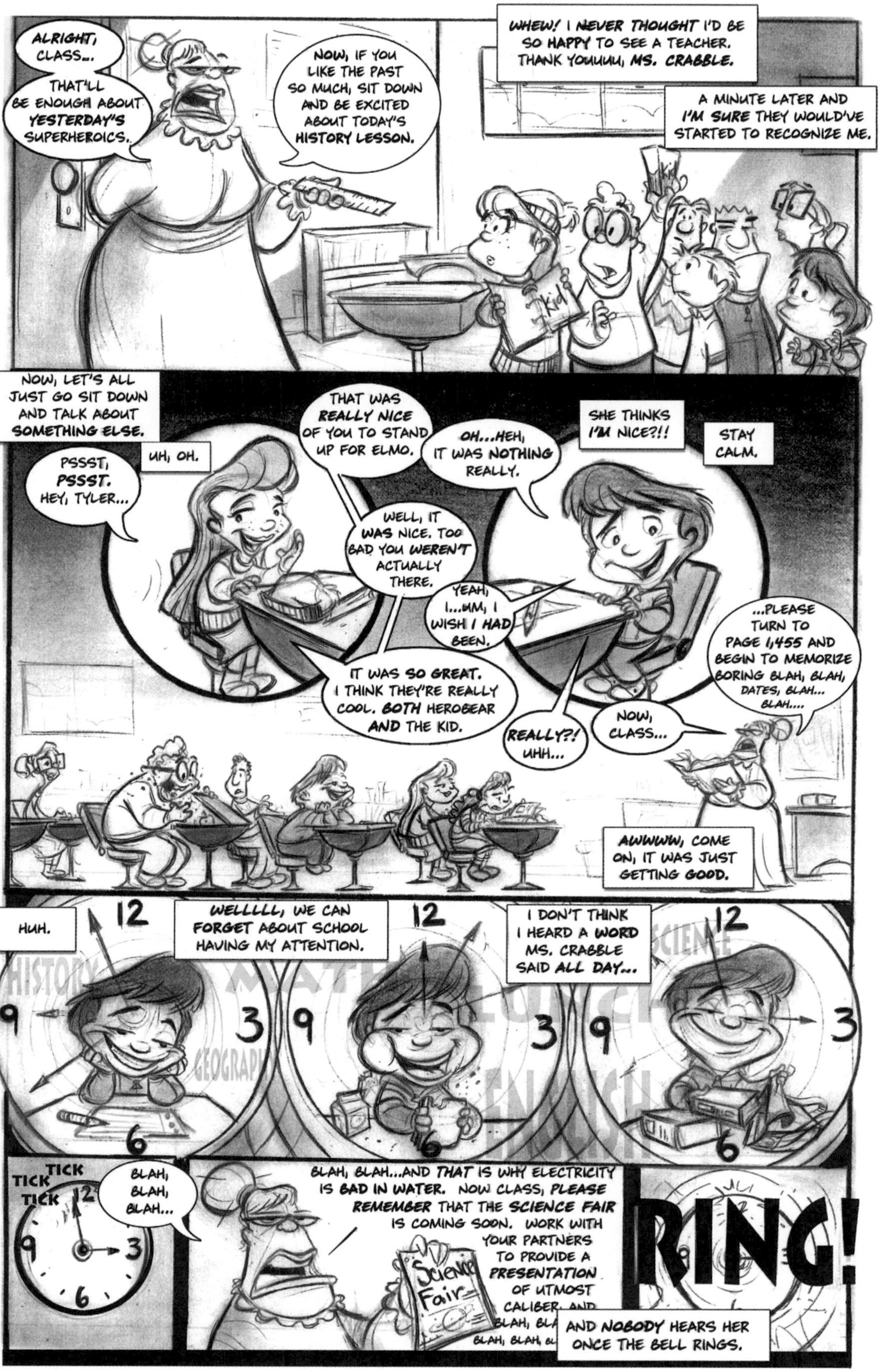
ALRIGHT, CLASS...
THAT'LL BE ENOUGH ABOUT YESTERDAY'S SUPERHEROICS.
NOW, IF YOU LIKE THE PAST SO MUCH, SIT DOWN AND BE EXCITED ABOUT TODAY'S HISTORY LESSON.
WHEW! I NEVER THOUGHT I'D BE SO HAPPY TO SEE A TEACHER. THANK YOUUUU, MS. CRABBLE.
A MINUTE LATER AND I'M SURE THEY WOULD'VE STARTED TO RECOGNIZE ME.
Kid
Kid
NOW, LET'S ALL JUST GO SIT DOWN AND TALK ABOUT SOMETHING ELSE.
PSSST, PSSST. HEY, TYLER...
UH, OH.
THAT WAS REALLY NICE OF YOU TO STAND UP FOR ELMO.
OH...HEH, IT WAS NOTHING REALLY.
SHE THINKS I'M NICE?!!
STAY CALM.
WELL, IT WAS NICE. TOO BAD YOU WEREN'T ACTUALLY THERE.
YEAH, I...UM, I WISH I HAD BEEN.
IT WAS SO GREAT. I THINK THEY'RE REALLY COOL. BOTH HEROBEAR AND THE KID.
REALLY?! UHH...
NOW, CLASS...
...PLEASE TURN TO PAGE 1,455 AND BEGIN TO MEMORIZE BORING BLAH, BLAH, DATES, BLAH... BLAH....
AWWWW, COME ON, IT WAS JUST GETTING GOOD.
HUH.
WELLLLL, WE CAN FORGET ABOUT SCHOOL HAVING MY ATTENTION.
I DON'T THINK I HEARD A WORD MS. CRABBLE SAID ALL DAY...
HISTORY
GEOGRAPHY
SCIENCE
ENGLISH
TICK TICK TICK
BLAH, BLAH, BLAH...
BLAH, BLAH...AND THAT IS WHY ELECTRICITY IS BAD IN WATER. NOW CLASS, PLEASE REMEMBER THAT THE SCIENCE FAIR IS COMING SOON. WORK WITH YOUR PARTNERS TO PROVIDE A PRESENTATION OF UTMOST CALIBER, AND BLAH, BLA BLAH, BLAH, BL
Science Fair
RING!
AND NOBODY HEARS HER ONCE THE BELL RINGS.

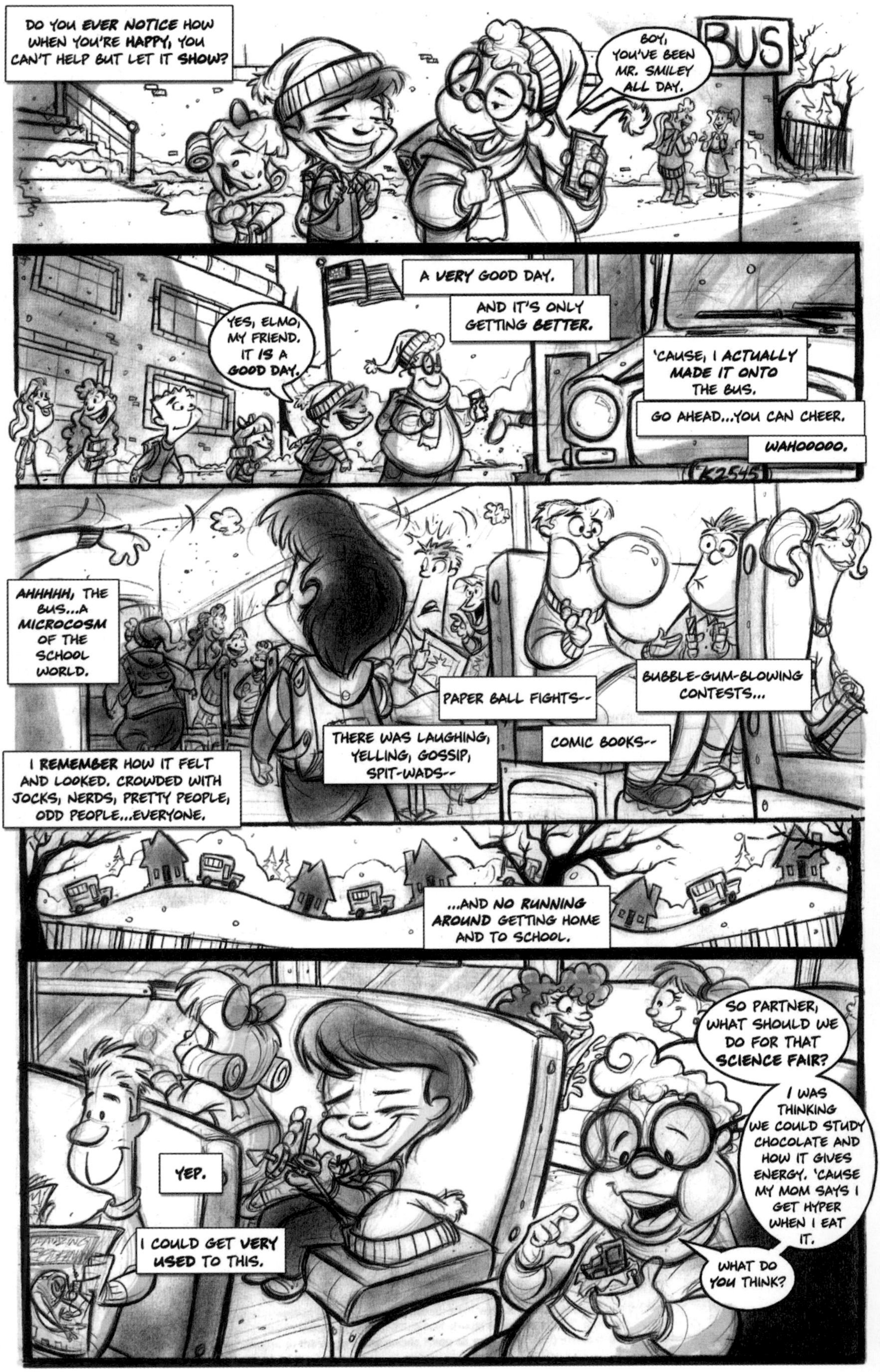

DO YOU EVER NOTICE HOW WHEN YOU'RE HAPPY, YOU CAN'T HELP BUT LET IT SHOW?
BOY, YOU'VE BEEN MR. SMILEY ALL DAY.
BUS
A VERY GOOD DAY.
AND IT'S ONLY GETTING BETTER.
YES, ELMO, MY FRIEND. IT IS A GOOD DAY.
'CAUSE, I ACTUALLY MADE IT ONTO THE BUS.
GO AHEAD...YOU CAN CHEER.
WAHOOOOO.
AHHHHH, THE BUS...A MICROCOSM OF THE SCHOOL WORLD.
BUBBLE-GUM-BLOWING CONTESTS...
PAPER BALL FIGHTS--
THERE WAS LAUGHING, YELLING, GOSSIP, SPIT-WADS--
COMIC BOOKS--
I REMEMBER HOW IT FELT AND LOOKED. CROWDED WITH JOCKS, NERDS, PRETTY PEOPLE, ODD PEOPLE...EVERYONE.
...AND NO RUNNING AROUND GETTING HOME AND TO SCHOOL.
SO PARTNER, WHAT SHOULD WE DO FOR THAT SCIENCE FAIR?
I WAS THINKING WE COULD STUDY CHOCOLATE AND HOW IT GIVES ENERGY. 'CAUSE MY MOM SAYS I GET HYPER WHEN I EAT IT.
WHAT DO YOU THINK?
YEP.
I COULD GET VERY USED TO THIS.

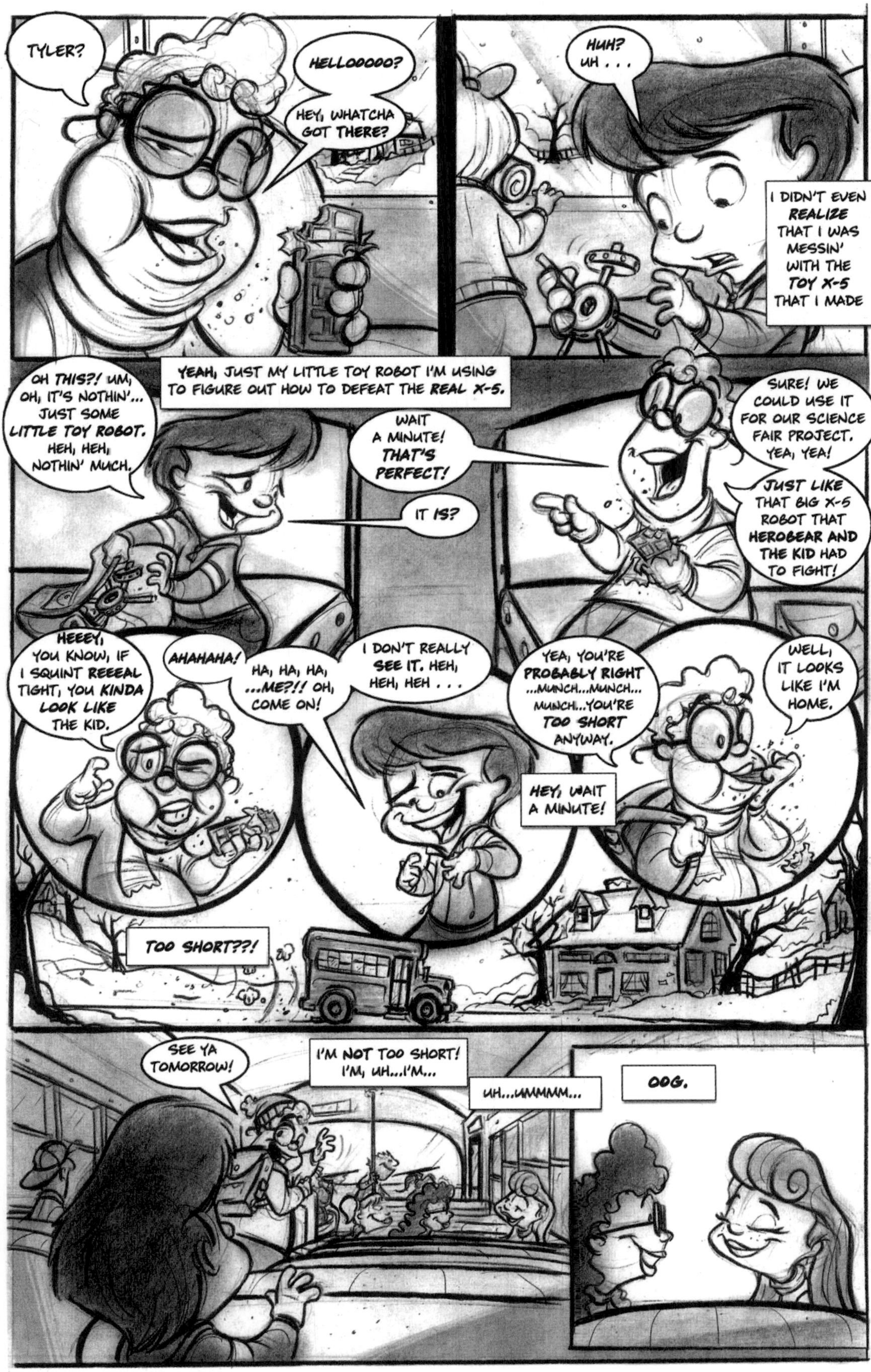
TYLER?
HELLOOOOO?
HEY, WHATCHA GOT THERE?
HUH? UH . . .
I DIDN'T EVEN REALIZE THAT I WAS MESSIN' WITH THE TOY X-5 THAT I MADE
OH THIS?! UM, OH, IT'S NOTHIN'... JUST SOME LITTLE TOY ROBOT. HEH, HEH, NOTHIN' MUCH.
YEAH, JUST MY LITTLE TOY ROBOT I'M USING TO FIGURE OUT HOW TO DEFEAT THE REAL X-5.
WAIT A MINUTE! THAT'S PERFECT!
IT IS?
SURE! WE COULD USE IT FOR OUR SCIENCE FAIR PROJECT. YEA, YEA!
JUST LIKE THAT BIG X-5 ROBOT THAT HEROBEAR AND THE KID HAD TO FIGHT!
HEEEY, YOU KNOW, IF I SQUINT REEEAL TIGHT, YOU KINDA LOOK LIKE THE KID.
AHAHAHA!
HA, HA, HA, ...ME?!! OH, COME ON!
I DON'T REALLY SEE IT. HEH, HEH, HEH . . .
YEA, YOU'RE PROBABLY RIGHT ...MUNCH...MUNCH... MUNCH...YOU'RE TOO SHORT ANYWAY.
WELL, IT LOOKS LIKE I'M HOME.
HEY, WAIT A MINUTE!
TOO SHORT??!
SEE YA TOMORROW!
I'M NOT TOO SHORT! I'M, UH...I'M...
UH...UMMMM...
OOG.

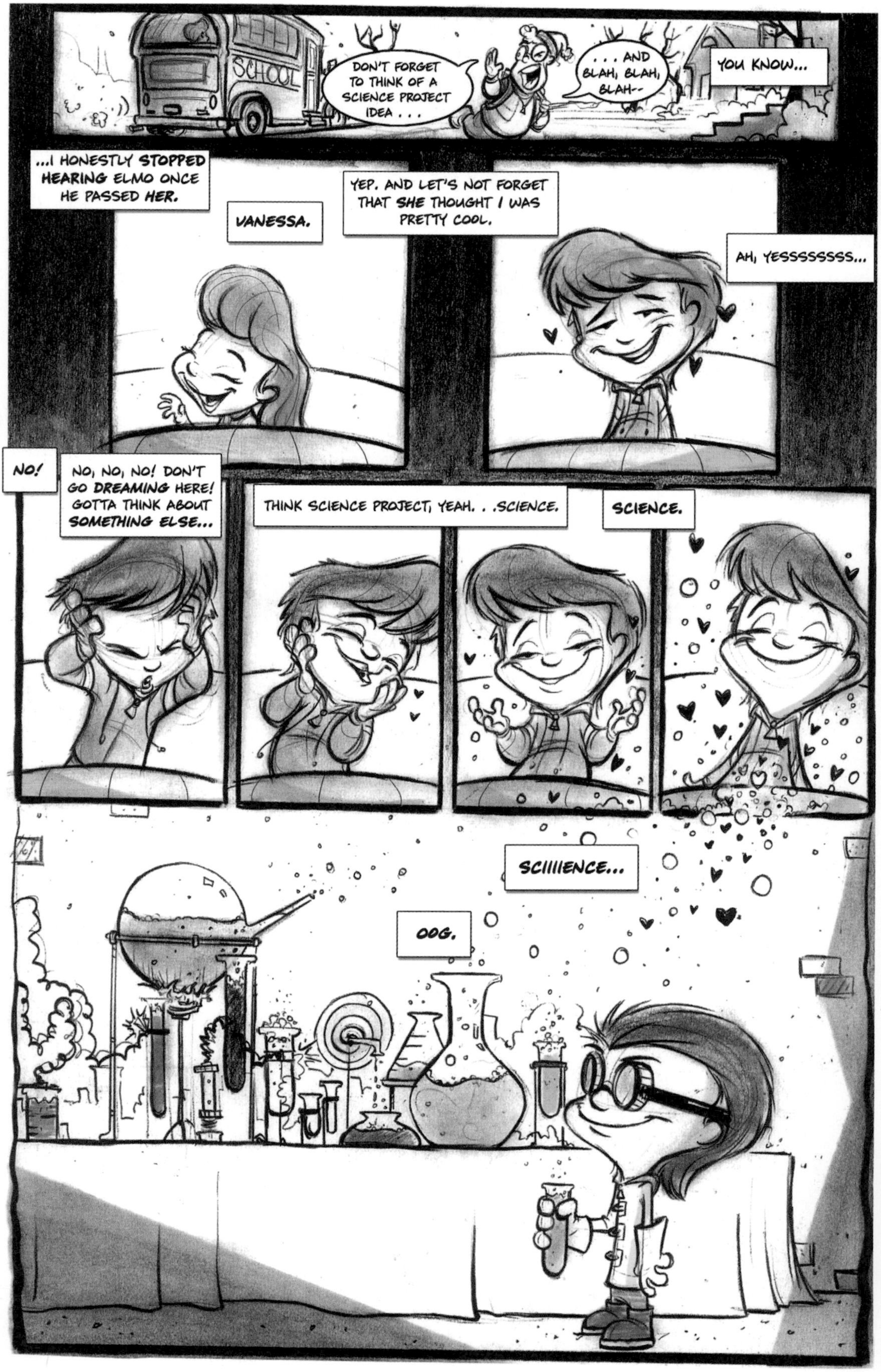

DON'T FORGET TO THINK OF A SCIENCE PROJECT IDEA . . .
. . . AND BLAH, BLAH, BLAH--
YOU KNOW...
...I HONESTLY STOPPED HEARING ELMO ONCE HE PASSED HER.
VANESSA.
YEP. AND LET'S NOT FORGET THAT SHE THOUGHT I WAS PRETTY COOL.
AH, YESSSSSSSS...
NO!
NO, NO, NO! DON'T GO DREAMING HERE! GOTTA THINK ABOUT SOMETHING ELSE...
THINK SCIENCE PROJECT, YEAH. . .SCIENCE.
SCIENCE.
SCIIIIENCE...
OOG.

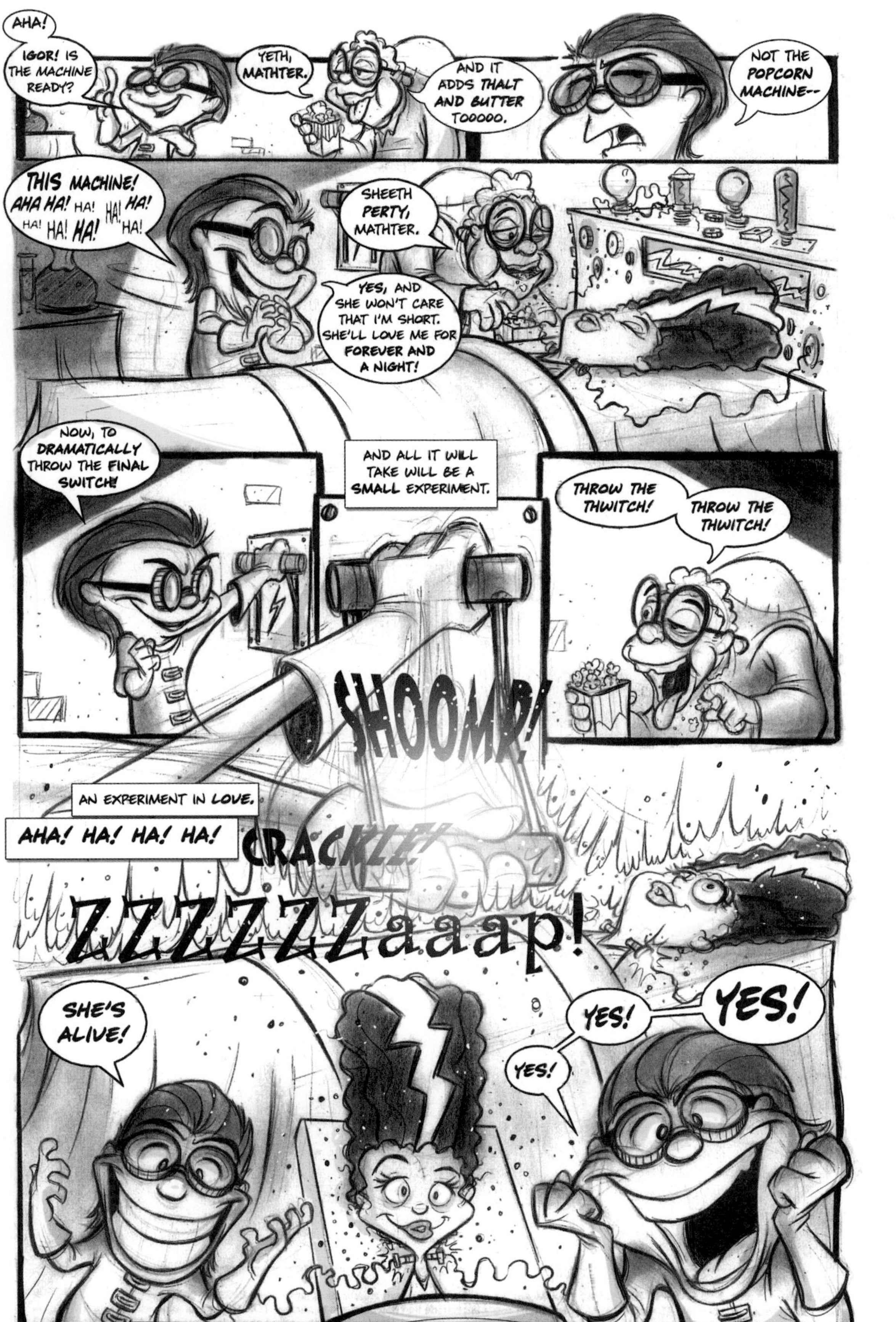
AHA!
IGOR! IS THE MACHINE READY?
YETH, MATHTER.
AND IT ADDS THALT AND BUTTER TOOOOO.
NOT THE POPCORN MACHINE--
THIS MACHINE! AHA HA! HA! HA! HA! HA! HA! HA! HA!
SHEETH PERTY, MATHTER.
YES, AND SHE WON'T CARE THAT I'M SHORT. SHE'LL LOVE ME FOR FOREVER AND A NIGHT!
NOW, TO DRAMATICALLY THROW THE FINAL SWITCH!
AND ALL IT WILL TAKE WILL BE A SMALL EXPERIMENT.
THROW THE THWITCH!
THROW THE THWITCH!
SHOOMP!
AN EXPERIMENT IN LOVE.
AHA! HA! HA! HA!
CRACKLE!
ZZZZZZZaaaap!
SHE'S ALIVE!
YES!
YES!
YES!

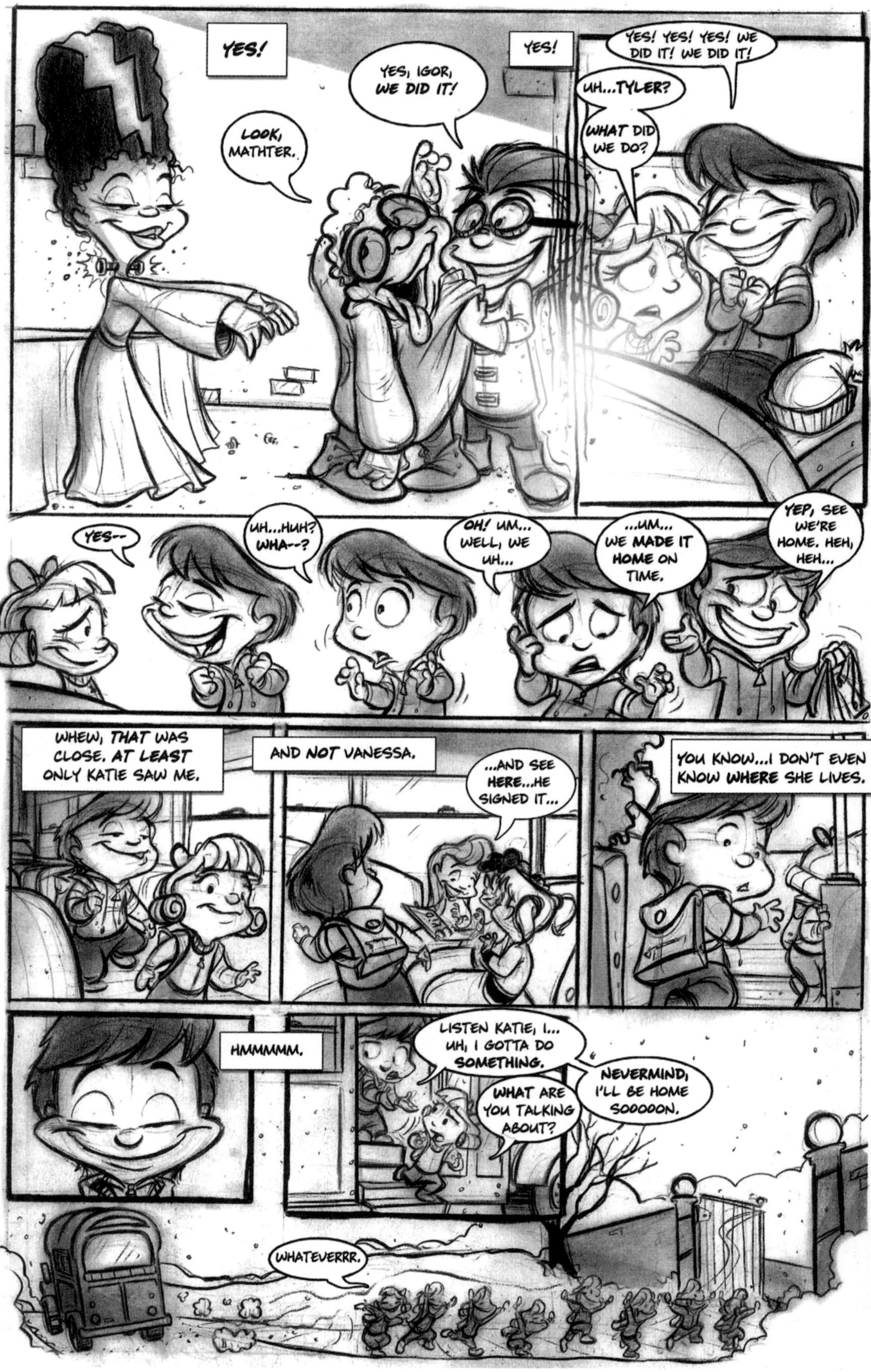
YES!
LOOK, MATHTER.
YES, IGOR, WE DID IT!
YES!
YES! YES! YES! WE DID IT! WE DID IT!
UH...TYLER?
WHAT DID WE DO?
YES--
UH...HUH? WHA--?
OH! UM... WELL, WE UH...
...UM... WE MADE IT HOME ON TIME.
YEP, SEE WE'RE HOME. HEH, HEH...
WHEW, THAT WAS CLOSE. AT LEAST ONLY KATIE SAW ME.
AND NOT VANESSA.
...AND SEE HERE...HE SIGNED IT...
YOU KNOW...I DON'T EVEN KNOW WHERE SHE LIVES.
HMMMMM.
LISTEN KATIE, I... UH, I GOTTA DO SOMETHING.
WHAT ARE YOU TALKING ABOUT?
NEVERMIND, I'LL BE HOME SOOOOON.
WHATEVERRR.

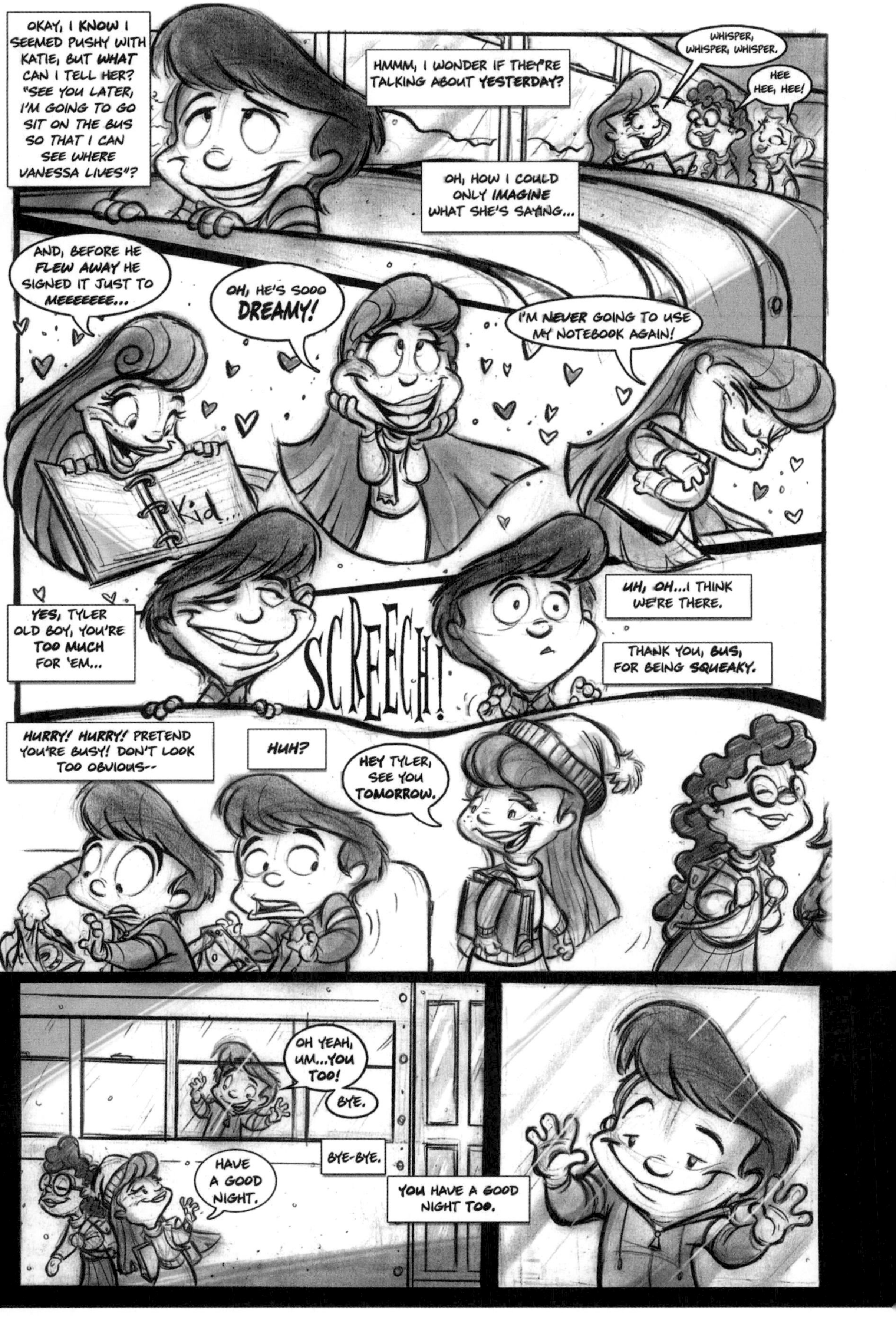
OKAY, I KNOW I SEEMED PUSHY WITH KATIE, BUT WHAT CAN I TELL HER? "SEE YOU LATER, I'M GOING TO GO SIT ON THE BUS SO THAT I CAN SEE WHERE VANESSA LIVES"?
HMMM, I WONDER IF THEY'RE TALKING ABOUT YESTERDAY?
WHISPER, WHISPER, WHISPER.
HEE HEE, HEE!
OH, HOW I COULD ONLY IMAGINE WHAT SHE'S SAYING...
AND, BEFORE HE FLEW AWAY HE SIGNED IT JUST TO MEEEEEEE...
Kid...
OH, HE'S SOOO DREAMY!
I'M NEVER GOING TO USE MY NOTEBOOK AGAIN!
YES, TYLER OLD BOY, YOU'RE TOO MUCH FOR 'EM...
SCREECH!
UH, OH...I THINK WE'RE THERE.
THANK YOU, BUS, FOR BEING SQUEAKY.
HURRY! HURRY! PRETEND YOU'RE BUSY! DON'T LOOK TOO OBVIOUS--
HUH?
HEY TYLER, SEE YOU TOMORROW.
OH YEAH, UM...YOU TOO!
BYE.
HAVE A GOOD NIGHT.
BYE-BYE.
YOU HAVE A GOOD NIGHT TOO.

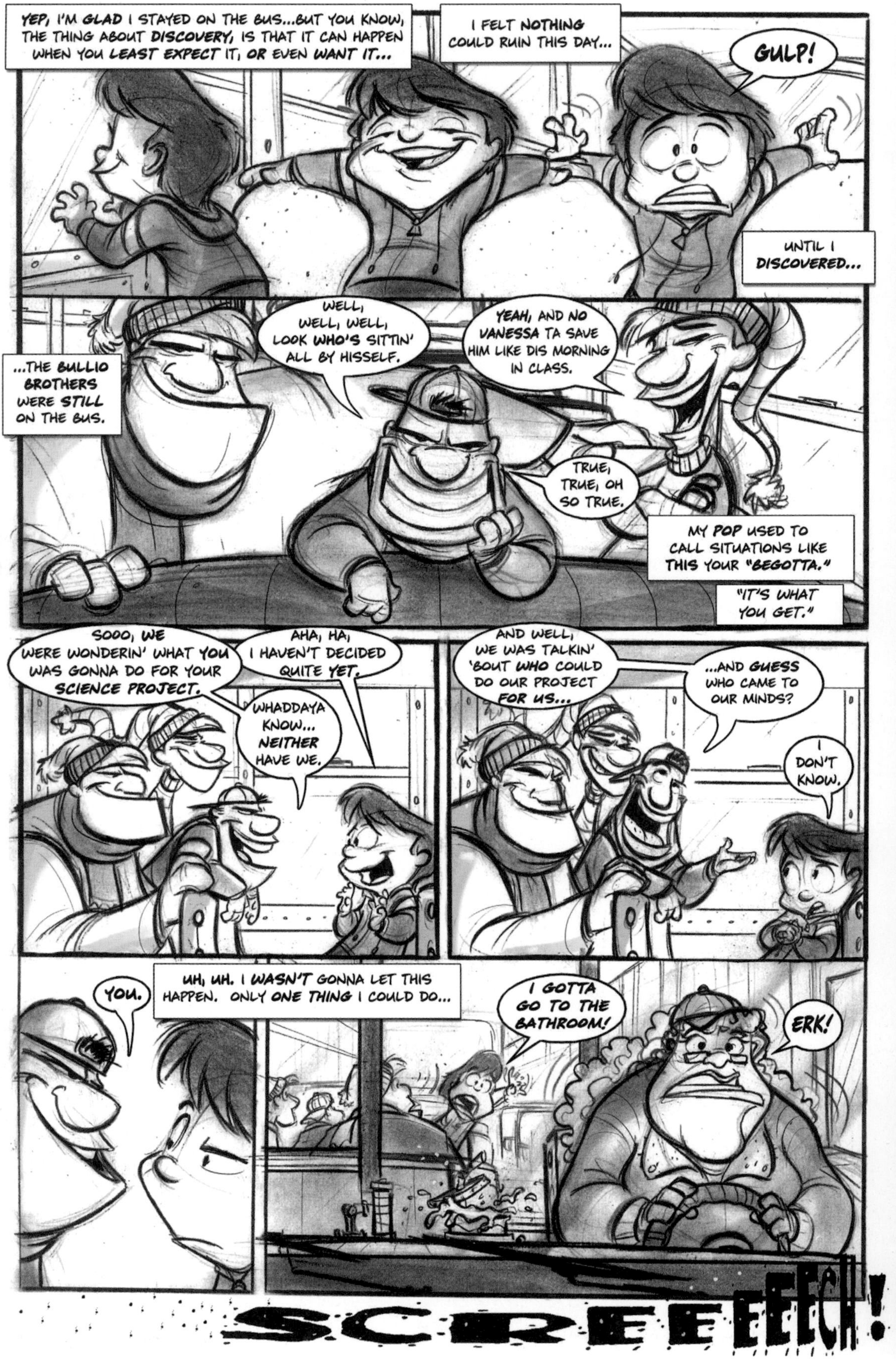

YEP, I'M GLAD I STAYED ON THE BUS...BUT YOU KNOW, THE THING ABOUT DISCOVERY, IS THAT IT CAN HAPPEN WHEN YOU LEAST EXPECT IT, OR EVEN WANT IT...
I FELT NOTHING COULD RUIN THIS DAY...
GULP!
UNTIL I DISCOVERED...
...THE BULLIO BROTHERS WERE STILL ON THE BUS.
WELL, WELL, WELL, LOOK WHO'S SITTIN' ALL BY HISSELF.
YEAH, AND NO VANESSA TA SAVE HIM LIKE DIS MORNING IN CLASS.
TRUE, TRUE, OH SO TRUE.
MY POP USED TO CALL SITUATIONS LIKE THIS YOUR "BEGOTTA."
"IT'S WHAT YOU GET."
SOOO, WE WERE WONDERIN' WHAT YOU WAS GONNA DO FOR YOUR SCIENCE PROJECT.
AHA, HA, I HAVEN'T DECIDED QUITE YET.
WHADDAYA KNOW... NEITHER HAVE WE.
AND WELL, WE WAS TALKIN' 'BOUT WHO COULD DO OUR PROJECT FOR US...
...AND GUESS WHO CAME TO OUR MINDS?
I DON'T KNOW.
YOU.
UH, UH. I WASN'T GONNA LET THIS HAPPEN. ONLY ONE THING I COULD DO...
I GOTTA GO TO THE BATHROOM!
ERK!
SCREEEEECH!

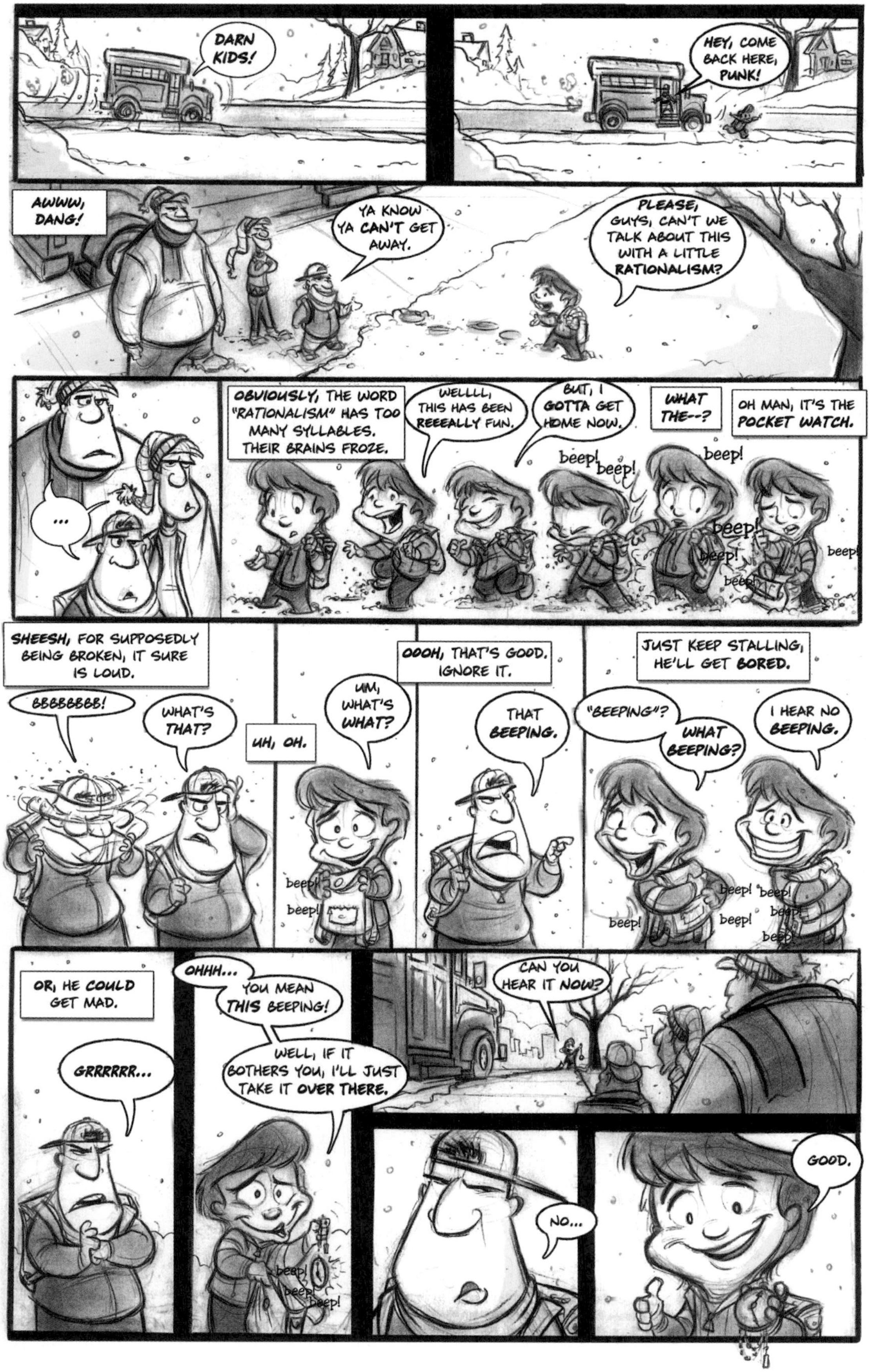
DARN KIDS!
HEY, COME BACK HERE, PUNK!
AWWW, DANG!
YA KNOW YA CAN'T GET AWAY.
PLEASE, GUYS, CAN'T WE TALK ABOUT THIS WITH A LITTLE RATIONALISM?
...
OBVIOUSLY, THE WORD "RATIONALISM" HAS TOO MANY SYLLABLES. THEIR BRAINS FROZE.
WELLLL, THIS HAS BEEN REEEALLY FUN.
BUT, I GOTTA GET HOME NOW.
beep! beep!
WHAT THE--?
beep!
OH MAN, IT'S THE POCKET WATCH.
beep! beep! beep! beep!
SHEESH, FOR SUPPOSEDLY BEING BROKEN, IT SURE IS LOUD.
BBBBBBBB!
WHAT'S THAT?
UH, OH.
UM, WHAT'S WHAT?
beep! beep!
OOOH, THAT'S GOOD. IGNORE IT.
THAT BEEPING.
JUST KEEP STALLING, HE'LL GET BORED.
"BEEPING"? WHAT BEEPING?
I HEAR NO BEEPING.
beep! beep! beep! beep! beep! beep!
OR, HE COULD GET MAD.
GRRRRRR...
OHHH... YOU MEAN THIS BEEPING!
WELL, IF IT BOTHERS YOU, I'LL JUST TAKE IT OVER THERE.
beep! beep! beep!
CAN YOU HEAR IT NOW?
NO...
GOOD.

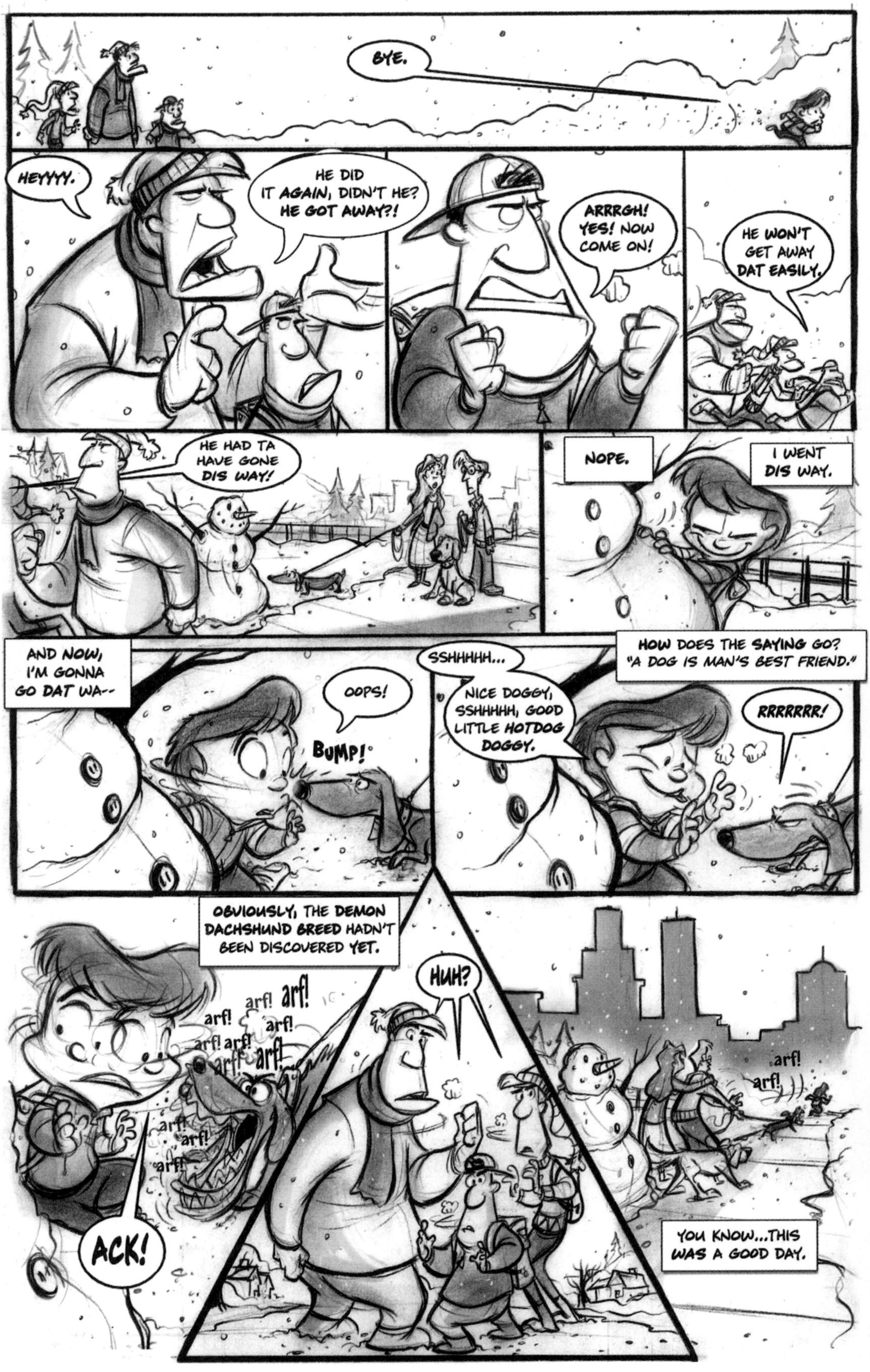
BYE.
HEYYYY.
HE DID IT AGAIN, DIDN'T HE? HE GOT AWAY?!
ARRRGH! YES! NOW COME ON!
HE WON'T GET AWAY DAT EASILY.
HE HAD TA HAVE GONE DIS WAY!
NOPE.
I WENT DIS WAY.
AND NOW, I'M GONNA GO DAT WA--
OOPS!
BUMP!
SSHHHHH...
NICE DOGGY, SSHHHHH, GOOD LITTLE HOTDOG DOGGY.
HOW DOES THE SAYING GO? "A DOG IS MAN'S BEST FRIEND."
RRRRRRR!
OBVIOUSLY, THE DEMON DACHSHUND BREED HADN'T BEEN DISCOVERED YET.
arf! arf! arf! arf! arf! arf! arf!
arf! arf! arf!
ACK!
HUH?
arf! arf!
YOU KNOW...THIS WAS A GOOD DAY.

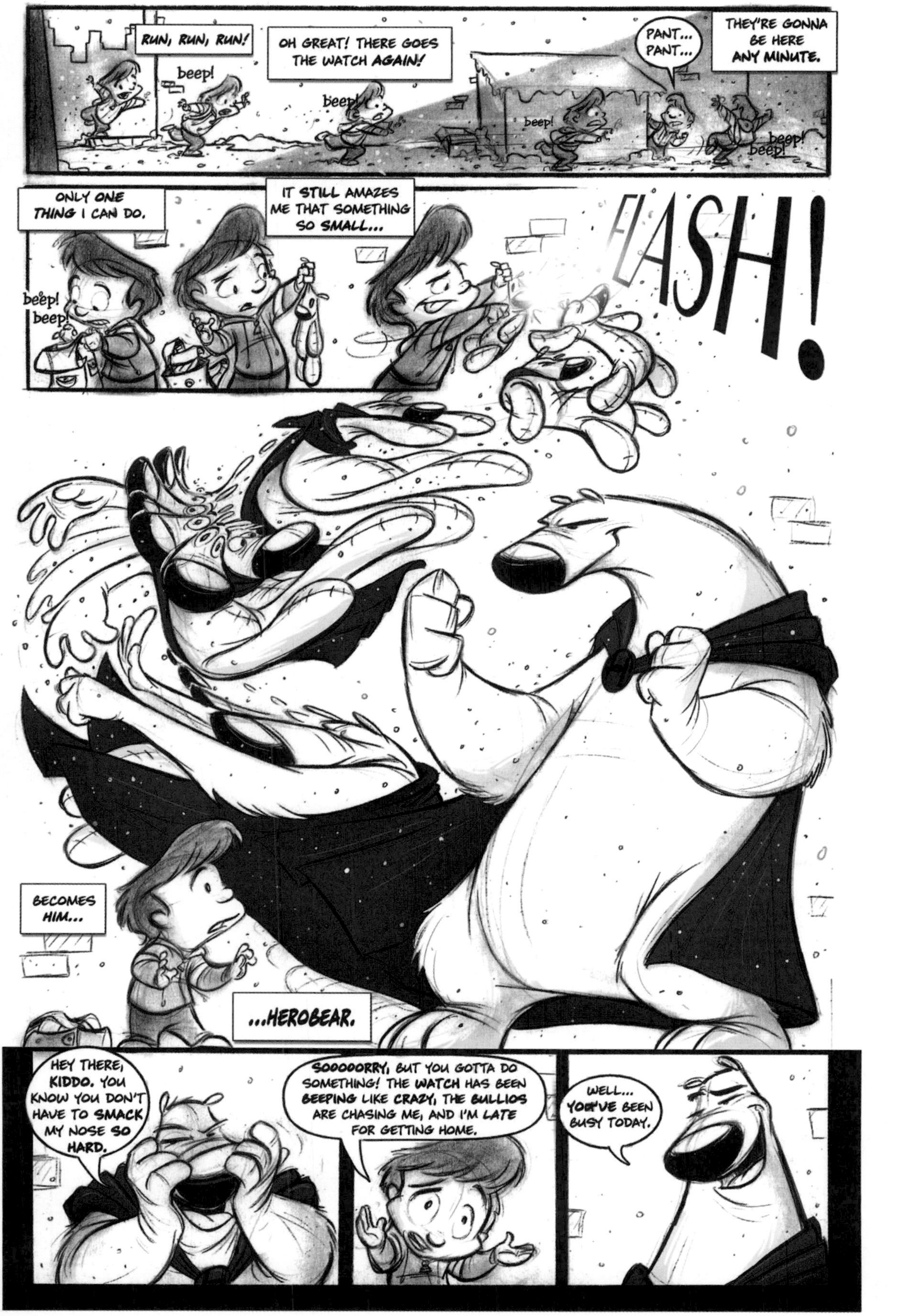
RUN, RUN, RUN!
beep!
OH GREAT! THERE GOES THE WATCH AGAIN!
beep!
beep!
PANT... PANT...
THEY'RE GONNA BE HERE ANY MINUTE.
beep!
beep!
ONLY ONE THING I CAN DO.
beep! beep!
IT STILL AMAZES ME THAT SOMETHING SO SMALL...
FLASH!
BECOMES HIM...
...HEROBEAR.
HEY THERE, KIDDO. YOU KNOW YOU DON'T HAVE TO SMACK MY NOSE SO HARD.
SOOOOORRY, BUT YOU GOTTA DO SOMETHING! THE WATCH HAS BEEN BEEPING LIKE CRAZY, THE BULLIOS ARE CHASING ME, AND I'M LATE FOR GETTING HOME.
WELL... YOU'VE BEEN BUSY TODAY.

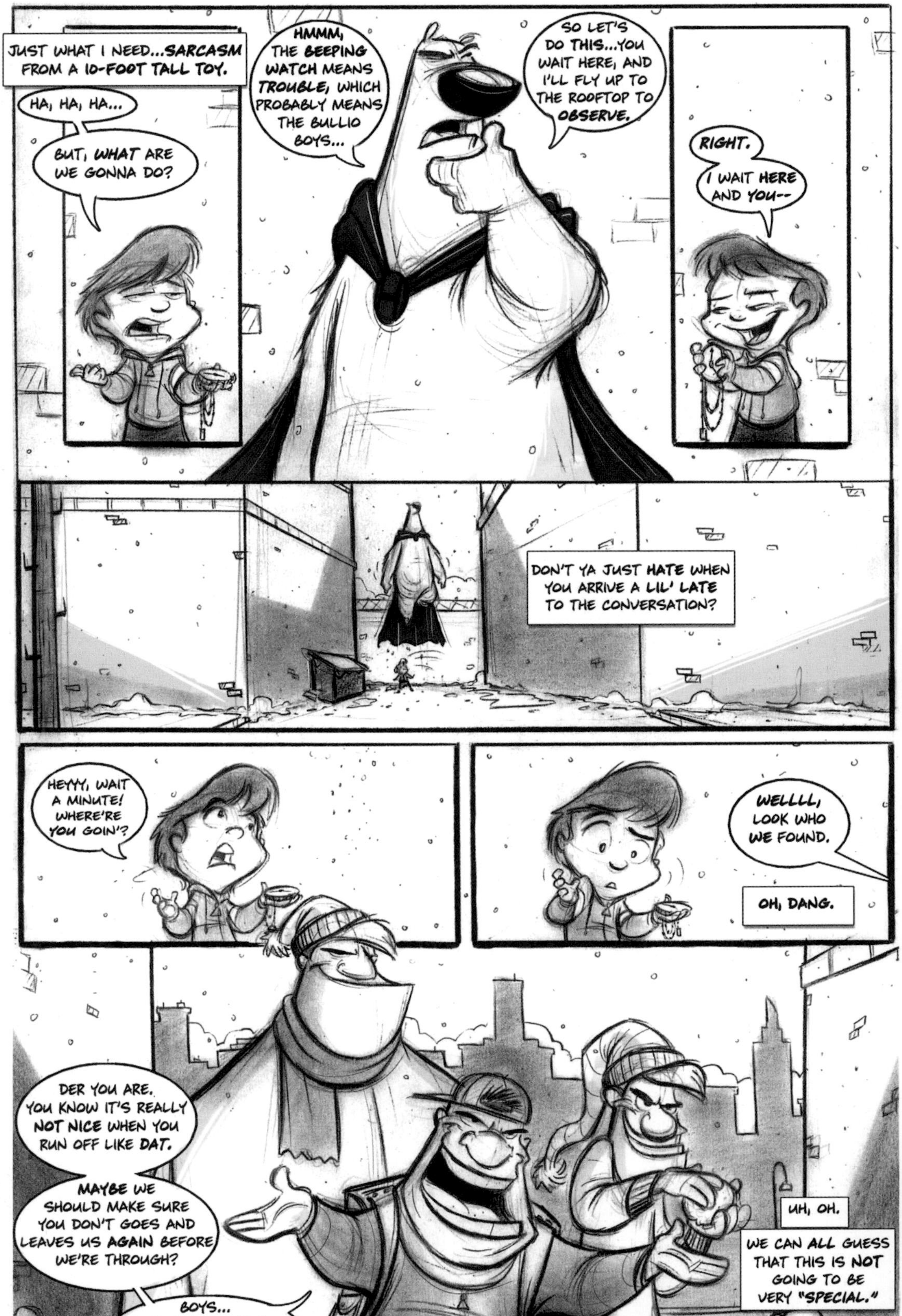
JUST WHAT I NEED...SARCASM FROM A 10-FOOT TALL TOY.
HA, HA, HA...
BUT, WHAT ARE WE GONNA DO?
HMMM, THE BEEPING WATCH MEANS TROUBLE, WHICH PROBABLY MEANS THE BULLIO BOYS...
SO LET'S DO THIS...YOU WAIT HERE, AND I'LL FLY UP TO THE ROOFTOP TO OBSERVE.
RIGHT.
I WAIT HERE AND YOU--
DON'T YA JUST HATE WHEN YOU ARRIVE A LIL' LATE TO THE CONVERSATION?
HEYYY, WAIT A MINUTE! WHERE'RE YOU GOIN'?
WELLLL, LOOK WHO WE FOUND.
OH, DANG.
DER YOU ARE. YOU KNOW IT'S REALLY NOT NICE WHEN YOU RUN OFF LIKE DAT.
MAYBE WE SHOULD MAKE SURE YOU DON'T GOES AND LEAVES US AGAIN BEFORE WE'RE THROUGH?
BOYS... I SAY WE MAKE A SNOW SPECIAL.
UH, OH.
WE CAN ALL GUESS THAT THIS IS NOT GOING TO BE VERY "SPECIAL."

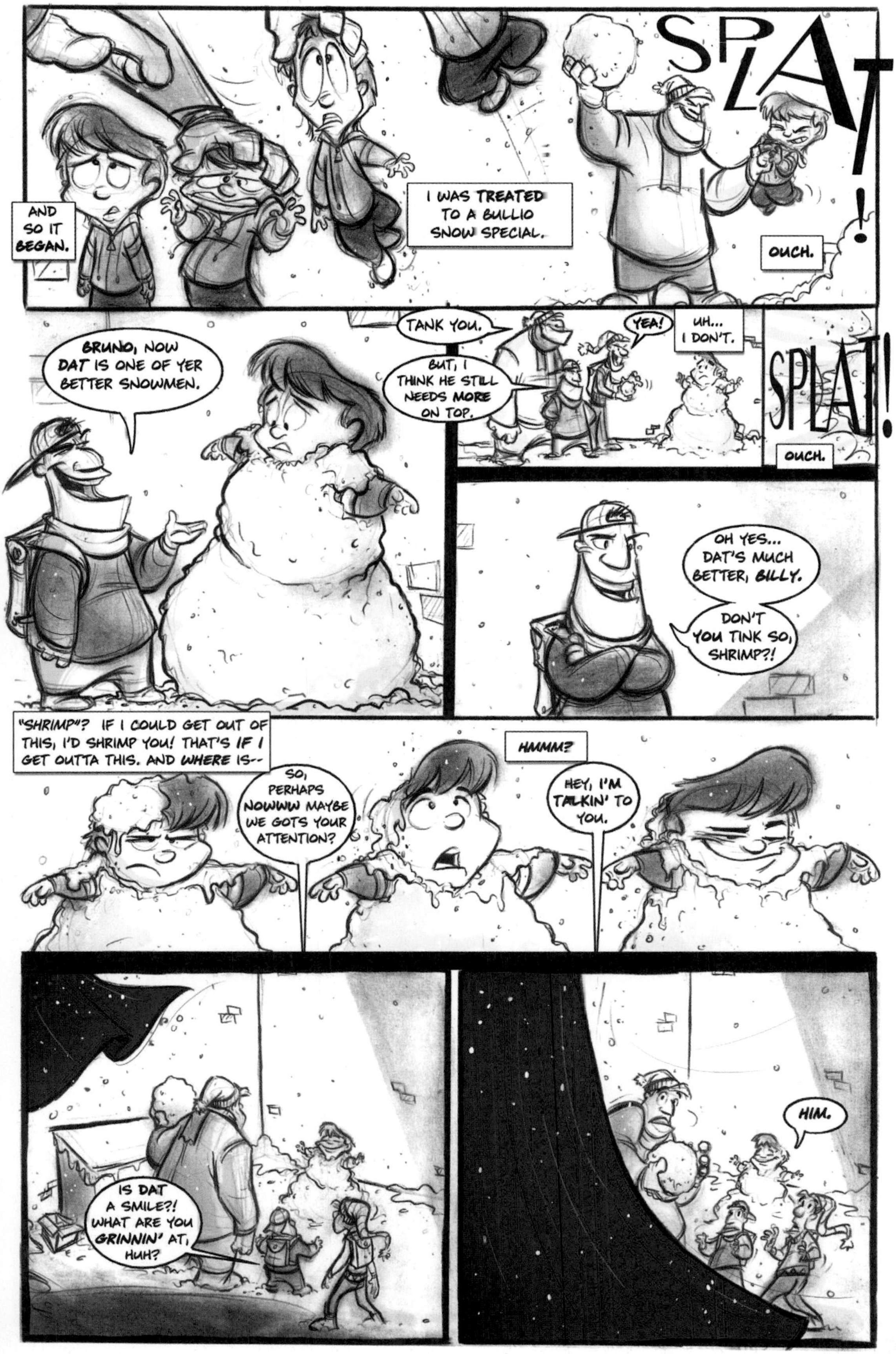
AND SO IT BEGAN.
I WAS TREATED TO A BULLIO SNOW SPECIAL.
SPLAT!
OUCH.
BRUNO, NOW DAT IS ONE OF YER BETTER SNOWMEN.
TANK YOU.
BUT, I THINK HE STILL NEEDS MORE ON TOP.
YEA!
UH... I DON'T.
SPLAT!
OUCH.
OH YES... DAT'S MUCH BETTER, BILLY.
DON'T YOU TINK SO, SHRIMP?!
"SHRIMP"? IF I COULD GET OUT OF THIS, I'D SHRIMP YOU! THAT'S IF I GET OUTTA THIS. AND WHERE IS--
SO, PERHAPS NOWWW MAYBE WE GOTS YOUR ATTENTION?
HMMM?
HEY, I'M TALKIN' TO YOU.
IS DAT A SMILE?! WHAT ARE YOU GRINNIN' AT, HUH?
HIM.

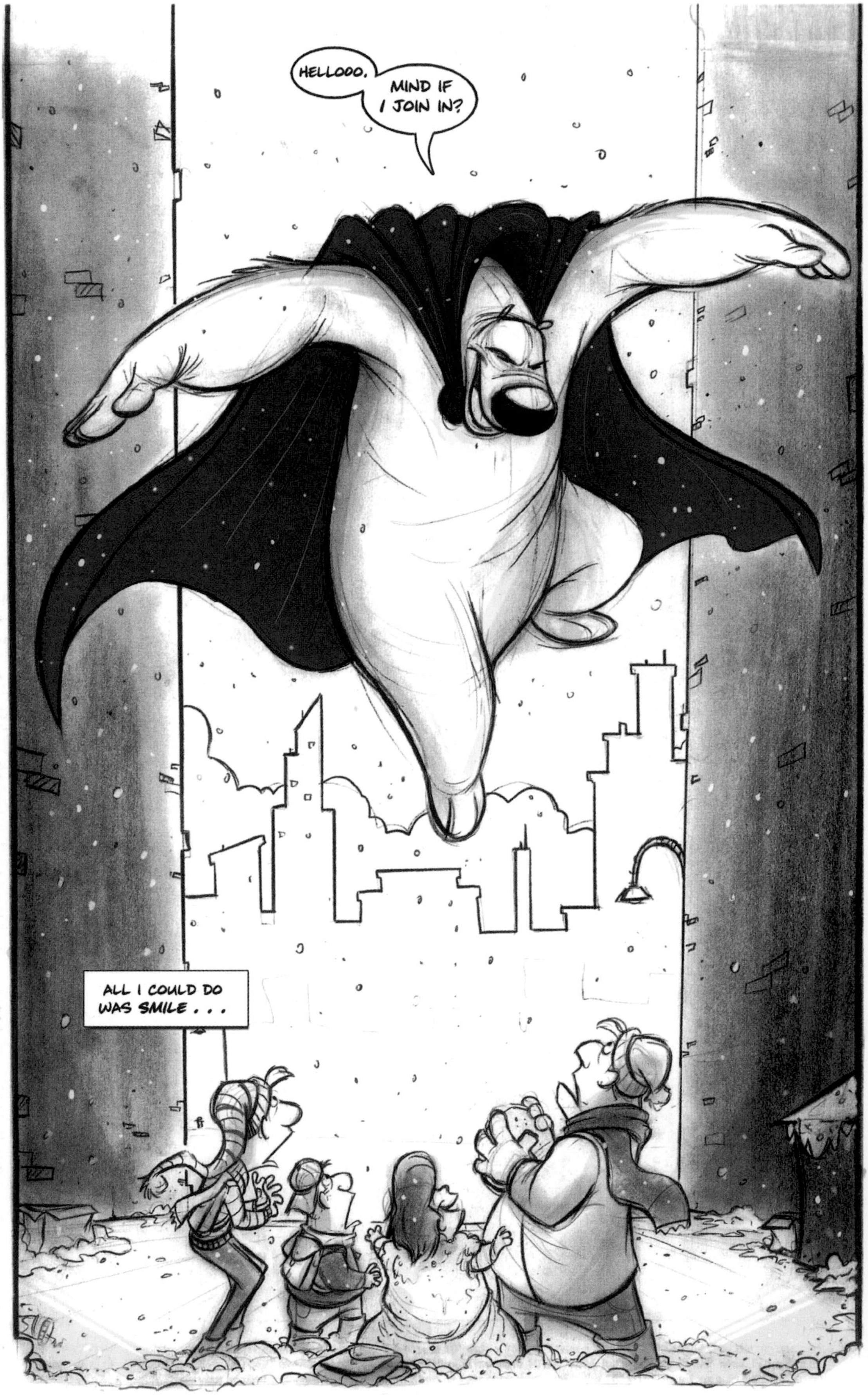
HELLOOO.
MIND IF I JOIN IN?
ALL I COULD DO WAS SMILE . . .

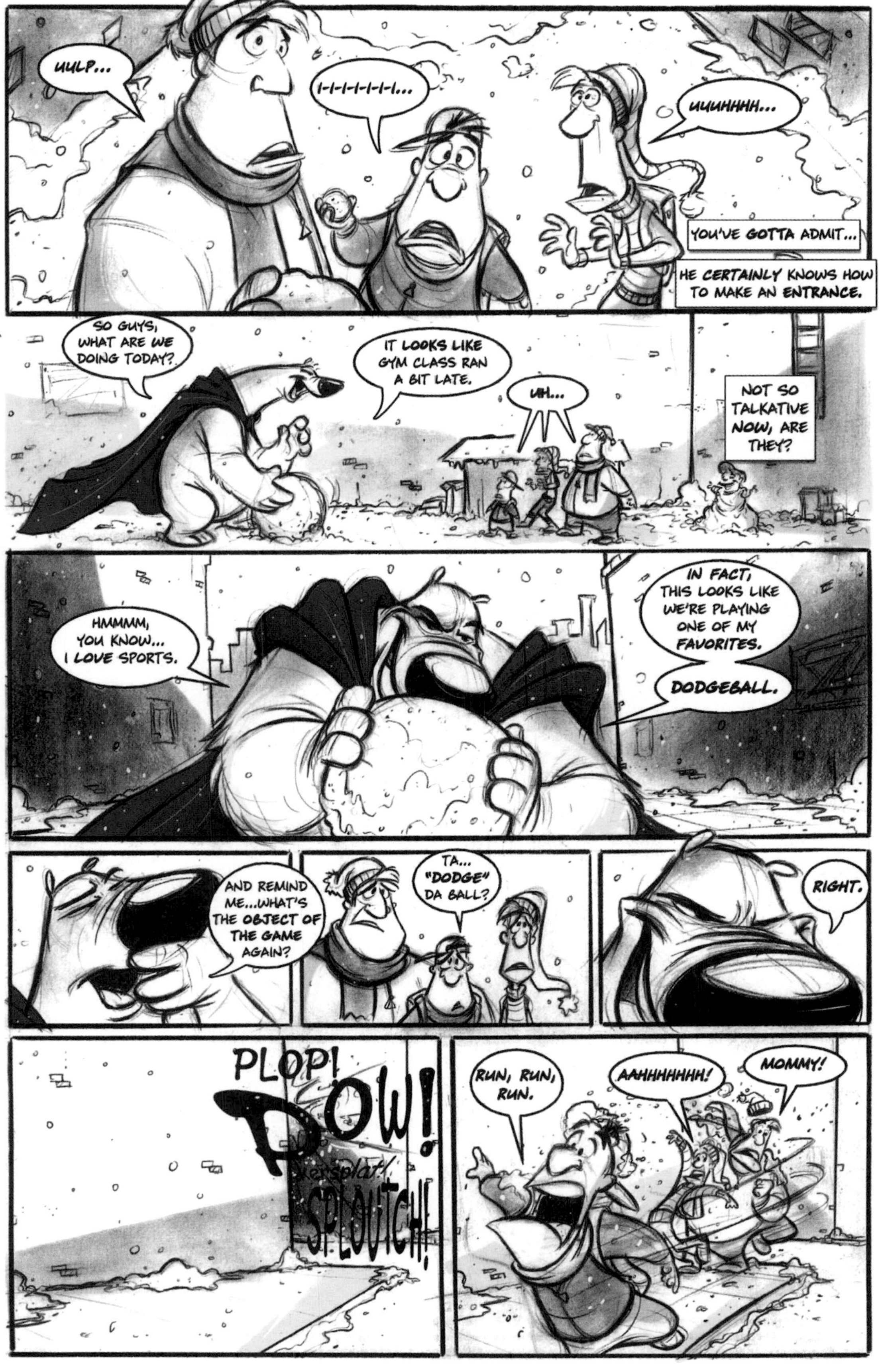
UULP...
I-I-I-I-I-I-I-I...
UUUHHHH...
YOU'VE GOTTA ADMIT...
HE CERTAINLY KNOWS HOW TO MAKE AN ENTRANCE.
SO GUYS, WHAT ARE WE DOING TODAY?
IT LOOKS LIKE GYM CLASS RAN A BIT LATE.
UH...
NOT SO TALKATIVE NOW, ARE THEY?
HMMMM, YOU KNOW... I LOVE SPORTS.
IN FACT, THIS LOOKS LIKE WE'RE PLAYING ONE OF MY FAVORITES.
DODGEBALL.
AND REMIND ME...WHAT'S THE OBJECT OF THE GAME AGAIN?
TA... "DODGE" DA BALL?
RIGHT.
PLOP!
POW!
SPLOUTCH!
RUN, RUN, RUN.
AAHHHHHHH!
MOMMY!

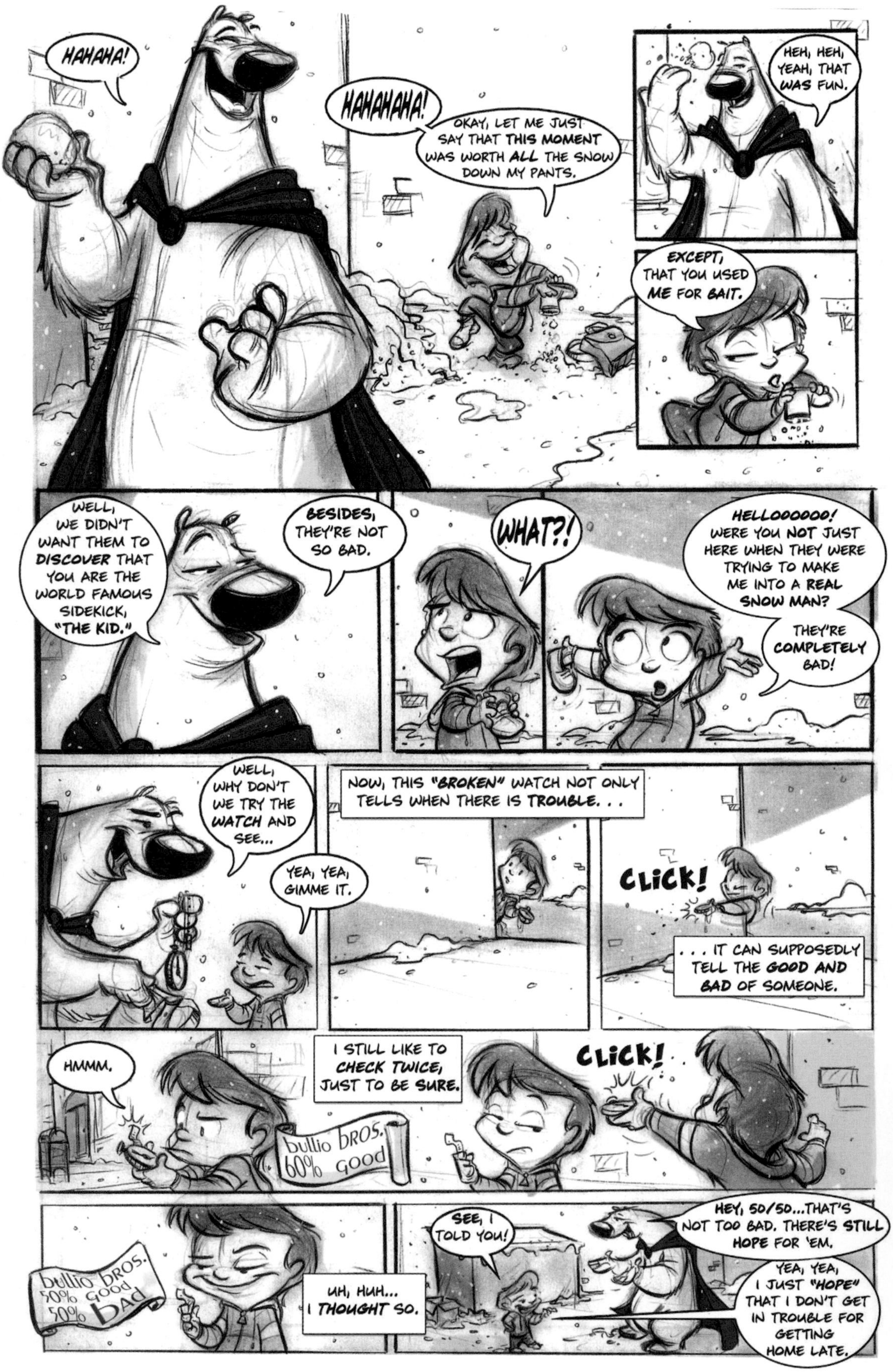
HAHAHA!
HAHAHAHA!
OKAY, LET ME JUST SAY THAT THIS MOMENT WAS WORTH ALL THE SNOW DOWN MY PANTS.
HEH, HEH, YEAH, THAT WAS FUN.
EXCEPT, THAT YOU USED ME FOR BAIT.
WELL, WE DIDN'T WANT THEM TO DISCOVER THAT YOU ARE THE WORLD FAMOUS SIDEKICK, "THE KID."
BESIDES, THEY'RE NOT SO BAD.
WHAT?!
HELLOOOOOO! WERE YOU NOT JUST HERE WHEN THEY WERE TRYING TO MAKE ME INTO A REAL SNOW MAN?
THEY'RE COMPLETELY BAD!
WELL, WHY DON'T WE TRY THE WATCH AND SEE...
YEA, YEA, GIMME IT.
NOW, THIS "BROKEN" WATCH NOT ONLY TELLS WHEN THERE IS TROUBLE. . .
CLICK!
. . . IT CAN SUPPOSEDLY TELL THE GOOD AND BAD OF SOMEONE.
HMMM.
bullio BROS. 60% Good
I STILL LIKE TO CHECK TWICE, JUST TO BE SURE.
CLICK!
bullio bros. 50% Good 50% bad
UH, HUH... I THOUGHT SO.
SEE, I TOLD YOU!
HEY, 50/50...THAT'S NOT TOO BAD. THERE'S STILL HOPE FOR 'EM.
YEA, YEA, I JUST "HOPE" THAT I DON'T GET IN TROUBLE FOR GETTING HOME LATE.

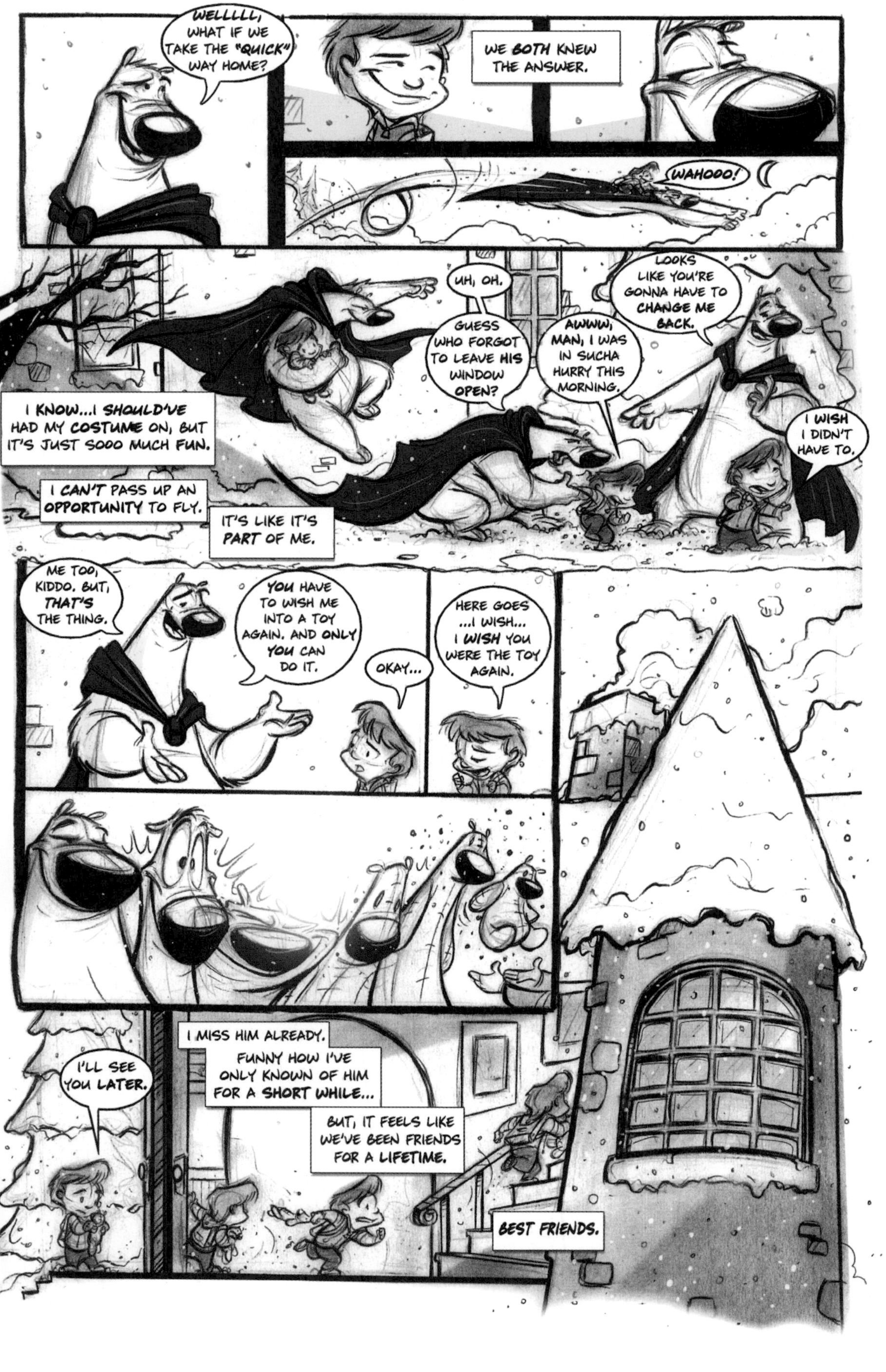
WELLLLL, WHAT IF WE TAKE THE "QUICK" WAY HOME?
WE BOTH KNEW THE ANSWER.
WAHOOO!
I KNOW...I SHOULD'VE HAD MY COSTUME ON, BUT IT'S JUST SOOO MUCH FUN.
I CAN'T PASS UP AN OPPORTUNITY TO FLY.
IT'S LIKE IT'S PART OF ME.
UH, OH.
GUESS WHO FORGOT TO LEAVE HIS WINDOW OPEN?
AWWW, MAN, I WAS IN SUCHA HURRY THIS MORNING.
LOOKS LIKE YOU'RE GONNA HAVE TO CHANGE ME BACK.
I WISH I DIDN'T HAVE TO.
ME TOO, KIDDO. BUT, THAT'S THE THING.
YOU HAVE TO WISH ME INTO A TOY AGAIN. AND ONLY YOU CAN DO IT.
OKAY...
HERE GOES ...I WISH... I WISH YOU WERE THE TOY AGAIN.
I'LL SEE YOU LATER.
I MISS HIM ALREADY.
FUNNY HOW I'VE ONLY KNOWN OF HIM FOR A SHORT WHILE...
BUT, IT FEELS LIKE WE'VE BEEN FRIENDS FOR A LIFETIME.
BEST FRIENDS.

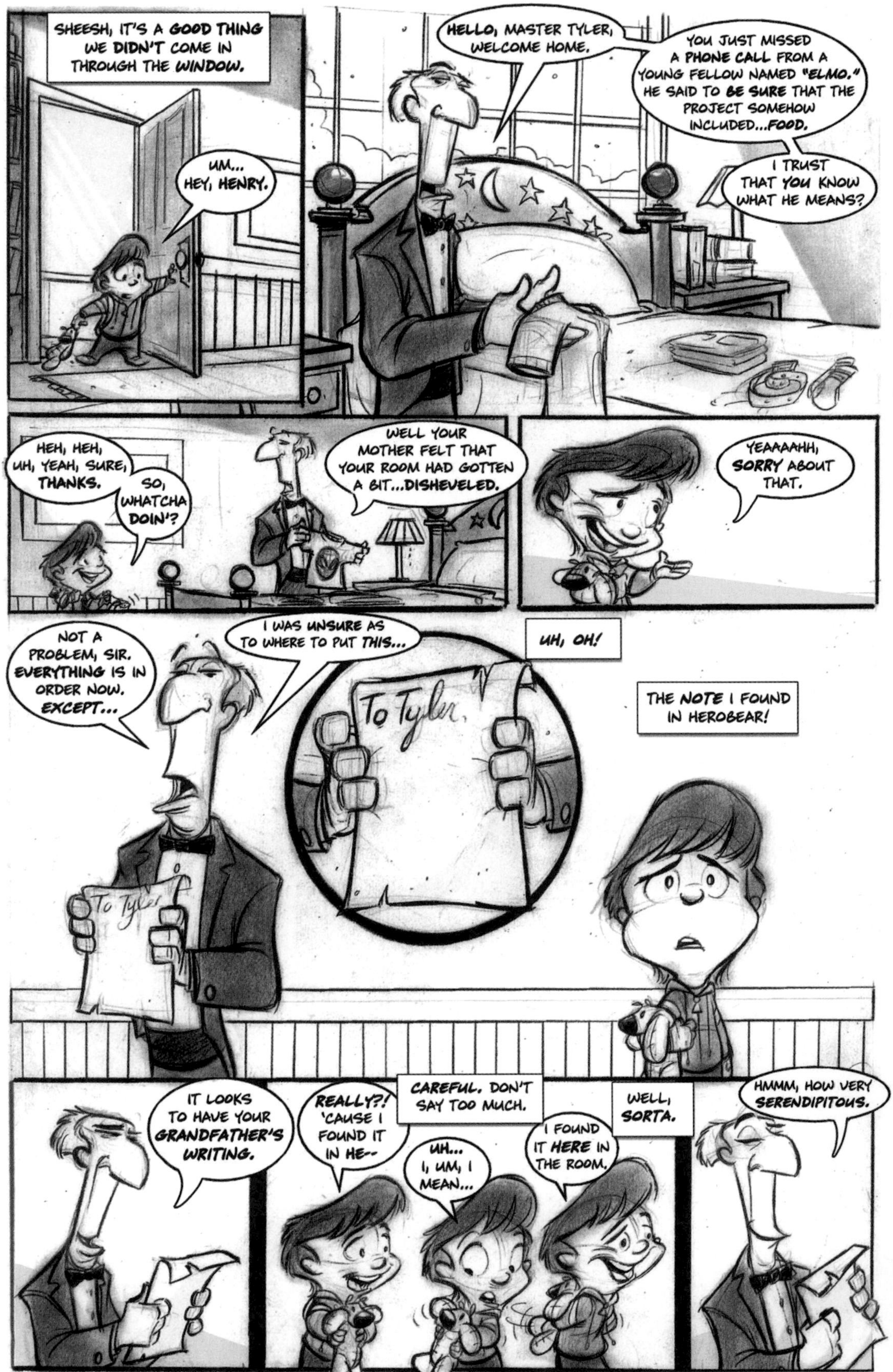
SHEESH, IT'S A GOOD THING WE DIDN'T COME IN THROUGH THE WINDOW.
UM... HEY, HENRY.
HELLO, MASTER TYLER, WELCOME HOME.
YOU JUST MISSED A PHONE CALL FROM A YOUNG FELLOW NAMED "ELMO." HE SAID TO BE SURE THAT THE PROJECT SOMEHOW INCLUDED...FOOD.
I TRUST THAT YOU KNOW WHAT HE MEANS?
HEH, HEH, UH, YEAH, SURE, THANKS.
SO, WHATCHA DOIN'?
WELL YOUR MOTHER FELT THAT YOUR ROOM HAD GOTTEN A BIT...DISHEVELED.
YEAAAAHH, SORRY ABOUT THAT.
NOT A PROBLEM, SIR. EVERYTHING IS IN ORDER NOW. EXCEPT...
I WAS UNSURE AS TO WHERE TO PUT THIS...
To Tyler
UH, OH!
THE NOTE I FOUND IN HEROBEAR!
To Tyler
IT LOOKS TO HAVE YOUR GRANDFATHER'S WRITING.
REALLY?! 'CAUSE I FOUND IT IN HE--
CAREFUL. DON'T SAY TOO MUCH.
UH... I, UM, I MEAN...
WELL, SORTA.
I FOUND IT HERE IN THE ROOM.
HMMM, HOW VERY SERENDIPITOUS.

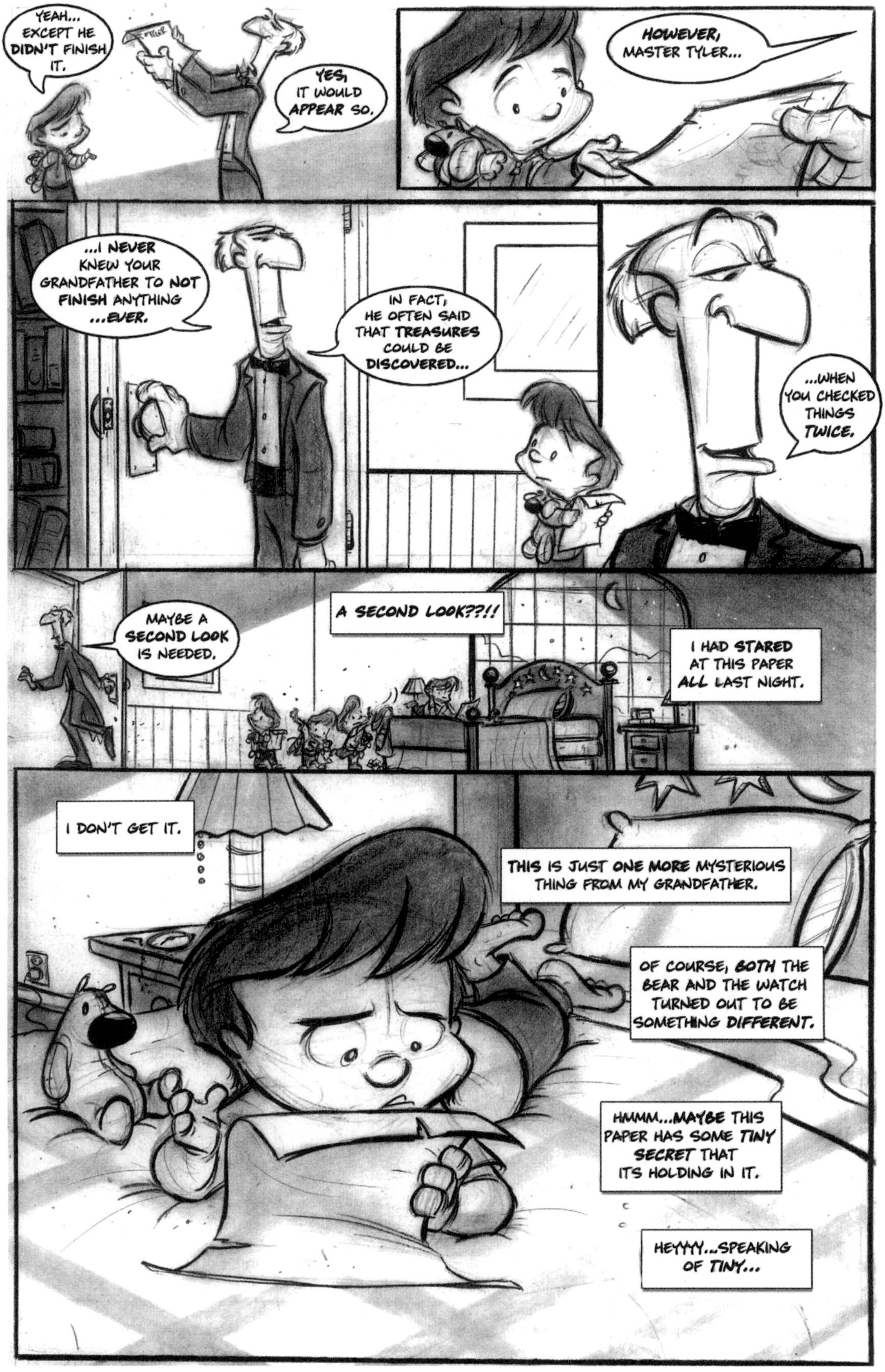
YEAH... EXCEPT HE DIDN'T FINISH IT.
YES, IT WOULD APPEAR SO.
HOWEVER, MASTER TYLER...
...I NEVER KNEW YOUR GRANDFATHER TO NOT FINISH ANYTHING ...EVER.
IN FACT, HE OFTEN SAID THAT TREASURES COULD BE DISCOVERED...
...WHEN YOU CHECKED THINGS TWICE.
MAYBE A SECOND LOOK IS NEEDED.
A SECOND LOOK??!!
I HAD STARED AT THIS PAPER ALL LAST NIGHT.
I DON'T GET IT.
THIS IS JUST ONE MORE MYSTERIOUS THING FROM MY GRANDFATHER.
OF COURSE, BOTH THE BEAR AND THE WATCH TURNED OUT TO BE SOMETHING DIFFERENT.
HMMM...MAYBE THIS PAPER HAS SOME TINY SECRET THAT ITS HOLDING IN IT.
HEYYYY...SPEAKING OF TINY...

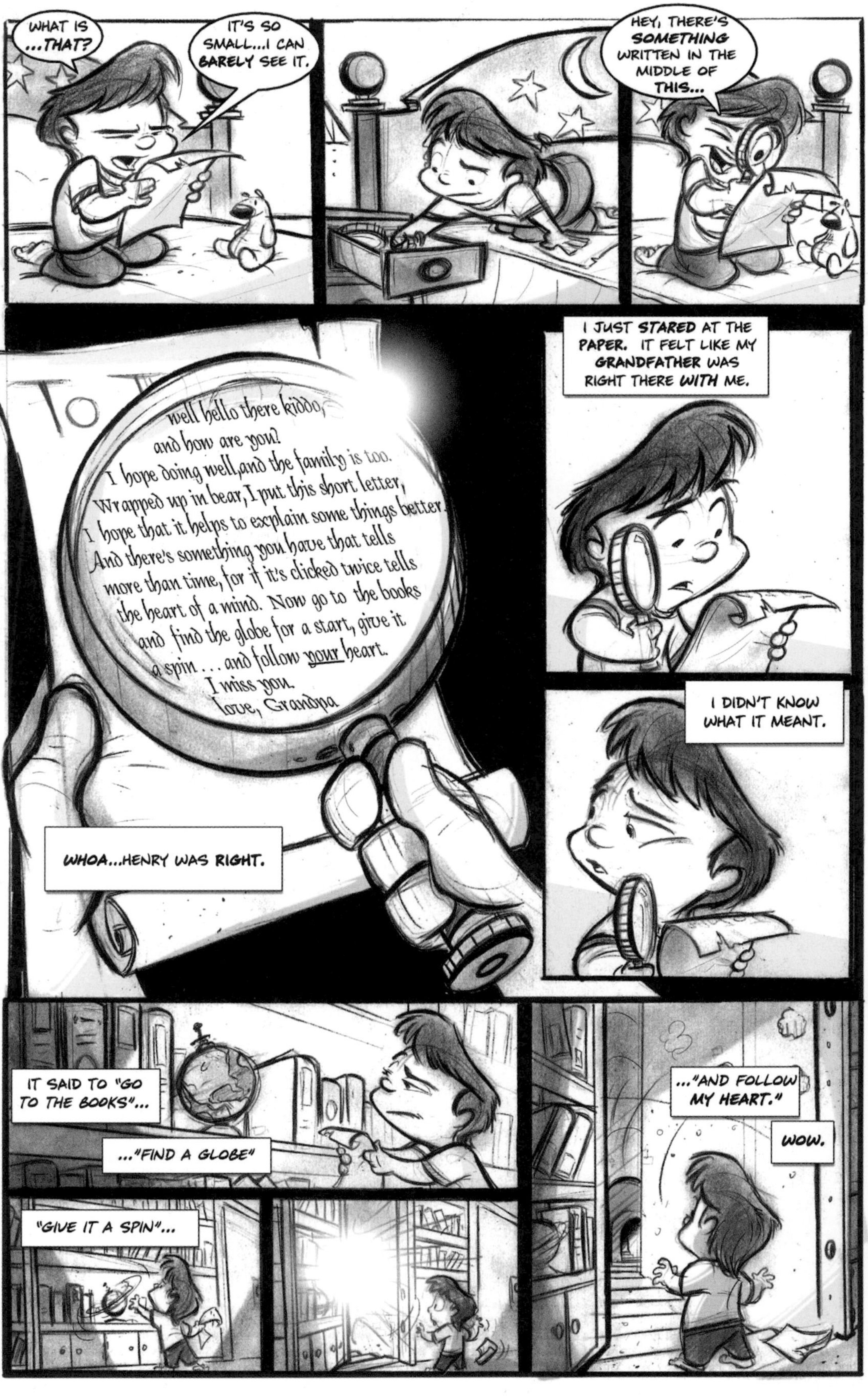
WHAT IS ...THAT?
IT'S SO SMALL...I CAN BARELY SEE IT.
HEY, THERE'S SOMETHING WRITTEN IN THE MIDDLE OF THIS...
well hello there kiddo, and how are you! I hope doing well, and the family is too. Wrapped up in bear, I put this short letter, I hope that it helps to explain some things better. And there's something you have that tells more than time, for if it's clicked twice tells the heart of a mind. Now go to the books and find the globe for a start, give it a spin . . . and follow your heart. I miss you. love, Grandpa
I JUST STARED AT THE PAPER. IT FELT LIKE MY GRANDFATHER WAS RIGHT THERE WITH ME.
I DIDN'T KNOW WHAT IT MEANT.
WHOA...HENRY WAS RIGHT.
IT SAID TO "GO TO THE BOOKS"...
..."FIND A GLOBE"
"GIVE IT A SPIN"...
..."AND FOLLOW MY HEART."
WOW.

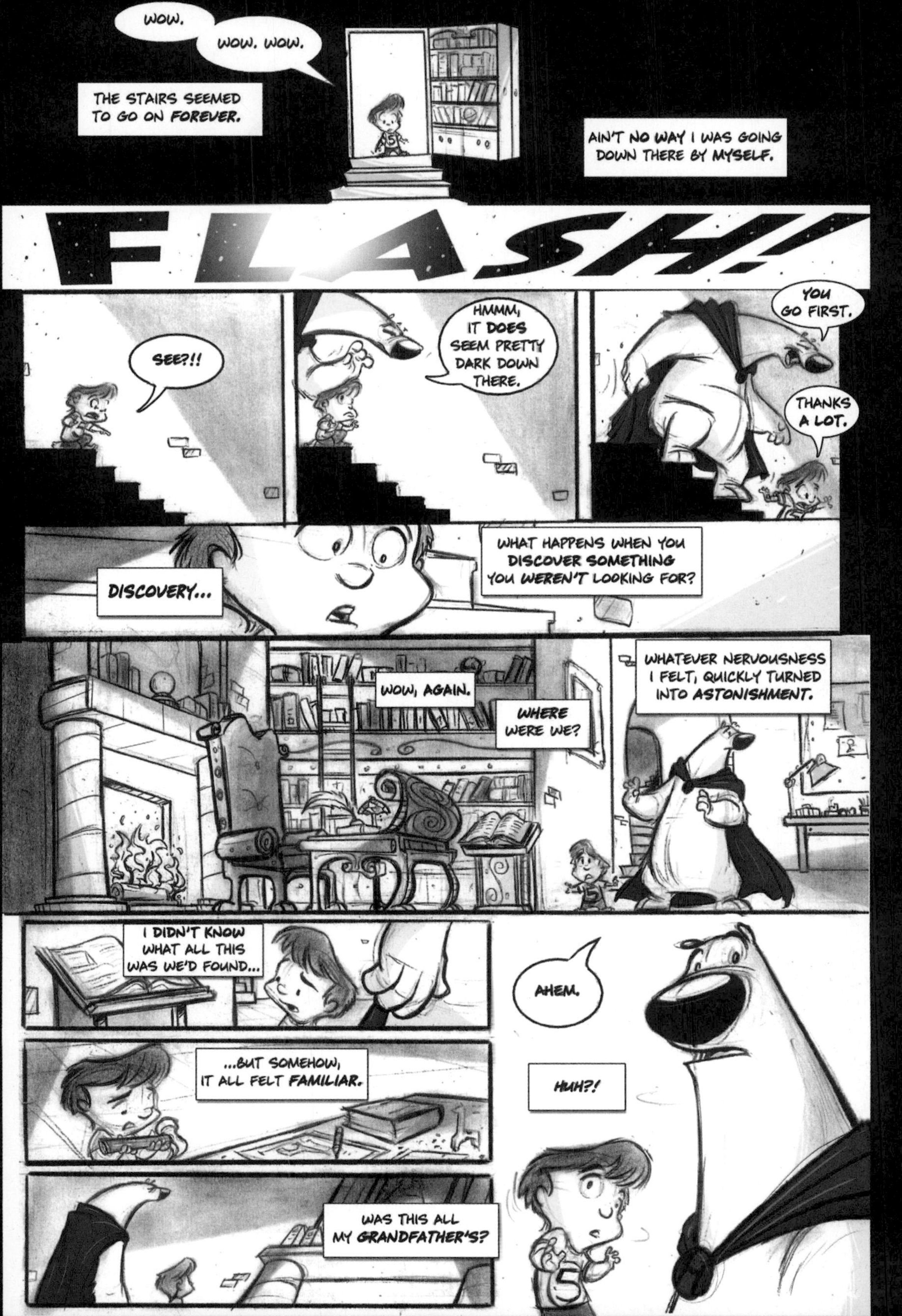
WOW.
WOW. WOW.
THE STAIRS SEEMED TO GO ON FOREVER.
AIN'T NO WAY I WAS GOING DOWN THERE BY MYSELF.
FLASH!
SEE?!!
HMMM, IT DOES SEEM PRETTY DARK DOWN THERE.
YOU GO FIRST.
THANKS A LOT.
DISCOVERY...
WHAT HAPPENS WHEN YOU DISCOVER SOMETHING YOU WEREN'T LOOKING FOR?
WOW, AGAIN.
WHERE WERE WE?
WHATEVER NERVOUSNESS I FELT, QUICKLY TURNED INTO ASTONISHMENT.
I DIDN'T KNOW WHAT ALL THIS WAS WE'D FOUND...
...BUT SOMEHOW, IT ALL FELT FAMILIAR.
WAS THIS ALL MY GRANDFATHER'S?
AHEM.
HUH?!

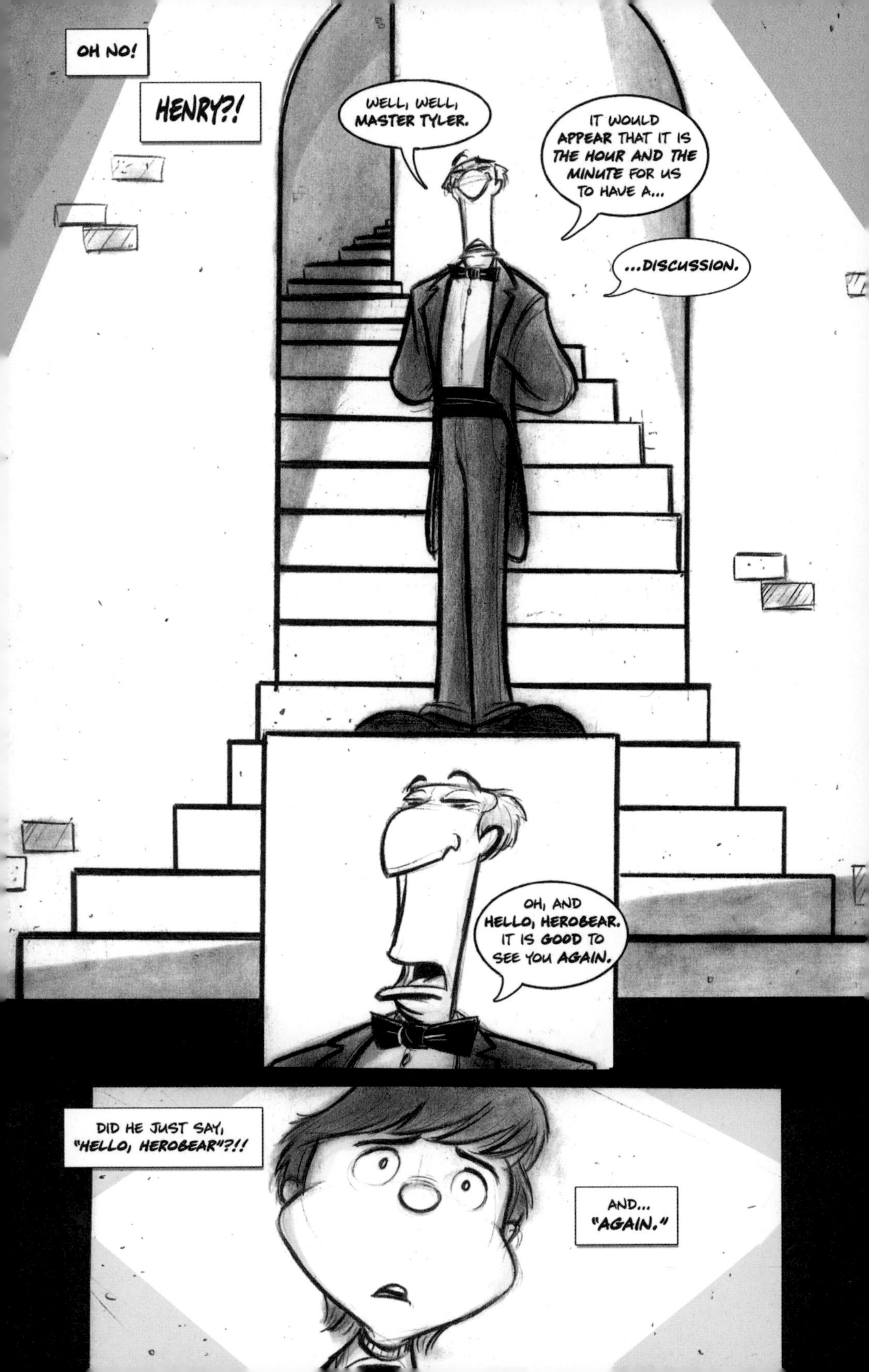
OH NO!
HENRY?!
WELL, WELL, MASTER TYLER.
IT WOULD APPEAR THAT IT IS THE HOUR AND THE MINUTE FOR US TO HAVE A...
...DISCUSSION.
OH, AND HELLO, HEROBEAR. IT IS GOOD TO SEE YOU AGAIN.
DID HE JUST SAY, "HELLO, HEROBEAR"?!!
AND... "AGAIN."

Chapter Five

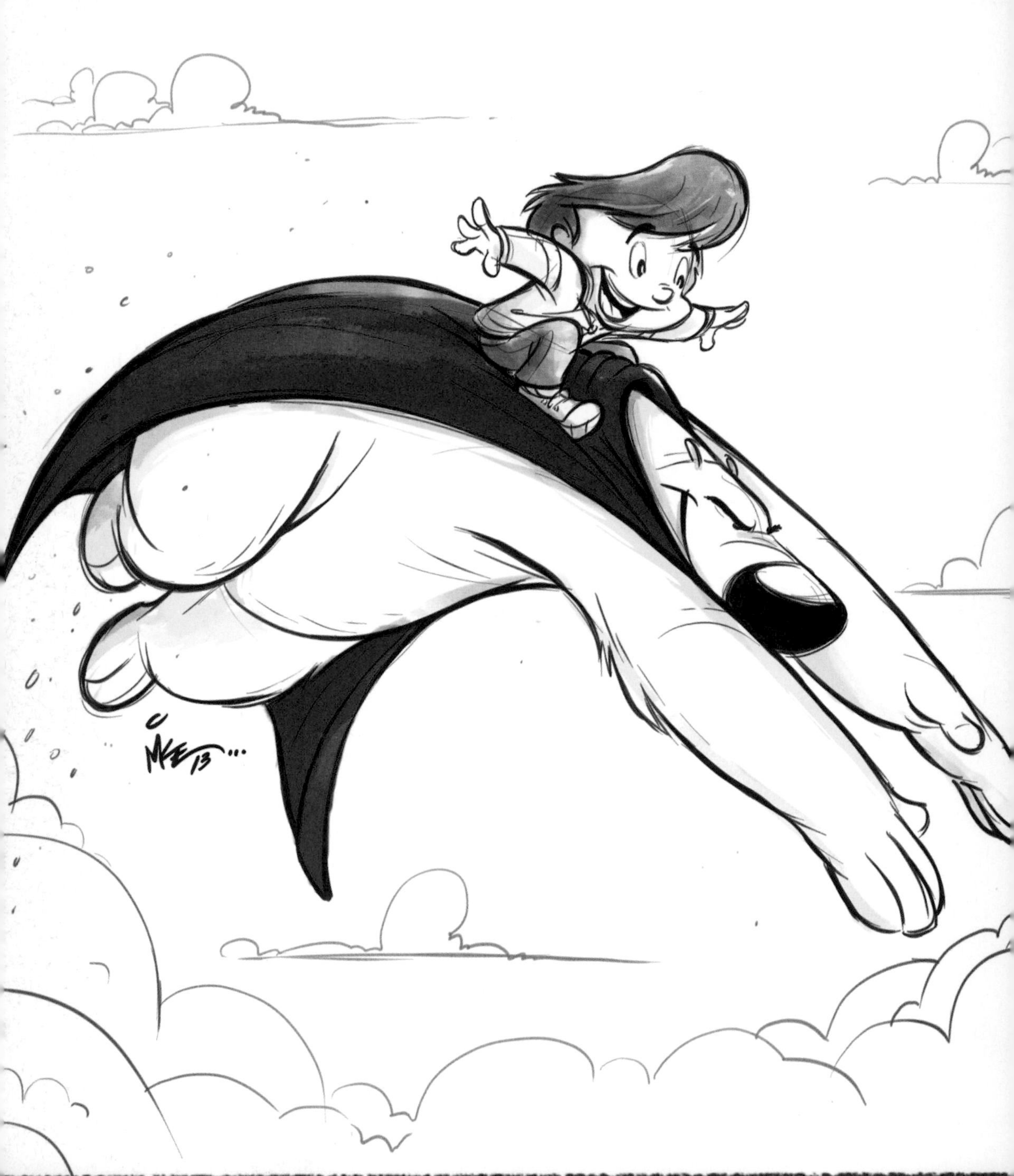

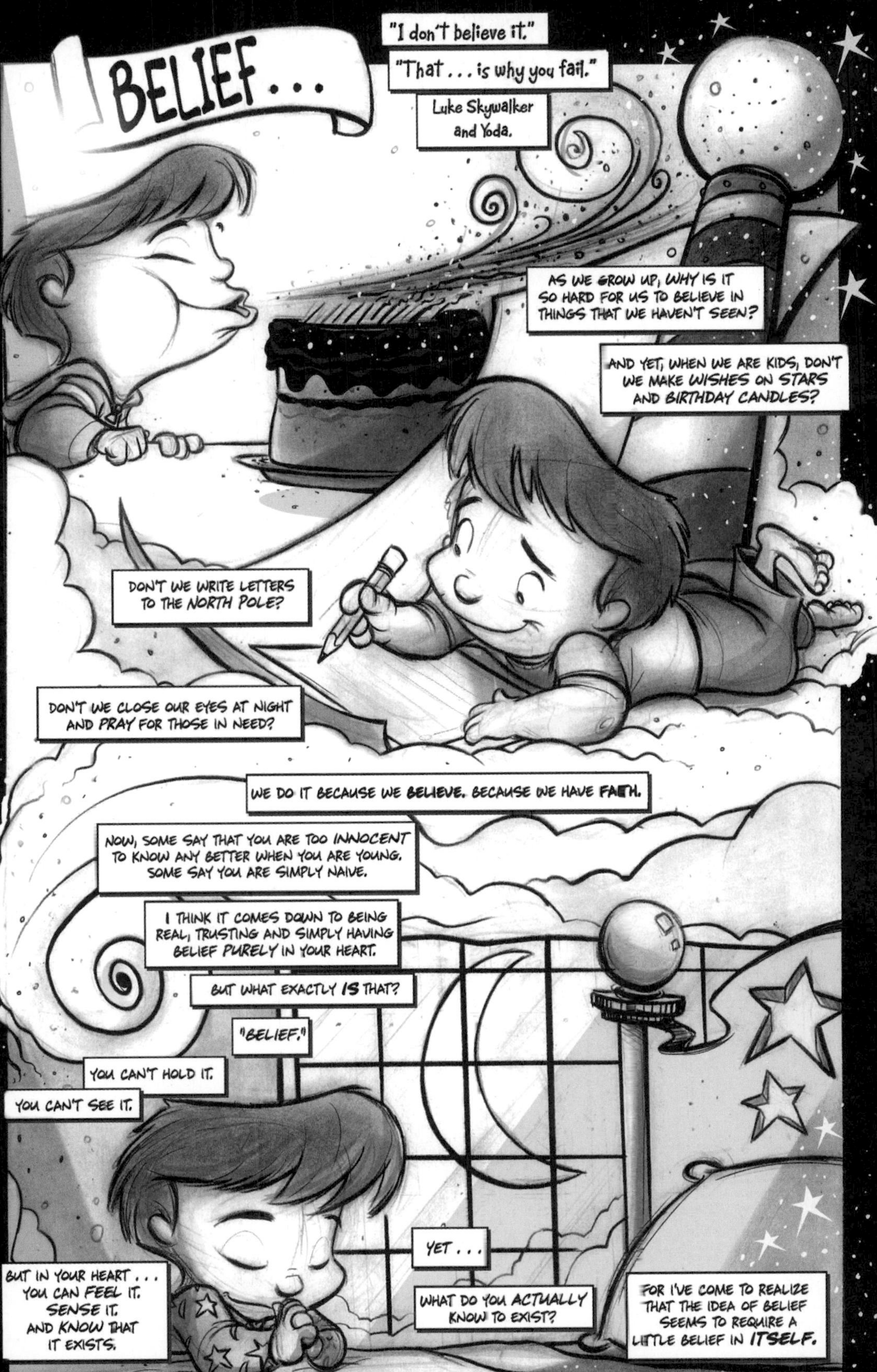
BELIEF . . .
"I don't believe it."
"That . . . is why you fail."
Luke Skywalker and Yoda.
AS WE GROW UP, WHY IS IT SO HARD FOR US TO BELIEVE IN THINGS THAT WE HAVEN'T SEEN?
AND YET, WHEN WE ARE KIDS, DON'T WE MAKE WISHES ON STARS AND BIRTHDAY CANDLES?
DON'T WE WRITE LETTERS TO THE NORTH POLE?
DON'T WE CLOSE OUR EYES AT NIGHT AND PRAY FOR THOSE IN NEED?
WE DO IT BECAUSE WE BELIEVE. BECAUSE WE HAVE FAITH.
NOW, SOME SAY THAT YOU ARE TOO INNOCENT TO KNOW ANY BETTER WHEN YOU ARE YOUNG. SOME SAY YOU ARE SIMPLY NAIVE.
I THINK IT COMES DOWN TO BEING REAL, TRUSTING AND SIMPLY HAVING BELIEF PURELY IN YOUR HEART.
BUT WHAT EXACTLY IS THAT?
"BELIEF."
YOU CAN'T HOLD IT.
YOU CAN'T SEE IT.
YET . . .
WHAT DO YOU ACTUALLY KNOW TO EXIST?
BUT IN YOUR HEART . . . YOU CAN FEEL IT. SENSE IT. AND KNOW THAT IT EXISTS.
FOR I'VE COME TO REALIZE THAT THE IDEA OF BELIEF SEEMS TO REQUIRE A LITTLE BELIEF IN ITSELF.

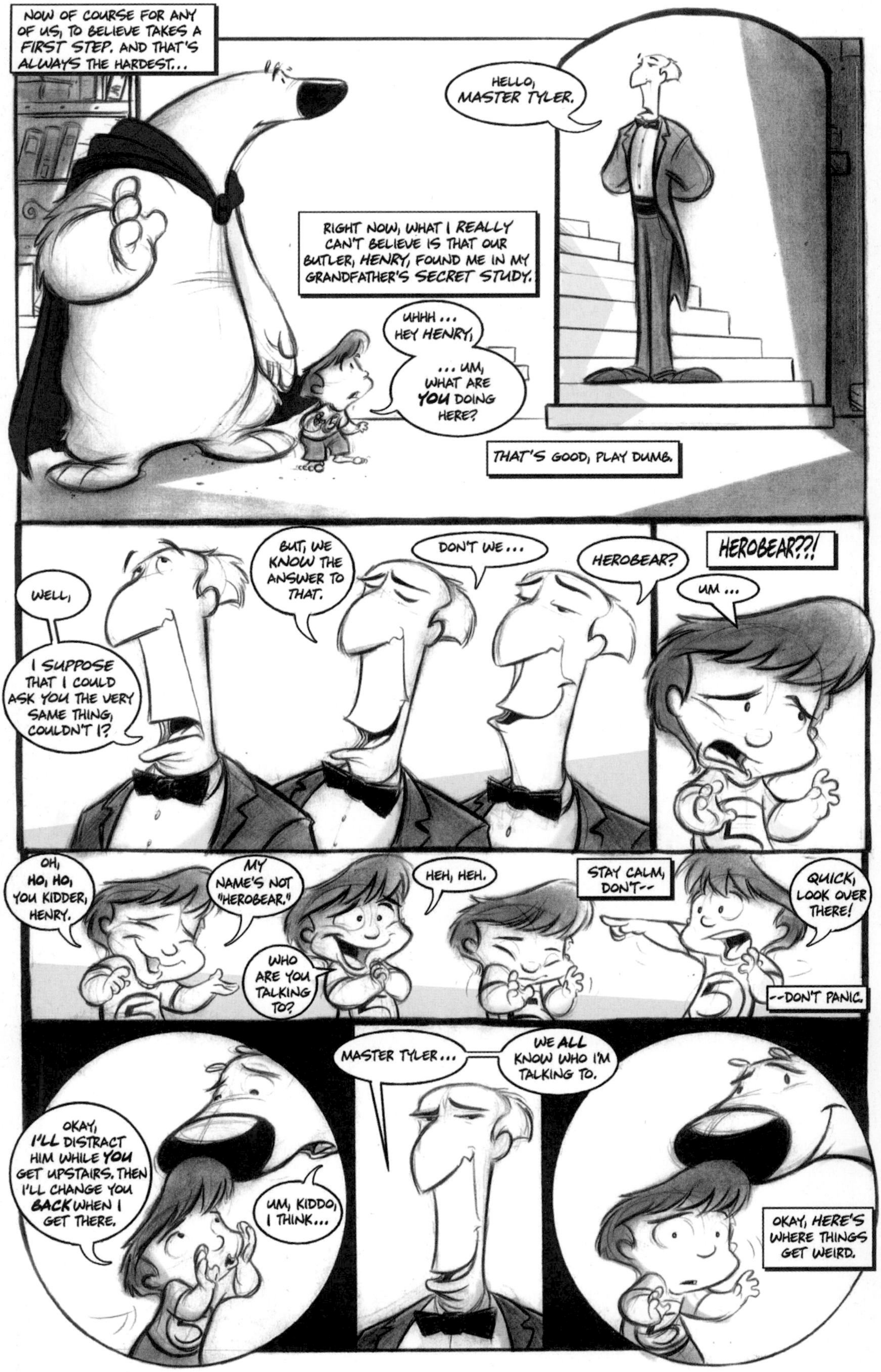
NOW OF COURSE FOR ANY OF US, TO BELIEVE TAKES A FIRST STEP. AND THAT'S ALWAYS THE HARDEST...
HELLO, MASTER TYLER.
RIGHT NOW, WHAT I REALLY CAN'T BELIEVE IS THAT OUR BUTLER, HENRY, FOUND ME IN MY GRANDFATHER'S SECRET STUDY.
UHHH... HEY HENRY,
...UM, WHAT ARE YOU DOING HERE?
THAT'S GOOD, PLAY DUMB.
WELL,
I SUPPOSE THAT I COULD ASK YOU THE VERY SAME THING, COULDN'T I?
BUT, WE KNOW THE ANSWER TO THAT.
DON'T WE...
HEROBEAR?
HEROBEAR??!
UM...
OH, HO, HO, YOU KIDDER, HENRY.
MY NAME'S NOT "HEROBEAR."
WHO ARE YOU TALKING TO?
HEH, HEH.
STAY CALM, DON'T--
QUICK, LOOK OVER THERE!
--DON'T PANIC.
OKAY, I'LL DISTRACT HIM WHILE YOU GET UPSTAIRS. THEN I'LL CHANGE YOU BACK WHEN I GET THERE.
UM, KIDDO, I THINK...
MASTER TYLER...
WE ALL KNOW WHO I'M TALKING TO.
OKAY, HERE'S WHERE THINGS GET WEIRD.

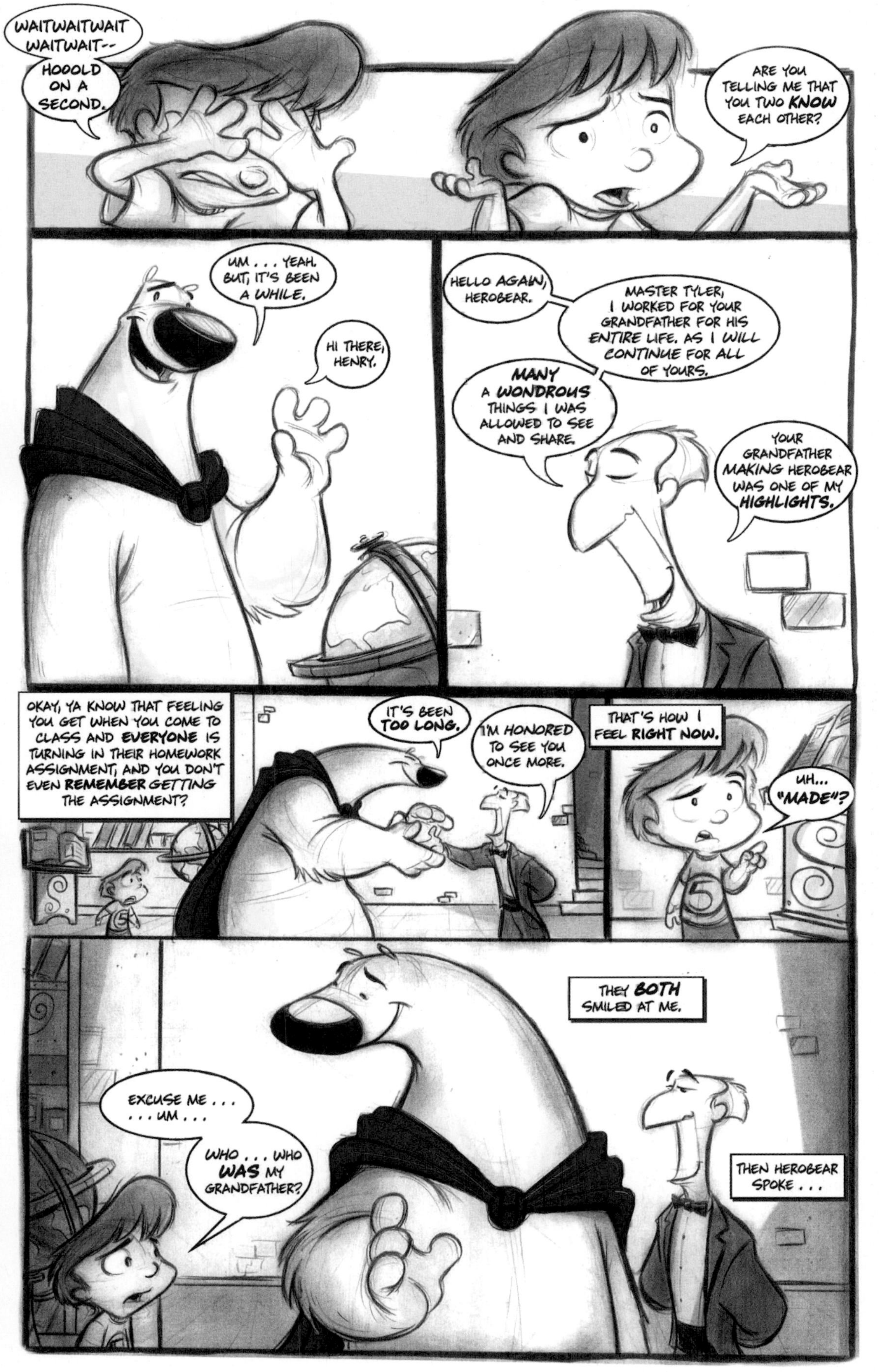

WAITWAITWAIT WAITWAIT--
HOOOLD ON A SECOND.
ARE YOU TELLING ME THAT YOU TWO KNOW EACH OTHER?
UM . . . YEAH. BUT, IT'S BEEN A WHILE.
HI THERE, HENRY.
HELLO AGAIN, HEROBEAR.
MASTER TYLER, I WORKED FOR YOUR GRANDFATHER FOR HIS ENTIRE LIFE. AS I WILL CONTINUE FOR ALL OF YOURS.
MANY A WONDROUS THINGS I WAS ALLOWED TO SEE AND SHARE.
YOUR GRANDFATHER MAKING HEROBEAR WAS ONE OF MY HIGHLIGHTS.
OKAY, YA KNOW THAT FEELING YOU GET WHEN YOU COME TO CLASS AND EVERYONE IS TURNING IN THEIR HOMEWORK ASSIGNMENT, AND YOU DON'T EVEN REMEMBER GETTING THE ASSIGNMENT?
IT'S BEEN TOO LONG.
I'M HONORED TO SEE YOU ONCE MORE.
THAT'S HOW I FEEL RIGHT NOW.
UH... "MADE"?
THEY BOTH SMILED AT ME.
EXCUSE ME . . . . . . UM . . .
WHO . . . WHO WAS MY GRANDFATHER?
THEN HEROBEAR SPOKE . . .

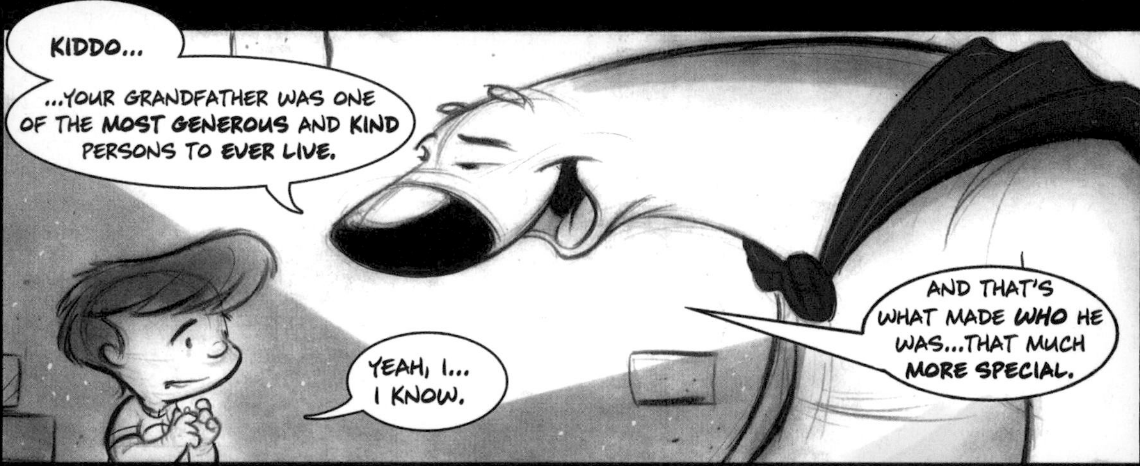
KIDDO...
...YOUR GRANDFATHER WAS ONE OF THE **MOST GENEROUS** AND **KIND** PERSONS TO **EVER LIVE.**
YEAH, I... I KNOW.
AND THAT'S WHAT MADE **WHO** HE WAS...THAT MUCH **MORE SPECIAL.**

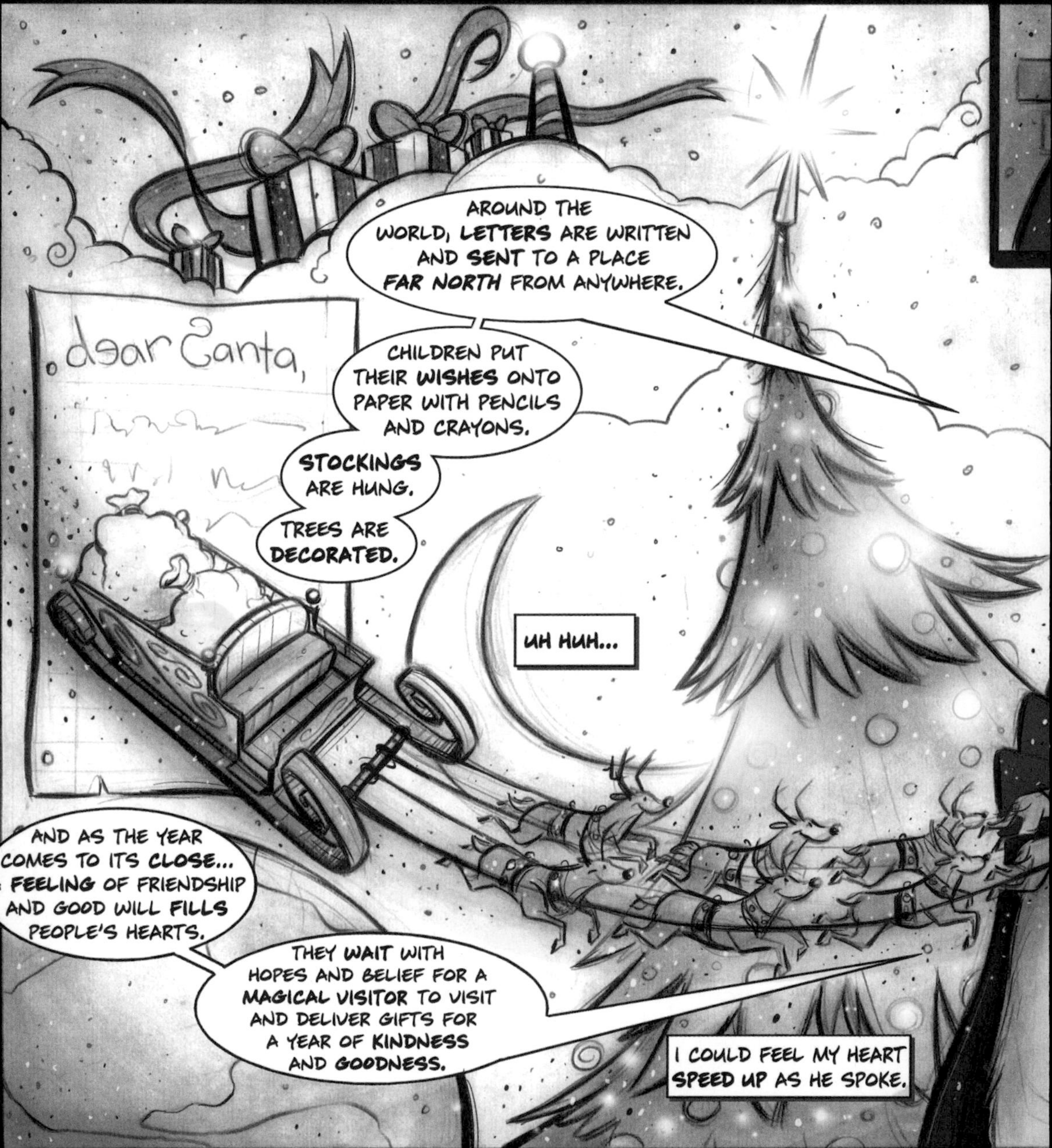
AROUND THE WORLD, **LETTERS** ARE WRITTEN AND **SENT** TO A PLACE **FAR NORTH** FROM ANYWHERE.
dear Santa,
CHILDREN PUT THEIR **WISHES** ONTO PAPER WITH PENCILS AND CRAYONS.
STOCKINGS ARE HUNG.
TREES ARE **DECORATED.**
UH HUH...
AND AS THE YEAR COMES TO ITS **CLOSE...** A **FEELING** OF FRIENDSHIP AND GOOD WILL **FILLS** PEOPLE'S HEARTS.
THEY **WAIT** WITH HOPES AND BELIEF FOR A **MAGICAL VISITOR** TO VISIT AND DELIVER GIFTS FOR A YEAR OF **KINDNESS** AND **GOODNESS.**
I COULD FEEL MY HEART **SPEED UP** AS HE SPOKE.

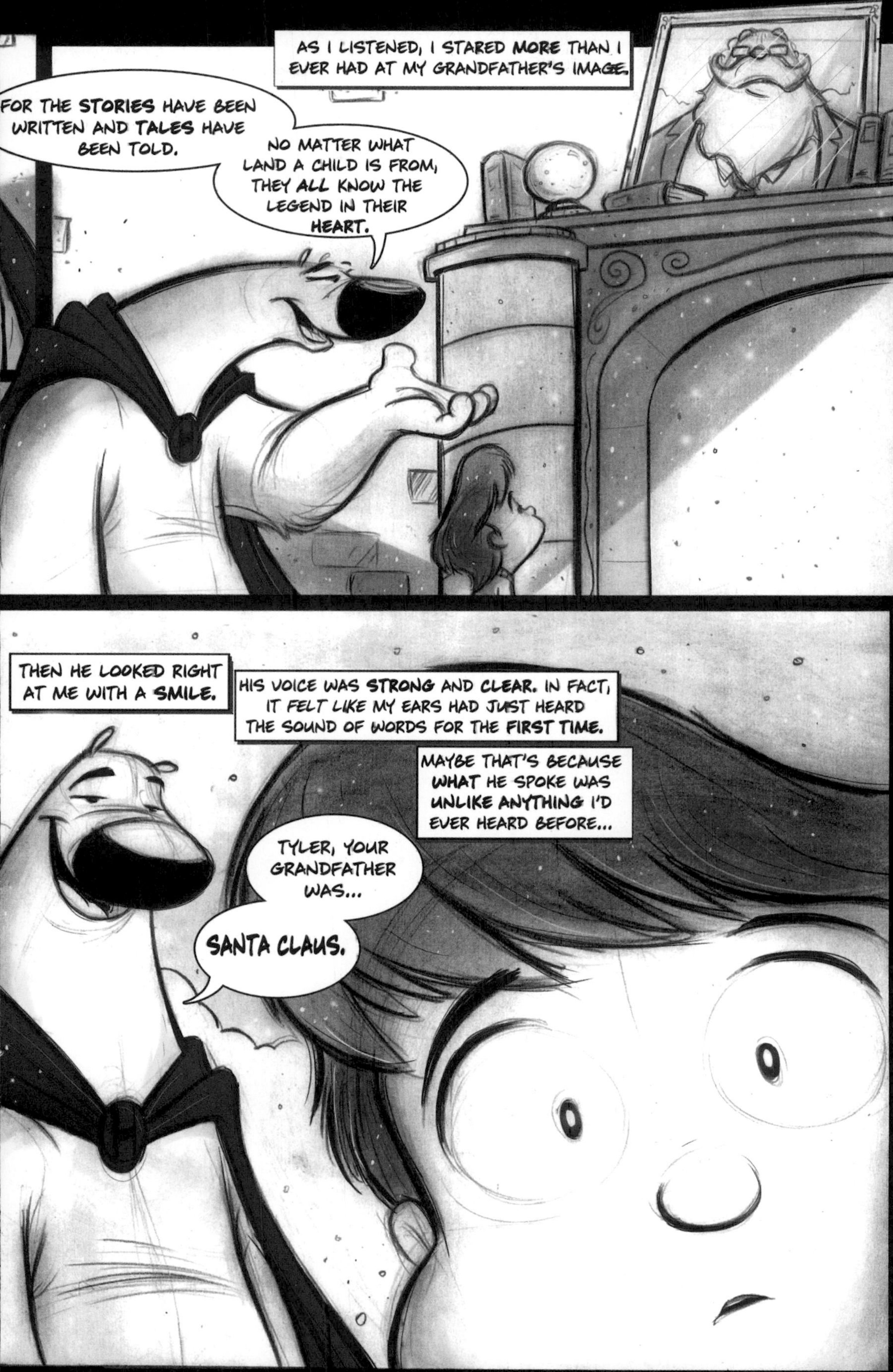
AS I LISTENED, I STARED MORE THAN I EVER HAD AT MY GRANDFATHER'S IMAGE.
FOR THE STORIES HAVE BEEN WRITTEN AND TALES HAVE BEEN TOLD.
NO MATTER WHAT LAND A CHILD IS FROM, THEY ALL KNOW THE LEGEND IN THEIR HEART.
THEN HE LOOKED RIGHT AT ME WITH A SMILE.
HIS VOICE WAS STRONG AND CLEAR. IN FACT, IT FELT LIKE MY EARS HAD JUST HEARD THE SOUND OF WORDS FOR THE FIRST TIME.
MAYBE THAT'S BECAUSE WHAT HE SPOKE WAS UNLIKE ANYTHING I'D EVER HEARD BEFORE...
TYLER, YOUR GRANDFATHER WAS...
SANTA CLAUS.

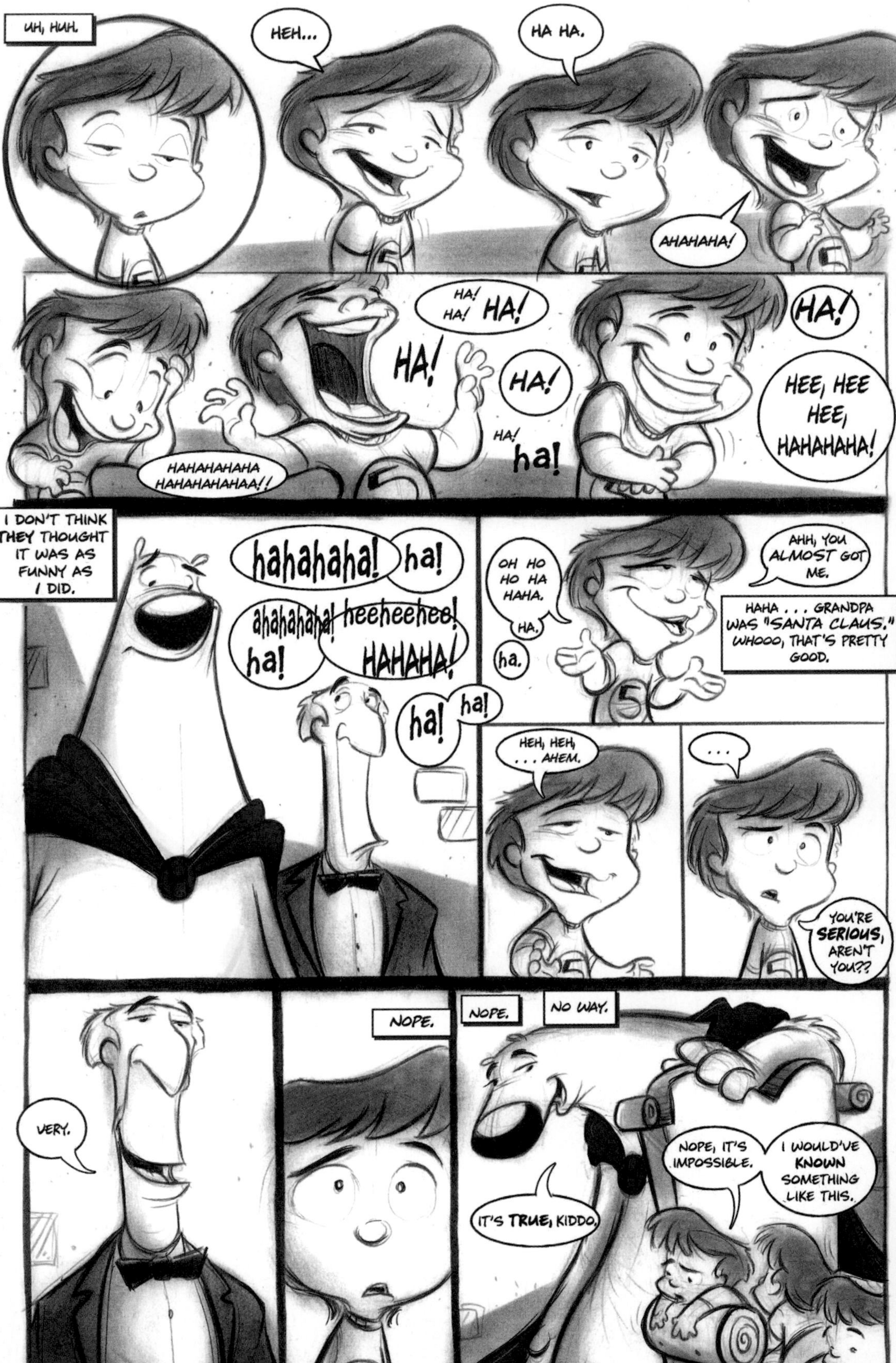
UH, HUH.
HEH...
HA HA.
AHAHAHA!
HAHAHAHAHA HAHAHAHAHAA!!
HA! HA! HA!
HA!
HA!
HA! ha!
HA!
HEE, HEE HEE, HAHAHAHA!
I DON'T THINK THEY THOUGHT IT WAS AS FUNNY AS I DID.
hahahaha! ha!
ahahahaha! heeheehee! ha! HAHAHA!
ha! ha!
OH HO HO HA HAHA.
HA.
ha.
AHH, YOU ALMOST GOT ME.
HAHA . . . GRANDPA WAS "SANTA CLAUS." WHOOO, THAT'S PRETTY GOOD.
HEH, HEH, . . . AHEM.
. . .
YOU'RE SERIOUS, AREN'T YOU??
VERY.
NOPE.
NOPE.
NO WAY.
IT'S TRUE, KIDDO.
NOPE, IT'S IMPOSSIBLE.
I WOULD'VE KNOWN SOMETHING LIKE THIS.

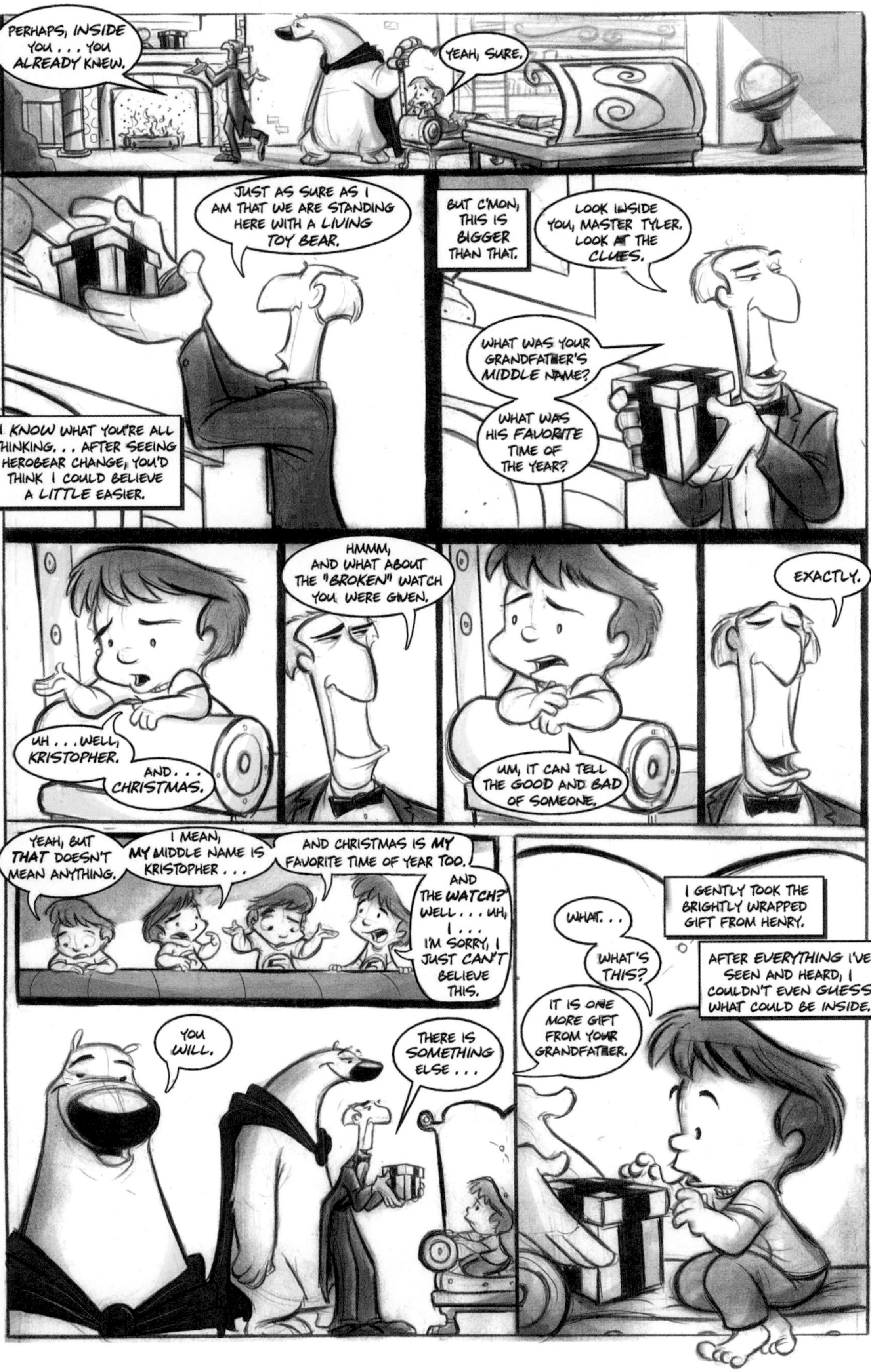

PERHAPS, INSIDE YOU . . . YOU ALREADY KNEW.
YEAH, SURE.
JUST AS SURE AS I AM THAT WE ARE STANDING HERE WITH A LIVING TOY BEAR.
I KNOW WHAT YOU'RE ALL THINKING. . . AFTER SEEING HEROBEAR CHANGE, YOU'D THINK I COULD BELIEVE A LITTLE EASIER.
BUT C'MON, THIS IS BIGGER THAN THAT.
LOOK INSIDE YOU, MASTER TYLER. LOOK AT THE CLUES.
WHAT WAS YOUR GRANDFATHER'S MIDDLE NAME?
WHAT WAS HIS FAVORITE TIME OF THE YEAR?
UH . . . WELL, KRISTOPHER.
AND. . . CHRISTMAS.
HMMM, AND WHAT ABOUT THE "BROKEN" WATCH YOU WERE GIVEN.
UM, IT CAN TELL THE GOOD AND BAD OF SOMEONE.
EXACTLY.
YEAH, BUT THAT DOESN'T MEAN ANYTHING.
I MEAN, MY MIDDLE NAME IS KRISTOPHER . . .
AND CHRISTMAS IS MY FAVORITE TIME OF YEAR TOO.
AND THE WATCH? WELL . . . UH, I . . . I'M SORRY, I JUST CAN'T BELIEVE THIS.
YOU WILL.
THERE IS SOMETHING ELSE . . .
I GENTLY TOOK THE BRIGHTLY WRAPPED GIFT FROM HENRY.
WHAT. . .
WHAT'S THIS?
AFTER EVERYTHING I'VE SEEN AND HEARD, I COULDN'T EVEN GUESS WHAT COULD BE INSIDE.
IT IS ONE MORE GIFT FROM YOUR GRANDFATHER.

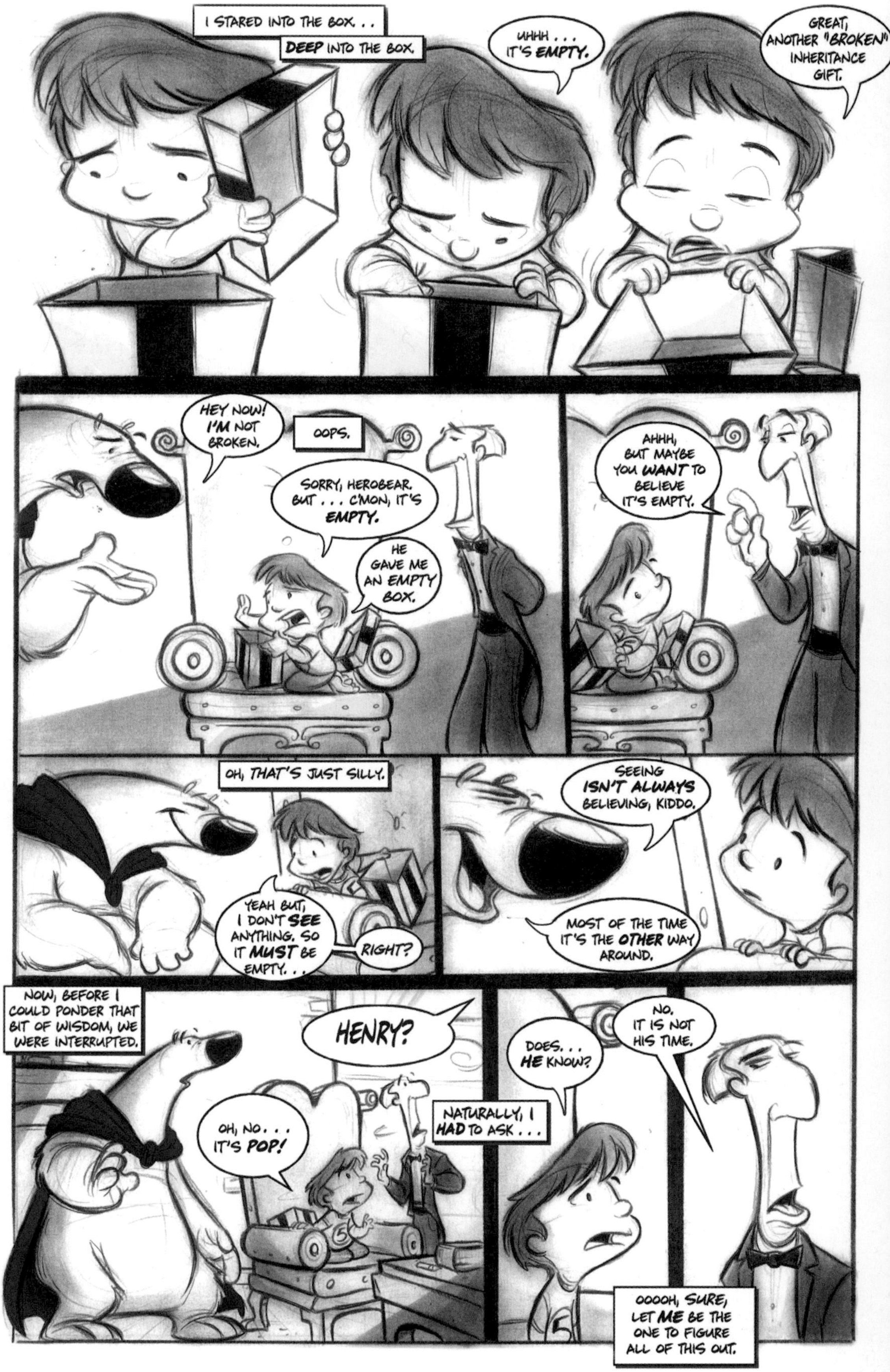
I STARED INTO THE BOX. . .
DEEP INTO THE BOX.
UHHH . . . IT'S EMPTY.
GREAT, ANOTHER "BROKEN" INHERITANCE GIFT.
HEY NOW! I'M NOT BROKEN.
OOPS.
SORRY, HEROBEAR. BUT . . . C'MON, IT'S EMPTY.
HE GAVE ME AN EMPTY BOX.
AHHH, BUT MAYBE YOU WANT TO BELIEVE IT'S EMPTY.
OH, THAT'S JUST SILLY.
YEAH BUT, I DON'T SEE ANYTHING. SO IT MUST BE EMPTY. . .
RIGHT?
SEEING ISN'T ALWAYS BELIEVING, KIDDO.
MOST OF THE TIME IT'S THE OTHER WAY AROUND.
NOW, BEFORE I COULD PONDER THAT BIT OF WISDOM, WE WERE INTERRUPTED.
HENRY?
OH, NO. . . IT'S POP!
NATURALLY, I HAD TO ASK . . .
DOES. . . HE KNOW?
NO. IT IS NOT HIS TIME.
OOOOH, SURE, LET ME BE THE ONE TO FIGURE ALL OF THIS OUT.

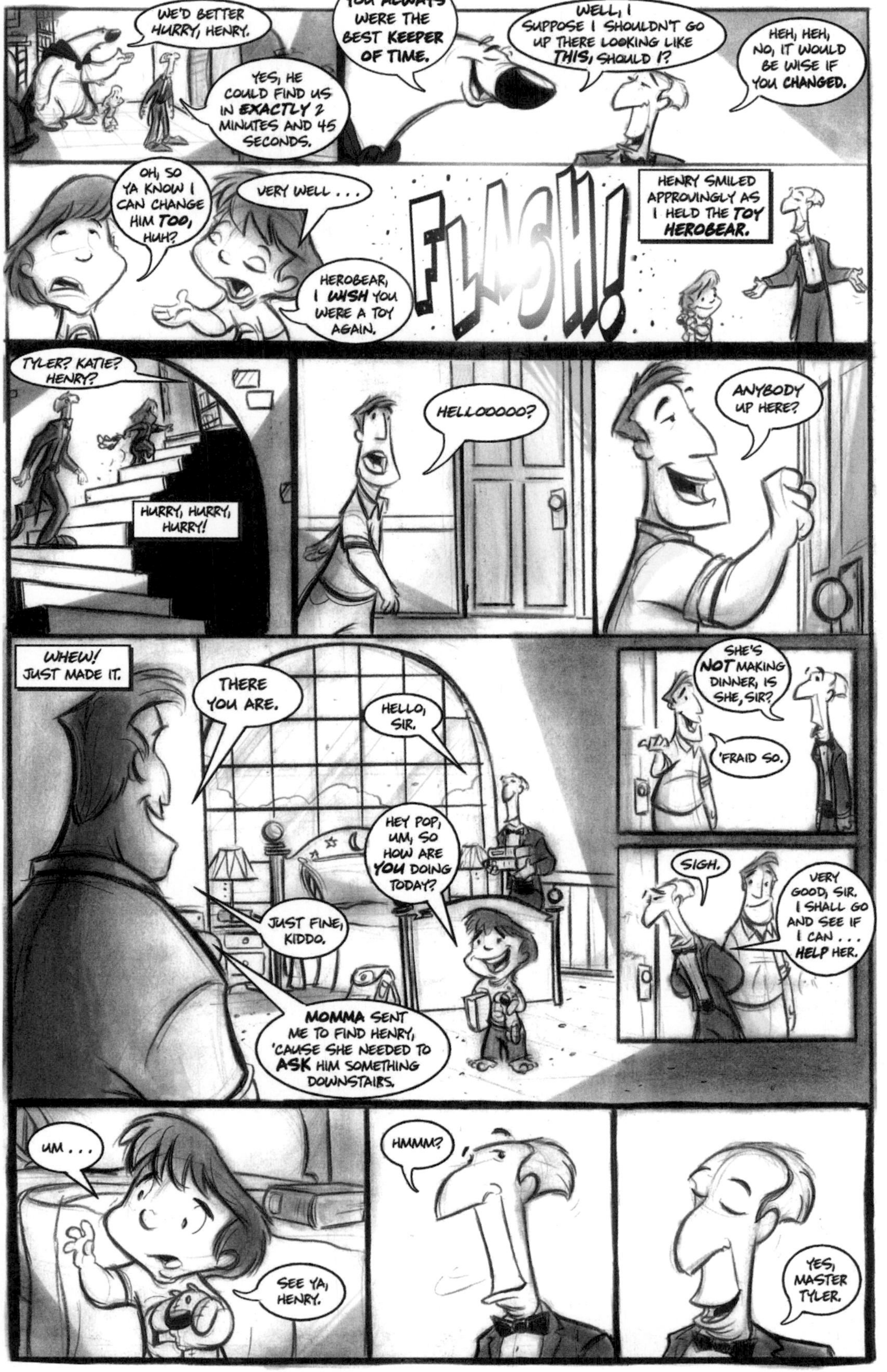

WE'D BETTER HURRY, HENRY.
YES, HE COULD FIND US IN EXACTLY 2 MINUTES AND 45 SECONDS.
HAH, YOU ALWAYS WERE THE BEST KEEPER OF TIME.
WELL, I SUPPOSE I SHOULDN'T GO UP THERE LOOKING LIKE THIS, SHOULD I?
HEH, HEH, NO, IT WOULD BE WISE IF YOU CHANGED.
OH, SO YA KNOW I CAN CHANGE HIM TOO, HUH?
VERY WELL . . .
HEROBEAR, I WISH YOU WERE A TOY AGAIN.
FLASH!
HENRY SMILED APPROVINGLY AS I HELD THE TOY HEROBEAR.
TYLER? KATIE? HENRY?
HURRY, HURRY, HURRY!
HELLOOOOO?
ANYBODY UP HERE?
WHEW! JUST MADE IT.
THERE YOU ARE.
HELLO, SIR.
HEY POP, UM, SO HOW ARE YOU DOING TODAY?
JUST FINE, KIDDO.
MOMMA SENT ME TO FIND HENRY, 'CAUSE SHE NEEDED TO ASK HIM SOMETHING DOWNSTAIRS.
SHE'S NOT MAKING DINNER, IS SHE, SIR?
'FRAID SO.
SIGH.
VERY GOOD, SIR. I SHALL GO AND SEE IF I CAN . . . HELP HER.
UM . . .
SEE YA, HENRY.
HMMM?
YES, MASTER TYLER.

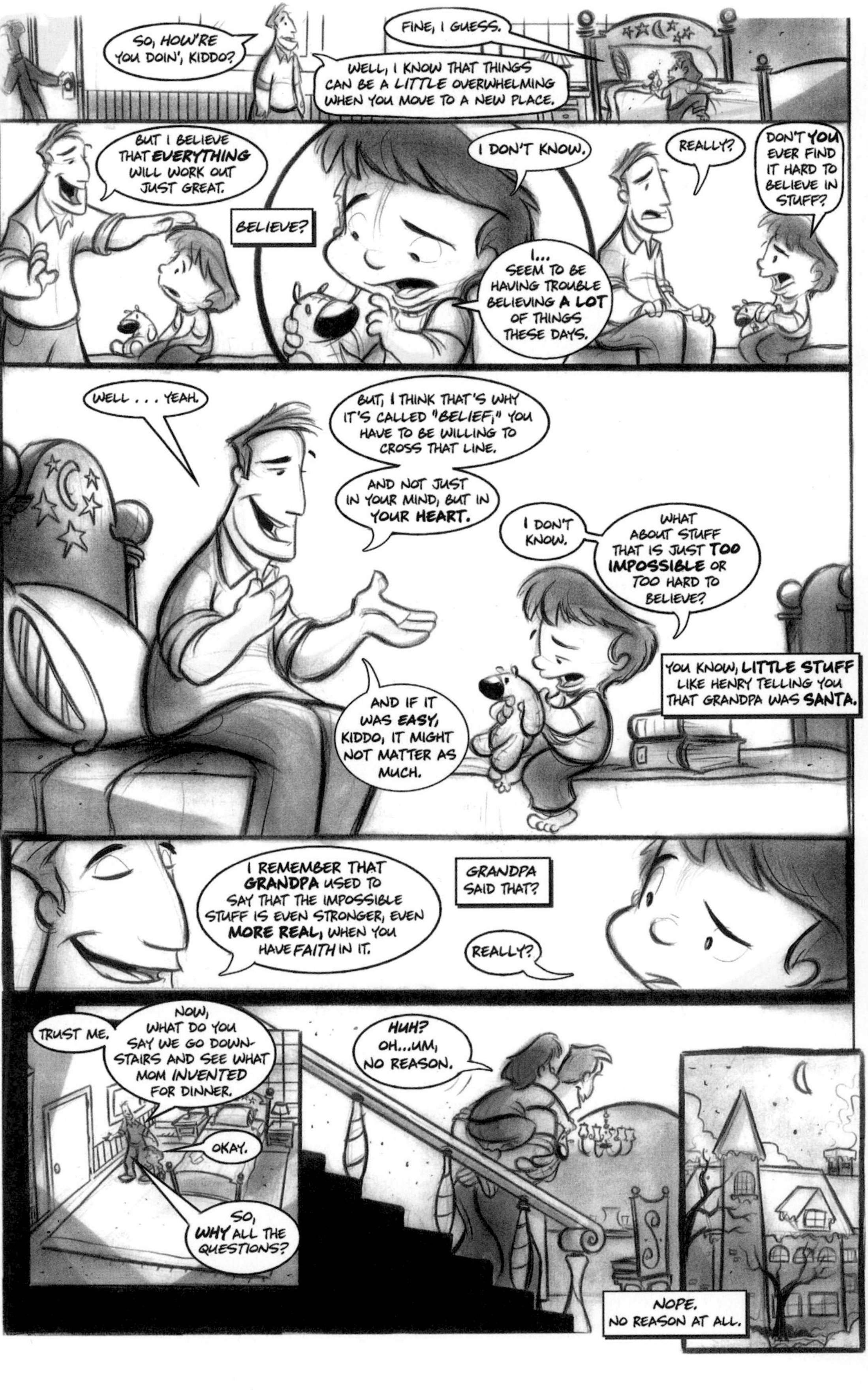
SO, HOW'RE YOU DOIN', KIDDO?
FINE, I GUESS.
WELL, I KNOW THAT THINGS CAN BE A LITTLE OVERWHELMING WHEN YOU MOVE TO A NEW PLACE.
BUT I BELIEVE THAT EVERYTHING WILL WORK OUT JUST GREAT.
BELIEVE?
I DON'T KNOW.
I... SEEM TO BE HAVING TROUBLE BELIEVING A LOT OF THINGS THESE DAYS.
REALLY?
DON'T YOU EVER FIND IT HARD TO BELIEVE IN STUFF?
WELL . . . YEAH.
BUT, I THINK THAT'S WHY IT'S CALLED "BELIEF," YOU HAVE TO BE WILLING TO CROSS THAT LINE.
AND NOT JUST IN YOUR MIND, BUT IN YOUR HEART.
I DON'T KNOW.
WHAT ABOUT STUFF THAT IS JUST TOO IMPOSSIBLE OR TOO HARD TO BELIEVE?
YOU KNOW, LITTLE STUFF LIKE HENRY TELLING YOU THAT GRANDPA WAS SANTA.
AND IF IT WAS EASY, KIDDO, IT MIGHT NOT MATTER AS MUCH.
I REMEMBER THAT GRANDPA USED TO SAY THAT THE IMPOSSIBLE STUFF IS EVEN STRONGER, EVEN MORE REAL, WHEN YOU HAVE FAITH IN IT.
GRANDPA SAID THAT?
REALLY?
TRUST ME.
NOW, WHAT DO YOU SAY WE GO DOWN-STAIRS AND SEE WHAT MOM INVENTED FOR DINNER.
OKAY.
SO, WHY ALL THE QUESTIONS?
HUH? OH...UM, NO REASON.
NOPE. NO REASON AT ALL.

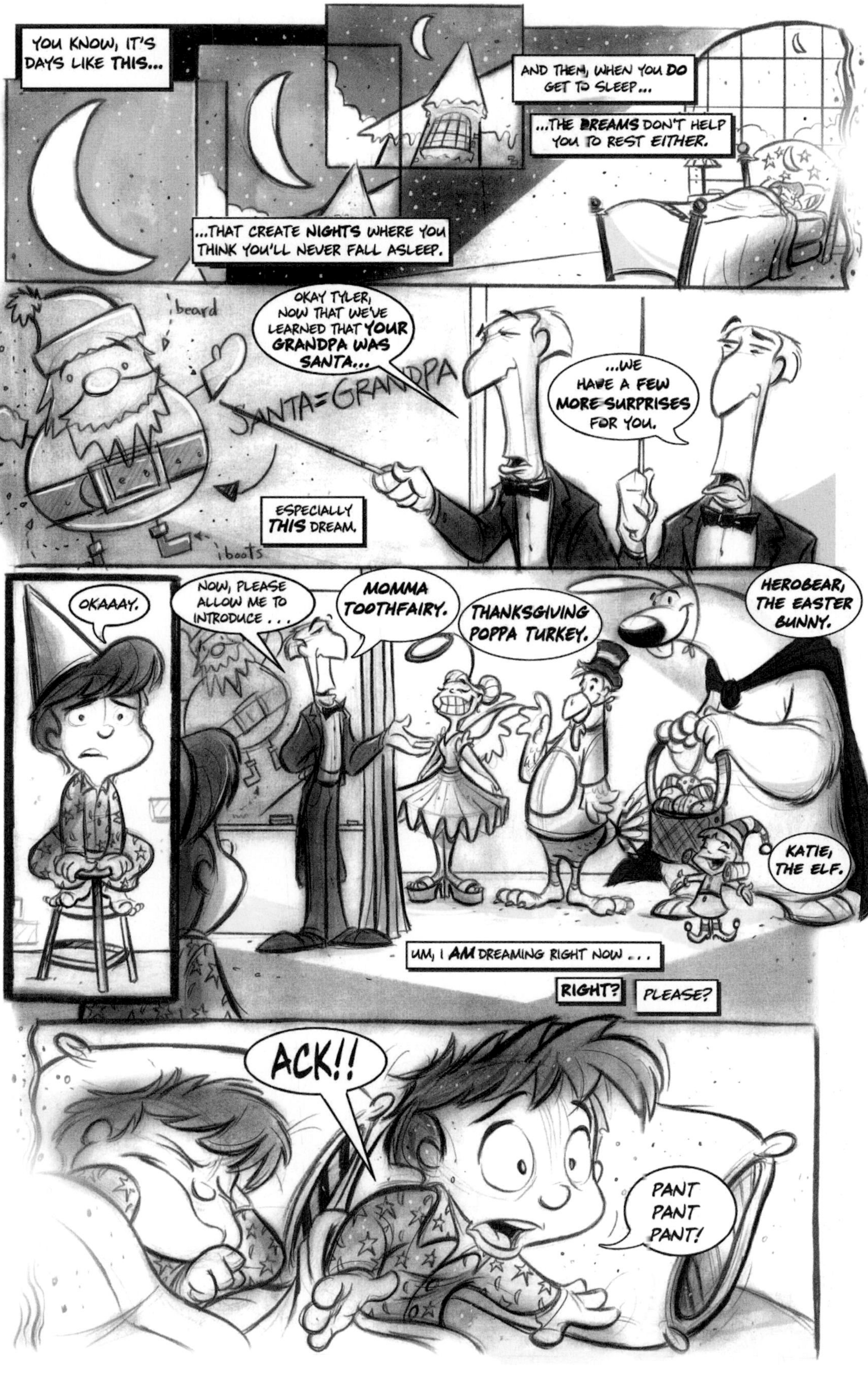
YOU KNOW, IT'S DAYS LIKE THIS...
...THAT CREATE NIGHTS WHERE YOU THINK YOU'LL NEVER FALL ASLEEP.
AND THEN, WHEN YOU DO GET TO SLEEP...
...THE DREAMS DON'T HELP YOU TO REST EITHER.
beard
boots
SANTA=GRANDPA
OKAY TYLER, NOW THAT WE'VE LEARNED THAT YOUR GRANDPA WAS SANTA...
...WE HAVE A FEW MORE SURPRISES FOR YOU.
ESPECIALLY THIS DREAM.
OKAAAY.
NOW, PLEASE ALLOW ME TO INTRODUCE . . .
MOMMA TOOTHFAIRY.
THANKSGIVING POPPA TURKEY.
HEROBEAR, THE EASTER BUNNY.
KATIE, THE ELF.
UM, I AM DREAMING RIGHT NOW . . .
RIGHT?
PLEASE?
ACK!!
PANT PANT PANT!

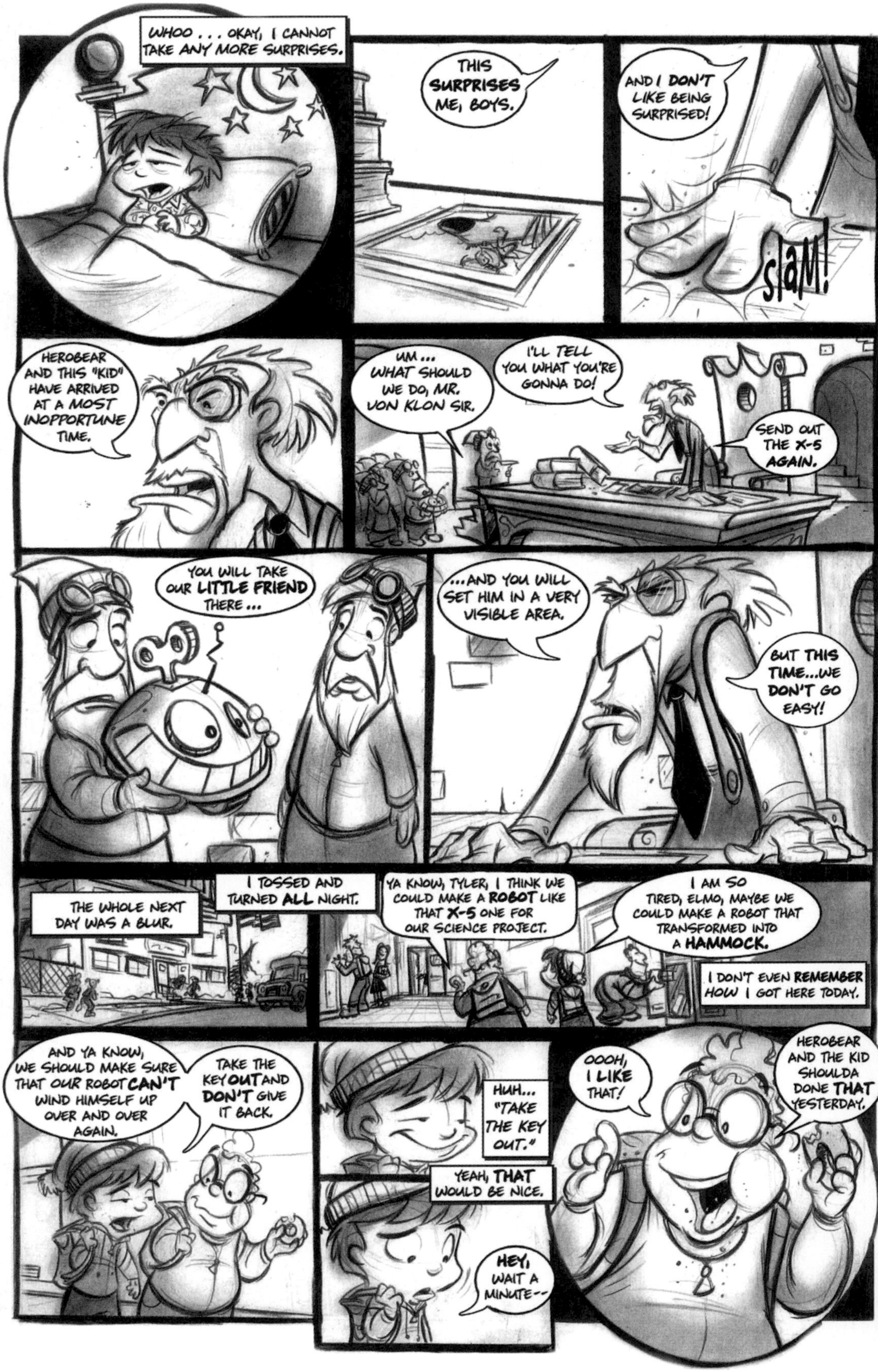
WHOO . . . OKAY, I CANNOT TAKE ANY MORE SURPRISES.
THIS SURPRISES ME, BOYS.
AND I DON'T LIKE BEING SURPRISED!
SLAM!
HEROBEAR AND THIS "KID" HAVE ARRIVED AT A MOST INOPPORTUNE TIME.
UM... WHAT SHOULD WE DO, MR. VON KLON SIR.
I'LL TELL YOU WHAT YOU'RE GONNA DO!
SEND OUT THE X-5 AGAIN.
YOU WILL TAKE OUR LITTLE FRIEND THERE...
...AND YOU WILL SET HIM IN A VERY VISIBLE AREA.
BUT THIS TIME...WE DON'T GO EASY!
THE WHOLE NEXT DAY WAS A BLUR.
I TOSSED AND TURNED ALL NIGHT.
YA KNOW, TYLER, I THINK WE COULD MAKE A ROBOT LIKE THAT X-5 ONE FOR OUR SCIENCE PROJECT.
I AM SO TIRED, ELMO, MAYBE WE COULD MAKE A ROBOT THAT TRANSFORMED INTO A HAMMOCK.
I DON'T EVEN REMEMBER HOW I GOT HERE TODAY.
AND YA KNOW, WE SHOULD MAKE SURE THAT OUR ROBOT CAN'T WIND HIMSELF UP OVER AND OVER AGAIN.
TAKE THE KEY OUT AND DON'T GIVE IT BACK.
HUH... "TAKE THE KEY OUT."
YEAH, THAT WOULD BE NICE.
HEY, WAIT A MINUTE--
OOOH, I LIKE THAT!
HEROBEAR AND THE KID SHOULDA DONE THAT YESTERDAY.

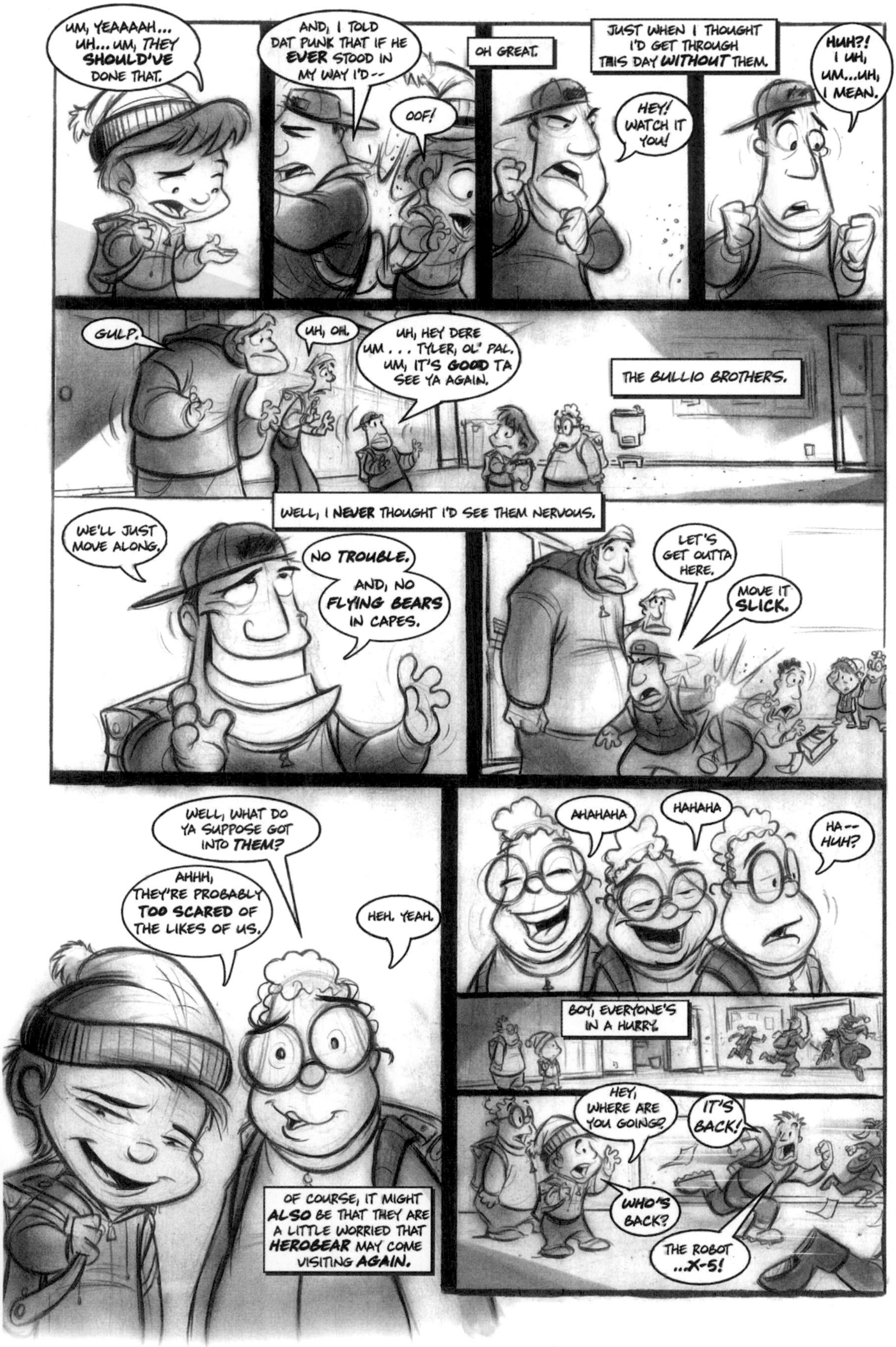
UM, YEAAAAH... UH... UM, THEY SHOULD'VE DONE THAT.
AND, I TOLD DAT PUNK THAT IF HE EVER STOOD IN MY WAY I'D--
OOF!
OH GREAT.
JUST WHEN I THOUGHT I'D GET THROUGH THIS DAY WITHOUT THEM.
HEY! WATCH IT YOU!
HUH?! I UH, UM...UH, I MEAN.
GULP.
UH, OH.
UH, HEY DERE UM . . . TYLER, OL' PAL. UM, IT'S GOOD TA SEE YA AGAIN.
THE BULLIO BROTHERS.
WELL, I NEVER THOUGHT I'D SEE THEM NERVOUS.
WE'LL JUST MOVE ALONG.
NO TROUBLE.
AND, NO FLYING BEARS IN CAPES.
LET'S GET OUTTA HERE.
MOVE IT SLICK.
WELL, WHAT DO YA SUPPOSE GOT INTO THEM?
AHHH, THEY'RE PROBABLY TOO SCARED OF THE LIKES OF US.
HEH. YEAH.
OF COURSE, IT MIGHT ALSO BE THAT THEY ARE A LITTLE WORRIED THAT HEROBEAR MAY COME VISITING AGAIN.
AHAHAHA
HAHAHA
HA-- HUH?
BOY, EVERYONE'S IN A HURRY.
HEY, WHERE ARE YOU GOING?
IT'S BACK!
WHO'S BACK?
THE ROBOT ...X-5!

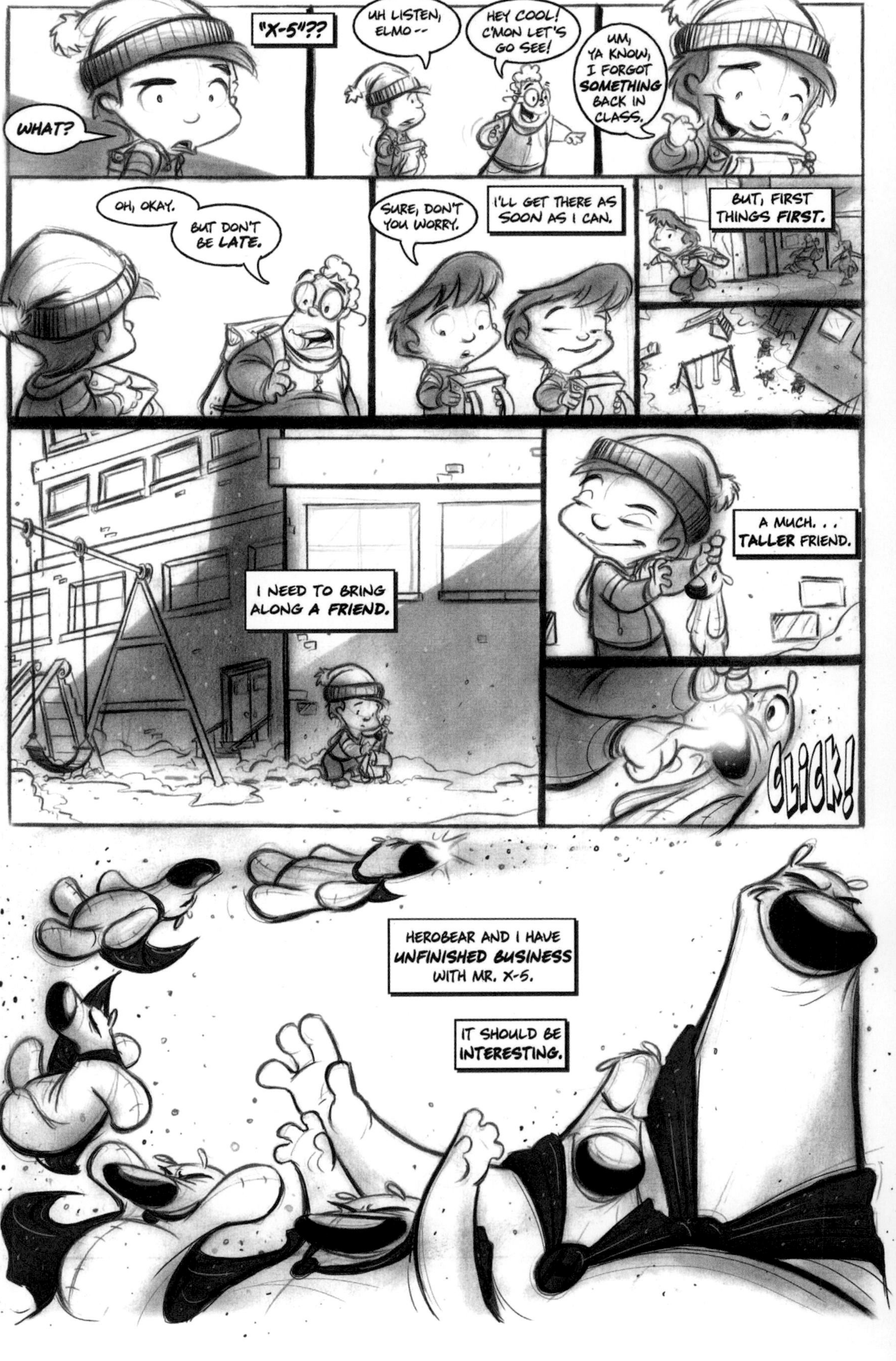
WHAT?
"X-5"??
UH LISTEN, ELMO --
HEY COOL! C'MON LET'S GO SEE!
UM, YA KNOW, I FORGOT SOMETHING BACK IN CLASS.
OH, OKAY.
BUT DON'T BE LATE.
SURE, DON'T YOU WORRY.
I'LL GET THERE AS SOON AS I CAN.
BUT, FIRST THINGS FIRST.
I NEED TO BRING ALONG A FRIEND.
A MUCH. . . TALLER FRIEND.
CLICK!
HEROBEAR AND I HAVE UNFINISHED BUSINESS WITH MR. X-5.
IT SHOULD BE INTERESTING.

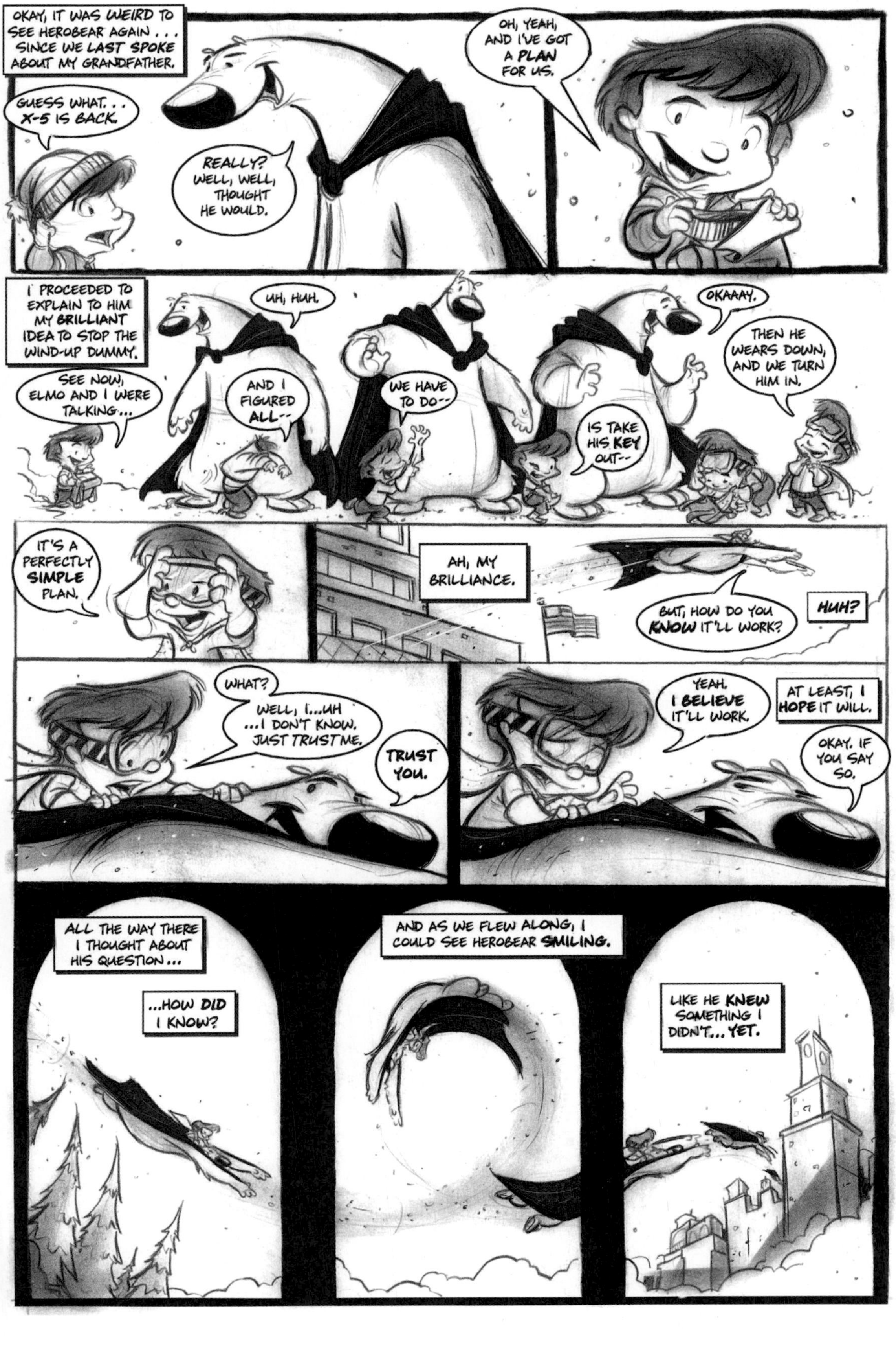

OKAY, IT WAS WEIRD TO SEE HEROBEAR AGAIN . . . SINCE WE LAST SPOKE ABOUT MY GRANDFATHER.
GUESS WHAT. . . X-5 IS BACK.
REALLY? WELL, WELL, THOUGHT HE WOULD.
OH, YEAH, AND I'VE GOT A PLAN FOR US.
I PROCEEDED TO EXPLAIN TO HIM MY BRILLIANT IDEA TO STOP THE WIND-UP DUMMY.
SEE NOW, ELMO AND I WERE TALKING...
UH, HUH.
AND I FIGURED ALL--
WE HAVE TO DO--
IS TAKE HIS KEY OUT--
OKAAAY.
THEN HE WEARS DOWN, AND WE TURN HIM IN.
IT'S A PERFECTLY SIMPLE PLAN.
AH, MY BRILLIANCE.
BUT, HOW DO YOU KNOW IT'LL WORK?
HUH?
WHAT?
WELL, I...UH ...I DON'T KNOW. JUST TRUST ME.
TRUST YOU.
YEAH. I BELIEVE IT'LL WORK.
AT LEAST, I HOPE IT WILL.
OKAY. IF YOU SAY SO.
ALL THE WAY THERE I THOUGHT ABOUT HIS QUESTION...
...HOW DID I KNOW?
AND AS WE FLEW ALONG, I COULD SEE HEROBEAR SMILING.
LIKE HE KNEW SOMETHING I DIDN'T... YET.

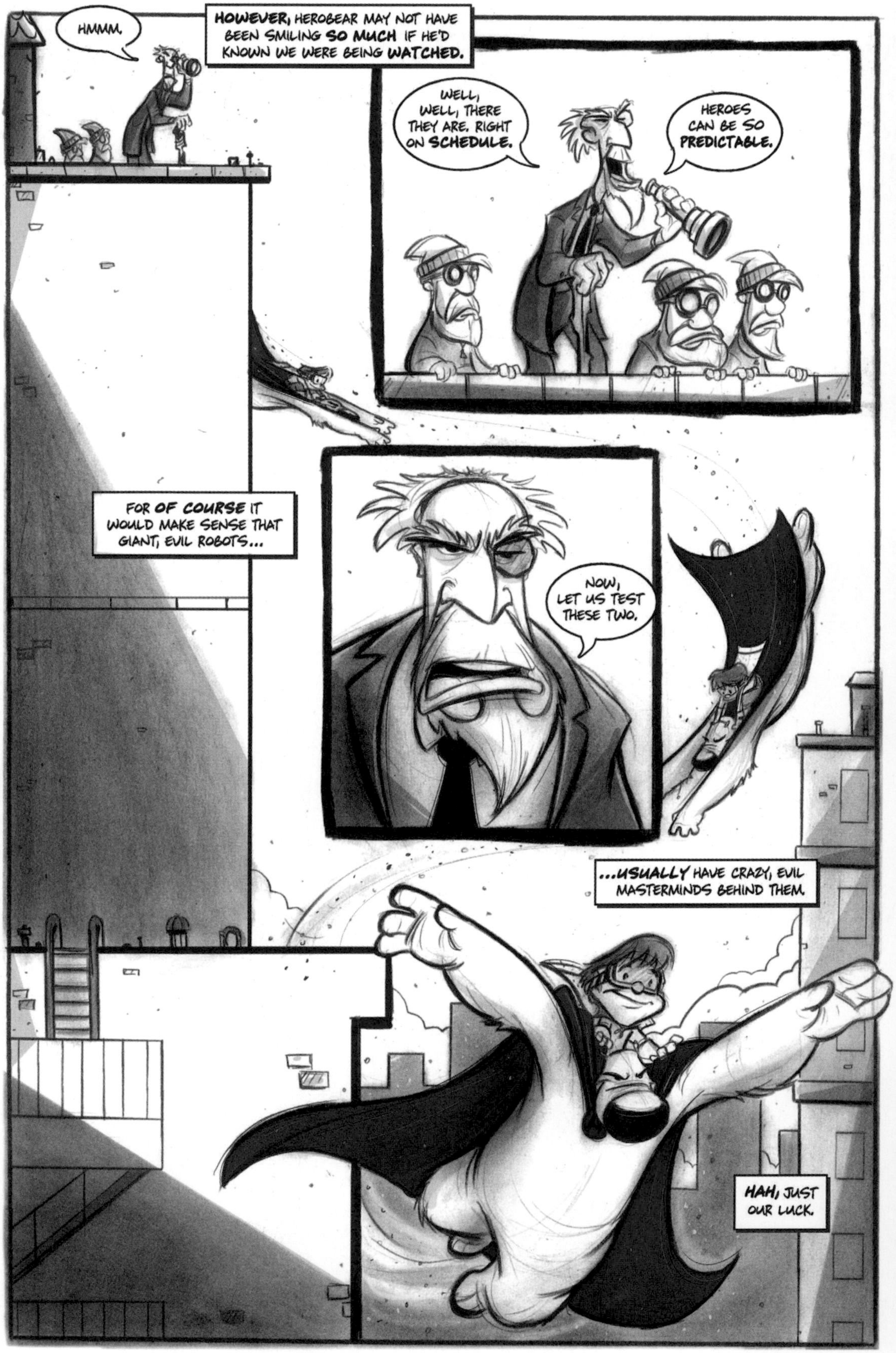
HMMM.
HOWEVER, HEROBEAR MAY NOT HAVE BEEN SMILING SO MUCH IF HE'D KNOWN WE WERE BEING WATCHED.
WELL, WELL, THERE THEY ARE. RIGHT ON SCHEDULE.
HEROES CAN BE SO PREDICTABLE.
FOR OF COURSE IT WOULD MAKE SENSE THAT GIANT, EVIL ROBOTS...
NOW, LET US TEST THESE TWO.
...USUALLY HAVE CRAZY, EVIL MASTERMINDS BEHIND THEM.
HAH, JUST OUR LUCK.

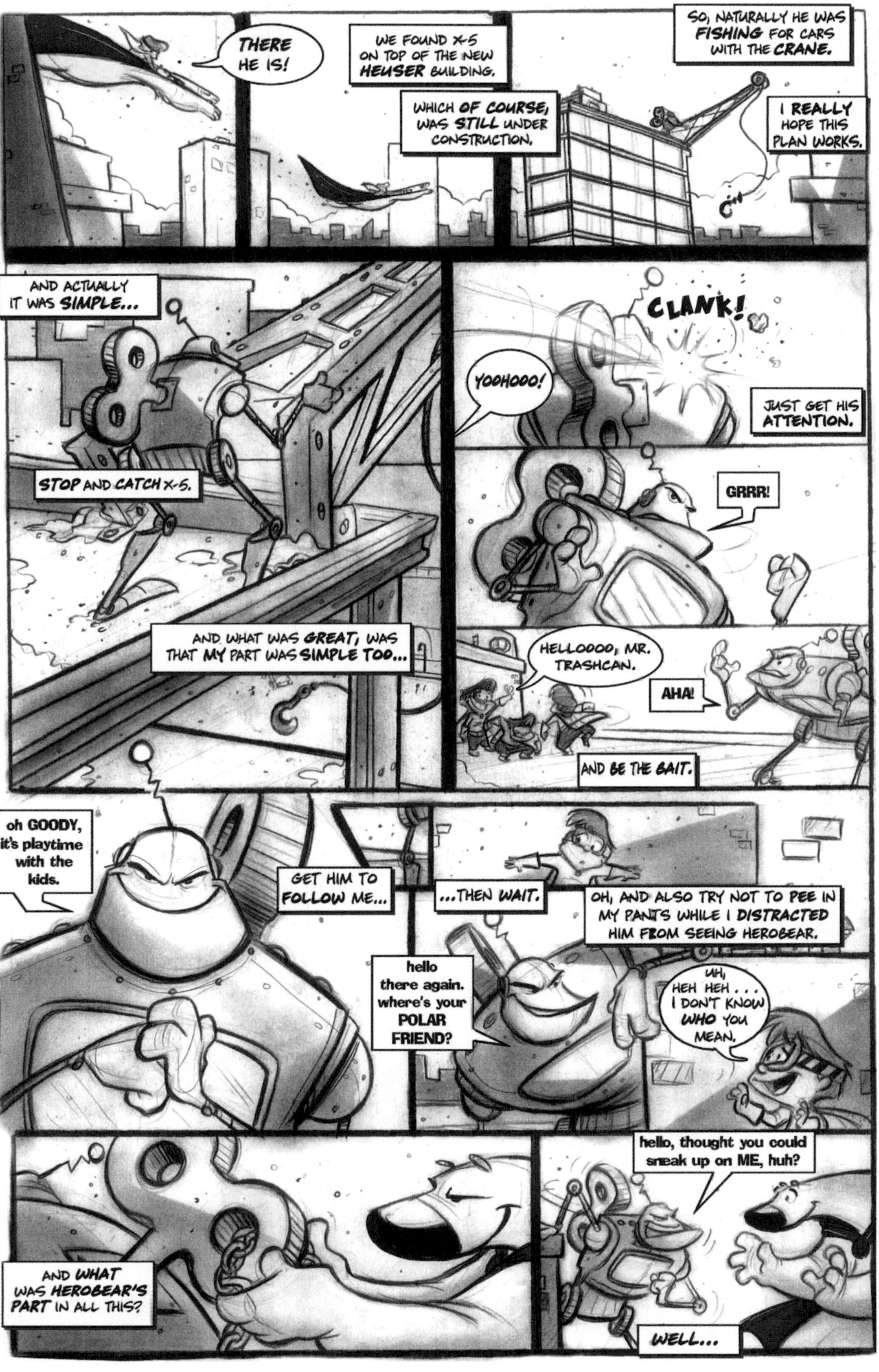
THERE HE IS!
WE FOUND X-5 ON TOP OF THE NEW HEUSER BUILDING.
WHICH OF COURSE, WAS STILL UNDER CONSTRUCTION.
SO, NATURALLY HE WAS FISHING FOR CARS WITH THE CRANE.
I REALLY HOPE THIS PLAN WORKS.
AND ACTUALLY IT WAS SIMPLE...
STOP AND CATCH X-5.
AND WHAT WAS GREAT, WAS THAT MY PART WAS SIMPLE TOO...
YOOHOOO!
CLANK!
JUST GET HIS ATTENTION.
GRRR!
HELLOOOO, MR. TRASHCAN.
AHA!
AND BE THE BAIT.
oh GOODY, it's playtime with the kids.
GET HIM TO FOLLOW ME...
...THEN WAIT.
OH, AND ALSO TRY NOT TO PEE IN MY PANTS WHILE I DISTRACTED HIM FROM SEEING HEROBEAR.
hello there again. where's your POLAR FRIEND?
UH, HEH HEH . . . I DON'T KNOW WHO YOU MEAN.
AND WHAT WAS HEROBEAR'S PART IN ALL THIS?
hello, thought you could sneak up on ME, huh?
WELL...

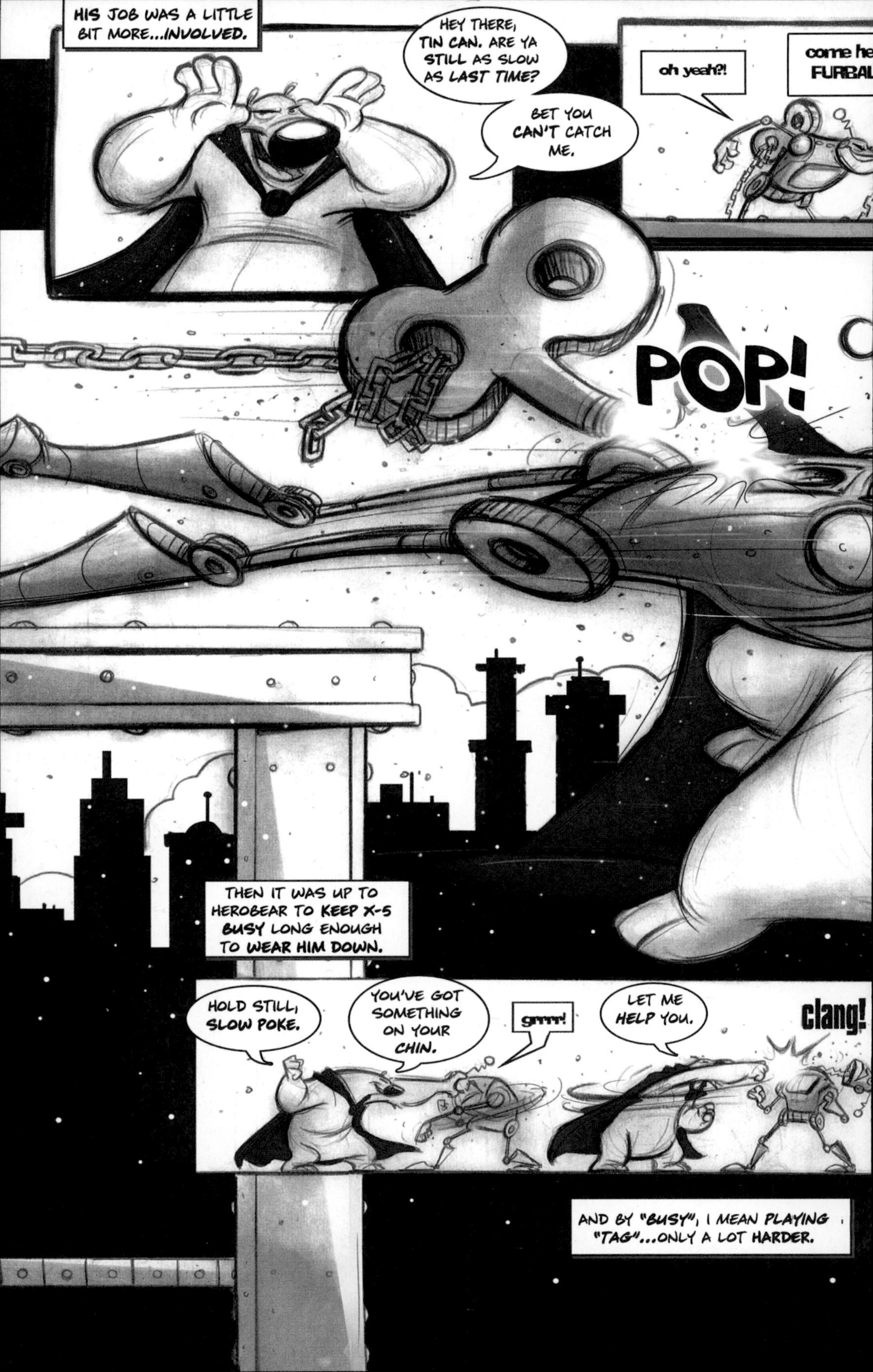
HIS JOB WAS A LITTLE BIT MORE...INVOLVED.
HEY THERE, TIN CAN. ARE YA STILL AS SLOW AS LAST TIME?
BET YOU CAN'T CATCH ME.
oh yeah?!
POP!
THEN IT WAS UP TO HEROBEAR TO KEEP X-5 BUSY LONG ENOUGH TO WEAR HIM DOWN.
HOLD STILL, SLOW POKE.
YOU'VE GOT SOMETHING ON YOUR CHIN.
grrrr!
LET ME HELP YOU.
clang!
AND BY "BUSY", I MEAN PLAYING "TAG"...ONLY A LOT HARDER.

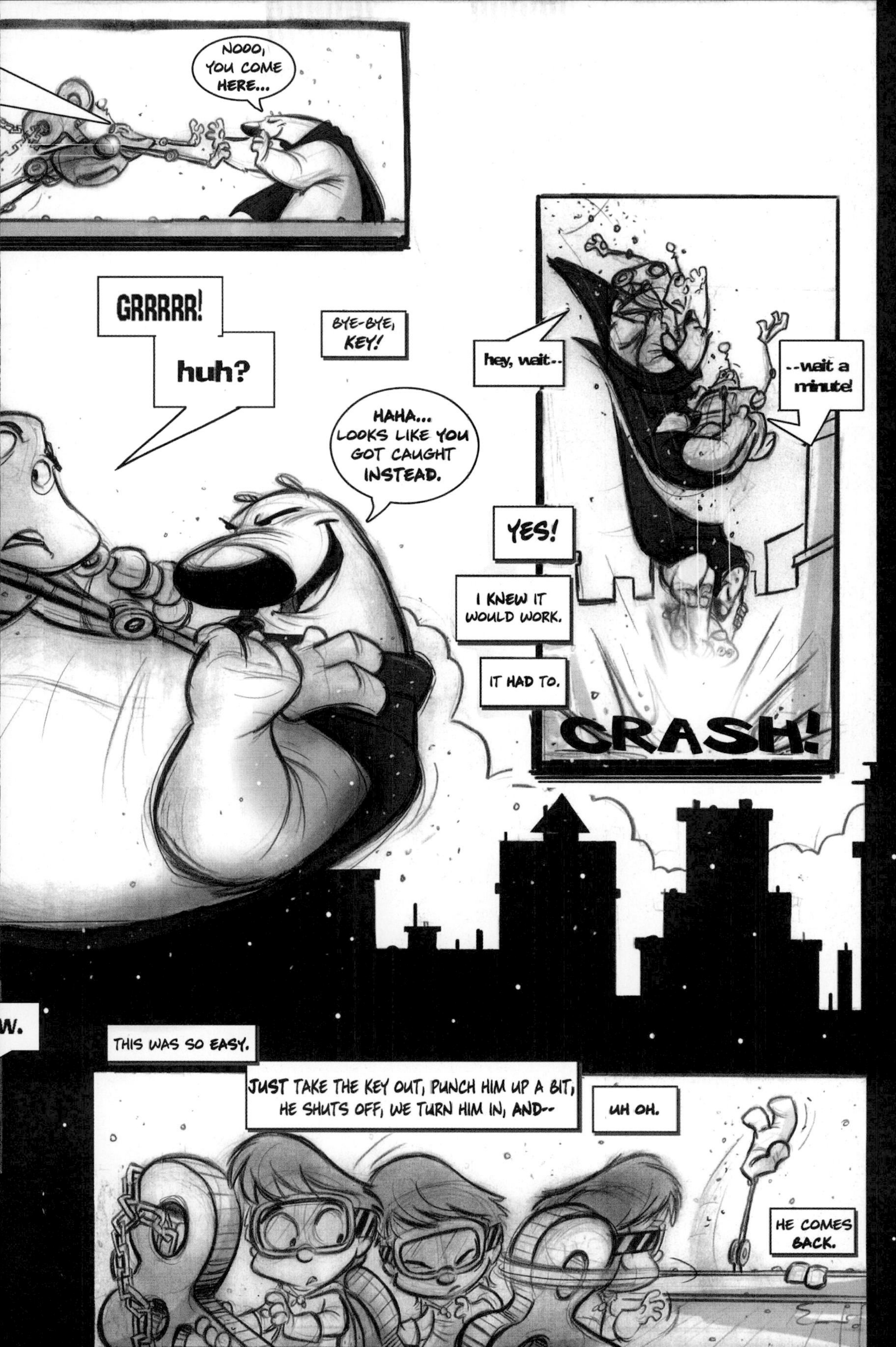
NOOO, YOU COME HERE...
GRRRRR!
huh?
BYE-BYE, KEY!
HAHA... LOOKS LIKE YOU GOT CAUGHT INSTEAD.
hey, wait--
--wait a minute!
YES!
I KNEW IT WOULD WORK.
IT HAD TO.
CRASH!
W.
THIS WAS SO EASY.
JUST TAKE THE KEY OUT, PUNCH HIM UP A BIT, HE SHUTS OFF, WE TURN HIM IN, AND--
UH OH.
HE COMES BACK.

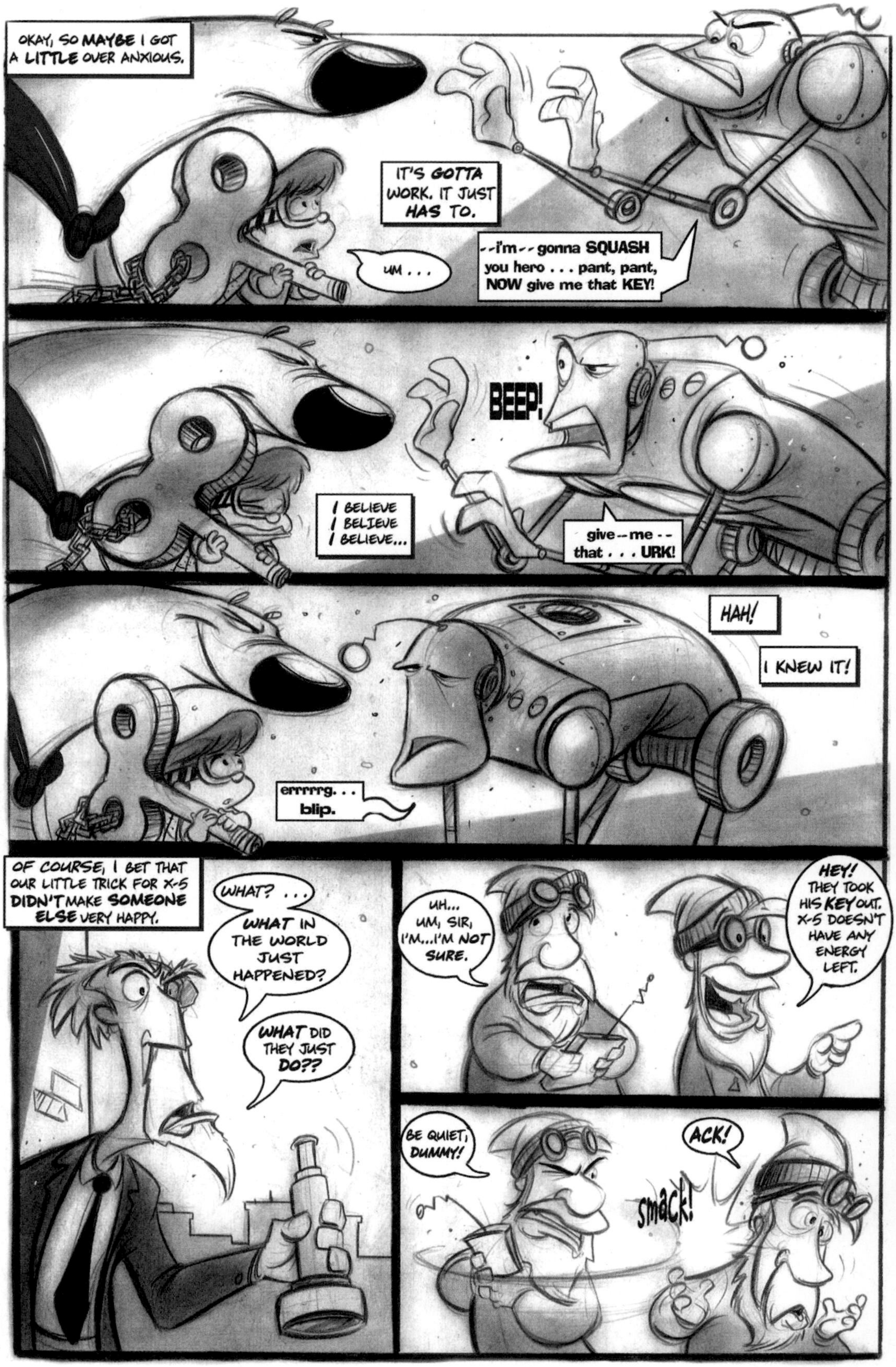
OKAY, SO MAYBE I GOT A LITTLE OVER ANXIOUS.
IT'S GOTTA WORK. IT JUST HAS TO.
UM . . .
--i'm-- gonna SQUASH you hero . . . pant, pant, NOW give me that KEY!
BEEP!
I BELIEVE I BELIEVE I BELIEVE...
give--me-- that . . . URK!
HAH!
I KNEW IT!
errrrrg. . . blip.
OF COURSE, I BET THAT OUR LITTLE TRICK FOR X-5 DIDN'T MAKE SOMEONE ELSE VERY HAPPY.
WHAT? . . .
WHAT IN THE WORLD JUST HAPPENED?
WHAT DID THEY JUST DO??
UH... UM, SIR, I'M...I'M NOT SURE.
HEY! THEY TOOK HIS KEY OUT. X-5 DOESN'T HAVE ANY ENERGY LEFT.
BE QUIET, DUMMY!
ACK!
smack!

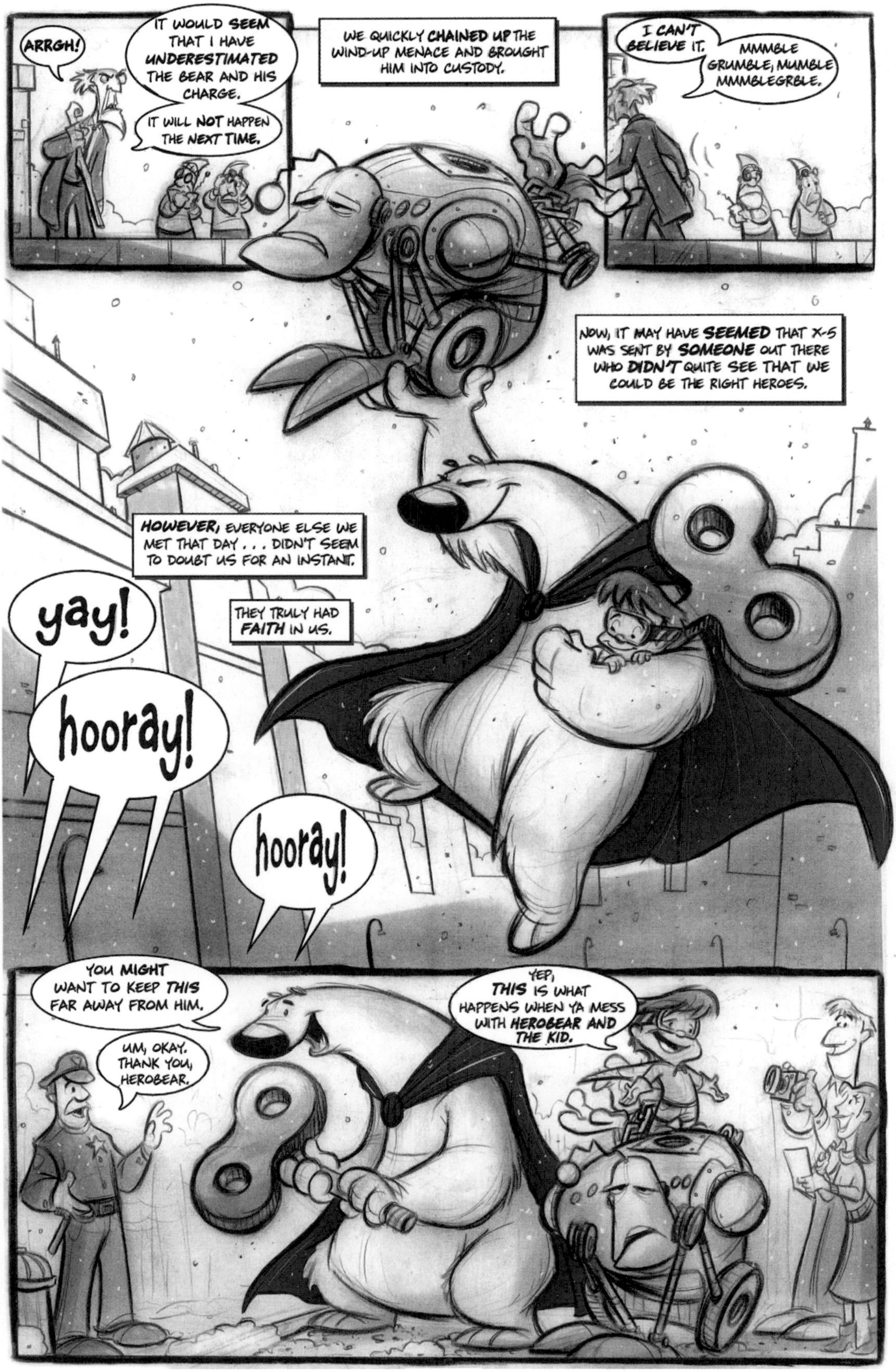
ARRGH!
IT WOULD SEEM THAT I HAVE UNDERESTIMATED THE BEAR AND HIS CHARGE.
IT WILL NOT HAPPEN THE NEXT TIME.
WE QUICKLY CHAINED UP THE WIND-UP MENACE AND BROUGHT HIM INTO CUSTODY.
I CAN'T BELIEVE IT.
MMMBLE GRUMBLE, MUMBLE MMMBLEGRBLE.
NOW, IT MAY HAVE SEEMED THAT X-5 WAS SENT BY SOMEONE OUT THERE WHO DIDN'T QUITE SEE THAT WE COULD BE THE RIGHT HEROES.
HOWEVER, EVERYONE ELSE WE MET THAT DAY . . . DIDN'T SEEM TO DOUBT US FOR AN INSTANT.
THEY TRULY HAD FAITH IN US.
yay!
hooray!
hooray!
YOU MIGHT WANT TO KEEP THIS FAR AWAY FROM HIM.
UM, OKAY. THANK YOU, HEROBEAR.
YEP, THIS IS WHAT HAPPENS WHEN YA MESS WITH HEROBEAR AND THE KID.

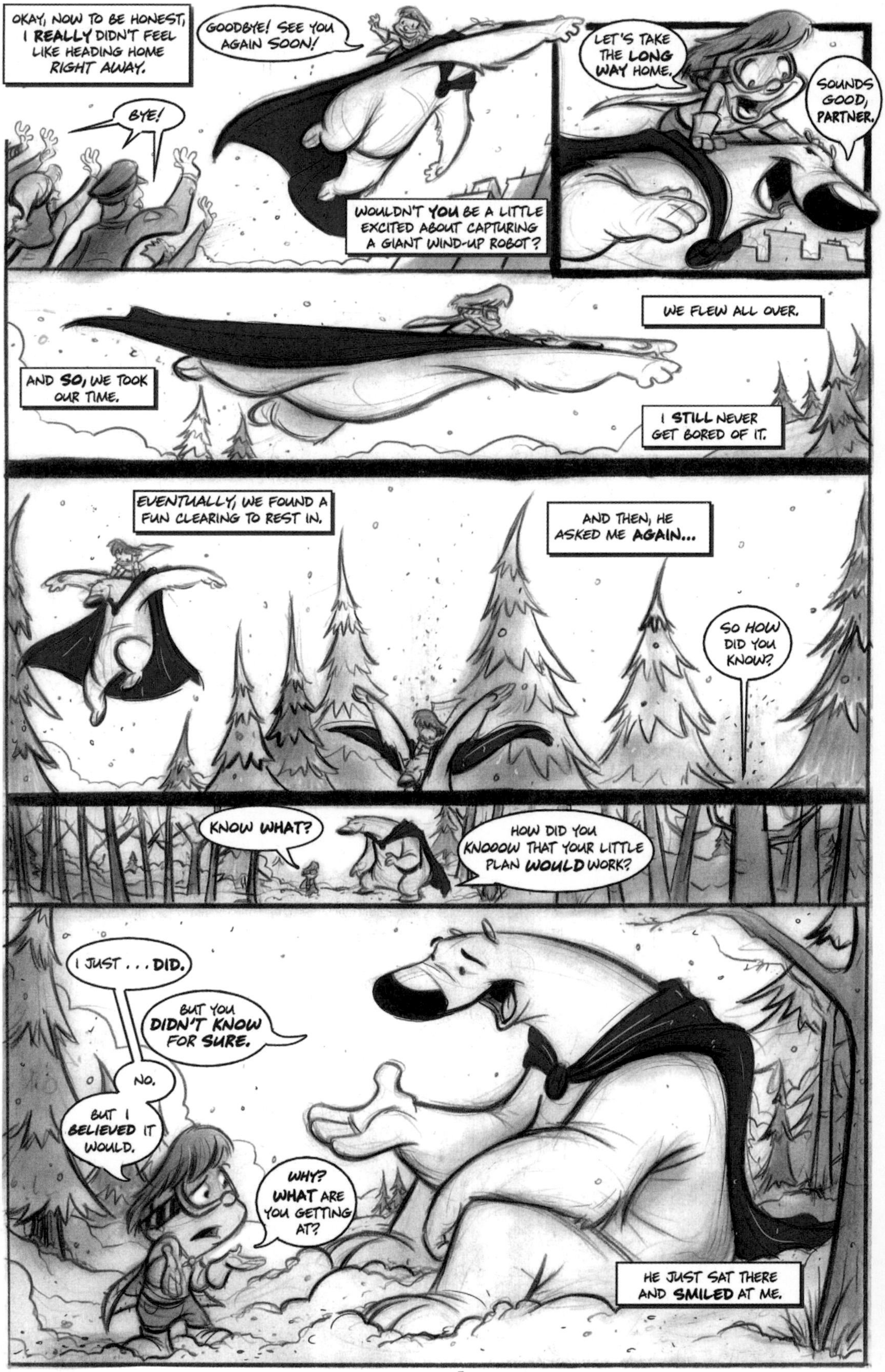

OKAY, NOW TO BE HONEST, I REALLY DIDN'T FEEL LIKE HEADING HOME RIGHT AWAY.
GOODBYE! SEE YOU AGAIN SOON!
BYE!
WOULDN'T YOU BE A LITTLE EXCITED ABOUT CAPTURING A GIANT WIND-UP ROBOT?
LET'S TAKE THE LONG WAY HOME.
SOUNDS GOOD, PARTNER.
AND SO, WE TOOK OUR TIME.
WE FLEW ALL OVER.
I STILL NEVER GET BORED OF IT.
EVENTUALLY, WE FOUND A FUN CLEARING TO REST IN.
AND THEN, HE ASKED ME AGAIN...
SO HOW DID YOU KNOW?
KNOW WHAT?
HOW DID YOU KNOOOW THAT YOUR LITTLE PLAN WOULD WORK?
I JUST . . . DID.
BUT YOU DIDN'T KNOW FOR SURE.
NO.
BUT I BELIEVED IT WOULD.
WHY? WHAT ARE YOU GETTING AT?
HE JUST SAT THERE AND SMILED AT ME.

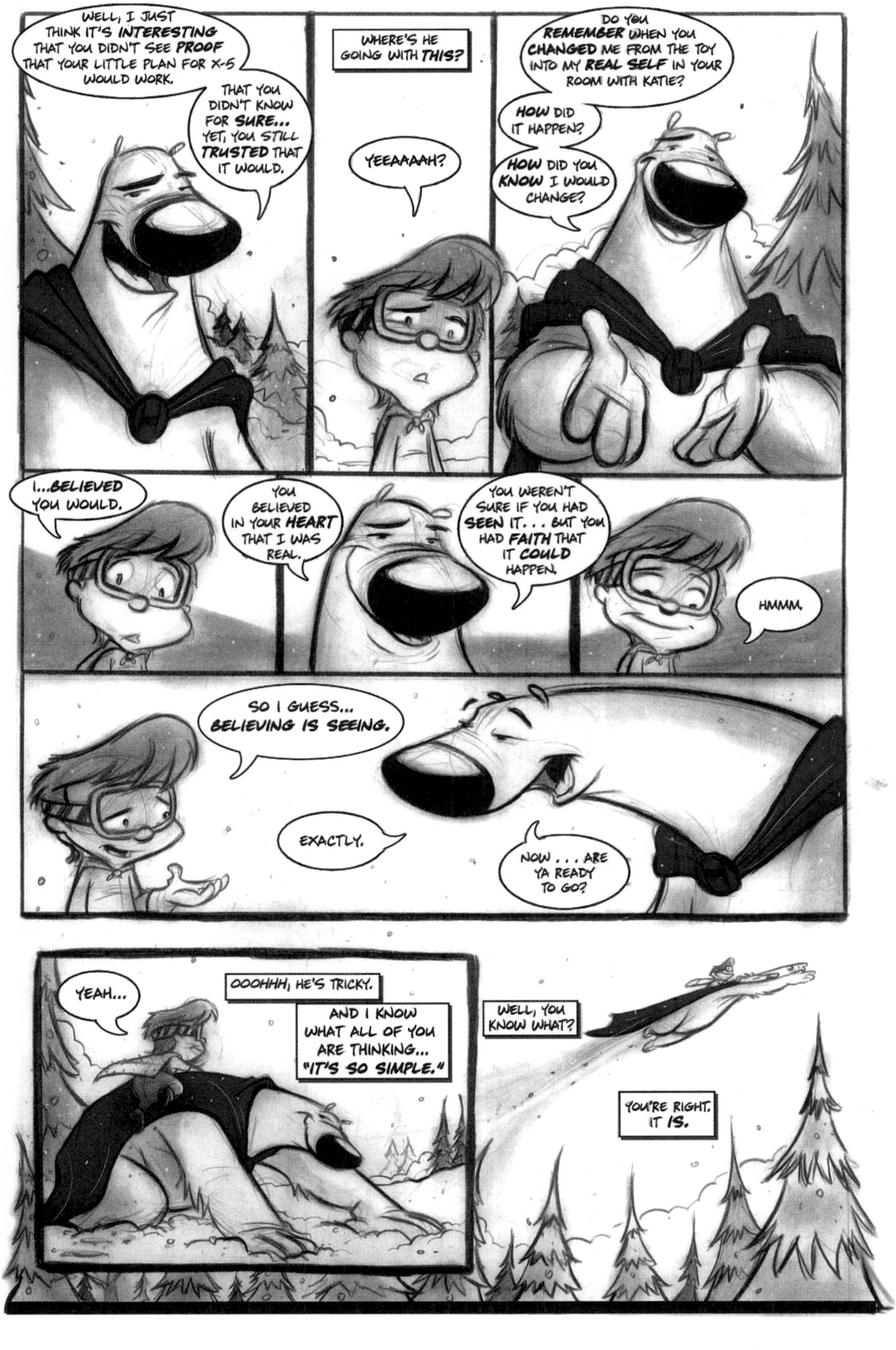
WELL, I JUST THINK IT'S INTERESTING THAT YOU DIDN'T SEE PROOF THAT YOUR LITTLE PLAN FOR X-5 WOULD WORK.
THAT YOU DIDN'T KNOW FOR SURE... YET, YOU STILL TRUSTED THAT IT WOULD.
WHERE'S HE GOING WITH THIS?
YEEAAAAH?
DO YOU REMEMBER WHEN YOU CHANGED ME FROM THE TOY INTO MY REAL SELF IN YOUR ROOM WITH KATIE?
HOW DID IT HAPPEN?
HOW DID YOU KNOW I WOULD CHANGE?
I...BELIEVED YOU WOULD.
YOU BELIEVED IN YOUR HEART THAT I WAS REAL.
YOU WEREN'T SURE IF YOU HAD SEEN IT. . . BUT YOU HAD FAITH THAT IT COULD HAPPEN.
HMMM.
SO I GUESS... BELIEVING IS SEEING.
EXACTLY.
NOW . . . ARE YA READY TO GO?
YEAH...
OOOHHH, HE'S TRICKY.
AND I KNOW WHAT ALL OF YOU ARE THINKING... "IT'S SO SIMPLE."
WELL, YOU KNOW WHAT?
YOU'RE RIGHT. IT IS.

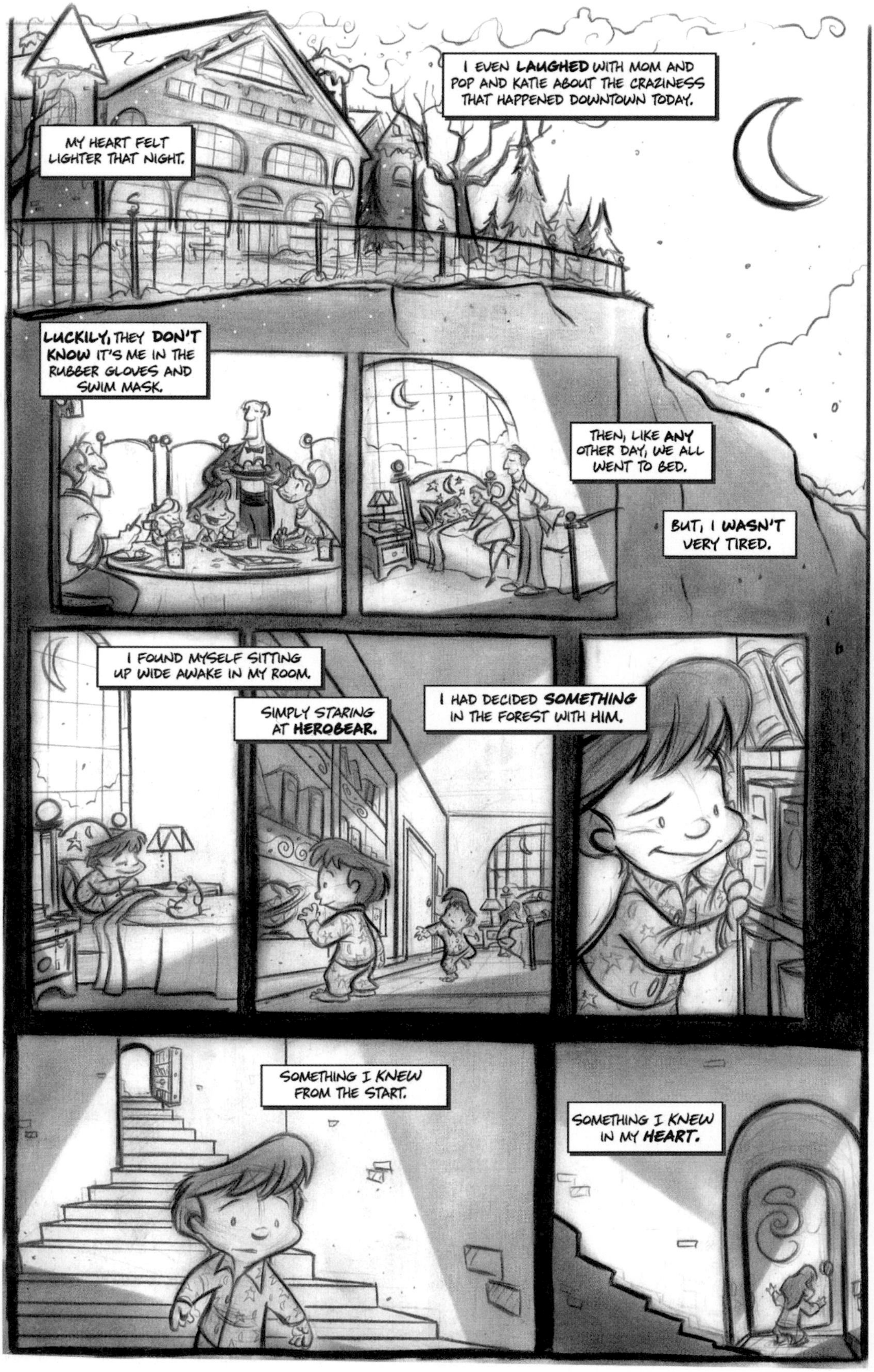

MY HEART FELT LIGHTER THAT NIGHT.
I EVEN LAUGHED WITH MOM AND POP AND KATIE ABOUT THE CRAZINESS THAT HAPPENED DOWNTOWN TODAY.
LUCKILY, THEY DON'T KNOW IT'S ME IN THE RUBBER GLOVES AND SWIM MASK.
THEN, LIKE ANY OTHER DAY, WE ALL WENT TO BED.
BUT, I WASN'T VERY TIRED.
I FOUND MYSELF SITTING UP WIDE AWAKE IN MY ROOM.
SIMPLY STARING AT HEROBEAR.
I HAD DECIDED SOMETHING IN THE FOREST WITH HIM.
SOMETHING I KNEW FROM THE START.
SOMETHING I KNEW IN MY HEART.

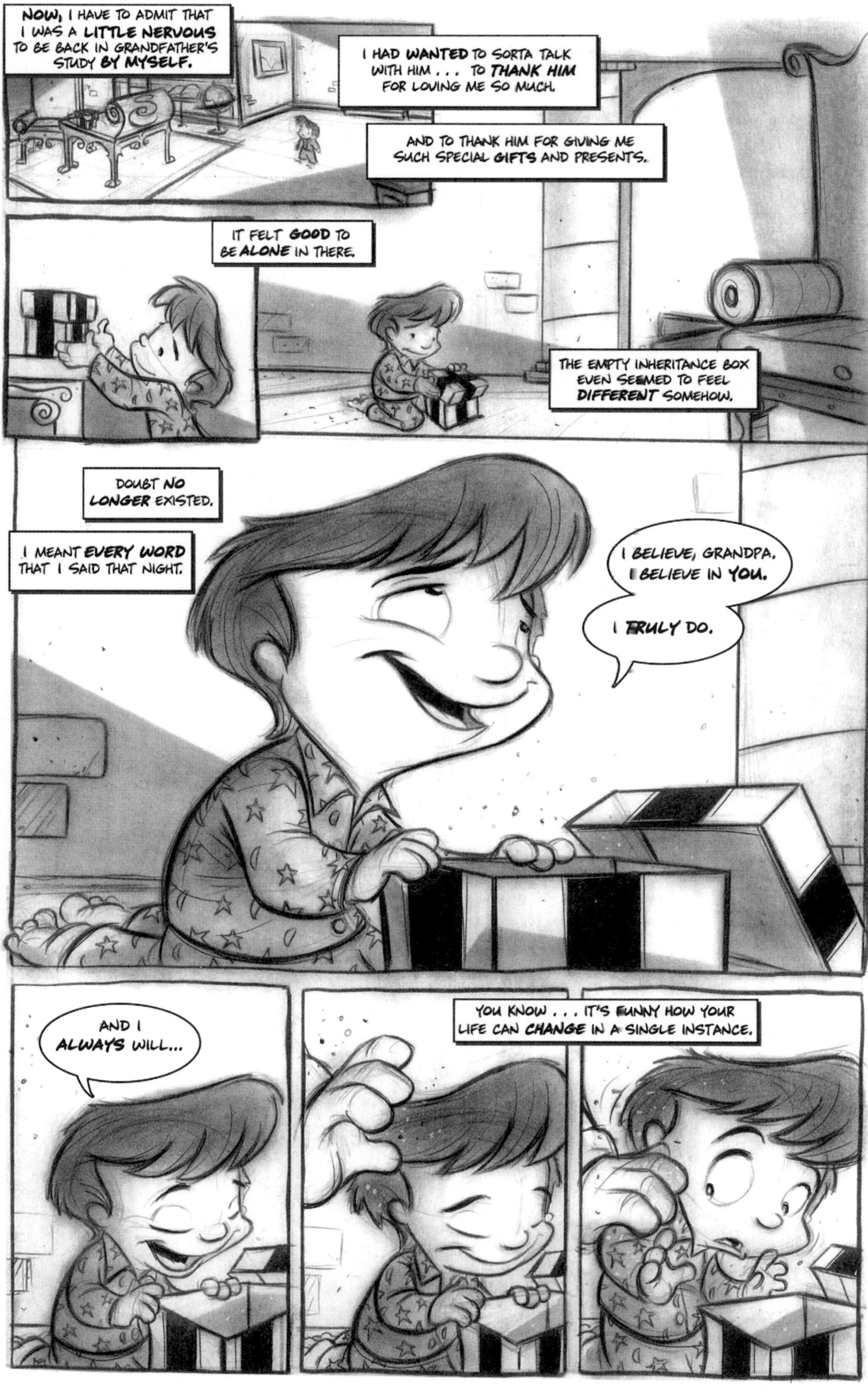
NOW, I HAVE TO ADMIT THAT I WAS A LITTLE NERVOUS TO BE BACK IN GRANDFATHER'S STUDY BY MYSELF.
I HAD WANTED TO SORTA TALK WITH HIM . . . TO THANK HIM FOR LOVING ME SO MUCH.
AND TO THANK HIM FOR GIVING ME SUCH SPECIAL GIFTS AND PRESENTS.
IT FELT GOOD TO BE ALONE IN THERE.
THE EMPTY INHERITANCE BOX EVEN SEEMED TO FEEL DIFFERENT SOMEHOW.
DOUBT NO LONGER EXISTED.
I MEANT EVERY WORD THAT I SAID THAT NIGHT.
I BELIEVE, GRANDPA. I BELIEVE IN YOU.
I TRULY DO.
AND I ALWAYS WILL...
YOU KNOW . . . IT'S FUNNY HOW YOUR LIFE CAN CHANGE IN A SINGLE INSTANCE.

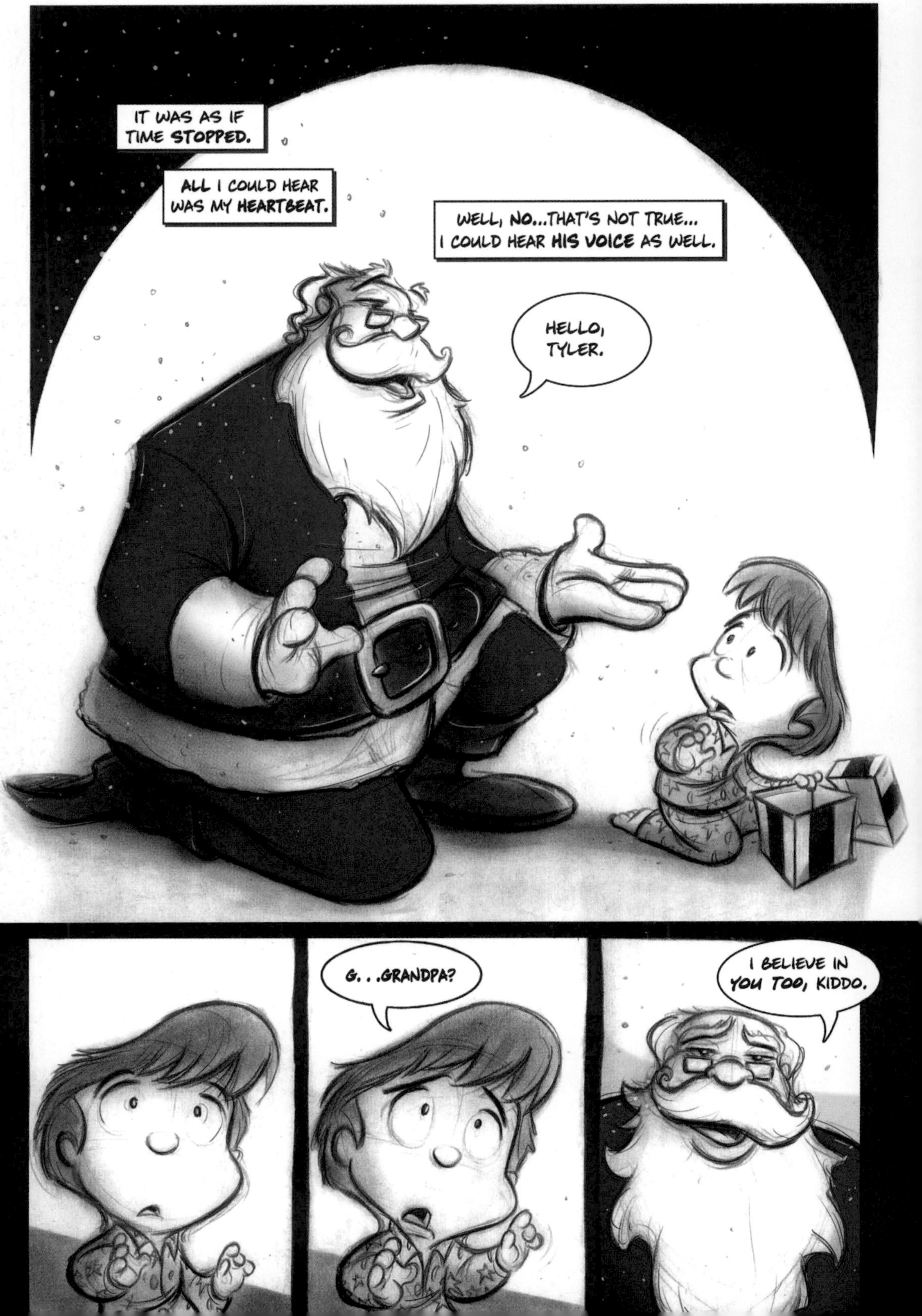
IT WAS AS IF TIME STOPPED.
ALL I COULD HEAR WAS MY HEARTBEAT.
WELL, NO...THAT'S NOT TRUE... I COULD HEAR HIS VOICE AS WELL.
HELLO, TYLER.
G. . .GRANDPA?
I BELIEVE IN YOU TOO, KIDDO.

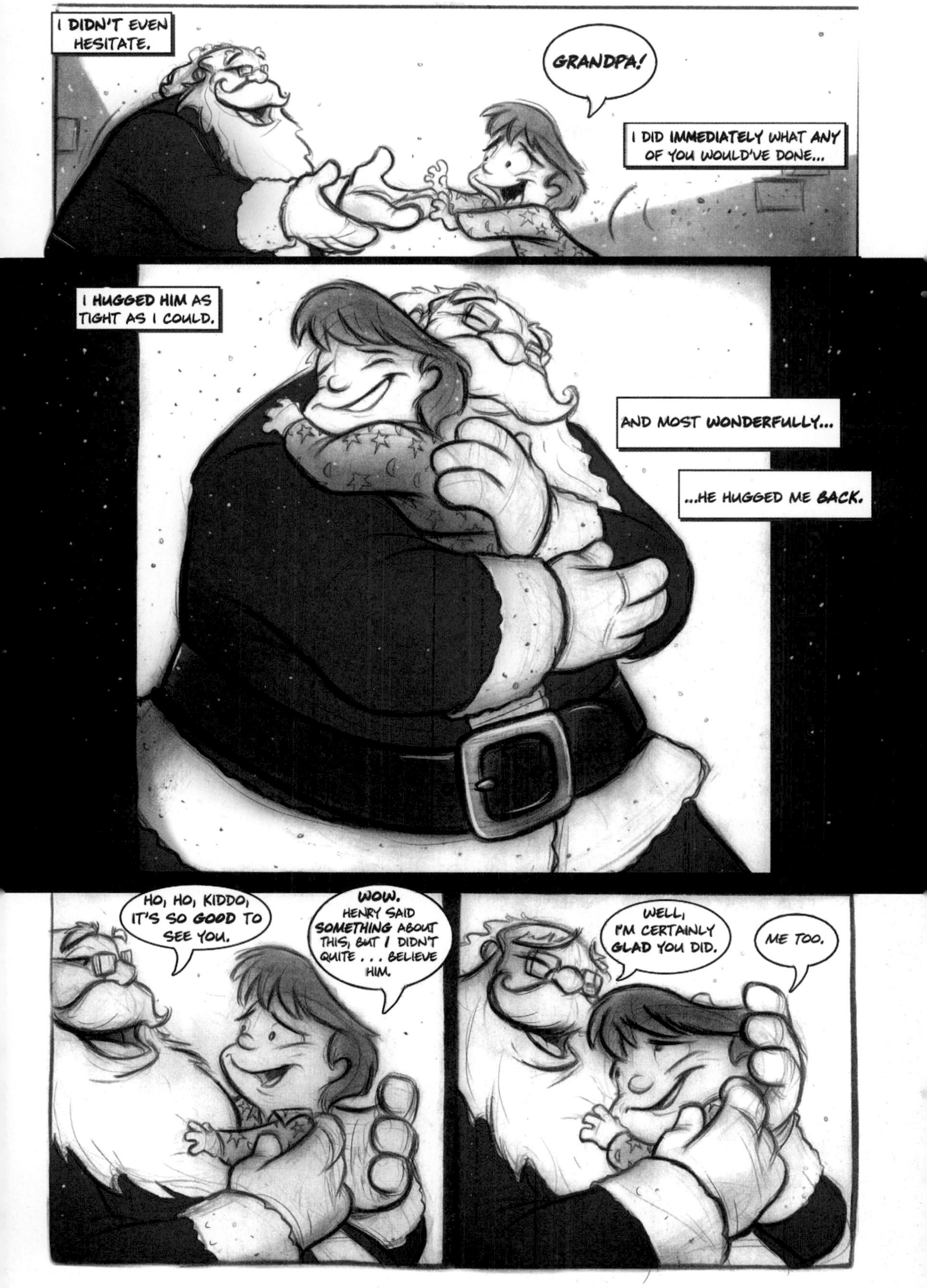
I DIDN'T EVEN HESITATE.
GRANDPA!
I DID IMMEDIATELY WHAT ANY OF YOU WOULD'VE DONE...
I HUGGED HIM AS TIGHT AS I COULD.
AND MOST WONDERFULLY...
...HE HUGGED ME BACK.
HO, HO, KIDDO, IT'S SO GOOD TO SEE YOU.
WOW. HENRY SAID SOMETHING ABOUT THIS, BUT I DIDN'T QUITE . . . BELIEVE HIM.
WELL, I'M CERTAINLY GLAD YOU DID.
ME TOO.

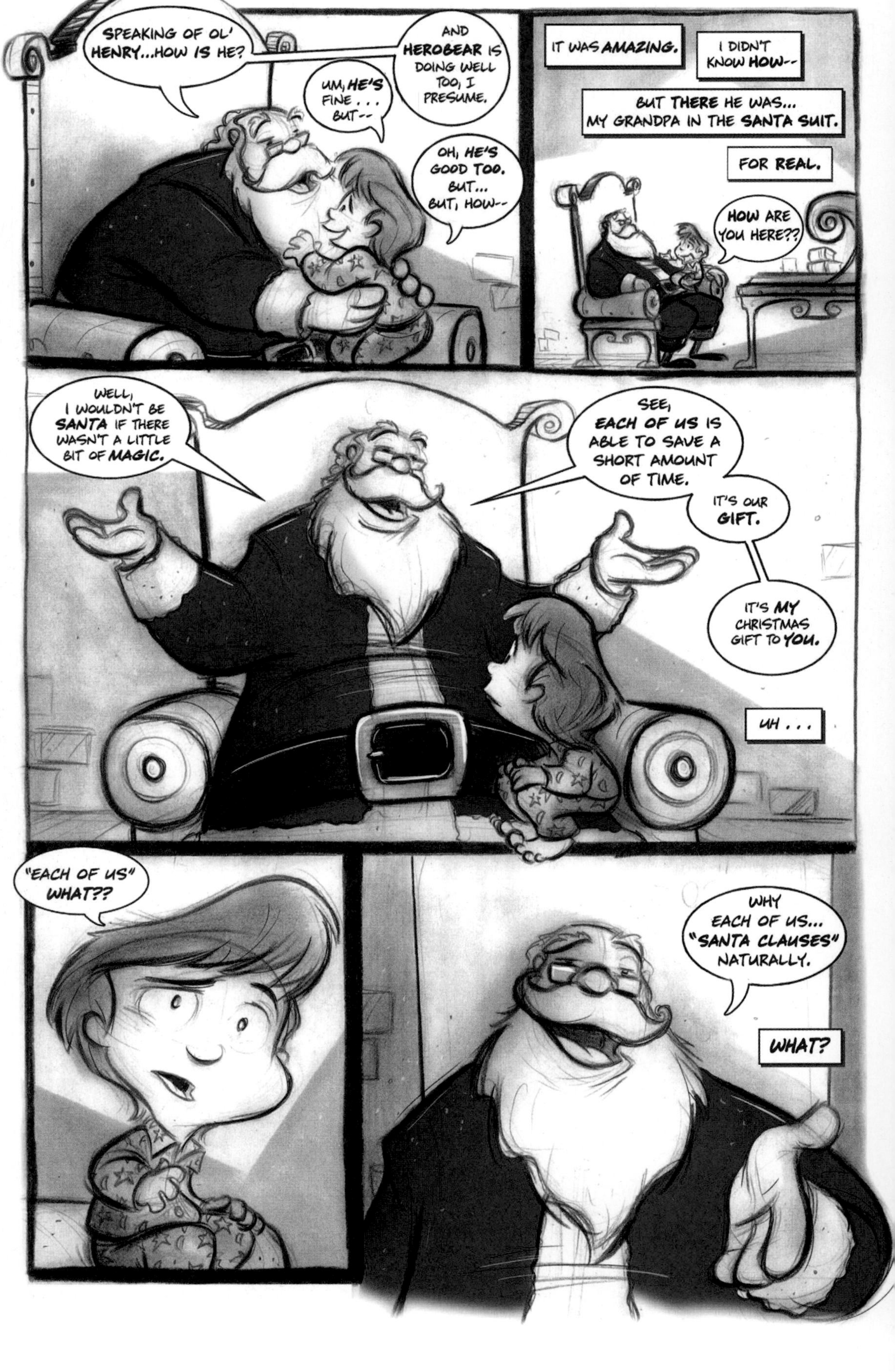

SPEAKING OF OL' HENRY...HOW IS HE?
UM, HE'S FINE . . . BUT--
AND HEROBEAR IS DOING WELL TOO, I PRESUME.
OH, HE'S GOOD TOO. BUT... BUT, HOW--
IT WAS AMAZING.
I DIDN'T KNOW HOW--
BUT THERE HE WAS... MY GRANDPA IN THE SANTA SUIT.
FOR REAL.
HOW ARE YOU HERE??
WELL, I WOULDN'T BE SANTA IF THERE WASN'T A LITTLE BIT OF MAGIC.
SEE, EACH OF US IS ABLE TO SAVE A SHORT AMOUNT OF TIME.
IT'S OUR GIFT.
IT'S MY CHRISTMAS GIFT TO YOU.
UH . . .
"EACH OF US" WHAT??
WHY EACH OF US... "SANTA CLAUSES" NATURALLY.
WHAT?

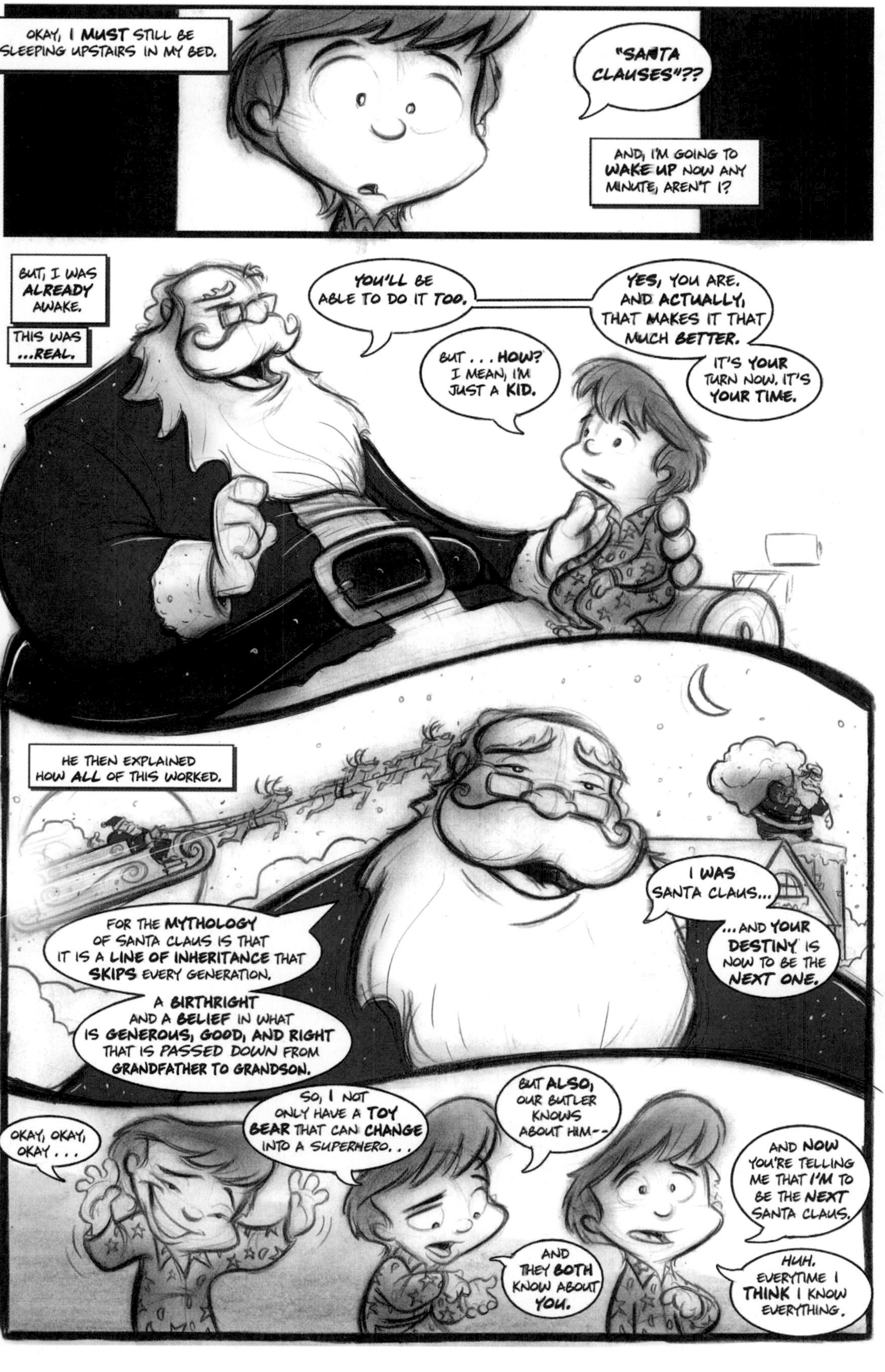
OKAY, I MUST STILL BE SLEEPING UPSTAIRS IN MY BED.
"SANTA CLAUSES"??
AND, I'M GOING TO WAKE UP NOW ANY MINUTE, AREN'T I?
BUT, I WAS ALREADY AWAKE.
THIS WAS ...REAL.
YOU'LL BE ABLE TO DO IT TOO.
YES, YOU ARE. AND ACTUALLY, THAT MAKES IT THAT MUCH BETTER.
BUT . . . HOW? I MEAN, I'M JUST A KID.
IT'S YOUR TURN NOW. IT'S YOUR TIME.
HE THEN EXPLAINED HOW ALL OF THIS WORKED.
I WAS SANTA CLAUS...
...AND YOUR DESTINY IS NOW TO BE THE NEXT ONE.
FOR THE MYTHOLOGY OF SANTA CLAUS IS THAT IT IS A LINE OF INHERITANCE THAT SKIPS EVERY GENERATION.
A BIRTHRIGHT AND A BELIEF IN WHAT IS GENEROUS, GOOD, AND RIGHT THAT IS PASSED DOWN FROM GRANDFATHER TO GRANDSON.
OKAY, OKAY, OKAY . . .
SO, I NOT ONLY HAVE A TOY BEAR THAT CAN CHANGE INTO A SUPERHERO. . .
BUT ALSO, OUR BUTLER KNOWS ABOUT HIM--
AND THEY BOTH KNOW ABOUT YOU.
AND NOW YOU'RE TELLING ME THAT I'M TO BE THE NEXT SANTA CLAUS.
HUH. EVERYTIME I THINK I KNOW EVERYTHING.

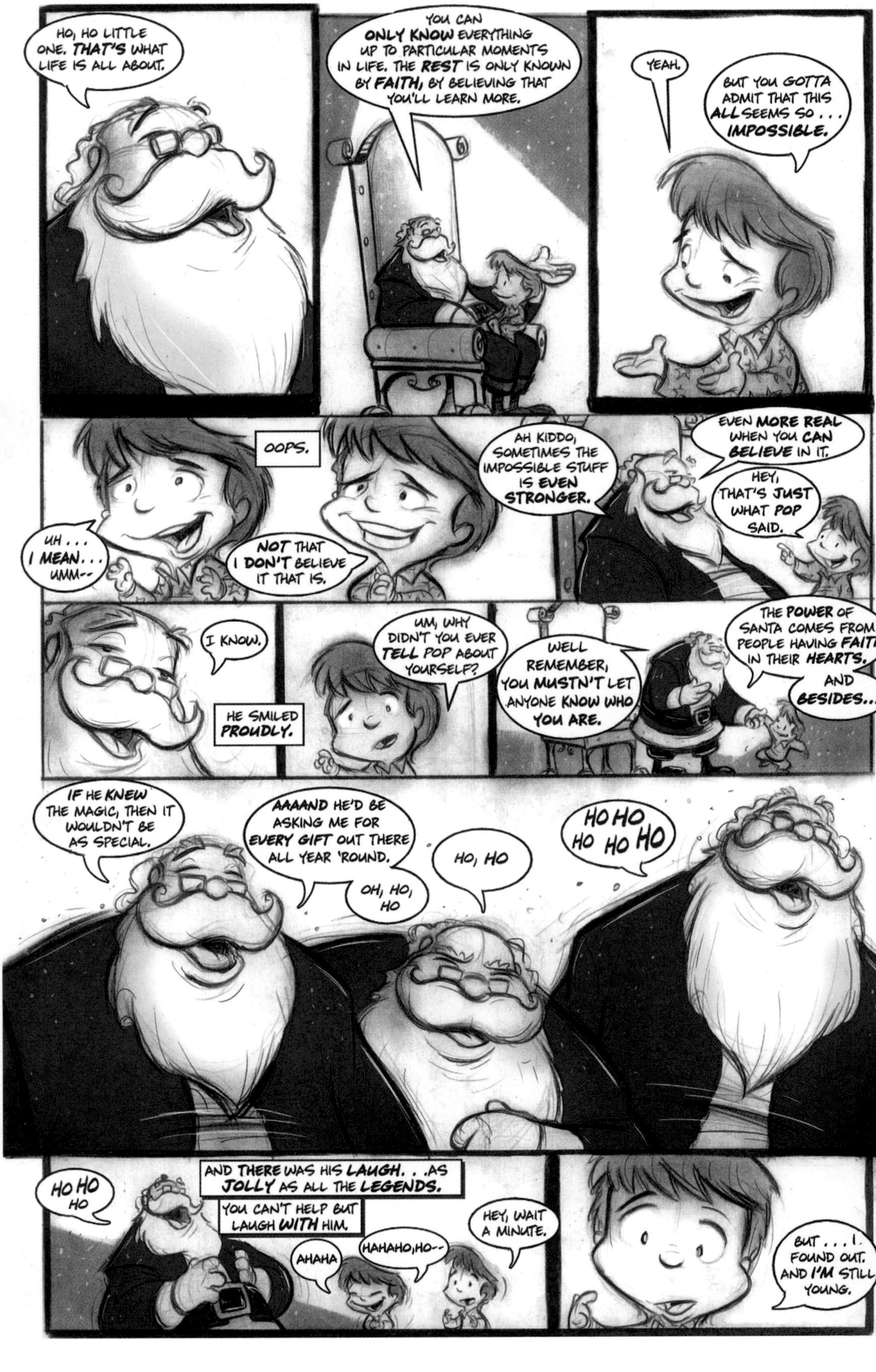
HO, HO LITTLE ONE. THAT'S WHAT LIFE IS ALL ABOUT.
YOU CAN ONLY KNOW EVERYTHING UP TO PARTICULAR MOMENTS IN LIFE. THE REST IS ONLY KNOWN BY FAITH, BY BELIEVING THAT YOU'LL LEARN MORE.
YEAH.
BUT YOU GOTTA ADMIT THAT THIS ALL SEEMS SO . . . IMPOSSIBLE.
UH . . . I MEAN . . . UMM--
OOPS.
NOT THAT I DON'T BELIEVE IT THAT IS.
AH KIDDO, SOMETIMES THE IMPOSSIBLE STUFF IS EVEN STRONGER.
EVEN MORE REAL WHEN YOU CAN BELIEVE IN IT.
HEY, THAT'S JUST WHAT POP SAID.
I KNOW.
HE SMILED PROUDLY.
UM, WHY DIDN'T YOU EVER TELL POP ABOUT YOURSELF?
WELL REMEMBER, YOU MUSTN'T LET ANYONE KNOW WHO YOU ARE.
THE POWER OF SANTA COMES FROM PEOPLE HAVING FAITH IN THEIR HEARTS.
AND BESIDES...
IF HE KNEW THE MAGIC, THEN IT WOULDN'T BE AS SPECIAL.
AAAAND HE'D BE ASKING ME FOR EVERY GIFT OUT THERE ALL YEAR 'ROUND.
OH, HO, HO
HO, HO
HO HO HO HO HO
HO HO HO
AND THERE WAS HIS LAUGH. . .AS JOLLY AS ALL THE LEGENDS.
YOU CAN'T HELP BUT LAUGH WITH HIM.
AHAHA
HAHAHO,HO--
HEY, WAIT A MINUTE.
BUT . . . I FOUND OUT. AND I'M STILL YOUNG.

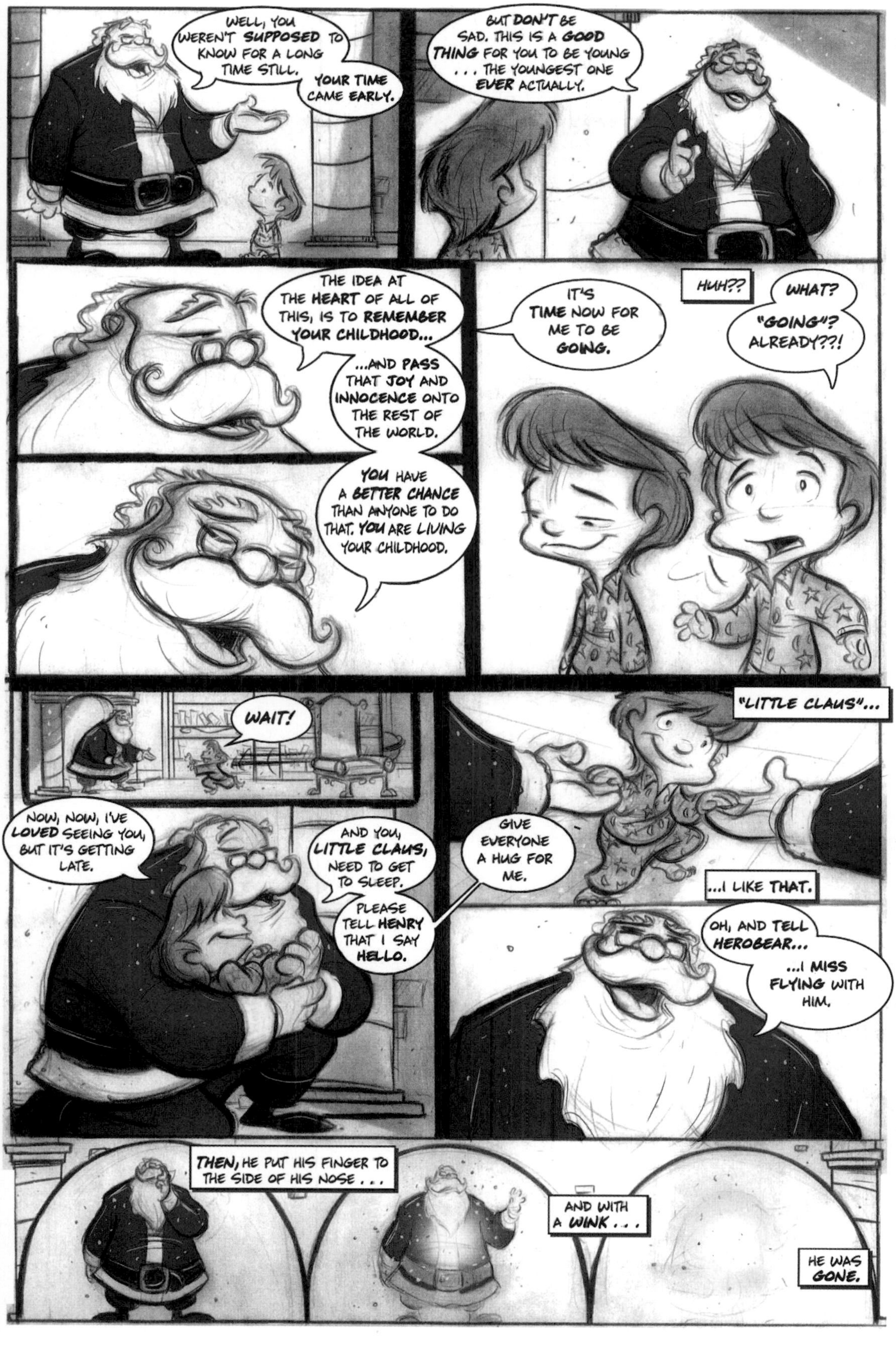
WELL, YOU WEREN'T SUPPOSED TO KNOW FOR A LONG TIME STILL.
YOUR TIME CAME EARLY.
BUT DON'T BE SAD. THIS IS A GOOD THING FOR YOU TO BE YOUNG . . . THE YOUNGEST ONE EVER ACTUALLY.
THE IDEA AT THE HEART OF ALL OF THIS, IS TO REMEMBER YOUR CHILDHOOD...
...AND PASS THAT JOY AND INNOCENCE ONTO THE REST OF THE WORLD.
YOU HAVE A BETTER CHANCE THAN ANYONE TO DO THAT. YOU ARE LIVING YOUR CHILDHOOD.
IT'S TIME NOW FOR ME TO BE GOING.
HUH??
WHAT? "GOING"? ALREADY??!
WAIT!
NOW, NOW, I'VE LOVED SEEING YOU, BUT IT'S GETTING LATE.
AND YOU, LITTLE CLAUS, NEED TO GET TO SLEEP.
PLEASE TELL HENRY THAT I SAY HELLO.
GIVE EVERYONE A HUG FOR ME.
"LITTLE CLAUS"...
...I LIKE THAT.
OH, AND TELL HEROBEAR...
...I MISS FLYING WITH HIM.
THEN, HE PUT HIS FINGER TO THE SIDE OF HIS NOSE . . .
AND WITH A WINK . . .
HE WAS GONE.

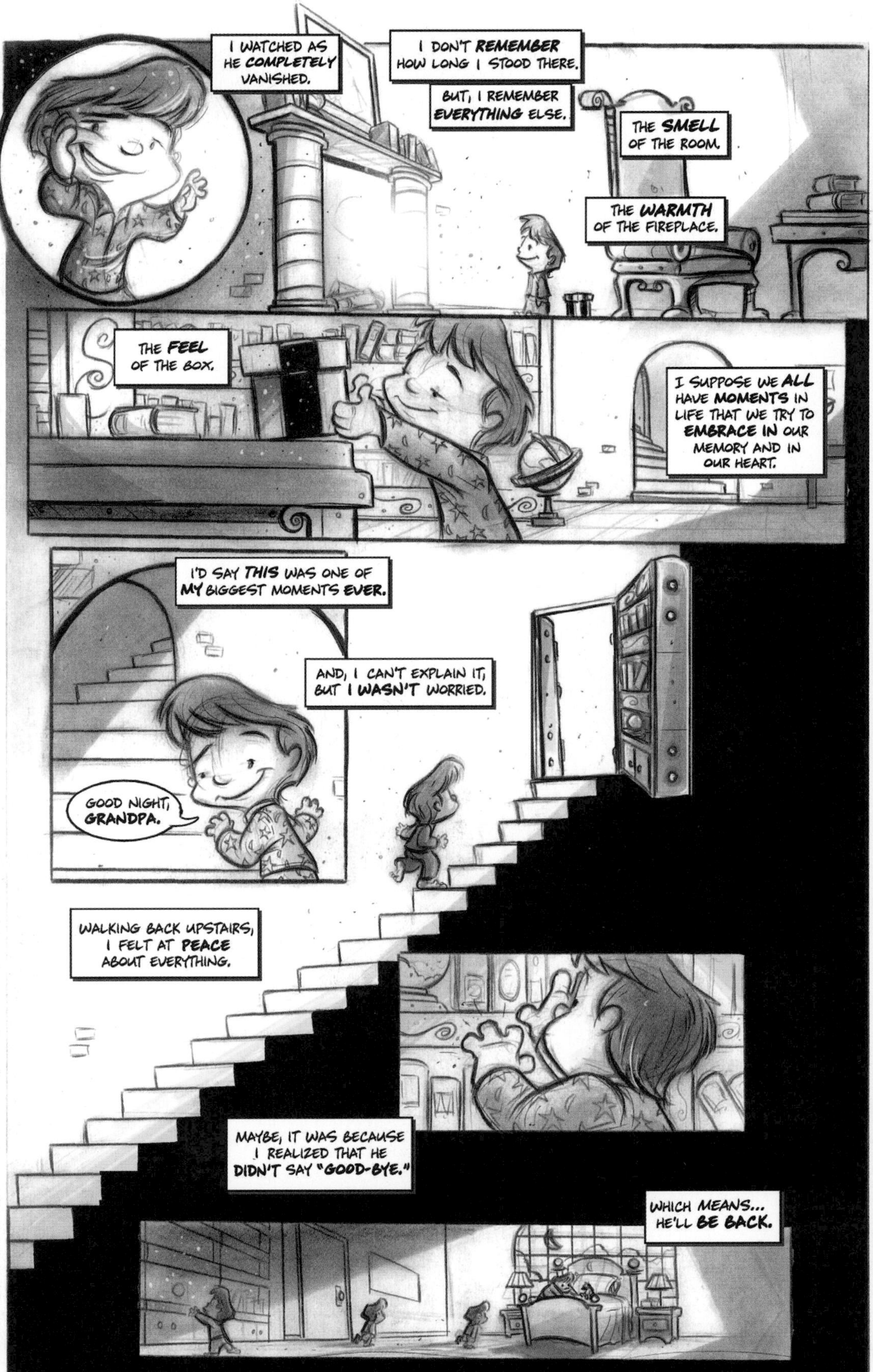
I WATCHED AS HE COMPLETELY VANISHED.
I DON'T REMEMBER HOW LONG I STOOD THERE.
BUT, I REMEMBER EVERYTHING ELSE.
THE SMELL OF THE ROOM.
THE WARMTH OF THE FIREPLACE.
THE FEEL OF THE BOX.
I SUPPOSE WE ALL HAVE MOMENTS IN LIFE THAT WE TRY TO EMBRACE IN OUR MEMORY AND IN OUR HEART.
I'D SAY THIS WAS ONE OF MY BIGGEST MOMENTS EVER.
AND, I CAN'T EXPLAIN IT, BUT I WASN'T WORRIED.
GOOD NIGHT, GRANDPA.
WALKING BACK UPSTAIRS, I FELT AT PEACE ABOUT EVERYTHING.
MAYBE, IT WAS BECAUSE I REALIZED THAT HE DIDN'T SAY "GOOD-BYE."
WHICH MEANS... HE'LL BE BACK.

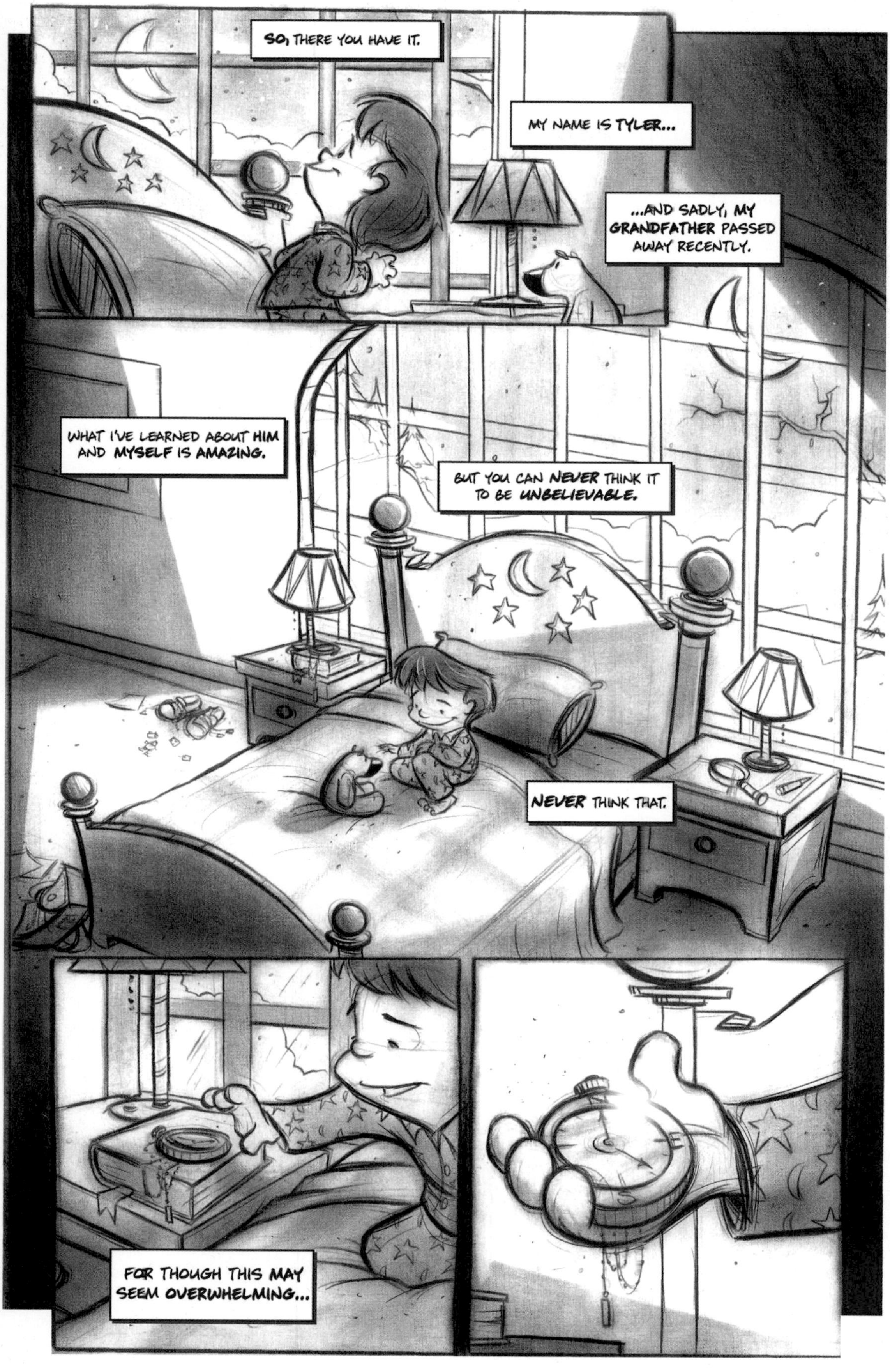
SO, THERE YOU HAVE IT.
MY NAME IS TYLER...
...AND SADLY, MY GRANDFATHER PASSED AWAY RECENTLY.
WHAT I'VE LEARNED ABOUT HIM AND MYSELF IS AMAZING.
BUT YOU CAN NEVER THINK IT TO BE UNBELIEVABLE.
NEVER THINK THAT.
FOR THOUGH THIS MAY SEEM OVERWHELMING...

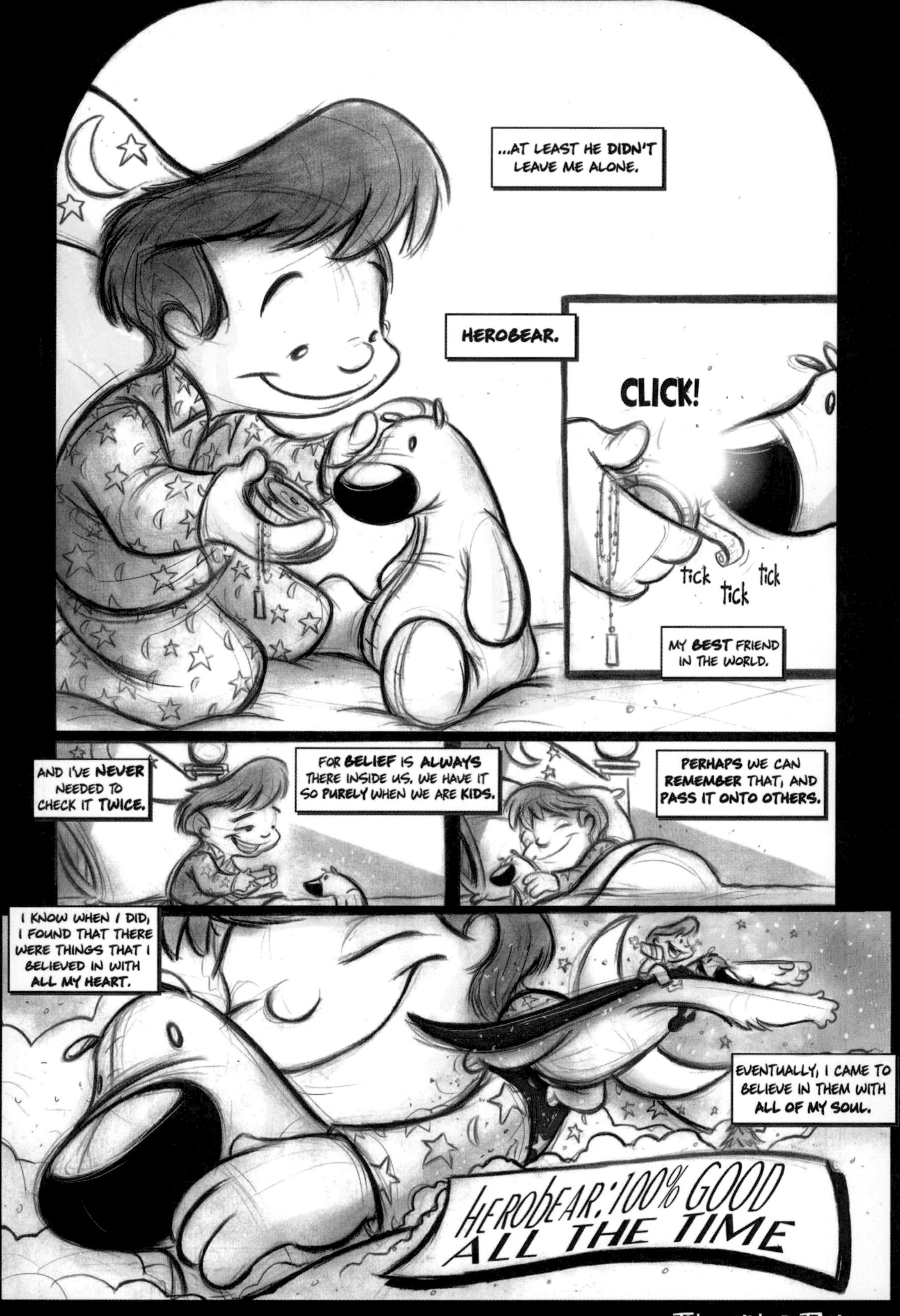
...AT LEAST HE DIDN'T LEAVE ME ALONE.
HEROBEAR.
CLICK!
tick
tick
tick
MY BEST FRIEND IN THE WORLD.
AND I'VE NEVER NEEDED TO CHECK IT TWICE.
FOR BELIEF IS ALWAYS THERE INSIDE US. WE HAVE IT SO PURELY WHEN WE ARE KIDS.
PERHAPS WE CAN REMEMBER THAT, AND PASS IT ONTO OTHERS.
I KNOW WHEN I DID, I FOUND THAT THERE WERE THINGS THAT I BELIEVED IN WITH ALL MY HEART.
EVENTUALLY, I CAME TO BELIEVE IN THEM WITH ALL OF MY SOUL.
HEROBEAR: 100% GOOD ALL THE TIME

THE END . . . OF THE INHERITANCE.

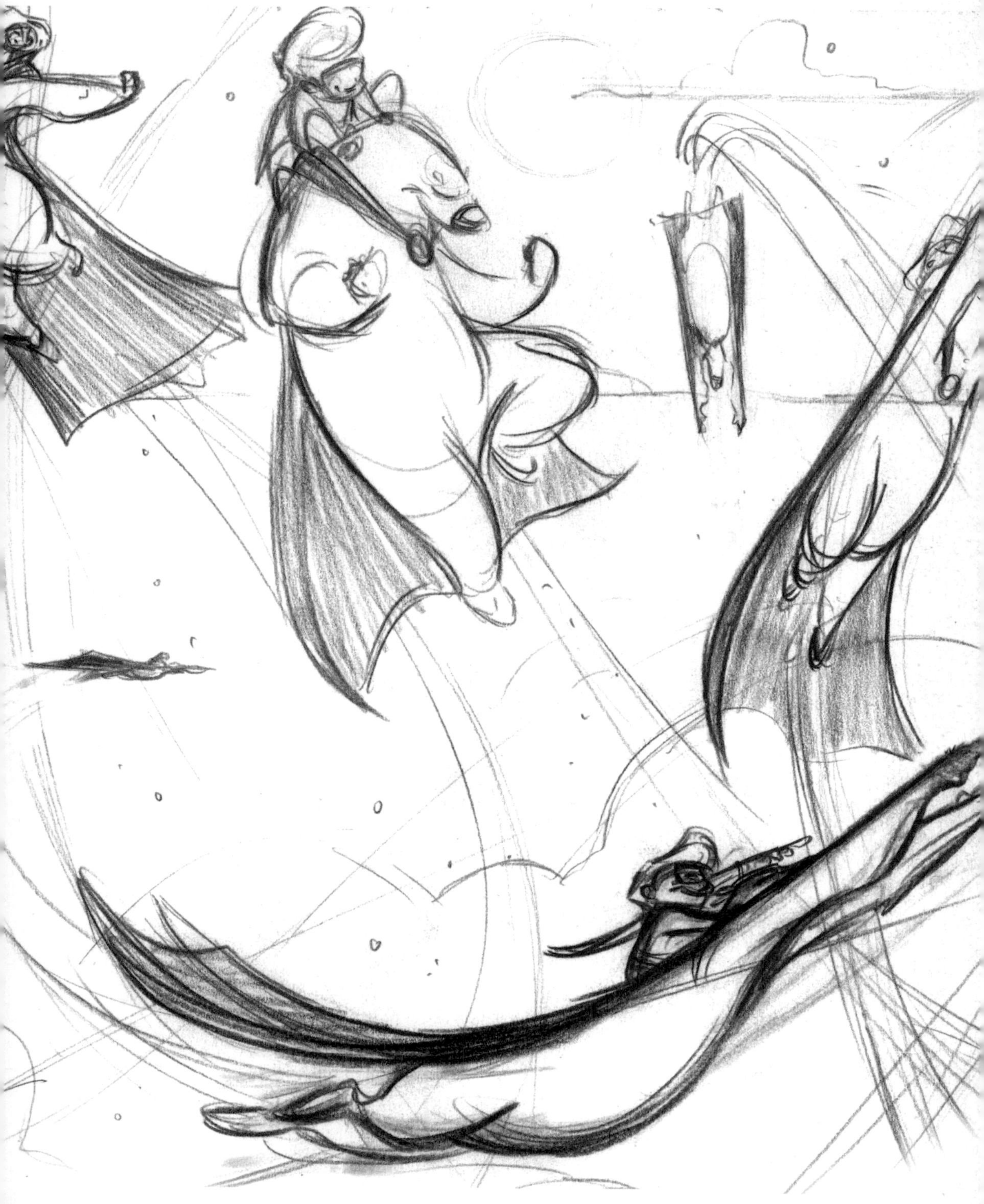

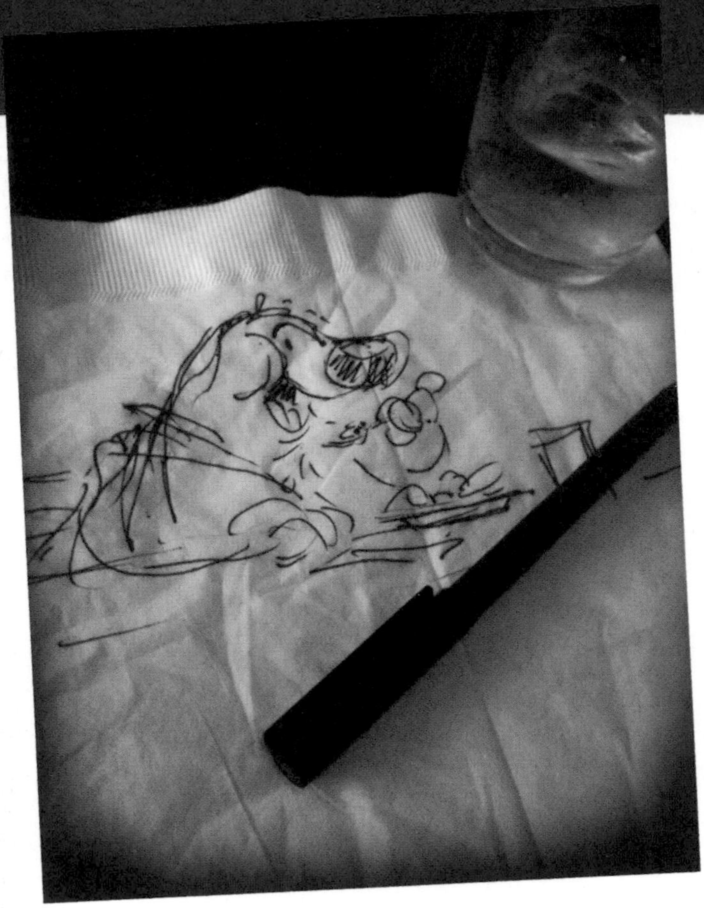

I can't help scribbling Herobear no matter where I am.

When I created the story of HEROBEAR AND THE KID, I originally planned for a panel in Issue #1 to have the villain Von Klon in the scene at the funeral. He's there to "pay his respects" to his "enemy"...Tyler's grandfather. Eventually, I wanted to tell the history and origin of Von Klon. I always assumed that Henry the butler would've seen him there and there would've been a little bit of an exchange.

When the time came for me to re-launch the series with BOOM!, I got very excited to tell this backstory. And, since most of my work is influenced by my animation background, this story quickly became an "in-between drawing/ story." I was able to tell the tale in-between the panel of the funeral on page three and the panel at the top of page four when we first meet Henry with the arrival of the family at the new house. Now, I could dip back into that part of the character's world, and take the audience into the house and show another side of Henry's personality and his personal connection to Fredrich Von Klon. This also sets up nicely with how our little character of Tyler is introduced into the story at that moment of Issue #1 and how Von Klon is connected to the factory and Tyler's family history.

I hope you all enjoy this extra little story. I had a great time getting the chance to tell it.

Mike...

From One Kid to Another

EPILOGUE

PART 1: the Arrival

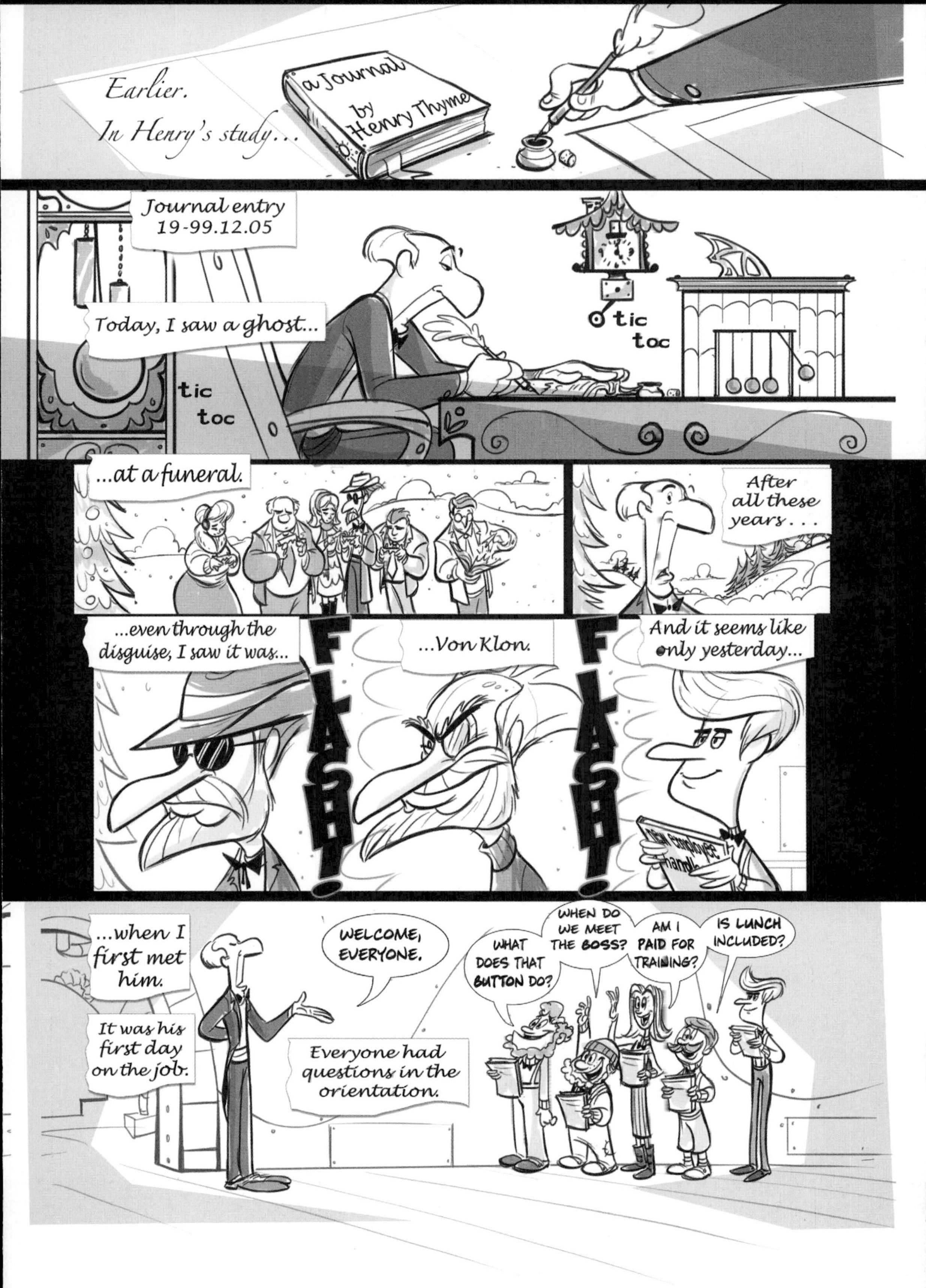
Earlier.
In Henry's study...
a Journal
by Henry Thyme
Journal entry
19-99.12.05
Today, I saw a ghost...
tic
toc
tic
toc
...at a funeral.
After all these years . . .
...even through the disguise, I saw it was...
FLASH!
...Von Klon.
FLASH!
And it seems like only yesterday...
...when I first met him.
It was his first day on the job.
WELCOME, EVERYONE.
Everyone had questions in the orientation.
WHAT DOES THAT BUTTON DO?
WHEN DO WE MEET THE BOSS?
AM I PAID FOR TRAINING?
IS LUNCH INCLUDED?

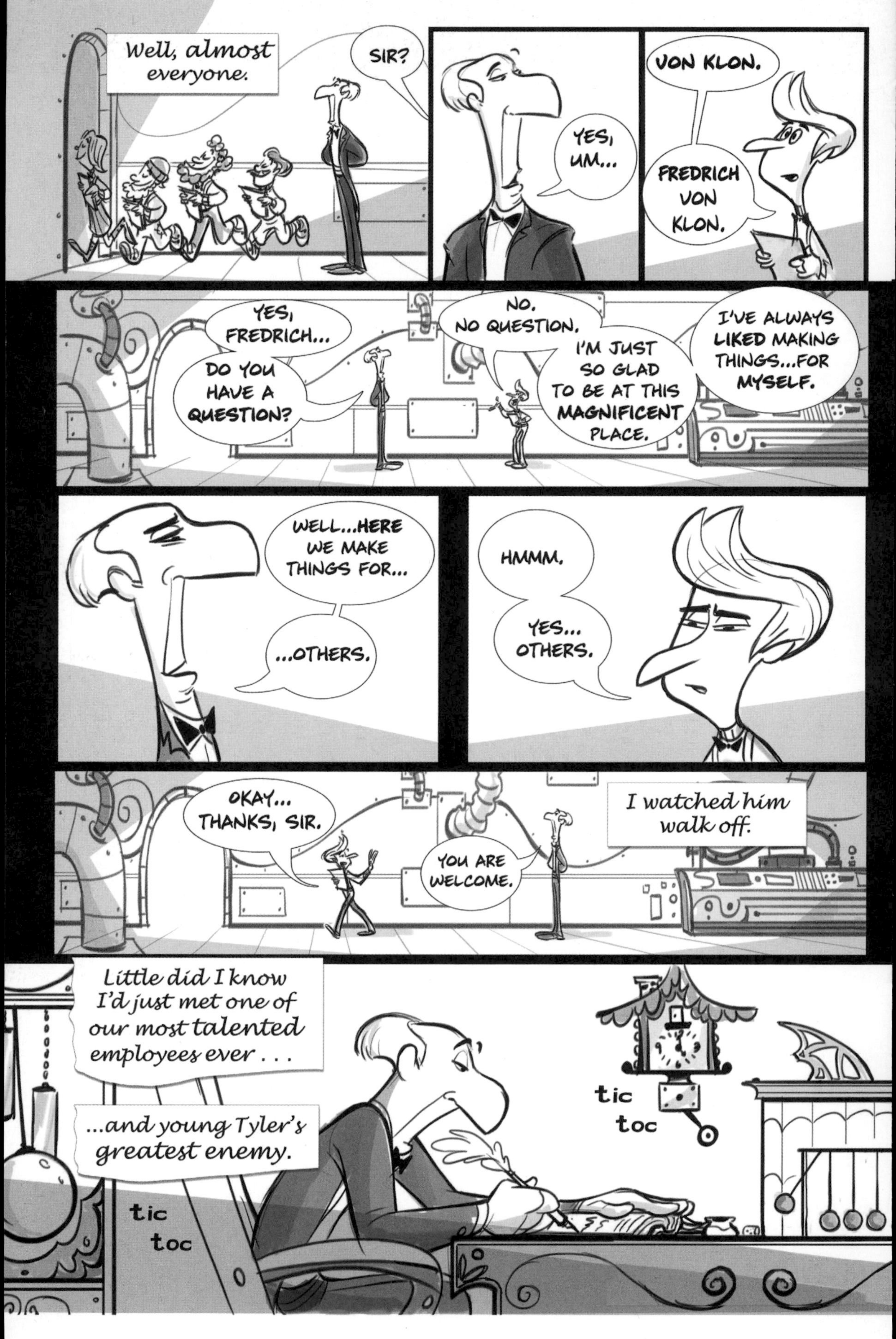
Well, almost everyone.
SIR?
YES, UM...
VON KLON.
FREDRICH VON KLON.
YES, FREDRICH...
DO YOU HAVE A QUESTION?
NO. NO QUESTION.
I'M JUST SO GLAD TO BE AT THIS MAGNIFICENT PLACE.
I'VE ALWAYS LIKED MAKING THINGS...FOR MYSELF.
WELL...HERE WE MAKE THINGS FOR...
...OTHERS.
HMMM.
YES... OTHERS.
OKAY... THANKS, SIR.
YOU ARE WELCOME.
I watched him walk off.
Little did I know I'd just met one of our most talented employees ever . . .
...and young Tyler's greatest enemy.
tic toc
tic toc

PART 2: the Potential

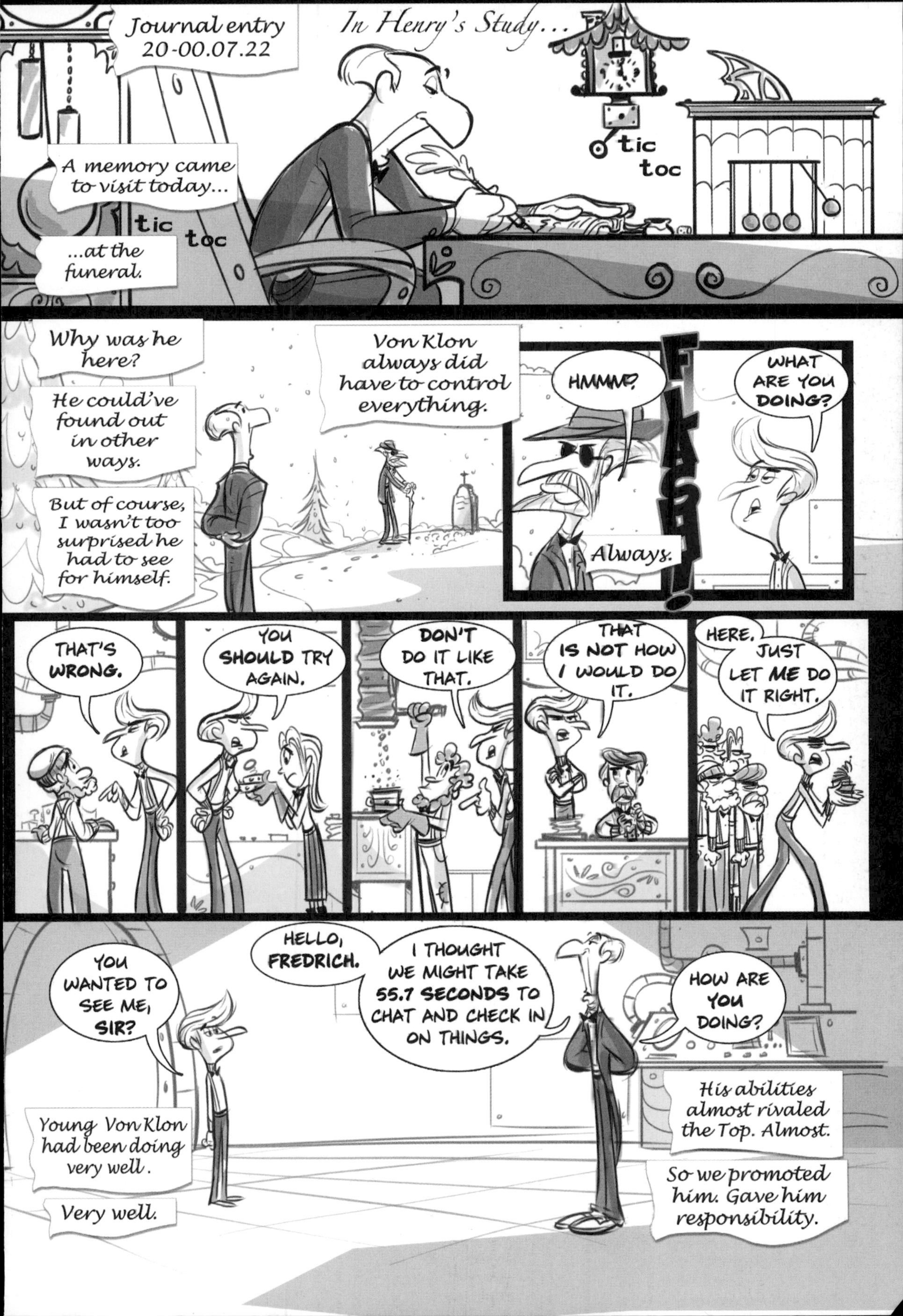

Journal entry
20-00.07.22
In Henry's Study...
A memory came to visit today...
tic
toc
tic
toc
...at the funeral.
Why was he here?
He could've found out in other ways.
But of course, I wasn't too surprised he had to see for himself.
Von Klon always did have to control everything.
HMMM?
FLASH!
WHAT ARE YOU DOING?
Always.
THAT'S WRONG.
YOU SHOULD TRY AGAIN.
DON'T DO IT LIKE THAT.
THAT IS NOT HOW I WOULD DO IT.
HERE.
JUST LET ME DO IT RIGHT.
YOU WANTED TO SEE ME, SIR?
HELLO, FREDRICH.
I THOUGHT WE MIGHT TAKE 55.7 SECONDS TO CHAT AND CHECK IN ON THINGS.
HOW ARE YOU DOING?
Young Von Klon had been doing very well.
Very well.
His abilities almost rivaled the Top. Almost.
So we promoted him. Gave him responsibility.

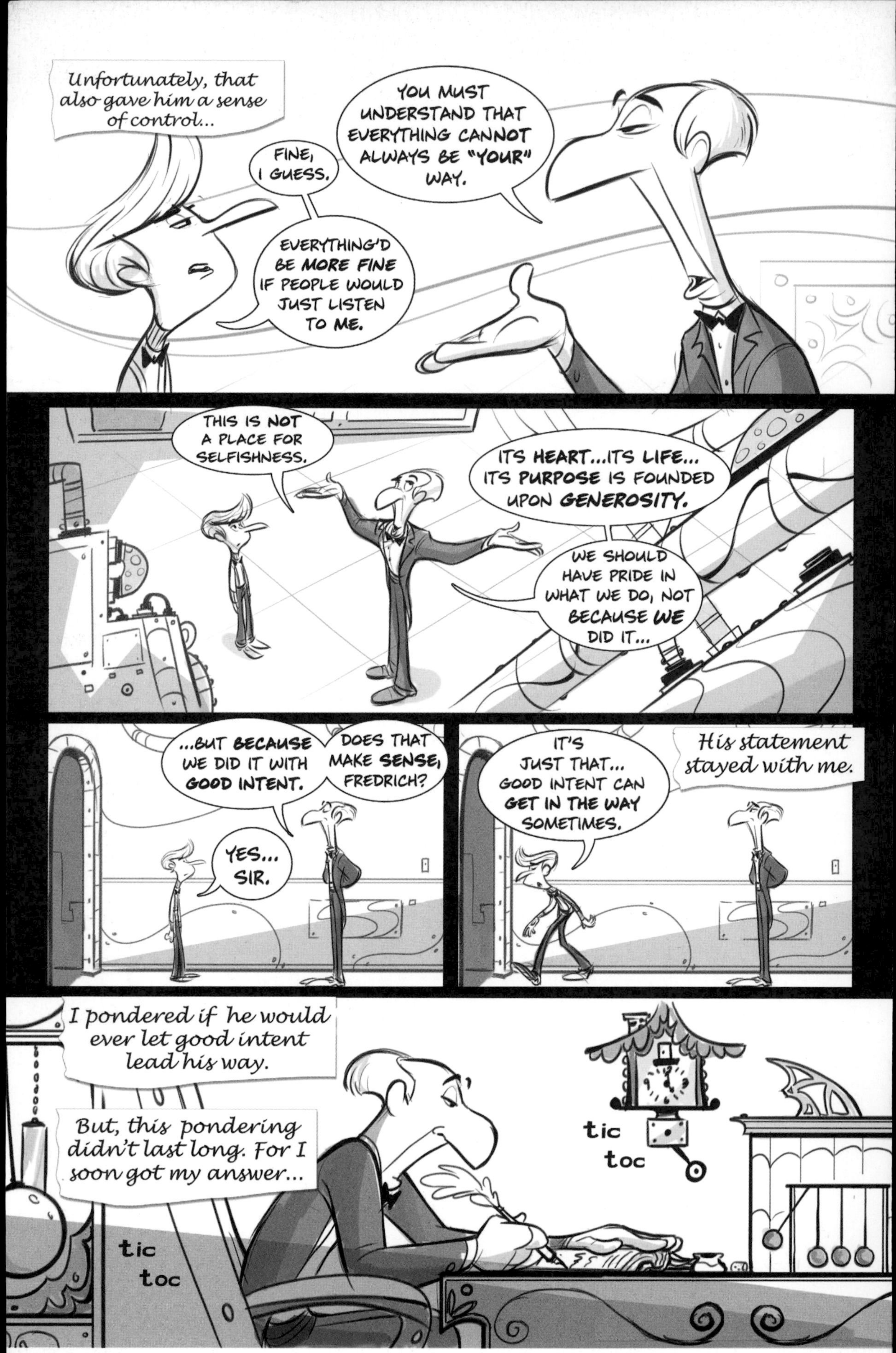
Unfortunately, that also gave him a sense of control...
FINE, I GUESS.
YOU MUST UNDERSTAND THAT EVERYTHING CANNOT ALWAYS BE "YOUR" WAY.
EVERYTHING'D BE MORE FINE IF PEOPLE WOULD JUST LISTEN TO ME.
THIS IS NOT A PLACE FOR SELFISHNESS.
ITS HEART...ITS LIFE... ITS PURPOSE IS FOUNDED UPON GENEROSITY.
WE SHOULD HAVE PRIDE IN WHAT WE DO, NOT BECAUSE WE DID IT...
...BUT BECAUSE WE DID IT WITH GOOD INTENT.
DOES THAT MAKE SENSE, FREDRICH?
YES... SIR.
IT'S JUST THAT... GOOD INTENT CAN GET IN THE WAY SOMETIMES.
His statement stayed with me.
I pondered if he would ever let good intent lead his way.
But, this pondering didn't last long. For I soon got my answer...
tic
toc
tic
toc

PART 3: the Assumption

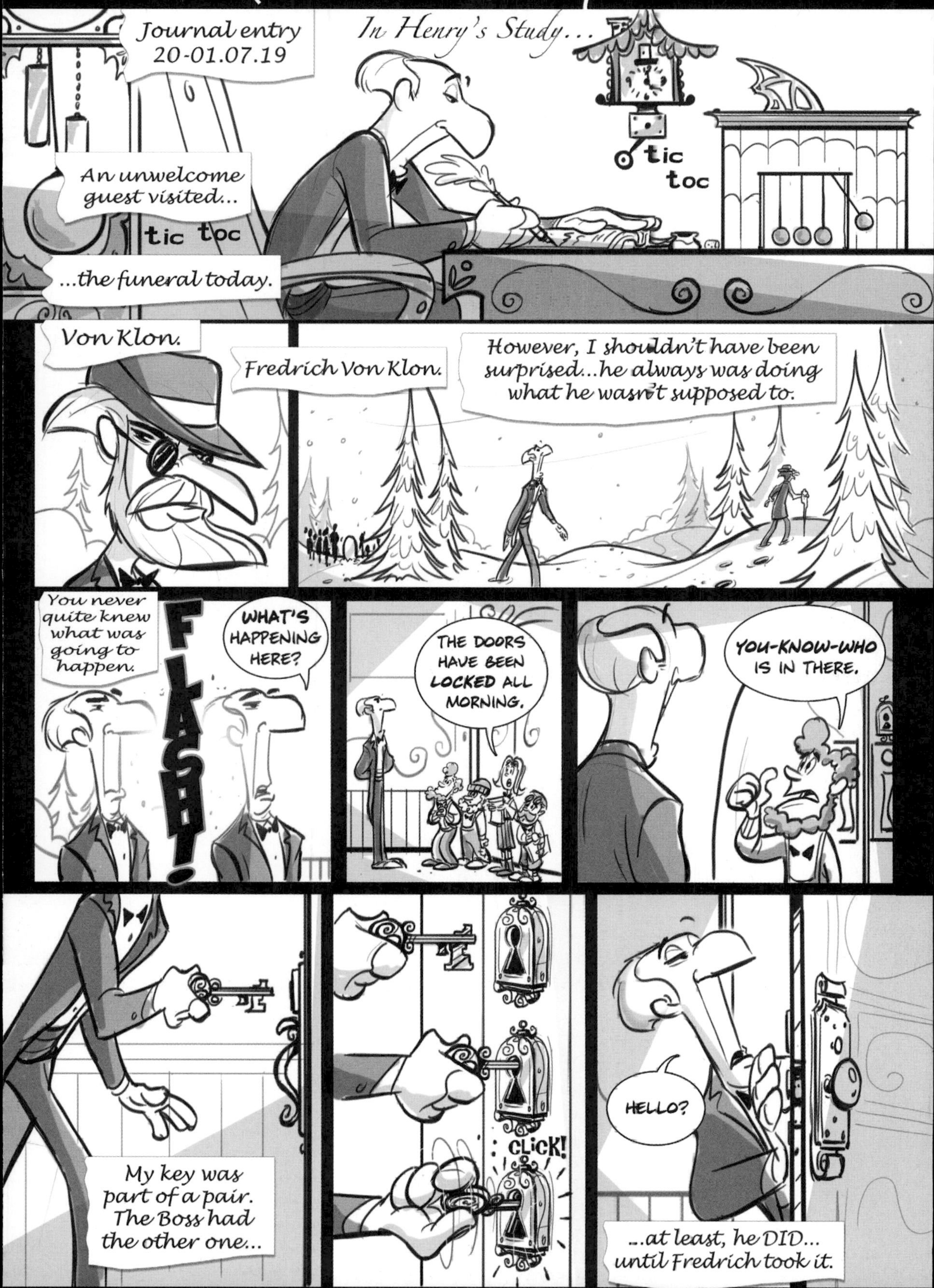

Journal entry 20-01.07.19
In Henry's Study...
tic toc
An unwelcome guest visited...
tic toc
...the funeral today.
Von Klon.
Fredrich Von Klon.
However, I shouldn't have been surprised...he always was doing what he wasn't supposed to.
You never quite knew what was going to happen.
FLASH!
WHAT'S HAPPENING HERE?
THE DOORS HAVE BEEN LOCKED ALL MORNING.
YOU-KNOW-WHO IS IN THERE.
My key was part of a pair. The Boss had the other one...
CLICK!
HELLO?
...at least, he DID... until Fredrich took it.

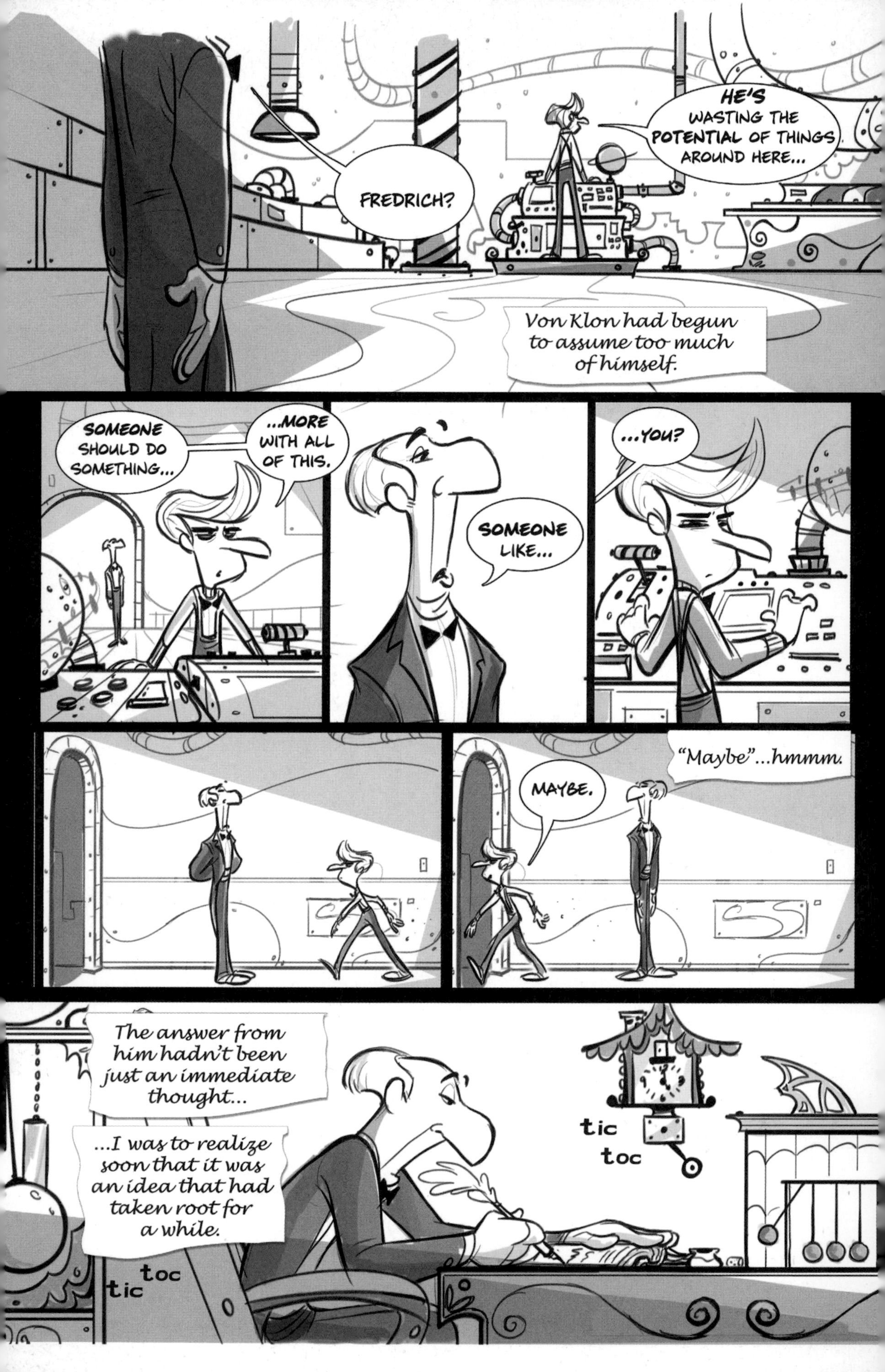
FREDRICH?
HE'S WASTING THE POTENTIAL OF THINGS AROUND HERE...
Von Klon had begun to assume too much of himself.
SOMEONE SHOULD DO SOMETHING...
...MORE WITH ALL OF THIS.
SOMEONE LIKE...
...YOU?
MAYBE.
"Maybe"...hmmm.
The answer from him hadn't been just an immediate thought...
...I was to realize soon that it was an idea that had taken root for a while.
tic
toc
tic
toc

PART 4: the Betrayal

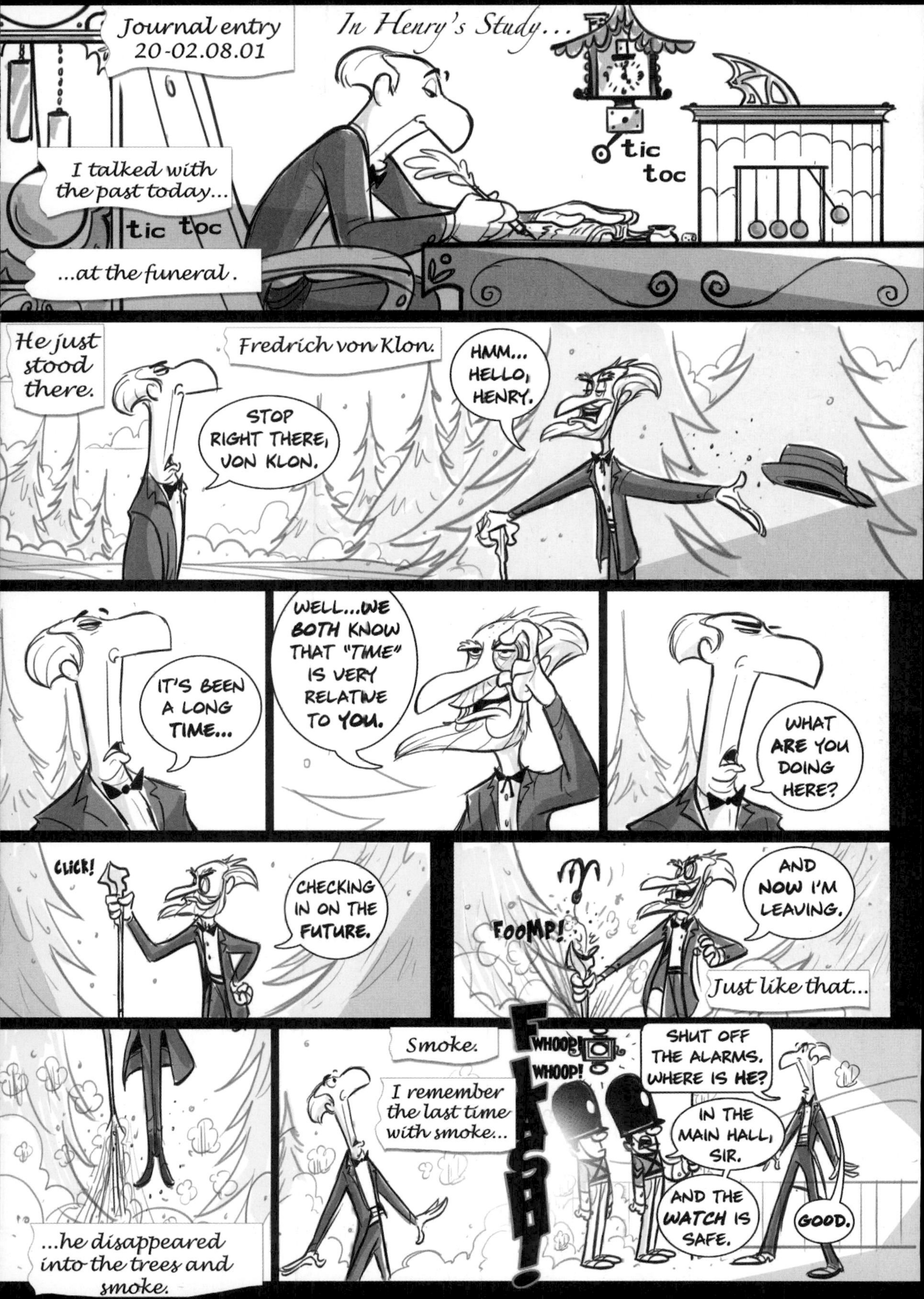
Journal entry 20-02.08.01
In Henry's Study...
tic toc
I talked with the past today...
tic toc
...at the funeral.
He just stood there.
Fredrich von Klon.
STOP RIGHT THERE, VON KLON.
HMM... HELLO, HENRY.
IT'S BEEN A LONG TIME...
WELL...WE BOTH KNOW THAT "TIME" IS VERY RELATIVE TO YOU.
WHAT ARE YOU DOING HERE?
CLICK!
CHECKING IN ON THE FUTURE.
FOOMP!
AND NOW I'M LEAVING.
Just like that...
...he disappeared into the trees and smoke.
Smoke.
I remember the last time with smoke...
FLASH!
WHOOP! WHOOP!
SHUT OFF THE ALARMS. WHERE IS HE?
IN THE MAIN HALL, SIR.
AND THE WATCH IS SAFE.
GOOD.

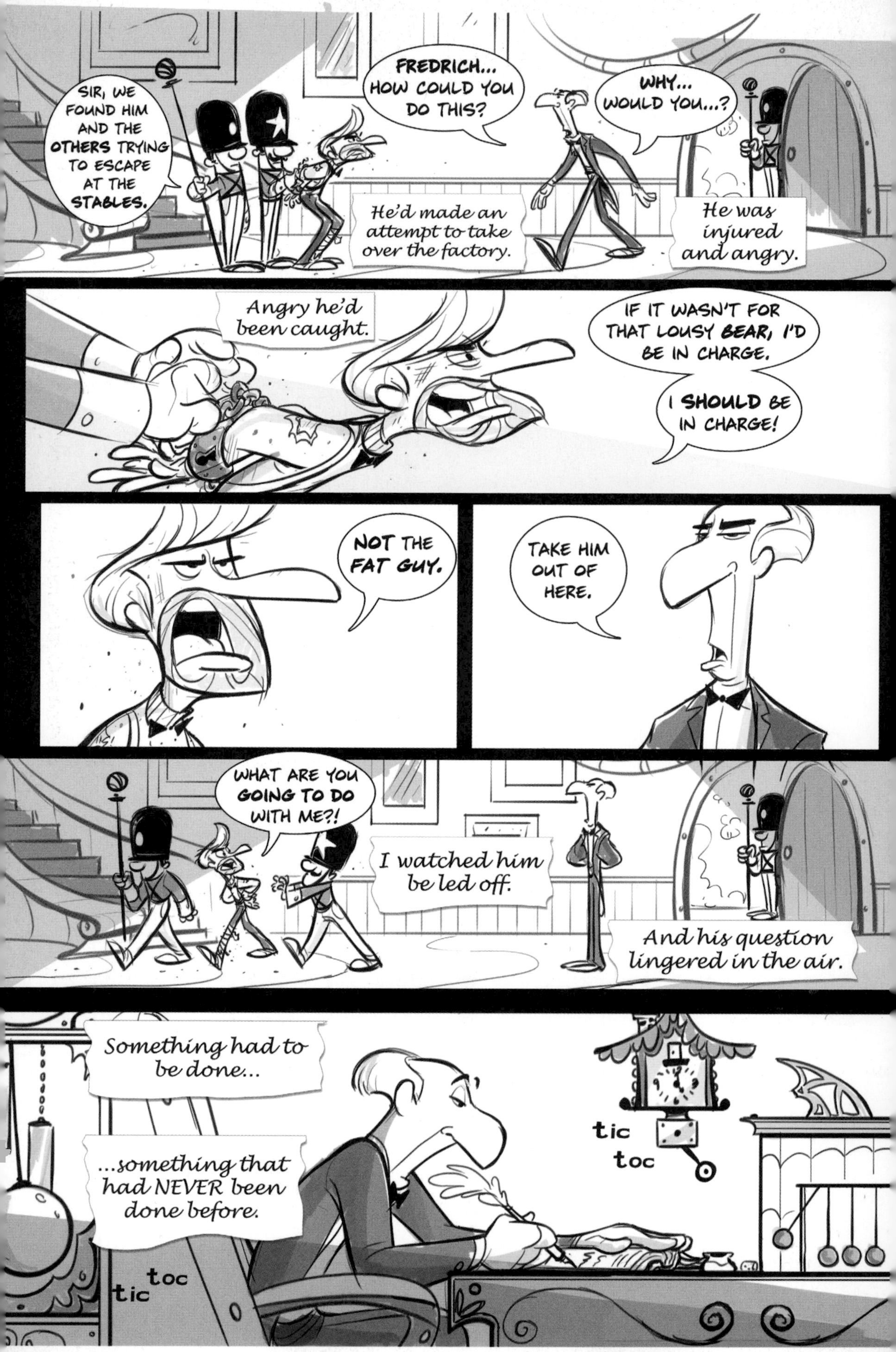
SIR, WE FOUND HIM AND THE OTHERS TRYING TO ESCAPE AT THE STABLES.
FREDRICH... HOW COULD YOU DO THIS?
He'd made an attempt to take over the factory.
WHY... WOULD YOU...?
He was injured and angry.
Angry he'd been caught.
IF IT WASN'T FOR THAT LOUSY BEAR, I'D BE IN CHARGE.
I SHOULD BE IN CHARGE!
NOT THE FAT GUY.
TAKE HIM OUT OF HERE.
WHAT ARE YOU GOING TO DO WITH ME?!
I watched him be led off.
And his question lingered in the air.
Something had to be done...
...something that had NEVER been done before.
tic
toc
tic
toc

PART 5: the Banishment

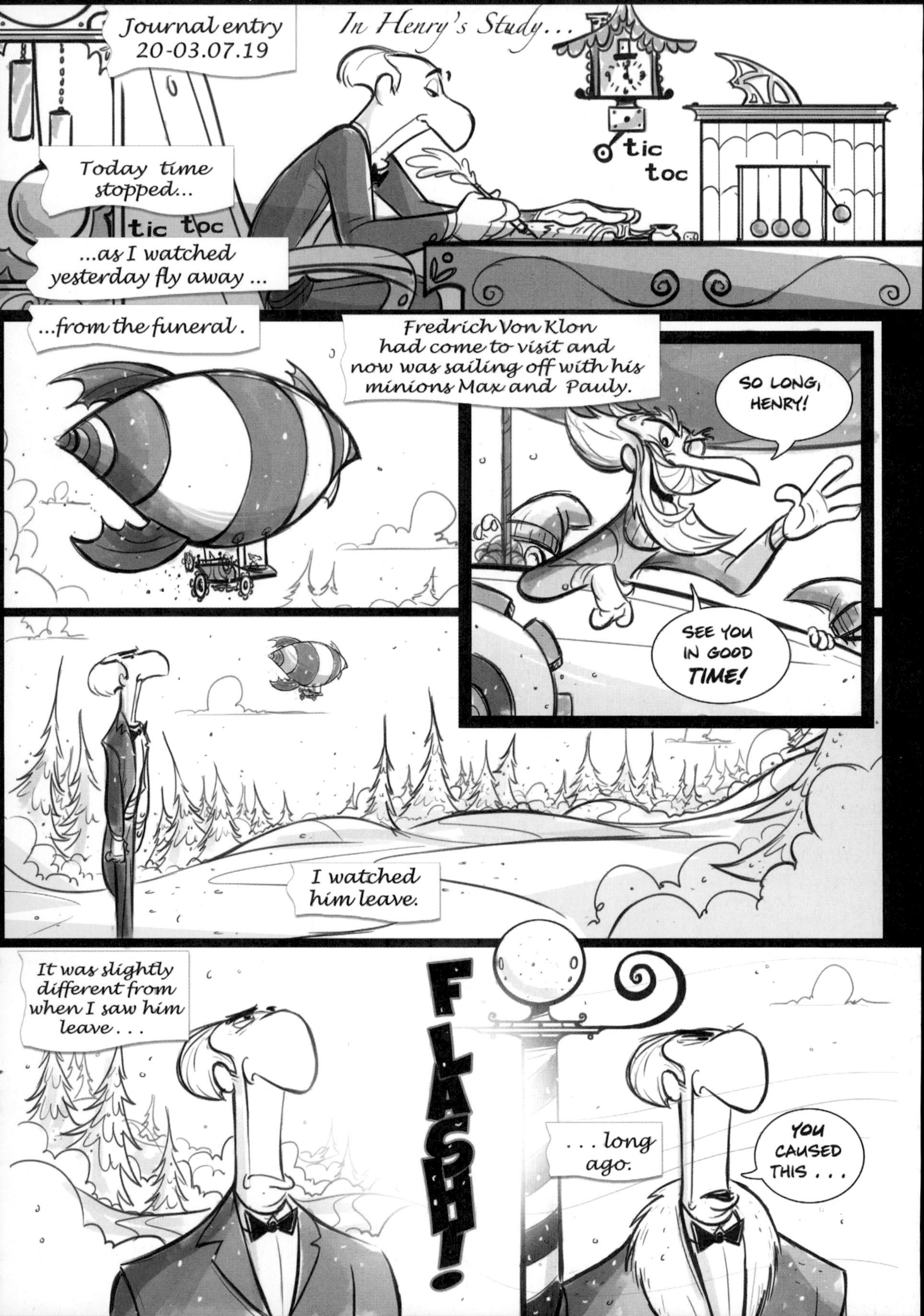

Journal entry 20-03.07.19
In Henry's Study...
tic toc
Today time stopped...
tic toc
...as I watched yesterday fly away ...
...from the funeral.
Fredrich Von Klon had come to visit and now was sailing off with his minions Max and Pauly.
SO LONG, HENRY!
SEE YOU IN GOOD TIME!
I watched him leave.
It was slightly different from when I saw him leave . . .
FLASH!
. . . long ago.
YOU CAUSED THIS . . .

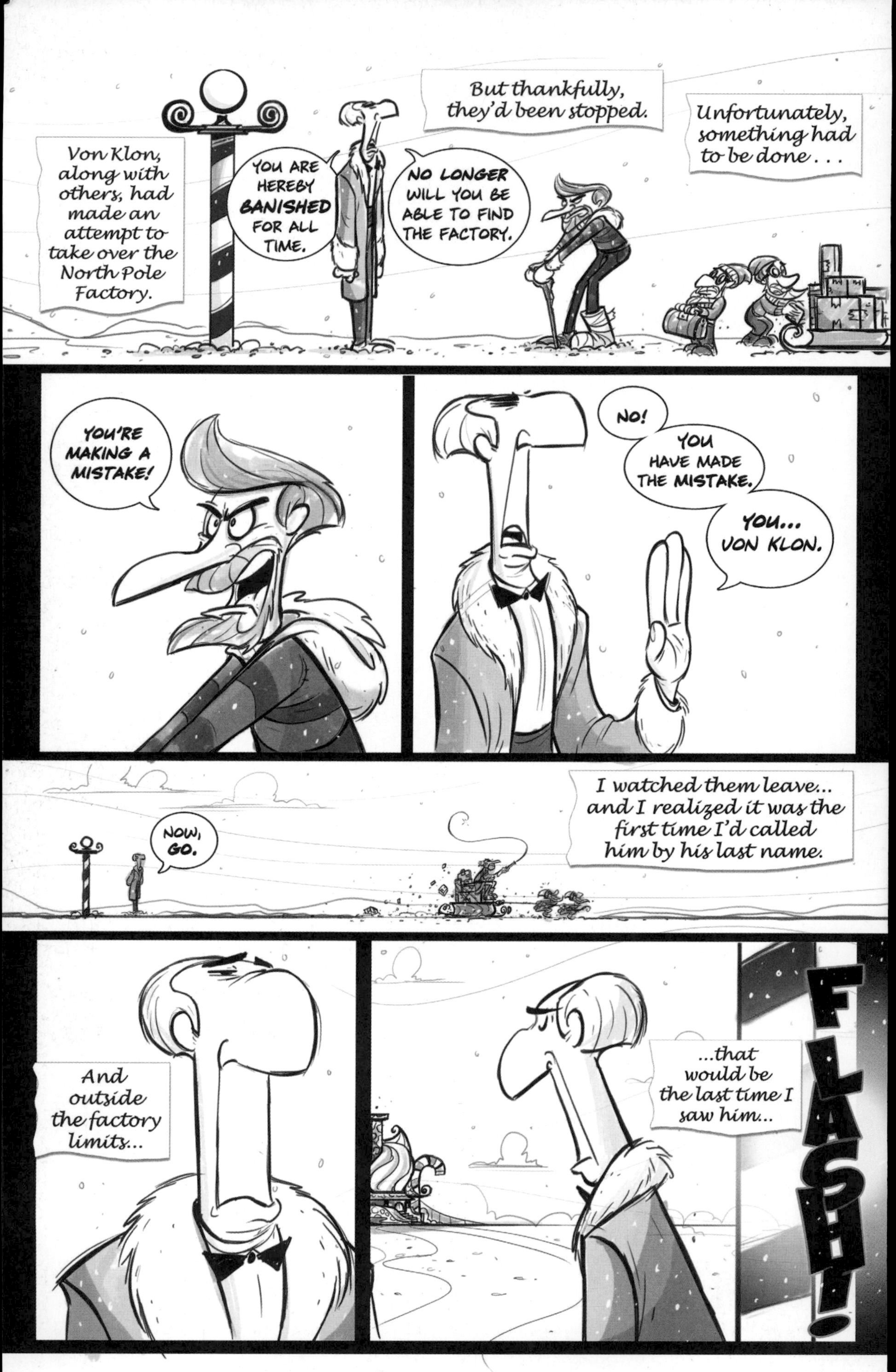

Von Klon, along with others, had made an attempt to take over the North Pole Factory.
YOU ARE HEREBY BANISHED FOR ALL TIME.
NO LONGER WILL YOU BE ABLE TO FIND THE FACTORY.
But thankfully, they'd been stopped.
Unfortunately, something had to be done . . .
YOU'RE MAKING A MISTAKE!
NO!
YOU HAVE MADE THE MISTAKE.
YOU... VON KLON.
NOW, GO.
I watched them leave... and I realized it was the first time I'd called him by his last name.
And outside the factory limits...
...that would be the last time I saw him...
FLASH!

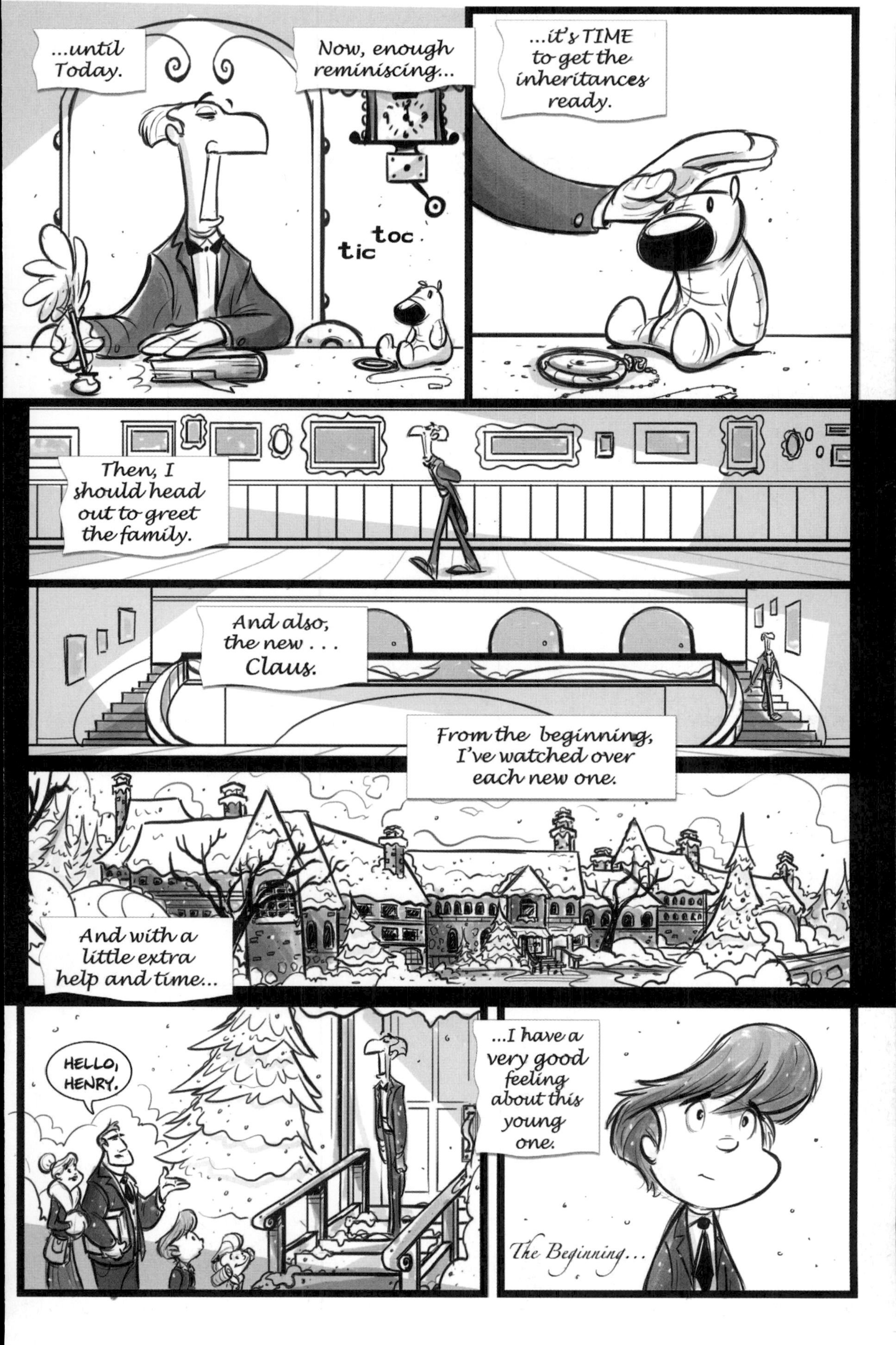
...until Today.
Now, enough reminiscing...
tic toc
...it's TIME to get the inheritances ready.
Then, I should head out to greet the family.
And also, the new . . . Claus.
From the beginning, I've watched over each new one.
And with a little extra help and time...
HELLO, HENRY.
...I have a very good feeling about this young one.
The Beginning...

Free Comic
Book Day
2013

At the core of HEROBEAR AND THE KID is the relationship between two best friends...Tyler and Herobear. When it came to relaunching with BOOM! I wanted to do a simple little story that captured the heart of their friendship...they look out for each other and they truly have fun together living through Tyler's childhood. When I was a kid, I dreamed of flying...I'd even sink under the water of the deep end of pools to float and imagine what flying felt like. The motto I've always had with my work is, "Remember your childhood...and pass it on."

Naturally, one of the most favorite things Herobear and Tyler love to share would be...flying. And of course, that had to be what the first story back was about. Simple and heartfelt. Pretty much the way I hope the world and stories of HEROBEAR AND THE KID are always presented.

— MIKE KUNKEL

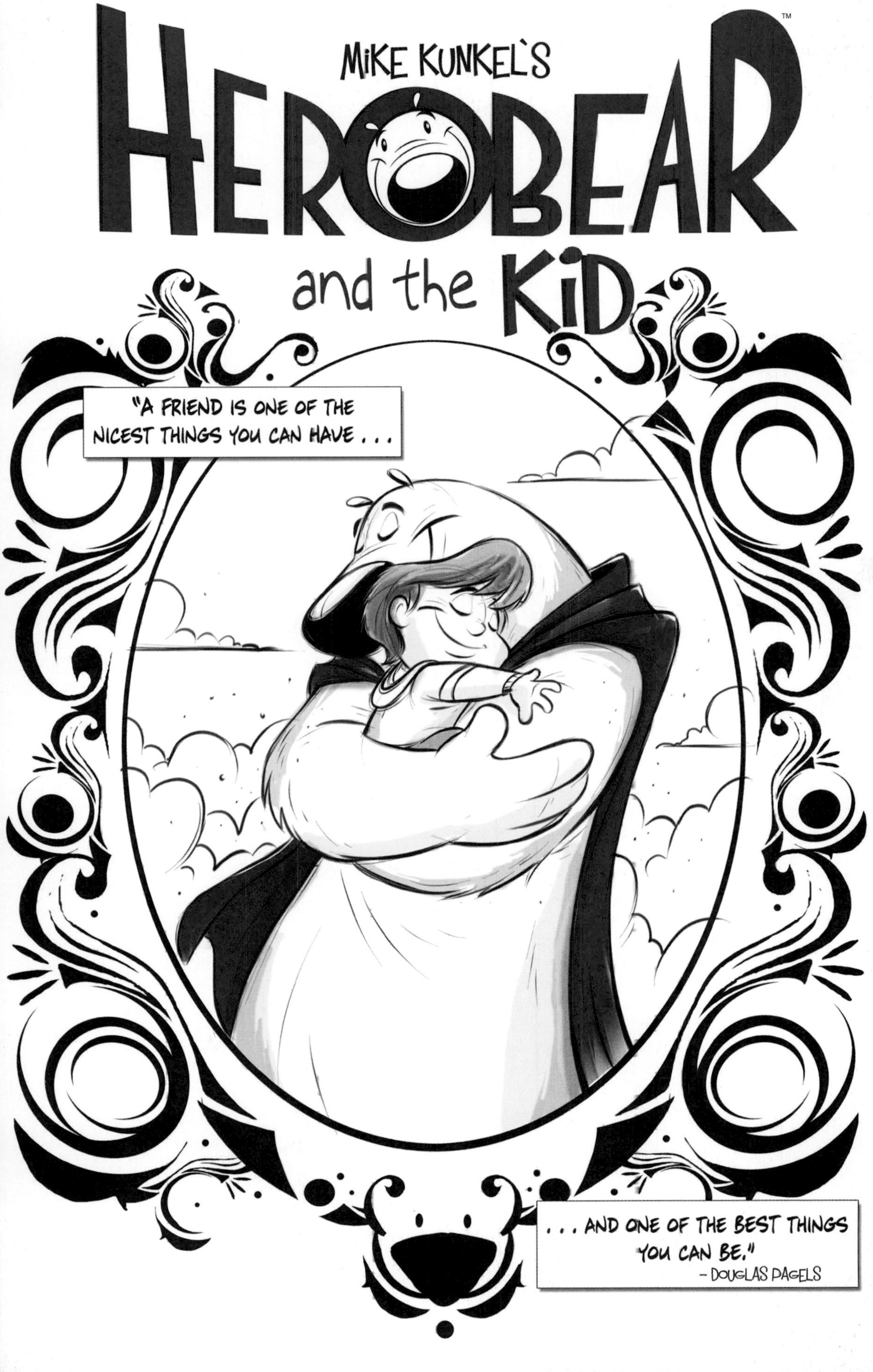
MIKE KUNKEL'S
HEROBEAR™
and the KID
"A FRIEND IS ONE OF THE NICEST THINGS YOU CAN HAVE . . .
. . . AND ONE OF THE BEST THINGS YOU CAN BE."
– DOUGLAS PAGELS

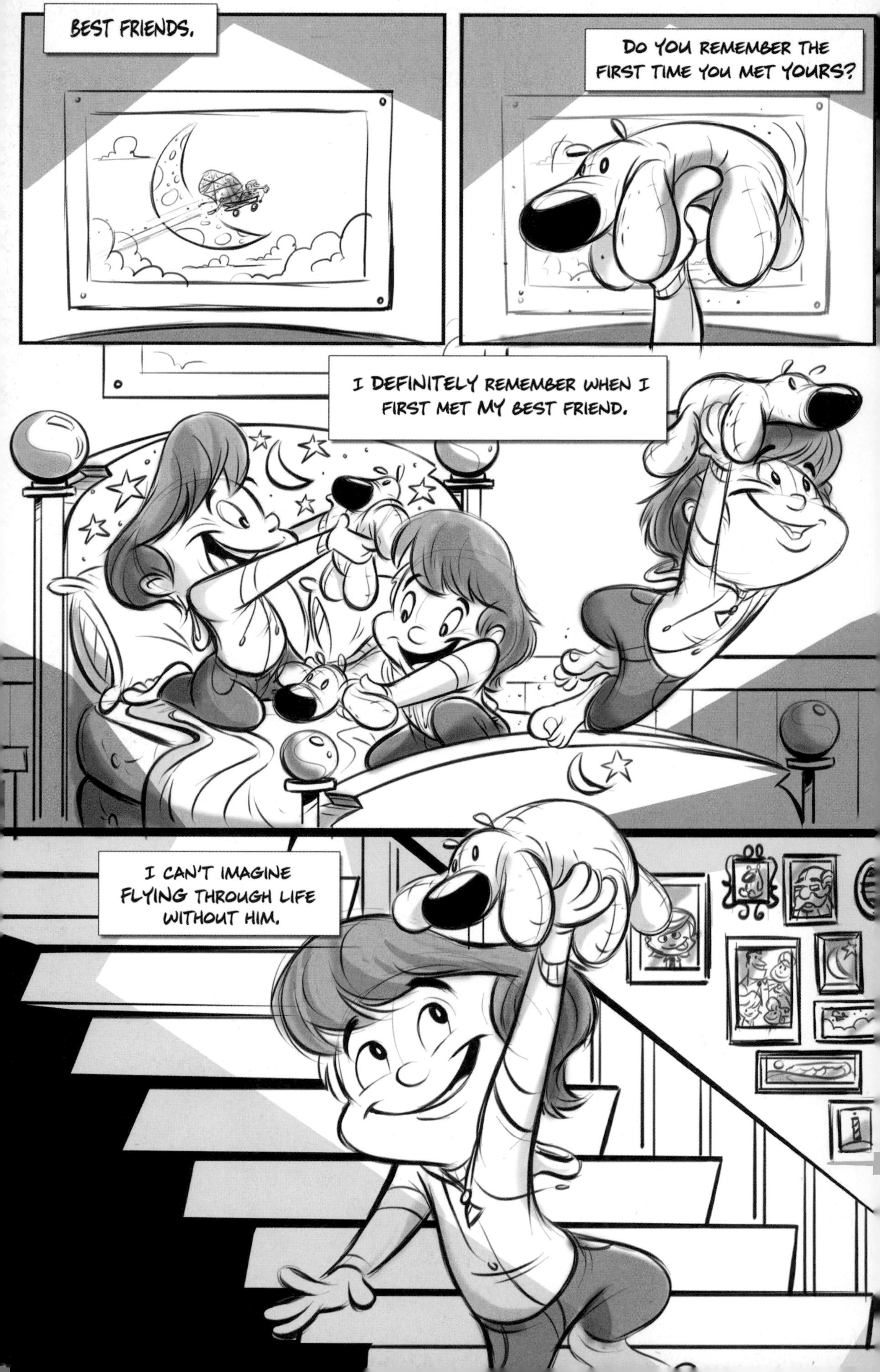
BEST FRIENDS.
DO YOU REMEMBER THE FIRST TIME YOU MET YOURS?
I DEFINITELY REMEMBER WHEN I FIRST MET MY BEST FRIEND.
I CAN'T IMAGINE FLYING THROUGH LIFE WITHOUT HIM.

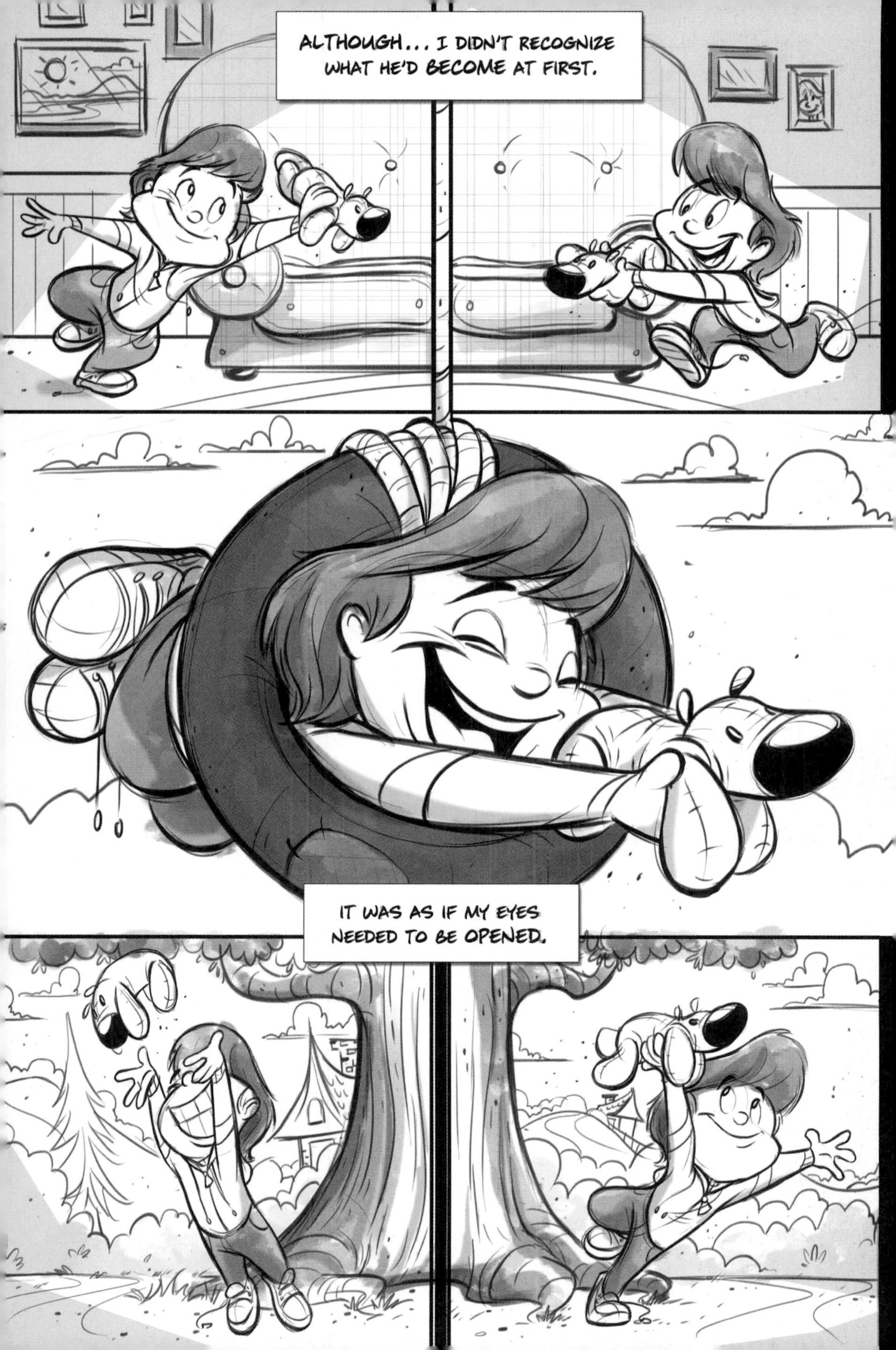
ALTHOUGH... I DIDN'T RECOGNIZE WHAT HE'D BECOME AT FIRST.
IT WAS AS IF MY EYES NEEDED TO BE OPENED.

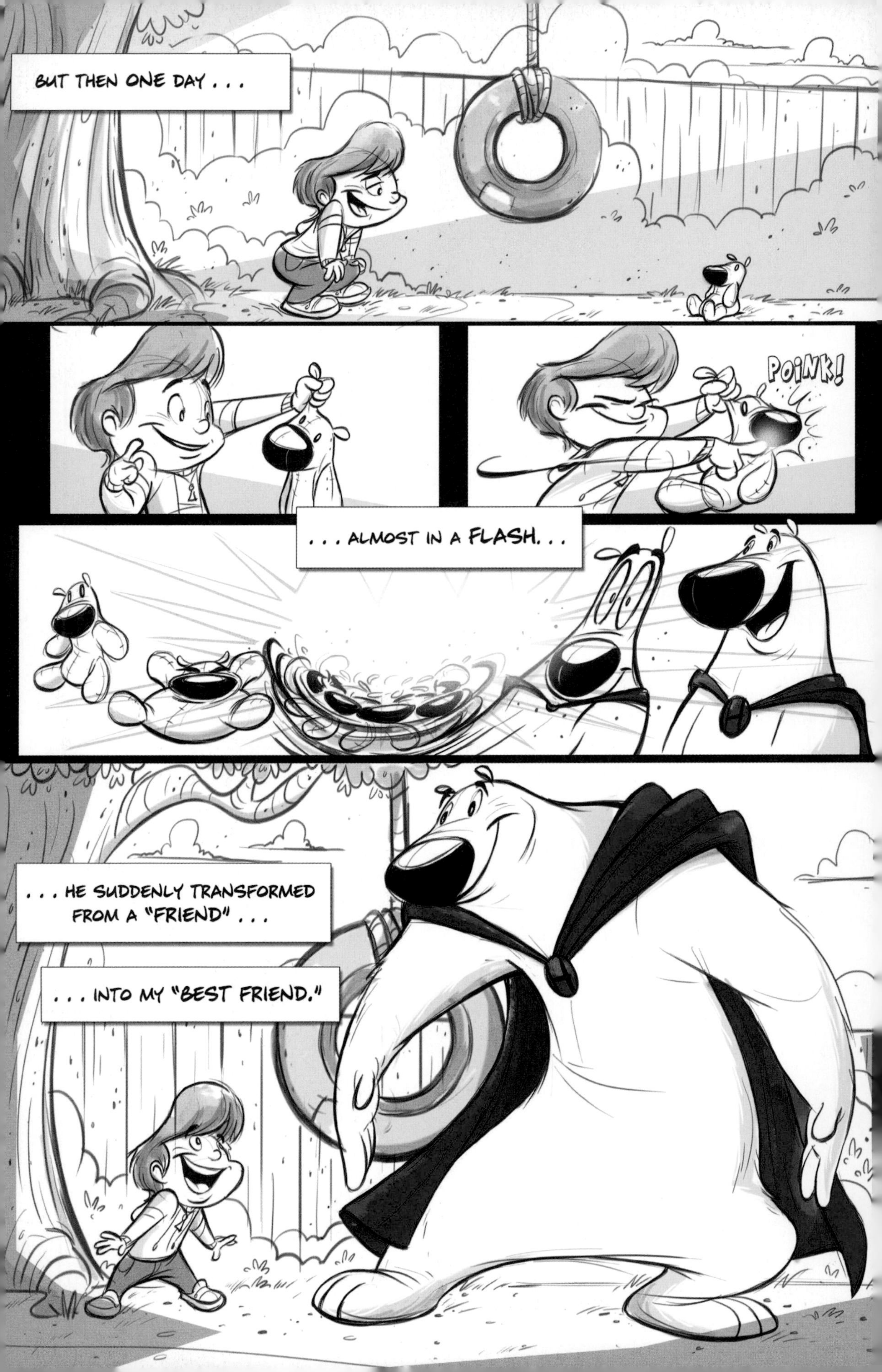
BUT THEN ONE DAY . . .
POINK!
. . . ALMOST IN A FLASH. . .
. . . HE SUDDENLY TRANSFORMED FROM A "FRIEND" . . .
. . . INTO MY "BEST FRIEND."

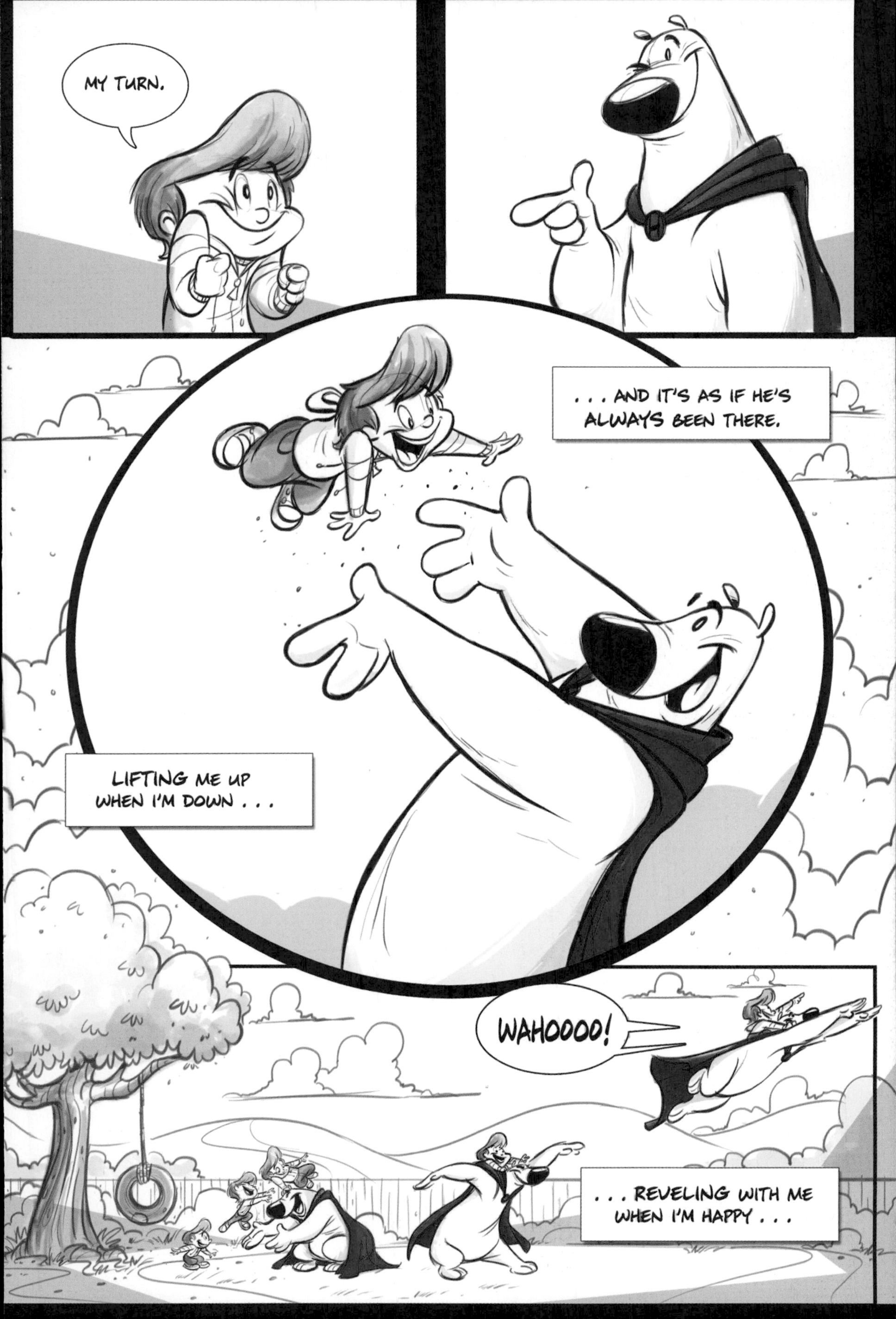

MY TURN.
. . . AND IT'S AS IF HE'S ALWAYS BEEN THERE.
LIFTING ME UP WHEN I'M DOWN . . .
WAHOOOO!
. . . REVELING WITH ME WHEN I'M HAPPY . . .

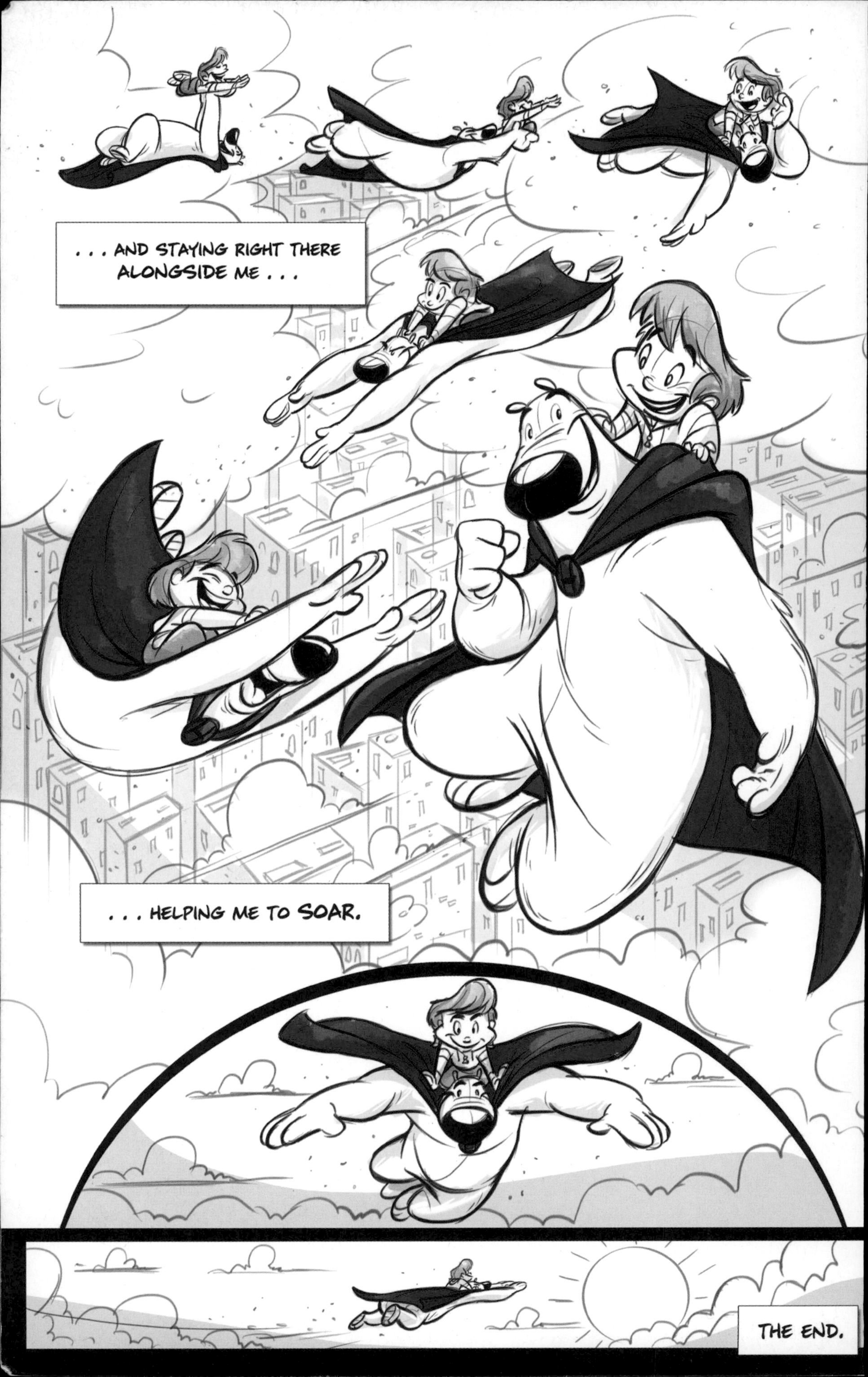
. . . AND STAYING RIGHT THERE ALONGSIDE ME . . .
. . . HELPING ME TO SOAR.
THE END.

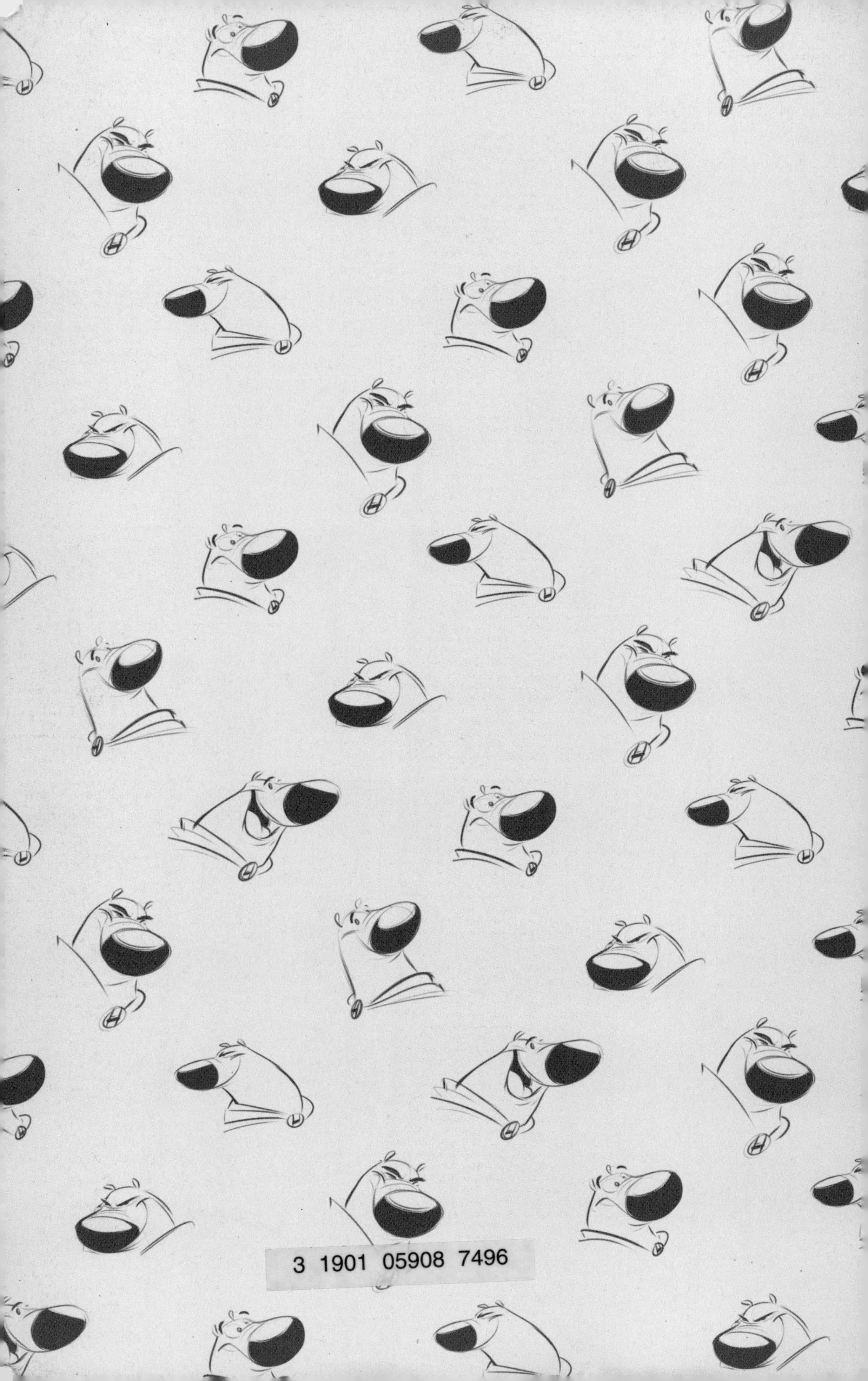